MAJOR
MISTAKE

MAJOR
MISTAKE

Rodney L. Baumberger

authorHOUSE®

AuthorHouse™
1663 Liberty Drive
Bloomington, IN 47403
www.authorhouse.com
Phone: 1-800-839-8640

First published by AuthorHouse   09/14/2011

ISBN: 978-1-4670-2685-7 (sc)
ISBN: 978-1-4670-2684-0 (hc)
ISBN: 978-1-4670-2683-3 (ebk)

Library of Congress Control Number: 2011916174

Printed in the United States of America

It was a very good dream, the kind of dream that a person hates to wake up from. He was back in high school and was exacting a sort of revenge from a minor high school bully that had pestered him in real life. He had just backed him into a corner by the lockers and could see the fear start to flicker in his eyes, when the buzzing from the alarm clock startled him awake.

Major lay there with his eyes closed, and allowed a faint smile to come to his lips. In his dream he was the size he was now, not the seventy-nine pound freshman he was back in his high school days.

He felt his wife of twelve years start to stir, so he leaned over his side of the bed and shut the alarm off and flicked the bedside light on.

"Morning babe, it's that time again," Major whispered, rolling over and putting his arm around her waist. He squeezed her slightly and kissed the nape of her neck.

Jill allowed him to caress and snuggle for a precious few seconds and then deftly flipped the covers from her and rose from the bed. Major watched her rise, enjoying the moment because she always slept without nightclothes. He watched her put her gown on and make her way to the bathroom. He listened as she completed her toiletry and she made her way down the dark stairway.

Major rose, stretched and felt then heard the ligaments and joints crack throughout his body. His back was a little sore this morning, but experience told him that the pain would work out soon.

He walked into the adjoining bedroom and gazed down at his two-year-old son. Brok was what Major and Jill considered their miracle baby. They had been married almost ten years before Brok was conceived and throughout all that time they never used protection.

He pulled the covers from Brok and carried him into the bathroom and slid him down between his legs and faced him towards the commode. Lifting up the seat with one hand and balancing Brok between his legs he pulled his pajama bottoms down with his other hand. "Pee, little buddy," he said and smiled as the little boy grabbed his winkee and let a small stream of urine splash into the bowl. When he was done, Major pulled his pajama bottoms back up and carried his son back to his bed and put him in still mostly asleep. "'Nite pal, I'll see you tonight after work." Major turned and went back into the bathroom, urinated, brushed his teeth, combed his hair and then dressed.

He padded down the steps and silently slid up behind Jill. He put his crotch into the middle of her buttocks and reached up with both of his hands and took her full breasts in his bands.

"You'd better stop that, or you won't go to work." Jill said and at the same time she pressed herself firmly against him and started to rotate her buttocks. Major chuckled and enjoyed the sensations Jill was sending through his body. "Yeah, you're right," he said, but still fondled her for a few more seconds.

Major sat down at the table and watched her finish packing his bucket, and place his bowl of Campbell's vegetable beef soup in front of him. Major always ate soup for breakfast. He couldn't stand to look at eggs in the morning.

"Think you'll work tomorrow? Remember, you promised Brok that if you had Saturday off, you and he were going to "pal" around together."

Major looked up from his soup and looked at his wife. "I hope I don't have to work, it would be nice to have the weekend off, but I won't know until today."

Jill came over and kissed Major on top of his head. Well, I'm going to bed now. See you tonight." She turned and glided up the steps.

Major finished up his soup and placed the empty bowl and spoon into the sink. He finished off his glass of Pepsi, another unusual taste; left the glass on the table grabbed his bucket and headed for the door.

He stepped outside and breathed deeply of the fresh summer air. He listened to the early morning sounds, crickets chirping, trees and grass rustling slightly from the breeze and his favorite sound, the sleepy chirps of the first birds starting to awaken.

Once again a smile crossed his face, as he walked over to his company vehicle supplied to him, climbed in, started it and let it warm up for a full minute. While he was waiting for the truck's engine to warm up he turned the F.M. radio to his favorite country station.

He backed out of the driveway and went to the site where he would pick up the two men working with him. He picked up his co-workers and headed to the work site, humming an old Hank Williams song, remade by George Strait.

They arrived and started up their machinery. They were strip miners, digging for coal. This was Major's main job. Although Major enjoyed working with heavy machinery, his true love was martial arts.

Major was a third degree black belt in the Korean art of Tae Kwon Do. He also held a black belt in the art of quarterstaff fighting. His wife Jill also held a black belt in Tae Kwon Do. Together they owned and operated a martial arts school called "Brown's Karate." They had been in business for three years.

Both Major and Jill enjoyed teaching. He had children's and adult classes twice weekly and Jill had a five year and younger class once a week. She also filled in when Major had to work late.

At five foot nine inches Major was a soft 180 pounds. He could free fight or spar for several minutes at a time, but lately he has been noticing a lack of air the last bit of time. He had fought tournaments when he was first into the arts and he had "retired" from fighting competitions the second year he owned the school. He had picked up the habit of smoking a pipe, and was smoking one now in fact.

He grimaced, knocked the live ashes from the bowl and put the pipe back into his pocket. "Going to have to quit one of these days," he thought as his mind drifted back to the martial arts.

Although he was a tournament champion several times and ranked in the state of Ohio and enjoyed a reputation as a good fighter, he still doubted his skills as a martial artist. He thought that everyone who does anything athletically doubted their skills somewhat, but in most sports you just lose the game. If you make a mistake using karate on the street or even in tournaments you could be seriously injured or even killed. Something most people don't even want to think about. "Oh well, everyone has doubts, he thought.

Ten hours later, he was on his way home.

CHAPTER TWO

Major pulled into his driveway and pulled the parking brake, switched off the engine and sat behind the wheel for a moment.

Friday night, and he had Saturday and Sunday off! Usually he had to work Saturday, but things worked out for this weekend.

Smiling, he reached for the door handle and his lunch bucket and slid from the truck. The sound of a door opening made him look to the house and his smile grew even wider as he seen Jill and Brok coming out the back door to greet him.

"Daddy! Daddy!" Sang Brok as he ran unsteadily toward Major with arms wind milling and plump little legs taking short chopping strides forwards.

Major sat his bucket down and reached down and picked his son up and tossed him in the air twice, gave him a quick kiss on the cheek, set him down on his feet towards his mommy and a quick pat on the butt sent him squealing with laughter towards Jill.

"Hi," Jill said, "you gotta work tomorrow?"

Major answered with a grin "No!"

"Great, then you are going to take Brok to the mall?" Although it came out as a question, Major knew that it was a statement. "Yeah, I was planning on it."

"Good," Brok will love it." She kissed him then and then they linked arms and went into the house.

Major grabbed a Pepsi and the local paper and headed up the steps to the bathroom.

"Dinner in half an hour, so don't take forever up there." Jill admonished her husband. She knew that it would take him all night to get a bath if she didn't hurry him a little.

Major started his tub and sat on the toilet as the water ran and started to read the paper. He read all the major stories on the front page; Middle East wars, drug wars and political wars, and then turned to the editorial pages, after the editorials he turned to the sports page, he always saved the comics for last.

He stood up and shut the water off flushed the toilet and climbed into the tub. He grabbed the sections of paper he hadn't read yet and leaned back. He kicked on the hot water and leaned back with just his head and his knees out of the water and started to read the rest of the paper.

He read about the Indians losing streak and about the Orioles winning streak and he grimaced as how much money was offered to a star ball player, almost five million dollars a year! Unreal!

He shut the water off with his foot threw the sports section on the floor and reached for the comic section. Glancing through he seen a small headliner about a kidnapping in St. Clairsville Mall, it had attracted his attention because he knew where it was, and had been there before. A three year old boy had been abducted from there, and his father assaulted. The article was weak in details. Major shook his head as he finished the article. Personally he thought people who did stuff like that ought to be shot or worse.

"Dinner's ready," Jill yelled up the steps, taking Major out of his musing.

"Be right there," Major said as he soaped up a washrag and quickly cleansed himself. He got out of the tub and dried himself while the tub was draining. He dressed himself in a sweat outfit and went down the steps.

Major, Jill and Brok sat at the table and ate their chicken dinner with gusto and Major told Brok that he would spend the day with him tomorrow. "Just man to man," laughed Major.

After the dinner dishes were done, and Brok was playing on the floor Major turned on the news. He was gently stroking Jill's leg when he heard the news caster mention the kidnapping that he read about. "Hey," Major blurted, "I read that in the paper."

"So did I," said Jill, "and I also read that this is not the first time it's happened! I've seen other stories similar to that."

"What do you mean?" Questioned Major.

"I mean that according to last nights paper that this is the fifth time its happened and there are similarities to each case, but no one's seen anything yet."

Major shook his head. "What about the parents? Surely they had to see something or someone suspicious. How could they lose a kid?"

Jill looked at Major, "Each of the kidnappings came at a mall, and each was connected with an assault of the parent, and it hasn't mattered if it's a mom or dad, they have been assaulted from behind, knocked unconscious and the child stolen. There has been no witnesses, no evidence, nothing. So what can the police do?"

"I don't know, but no one had better try to take my kid." Major said. "I'm liable to really hurt someone for that."

"Yeah, I know Major, but it's time for Brok's bedtime, and after he's sleeping you can rub my back."

"Good idea," Major said, reaching over and with his index finger sent shivers running down Jill's spine.

After a satisfying bout of love making, Major and Jill laid side by side on their backs lightly stroking each other. Jill whispered "Don't let anything happen to my baby tomorrow!"

"What is going to happen with a big, tough karate guy guarding him?" Asked Major. Jill didn't answer, she turned and laid her head on Major's chest and let herself drift off to sleep.

INTERLUDE

Theodore was looking at the money. Leaning back in his high top swivel chair, arms folded behind his head, his eyes glistening at the pile of tens, twenty's, fifty's and one hundred dollar bills piled haphazardly in front of him on his huge oak desk. Slightly less then two hundred fifty thousand dollars was in that pile of green.

Breathing in deeply through his nose and then exhaling through his mouth, Theodore could almost imagine he could smell the good life the money was going to bring to him. Fine cuisine, good liquor; elegant women, and tropical locales were all represented in that single breath.

But it wasn't enough! No sir! Theodore wanted more. He didn't want to worry about money for the rest of his life. Fifty years old and forced into an early retirement from the education system, because of an accused dalliance with a fourteen-year-old student, who by any account should have been considered at fault.

She was the one who seduced him, not the other way around. He had tried to end it several times, but in the end, she was the one who ended it. When she didn't get the A she was seeking in his history course, she told her parents that he had been molesting her. The resulting furor ended his teaching career.

Although he received a small retirement fund he was extremely angered at what he called "a shot gun to my head" and left the area he lived in all his life. He kept a post office box in a small town fifty miles away from his current address to receive his retirement check and personal correspondence.

Theodore sat up and reached for a bottle of scotch that was in the open desk drawer. He filled a water glass full and put the bottle back. He picked up the glass and suddenly downed it without a pause. Using the back of his hand to wipe his mouth and his fingers to rub the tears from his eyes, he let out a short bark of laughter.

Well, he had lost his preferred career, but his new career was going to make him rich, but the greatest thing of all was revenge! Revenge on kids, and revenge on parents.

There were a lot of rich people who couldn't have children and wouldn't trust the system to adopt a child. Extremely lengthy periods of time were required and the type of clients that Theodore was serving did not like any one prying in their private concerns. Also it was hard to find the exact type of child in an orphanage that most clients wanted and Theodore was more than happy to snatch a child that suited a prospective clients taste.

Ring-ring-ring-ring!!! The stillness of the room was shattered by the black dial telephone on the corner of the desk. Theodore let it ring four times before he picked up.

"Yes?" He answered.

"Gotta another job fer ya," a graveled voice said, "an it's worth a lot more to ya."

"How much more?" Theodore questioned.

"A hundred grand," growled the voice.

"What do you need and when?" Theodore trembled with excitement.

"Two to three year old, blond hair, and blue eyes, gotta be a good looking kid, and it's set up for Sunday night.

"Sunday night?" Sputtered Theodore. "But that's too soon! I need time to look around an set up the snatch!"

"Look," said the gravel voice, "that's why it's worth a hundred grand. It's for some one's birthday. If you don't want to do it I'll get someone else to do my jobs!"

"No, no, I'll do it, no problem. Same arrangement?"

"Yeah!" And then the connection was broken.

Theodore fumbled for the bottle of scotch and poured himself another glass full. A hundred grand! For that kind of money Theodore would take the risk. Besides all the other jobs had gone so smoothly, what could go wrong now? Theodore threw down his glass of scotch and sat back in his chair and owlishly stared at his pile of money.

END OF INTERLUDE

Major woke early Saturday morning, completed his morning hygiene, dressed in a sweat outfit and walked across his yard to his dojo. A dojo is a martial arts training hall.

He went inside and spent a few minutes stretching out his legs and loosening up his upper body.

Then stepping back with a hard "kiaaaa!" he started to run through his hand defends. Single knife defends, double knife defends, low inside and high inside defends, high and low blocks forearm and outside defends, he ran through them all with power. When he was through all of his defends he started in on his kicks. Roundhouse and side kicks, front and spin kicks, and after those four basic kicks he went into the variations of each. Outside crescents, inside crescents, flying front kicks, step behind sidekicks, step in front round houses. Spinning crescents, wheel kicks and finished up with flying spin kicks.

Sweating profusely now, he stepped up to the heavy bag, pulled on a pair of bag gloves and a pair of cloth shin and instep protection and proceeded to work out on it. "Huh! Huh! Huh!" he breathed out of his mouth with every punch. "Kiaaaa!" He shouted with every kick. He punched, kicked and pummeled the bag for three hard minutes before he was satisfied. He took off the bag gloves off wiped the sweat from his face and then started to shadow fight. He imagined there was an opponent in front of him and threw his whole arsenal at him. Kicks uppercuts and intricate combinations were all used. When Major was finished shadow boxing, he sat on the floor with his legs crossed and allowed his arms to lie loosely across his legs. He straightened his back and head in one line and breathed deeply through his nose and sent the air back through his mouth. At first he felt he wasn't getting enough air and the temptation to breath in through his mouth strong. He ignored the feeling knowing that within thirty seconds, he would be breathing normally again. With his breath starting to normalize, he allowed himself to start meditating. He forced himself not to think of anything and to clear his mind of all thoughts and clutter. He reached his goal, his body relaxed and all pain and soreness from his workout was now gone. He was floating on a cloud; he didn't feel the sweat dripping off of him or the hardness of the floor. Major sat there for a few minutes, before he allowed himself to open his eyes. He felt completely refreshed.

He got up from the floor and put his equipment away. Major walked back to the house and went in.

Jill was preparing breakfast for her and Brok. Major watched her make oatmeal cereal for her and Brok's lucky charms.

"Morning babe, I'm going up and shower."

"O.k. Major, Brok's watching cartoons right now, will you take his cereal into him please?"

Major walked over and drew her to his chest, kissed her deeply and released her. He took Brok's cereal into him and hugged him and kissed his little cheek.

"Going to the mall with me today buddy?" Major asked his son. "Mall, mall, daddy" Brok said with a four toothed grin.

"Good." Major said and then went up stairs.

Up stairs, Major quickly stripped the sweaty clothes from his body and set the water faucets on the shower. When the water was at the right temperature he opened the shower stall and went in.

He showered quickly and got back out. After drying himself off he wrapped he towel around his waist and went to his bedroom to get dressed. Dropping the towel, he put on a pair of playboy briefs and his socks, pulled on a pair of 501 jeans and picked a tee shirt out of his drawer with the Brown's karate logo on it. Going to his closet he grabbed his favorite pair of Nike tennis shoes out and put them on.

He went back to his dresser and grabbed his wallet and change from the top and opened up the second drawer and grabbed a handkerchief. He looked at his pipe and tobacco pouch and decided that just for today he wasn't going to smoke.

Going back downstairs, Major was ready for the day with his boy. "As soon as Bugs Bunny is over, we'll be leaving for the mall." "O.K. daddy." Brok said, his eyes never leaving the screen.

INTERLUDE

While Major was working out at home, Theodore was also at work. He had arrived at the King Mall before it had opened. He drove around it twice checking out the entrances to each store and marking them down on a store map. Although the mall had opened only a couple of years ago, that's when Theodore had gotten the map. Some of the stores had changed. He made the proper notations and parked in front of the big Sears store.

Other cars were parked around him now and the drivers were waiting for the stores to open.

At ten o'clock an employee came to the door of the Sears door entrance and opened it up, and the customers who were standing around the doors and the ones in their cars all went inside.

Theodore backed his gray Ford LTD out of the parking place and moved it catty cornered and half way back from the Sears door. If he was lucky enough to make a snatch he didn't want people looking straight out he door and seeing him get in his car. Locking the passenger side door, but leaving the driver side door unlocked he went inside.

Theodore was dressed nicely. He was tall, thin, silver haired with a well-trimmed mustache. He wore black horn rimmed glasses and although he wouldn't admit it, he bore an uncanny resemblance to Alfred Pennyworth, Bruce Wayne's butler on the old campy series of Batman that was on in the sixties.

He wore a fitted suit and tie and looked like an elegant man out for a stroll through the mall.

Keeping an eye out for a likely child, he slowly meandered around the stores checking for security officers and dead-ends.

He found the public restrooms and went in to use it. When he was done he flushed he urinal and went to the sink and washed his hands. It was perfect, he could keep an eye on anyone coming in the restroom and there was an entrance door twenty feet away from the restroom doors. Theodore went back to his car and moved it over by the entrance near the restroom. Now all he had to do was wait and hope for the right child to come along.

END OF INTERLUDE

Major and Brok pulled in the mall and parked around the main entrance. He couldn't get as close as he liked but he wasn't going to let anything bother him today. He and Brok were going to enjoy themselves.

Locking up his small truck {a Chevrolet S-10}, he led Brok into the mall by the hand.

Major did not come to the mall often, so he still liked to walk around and go into each store and check out their merchandise. The sights and sounds of the mall were exciting and stimulating to both him and Brok.

They walked past the entrance to a Hill's store and could smell the trademark popcorn. The smell of it reminded Major that he hadn't ate anything yet and started his stomach to rumbling. "Let's amble over to the food court area," he said to Brok.

"Not hungry, wanna ride toys," Brok was referring to the rides set up in the foyer of the mall.

"Okay pal, but as soon as you ride them, we're going to get something to eat."

"O.K. daddy."

Major fed quarters into the pony ride, then the pig ride followed by the space rocket and finally the antique car. He really loved to watch Brok's face as he made the accompanying noises with each ride.

When the last ride finally wound down, Major pulled Brok from the seat and said "Time to eat pal."

"Wanna ride more daddy!"

"We'll come back, pal."

Hand in hand they walked over to the food court and finally settled on hamburgers and French fries with cokes to wash them down with, unaware that they were being observed by a evil man who was watching them with a greedy and speculative eye.

Theodore was sitting on a bench away from the food court, but where he could keep an eye on the men's restroom. He had been there for about a half an hour and hadn't seen any potential child yet, and suddenly there he was, a handsome blond haired boy around two to three years old with his father. Theodore knew that this was the child he needed. He also knew that after they ate, the father would probably take his boy to the restroom with a little luck he would have his hundred grand by this evening. When they go to the restroom, Theodore thought, I would follow them in and make my move.

CHAPTER THREE

Major and Brok ate their hamburgers and French fries and watched the people come and go. Major thought that this was one of the main attractions of the food court. They finished up their meal and cleaned up their table, throwing their trash in the waste can positioned around the area.

"You have to pee Brok?" Major asked.

"Gotta pee daddy."

"Okay pal, let's go to the restroom."

He led Brok by the hand towards the restroom door smiling and nodding his head to people. He noticed the nicely dressed gentleman by the door and nodded his head to him and walked by him. They went into the restroom with Major holding the door open for Brok. The restroom was a big spacious, modern facility with the washbasins on the left, urinals on the right and closeted commodes in back.

He led Brok over the urinals and unsnapped his button and unzipped his zipper and lifted Brok up to the urinal. Brok put his feet on the sides of the urinal leaning on daddy's chest grabbed his winkie and started to pee. Major heard the door open and he glanced over to see the nicely dressed gentleman that was sitting outside coming in. Major grinned at him and turned back to watch his son pee. Sensing the gentleman moving to his right side, Major started to turn his head that way, when he was suddenly staggered. Not knowing what had happened to him he swayed backwards, grabbing Brok around the middle so he wouldn't fall.

Brok let out a startled squawk and peed on his daddy's hands.

Trying to maintain his feet and not dropping Brok, Major looked at the man again, just in time to see him swing a short club at his head. The stranger hit him just above the left eye with what looked like a table leg and Major went down to the floor with Brok on his belly.

The last thing Major remembers was a foot coming towards his head.

When Theodore walked into the restroom, he knew he had very little time to accomplish what he had to do. No one was coming when he went in, so he figured he had thirty seconds to get in and out. The man looked at him when he came in and grinned at him. Well he wouldn't be grinning in a second. Pulling a sawed off end table leg from under his coat, Theodore stepped up behind him and swung the club. In mid swing the man turned his head and Theodore hit him on back of the head by the crown instead of on top. The man staggered back holding the child and Theodore swung the club like a one-handed baseball player catching him above the eyes and dropping him backwards to the floor. Theodore couldn't believe it. He was still conscious! He drew back his foot and kicked him in the side of the head as hard as he could. That did it the man twitched and then was still. Blood was pouring from above his eye and dripping to the tiled floor. The child was sitting spread eagle on the unconscious man's chest and was looking up owlish at Theodore.

Theodore reached down for the child saying, "Your daddy had a accident, and we had better go find your mommy."

Brok looked at Theodore still not comprehending what was going on. "Ma-Ma home."

"Well, we better go get her." Theodore picked him up and pulled his pants up at the same time. Cradling the child as he walked out the rest room door. He looked up and down the hallway towards the main part of the mall and towards the exit doors. No one was coming either way.

"What a stroke of luck," thought Theodore as he nonchalantly walked to the exit and went out. People were walking towards the doors he had just left, but not a one gave him even a passing glance. Thank goodness the boy wasn't raising a fuss.

Theodore walked calmly to his LTD and opened the drivers' side door and set the boy inside.

"Scoot over," Theodore told him.

The boy moved over enough for Theodore to get into the car.

"What's your name, son?" He asked.

"I, Brok. Say like rock."

"Why that's a real nice name. "Brok, I like it, how old are you, Brok?"

Brok didn't answer, he held up his index finger and middle finger for the number two, just like mommy and daddy always showed him.

"Two years old, why that's real good Brok." Theodore intoned with a gentle voice. "Well, sit back and I'll buckle your seat belt for you."

Brok leaned back and Theodore buckled him in. Ohio had passed a mandatory seat belt law a couple of years ago and Theodore didn't want to get pulled over for something as trivial as that.

Theodore put the LTD in gear and drove carefully away from the King Mall. Obeying all stop signs, traffic signals and maintaining the speed limit he drove across town away from the mall until he found a telephone from which he could place a call without leaving his vehicle.

He pulled up beside the phone, rolled his window down and reached for the telephone.

"Where Ma-Ma at?" Brok asked looking around.

"We will find her in a little bit, Brok, don't you like being with me?"

"Want Ma-Ma an' daddy." Brok started to cry then, his face pinched up and big tears rolled down his cheeks.

"Don't cry Brok, I'm going to call your Ma-Ma right now." Lied Theodore. Brok settled back down in his seat sniffling.

Theodore reached across his car and opening up the glove box pulled out a cool-whip container full of quarters. He fed five dollars worth of quarters into the slot and then punched out the number he had memorized.

The phone rang through five times before it was picked up. "Yes?" It was the graveled voiced man again.

"It's a go," said Theodore, "Can we meet tonight?"

"No! I told you Sunday night and Sunday night is when it's gonna be!" Snarled the voice.

"But I got him now!" "What am I going to do with a kid for twenty four hours?" Whined Theodore.

"That's your problem, asshole! You just better have him at the usual place at the right time if you want your money. I don't pay or go out of my way if you're early!"

Click . . . . The connection was broken. Theodore slammed the phone against the steering wheel and sat staring straight ahead for a moment his jaws were clenched tight and his face was a furious cloud.

"One of these days he is going to regret talking to me like that." Theodore thought.

He hung up the phone and rolled his window back up. Brok, who was listening to the conversation started to cry.

"Brok want my Ma-Ma, where my Ma-Ma at?"

It was all Theodore could do to control himself. He wanted to backhand the little child as hard as he could, he wanted to shake him and slap him until he shut his mouth. Theodore actually drew his hand back for the initial strike, before his fury broke. He didn't think anyone would pay one hundred thousand dollars for abused merchandise. Taking in a deep breath through his mouth and releasing it softly through his nose, Theodore looked over at Brok and reached across with his right hand rubbed his head and told him, "I just talked to your Ma-Ma, Brok. She has to go help your daddy, so she wants you to spend a couple of days with me."

"Want to go home."

"I'll take you home later then Brok, but first I'm going to take you to my house and we'll have fun together."

"Want Ma-Ma."

"We'll see about that later." Lied Theodore.

He dropped the transmission in drive and headed for a little town about thirty miles north of Marietta, Ohio.

It was a bad dream, not a nightmare, but the kind of dream you hate to have. Someone, whom he didn't know, was chasing him. He couldn't run he couldn't even turn his head to see who was chasing. All he knew was he was scared to death and someone was after him.

Somewhere far away he could hear someone calling his name. "Maaa Jooor, wake uuuupp!" The voice was one he knew, but he started to concentrate on it and to follow it away from his dream. Anything had to be better than this.

With a start, Major opened up his eyes to the worst headache he had ever had in his life. It was worse than any hang over headache he had ever suffered, even though he had quit drinking years ago. He still remembered some of the worst cases.

Major opened his eyes to mere slits and even that let too much light in. He closed them again and took an inventory of his body. Everything seemed to check out okay but his head was throbbing to his pulse. He started to reach up with his left hand to check for the cause of his pain when he felt something move on his arm. He opened up his eyes again and was startled to see an I.V. in his arm. Major closed his eyes again, trying to make sense of what was happening. An I.V. in his arm meant hospital and he couldn't remember what had happened to him. Using caution, he opened up his eyes again. The light wasn't hurting him near as bad as it did when he first came awake. He looked at his right arm and there seemed to be nothing wrong there. Slowly he reached up to his face and felt around. "What's this?" He murmured feeling the bandages above his left eye. "What has happened to me?" He wondered. He lay there trying to remember what had happened. Was he in an accident? Did he fall? He couldn't remember. He opened up his eyes and looked around the room. "Yes, definitely a hospital," he thought, "but how did I get here?" He looked to the side of the bed and seen the nurse call light. Reaching over gingerly with his left hand, he pushed it. The effort caused him to fall back in the bed with an audible moan.

Suddenly, the nurse swept in and came to his bedside. She was a young girl in a white uniform with a kind expression on her face.

"What's going on?" "What happened to me?" Major asked before the nurse could say anything.

"You've had as accident." She reached over his head and looked at the bandaged section. "I just came on shift and I don't really know what is going yet, but I do know your wife is here with some policeman." She walked to the other side of the bed and checked the machine hooked up to the I.V in his arm.

"Where is she? I'd like to see her." Major asked.

The nurse took his pulse, and stuck a thermometer into his mouth and wrapped his arm for the blood pressure reading.

"As soon as I take your vitals, I'll let them know you are awake, by the way, my name is Sandy, and I'll be your nurse on this shift." She paused and said, "Can I get you anything? Water perhaps?" Are you in much pain?"

"Yes, you can bring my wife in here. I have to know what's going on." Said Major.

Sandy smiled at him and left the room.

Major leaned back and closed his eyes. He wished that he could have some type of painkiller, but he had to see Jill first.

The door opened silently and Major opened his eyes in time to see Jill and a stranger walk through the door.

Someone had said a policeman and Major was expecting a uniformed cop, but this guy looked like one of those fancy detectives you see on T.V. He was wearing a tailored gray pin striped suit with black shoes on, polished bright enough to blind a man. His hair was a mixture of black sprinkled with gray. "Salt and pepper," Major thought. "About my age, mid thirties. His jacket was unbuttoned and Major could see the holster for a gun and the butt of it peeking out from under the lapel. The detective looked like he was in good shape, well anyway the suit hid it well if he wasn't. "One thing for sure," Major thought, "he looks capable."

Jill was standing beside the detective all the time Major was appraising him. She was looking at Major with a look he had never seen from her before. It looked like she had been crying and she had no makeup on and her hair was a mess.

But that wasn't what was bothering Major. It was that look in her eyes. It looked like . . . . Well what? Hatred? Yes! That's the word. It looked like she hated him with all of her heart.

Time was transfixed for a moment. Major and Jill was staring at each other s eyes and Major couldn't see the woman he had loved and married there. Why wasn't she coming to him? He needed her touch and soothing words. He didn't know what was going on yet but things didn't look good.

"Jill?" Major said her name as a question.

The detective stepped up to the side of the bed hand extended for a handshake.

Major shook hands with him although he couldn't manage a good grip. His head was really starting to pound now.

"Mr. Brown, my name is Richard Breeler from the F.B.I."

"F.B.I.?" Asked Major, now he was more confused. "What's going on here?"

"Do you remember going to King's Mall this morning with your son, Brok?" Queried the detective.

"Yeah, I took him to the mall. Where is he? Is he all right? What happened to me?" Demanded Major, his voice starting to rise as he sat up in the bed. His head started pounding like bass drum.

"I'm sorry to inform you that your son has been kidnapped."

"Kidnapped?" Gasped Major looking to Jill for affirmation. She barely nodded her head and her eyes grew harder still.

Suddenly Major knew why that look was in her eyes. She was blaming him for the loss of their child.

"Yes Sir, It looks like the same M.O. that has been used for several other kidnapping around the state." Detective Breeler reached into his shirt pocket and pulled out a pen and a pad.

"I need to ask you some questions, sir."

"Okay," Major looked at Jill and his heart broke as she looked away from him and walked over to the chair and sat down to listen, averting her face from him.

"Can you tell me what you did chronologically after you arrived at the mall, please?"

Major leaned back in the bed closed his eyes and tried to bring the morning back. "If only this headache would go away!" He thought.

"We arrived at the mall at about twelve thirty and walked around the stores a little bit. I let him ride all of the rides in the foyer and we went to get something to eat."

"What time was that?"

"Around one forty five or so."

The detective made a notation on his pad.

"Then what?"

"Well, we finished eating and I asked him if he had to go to the restroom and he said, "Yes," Major told him.

"Do you remember anything unusual?"

"No," said Major.

"No one was hanging around the restrooms or anyone looking suspicious?" Questioned the detective trying to be helpful.

"Well, wait a minute, everything is pretty hazy, let me think a minute." Major closed his eyes his head was pounding like a sledgehammer on steel now.

Major let his mind wonder back to this morning at the mall. Was it really this morning? It seemed like years.

He was remembering everything now, and it hit him like a punch in the stomach.

He opened his eyes to see the detective writing in his pad and he looked over at Jill, who still hadn't said a word to him. She was still looking away from him, looking at a spot on the wall as if her mind was a million miles away from the hospital room.

"I remember what happened now, all of it," said Major and an empty feeling invaded his very soul.

"You remember what?" Asked Breeler.

"There was a guy sitting on the bench before we went into the restroom, he followed us in."

"Do you remember what he looked like? Can you give a description of him?"

"Did you ever watch that old Batman series that used to be on?"

"Yes, but what does that have to do with it?"

"Well, that guy looked exactly like the butler Alfred."

"Okay," said Breeler scratching in his pad. "Can you tell me what happened?"

"Brok was peeing in the urinal, I was holding him up and this guy came up beside me."

"What then?"

"He must have hit me then. I remember seeing a club, like a table leg coming at me, and I remember going down, and the last thing I could see was a foot coming at me."

"Could you tell me what type of clothing he wore, any distinguishing marks, scars, tattoos, anything?"

"No, all I can tell you is that he was dressed nice."

"Okay Sir, you say he looked like Alfred?" He asked, looking at his notes.

"Yes, that's right. I remember thinking it could have actually been him."

"Okay, you get some rest now, and if you can think of anything else that will help us, let me know. If we have any more questions for you we'll get back to you."

The detective turned to leave, but Major stopped him.

"Have any of these cases been solved yet?"

The detective looked at Major with pity in his eyes. "No, but at least this time we got a description of the suspect. That's more than we ever had before. "Good day to you, sir."

Breeler nodded his head at Jill and left.

Major looked over at Jill as she left her seat and came to the front of the bed.

"Honey, I . . . ."

"Don't honey me!" Jill said in an eerie voice. "I told you last night not to let anything happen to my child!"

"But . . ."

"No Major! What's going to happen to him with a big tough karate guy guarding him?" She mimicked his words from last night.

"I'm done with you! I don't want anything more to do with you!" "Do you understand me?"

"But Jill," Major tried to calm her down. "We'll get him back, you'll see, and then it will be alright!"

"No! When I leave here I'm filing for a divorce, we're done!"

"What are you talking about?" Asked Major, starting to get angry.

"You are on your own from now on! I don't ever want to see you again! Never!"

Major flinched as she came around the bed and grabbed him by the hospital gown top he had on, and jerked him to a sitting position. "I hate you! I hate your guts! Stay away from me!" With that, she released his gown letting him flop to the bed, turned and angrily strode to the door and went through without a backward glance.

Major lay in the bed, eyes opened, staring at the ceiling as the nurse came running in.

"You okay?" She asked looking at the tears rolling down Major's face. She had heard everything.

"No, I'll never be okay again." Without looking at Sandy he said, "Get me something that will knock me out for awhile. Sandy left the room to get him an injection, Major relived the scene in his mind over and over again.

Sandy came back in and administered the medication. She stood by his bed until it took effect.

"Poor man," she said as Major finally succumbed.

CHAPTER FOUR

It took Theodore about an hour to drive to his house. He pulled up to his lane, which led back to his secluded home.

The closest town was only a five-minute drive, but he lived back far enough away from people that no one would come casually calling.

Theodore was a private individual and he liked being left alone. He looked across the seat at the little boy who had finally drifted off to the safety of sleep.

"It's going to be a long night and day with this crybaby kid," mused Theodore. He didn't have much patience with children this size having never been around them much. He had been an only child and his parents never went anywhere to expose him to other children. Even in grade school he had been pretty much a loner.

No traffic was coming either way, so Theodore turned left across the roadway and pulled up to his one level cottage. He parked along side of his house and shut the ignition off. Reaching across the sleeping child he unlocked the door. Theodore then got out on the driver's side, took his keys from the ignition and put them in his right front pocket. Walking around the front of the LTD, Theodore was careful not to mar his shoes on the limestone laid down for his driveway. He opened up the passenger door and immediately locked the door. That was a habit he always made use of. He didn't want to come out one morning and find his car stolen.

Theodore then reached down and picked up the sleeping child and started for the cottage.

Halfway to the door, Theodore realized he couldn't unlock the door with the child cradled in his arms.

Cursing under his breath he tried to shift Brok over his left shoulder so he could get into his pants pocket and retrieve the keys, when Brok started to wake up. The little boy lifted his head and looked around not knowing where he was.

"Where Ma-Ma?" He asked.

Theodore made a conscious effort not to be upset. He put Brok down on the cement stoop and dug the keys from his pocket.

"Where Ma-Ma?" Brok asked again his face starting to pinch up to cry.

"Ma-Ma is not here Brok." Theodore put the key in the lock and opened the door. "Come on in and let's see if we can call her on the phone, okay with you?"

"Okay." Brok agreed with a sniffle.

They entered the cottage, Theodore guiding Brok in by the back of his head.

Theodore glanced at the clock above the mantle located on the right of the front door. Three o'clock. "Good." Thought Theodore, maybe there's something on television for the little brat to watch."

Shutting the door behind them Theodore turned and fastened the dead bolt and also making sure the latch was locked. "Can't be too careful."

He walked past the child again, looking at him out of the corner of his eye. Although he looked like he was going to let loose with a wail he hadn't yet.

He went in the kitchen, which was adjacent to the living room and opened up the refrigerator door. Peering inside he spotted a can of diet Pepsi that had been in there for quite awhile. He grabbed it and shut the door. Looking up in the cupboard for something sweet to give Brok, Theodore came up with nothing. Muttering under his breath he peered in the lower cabinets and spotted the familiar blue and white box of

Nabisco saltine crackers. He pulled the box and was happy to see one whole sleeve of crackers was still sealed.

He took the pop and crackers out to Brok and said, "Come with me to my den and we'll see if there is anything on television."

"Okay," Brok agreed. He loved T.V.

Theodore led the way to the back of the cottage to the small bedroom he had converted to his den. He opened the door and led Brok in. He went over to his nineteen-inch remote controlled color zenith and grabbed the remote from the top of it. Hitting the power button he switched the T.V. on and began flipping through the channels. Theodore had no idea what was on, because he didn't watch much T.V. preferring instead to play with his money and daydreaming about his future.

Brok sat in front of the set and watched the images flicker across the screen.

"Burt and Ernie," he said suddenly.

Theodore had already passed the channel and instantly flipped back to the channel that Brok had noticed.

"Burt and Ernie," Brok said again, when Theodore regained the channel.

Theodore reached down to his rotor box and switched it to west and watched the screen clear up as his antennae slowly swiveled to the strongest signal. The program Brok was interested in was on a PBS station from a town thirty miles from his home.

Theodore recognized the characters. They were from a puppet show on a program called Sesame Street.

Hoping that the show would keep the young boy occupied Theodore went back to the kitchen to fix him and the boy something substantial to eat. Rummaging through the refrigerator, he was startled to find Brok behind him.

"Thirsty," he said.

Theodore sighed and went back to the den and opened up the can of Diet Pepsi and to take the little red clip off of the sleeve of crackers.

"There you go, eat there until I get something cooked up for us both," he said.

Brok sat down in front of the T.V. again took a small drink from the can and started to stuff crackers in his mouth. Theodore watched him for a minute and then went back to the kitchen.

Theodore plugged his Fry Baby in and went back to the potatoes bin and started to peel potatoes so he could make French fries up. What kid didn't like French fries?

He French-fried a bowl full of potatoes and grabbing the bottle of Heinz's ketchup from the refrigerator he headed back to the den. Walking through the door, Theodore stopped and couldn't believe what his eyes were seeing. There was the little punk weasel of a kid up on his beautiful oak desk and he had a pen in his hand! Trying desperately to control his temper he stepped over to where the little boy was scribbling all over his desktop.

"No! No! No!" Shouted Theodore. Putting the bowl of fries and the bottle of ketchup to the floor, he reached over to the boy and jerked him from the top of the desk.

"Look what you did!" he squealed. "Just look!" He grabbed Brok's head and forced the stunned child to look at his handiwork.

"No! No! No!" Shouted Theodore again. "Don't' you touch my things! No!" He cracked Brok's bottom three good whacks and put the terrified and screaming child to the floor.

Ignoring the screaming cries, Theodore went to the kitchen and grabbed some towels and a bottle of Murphy's oil soap.

He went back to his desk ignoring the sobbing child on the floor. He started scrubbing trying to get the cursed ink marks off his desk. After some strenuous scrubbing he managed to get most of the marking off, but no matter how much scrubbing he did, he couldn't get the scratch marks off the top.

Needing a drink, Theodore walked around to the drawer side of the desk and moving the swivel chair aside, he bent down to the drawer containing the scotch and his water glass. Filling it up to the top, he downed half of it in a single gulp. The liquor exploded in his stomach like a bomb. Wiping the tears from his eyes with the back of his hand, Theodore started to lose some of his intense anger.

Looking over the top of his marred desk he could see the little rug rat that drove him to such a rage.

He downed the other half of his drink and poured another one, but only a third of a glass.

"This kid is going to drive me crazy," he mumbled. "I'll be glad to be rid of him!" "Good thing it's only for eighteen hours more, or the boy would be damaged goods."

He would have to control his temper better. This kid was worth a 100 g's to him.

Taking a sip from the glass, Theodore looked at his desk once again. Shaking his head, he picked up the remote control from the corner of the desk, he flipped through the channels again until he came to a cartoon starring some cat named Heathcliff, and he walked around the desk to try to make friends with Brok again.

CHAPTER FIVE

Major was given his final check up by his family doctor at nine thirty Monday morning and was given the okay for his release.

He hadn't seen Jill since last Saturday afternoon. Major's face grew red as once again he recalled the rebuke that Jill had given him.

He had been hoping that Jill would relent and come and pick him up. That probably was probably too much to ask for though. Since he hadn't seen or heard from her, he had to believe that she meant every word she had said.

His parents had came up to see him yesterday and they assumed that he had a ride with Jill, and Major was so embarrassed by his wife leaving him that he didn't enlighten them of the separation effected by Jill.

Although his parents were very supporting of him, "It's happened to other people, you're not the first and won't be the last until they catch the man." His mother has said when they were leaving, Major was still acutely aware of the cheerful chatter she had put in the conversation, and the careful avoidance of Brok's name.

His father had just sat there and grunted when he should of. Major had never felt so alone before in his life. He was thankful when they left. He could never tell them of the scene from the day before.

Major shook himself from his reverie and watched as a nurse pushed a wheelchair into his room.

"Time to go." She said brightly.

Major looked around the room for a second, blinking back a mist from his eyes. He lost so much here. It's hard to believe he lost his wife and child in a single day.

He swung his feet to the side of the bed and climbed into the wheelchair.

"Watch your feet as we go," the nurse said, as Major settled into the chair.

She wheeled him out into the corridor and expertly wheeled him to the elevator and pushed the call button. When the elevator arrived and the door opened with a ding, she pushed him inside and pushed the ground floor button.

"There is a reporter on the first floor wanting to talk to you," she said. "I brought you to the ground floor, so you can leave if you didn't want to talk to him."

"Thanks I don't feel like talking right now."

"That's okay Sir, good luck."

Major got up from the wheelchair and looked at the glass door.

"Where is your ride Sir?" "I can wait until they arrive and keep you company."

"No thanks," Major kept his eyes looking out the door.

The nurse stood there for a second, shrugged her shoulders and turned and left.

Major stood there for several more minutes and finally realized that she wasn't coming. He checked his pants pockets and found his truck keys. And went out through the doors. Hands in his front pants pockets and head down he started to walk.

He was several miles from the mall where the abduction took place and he had no idea if is truck would even be there, but he didn't want to call anyone for a ride and he didn't want to call a cab. So he walked.

As he walked, he thought about how quickly his happy and secure home had disintegrated around him.

Losing Brok in such a violent way was bad enough, but the way he and Jill had separated was worse.

Walking down the sidewalk and streets and through intersections and across grassy lawns, Major barely glanced around at the cars, bicycles other pedestrians or the occasional cat or dog. He was a picture of a broken man. People who knew him would have never recognized him by his dejected shuffle.

All he could think of was the loss of his family. Five hours later he reached the vast parking lot of the King Mall. Walking around the sidewalk that encompassed the huge mall, he soon came to where he left his truck parked. Major looked and didn't see his pick-up through the first section of cars that were parked there.

Listless he scanned the section of parking around again and again he failed to see his S-10. He had just about made his mind up that it was towed when he caught a glimpse of a silver S-10 parked over closer to Hill's Store entrance.

Walking over he recognized his little truck. Major walked over to verify to his mind that it was his truck. It was. The twisted bumper testified to that fact. He had twisted it helping a stranded motorist from a ditch last winter.

Major pulled the keys from his pocket and had the key in the lock and was just starting to unlock the truck when he stopped.

He looked up at the Hill's entrance an in a split second decision decided to go inside and check out the restroom where he had been so brutally assaulted.

Walking past the Hill's entrance and smelling the popcorn gave Major a rather sinister feeling of deja vu. He went through the food court where he and Brok had ate their hamburger and walked into the restroom where his happiness had been so violently murdered.

Major looked around the restroom and at the partition and the urinals and the air machine that dried your hands.

His fists began to open and close, open and close and his body tightened up, his eyes closed, and his head went back, and his nostrils flared open, and heart pounded fiercely in his chest. The memory of the kidnapping assaulted him from all side. Major snapped his eyes open. His whole body was tense, ready to strike and to strike hard. But there was nothing to strike out at. Nothing! An animal growl started from deep within his chest and threatened to tear it self from his throat.

With an effort that left the muscles of his neck sore for days afterward to suppress it.

"By the life of my son, and for the death of my family, someone is going to pay for this!" Major breathed. "Some one is going to pay!" He turned and stalked out the restroom doors.

CHAPTER SIX

Theodore was drunk. He sat at his desk and stared owlishly at the bottle of scotch in front of him.

He had taken Brok to the small airfield where he usually met the buyer of his unusual merchandise.

He had shown up on time and he had a cardboard box with him full of fives, tens and twenty-dollar bills, just like Theodore preferred!

"Good looking kid," was all he said as he handed the box to Theodore.

"Let me know when you need more," Theodore had intoned. Being around the big man made Theodore nervous.

"Okay," the graveled voiced man turned to leave with Brok who now realized that once again he was going with someone new, had just started to pinch his face up to cry, he held his hands out to Theodore in the classic "pick me up" gesture used by children everywhere.

For once, since Theodore started his lurid sideline business he felt a pang of sorrow. He had enjoyed the little boy after the kid had settled down. That was after the desk incident. Thinking of the desk brought a hard glint to Theodore's eyes and suddenly he didn't feel sorry for the kid anymore.

Theodore turned to leave, ignoring the cries that started to issue from behind him. Good riddance was all he could say.

But . . . Theodore turned around and watched the big man pick Brok up and try to comfort him.

"Where is he going to?" Theodore asked.

"You know better then to ask something like that."

"Where's he going?" Theodore asked again and he gripped the big man's eyes with his own.

The big man tried to stare Theodore down but for the first time in their association he was unable too.

Their eyes remained locked for an undeterminable amount of time before the big man turned away.

"West Virginia," he said in a husky voice. "Just read the paper."

He turned and walked away from Theodore, Brok tucked under his arm.

And now Theodore was drunk and feeling a little dirty. He poured another drink and capped the bottle and stuck it in his lower desk drawer.

The bottle clinked against something and Theodore looked down to see what it was. It was a novelty cigarette lighter, shaped like a small derringer. You pull the trigger and a flame came out of the barrel. Theodore clicked it a few times and it didn't light. He searched around and found some lighter fluid and filled the gauze to saturation. Shaking the excess naphtha out, he put the lighter back together and flicked the trigger again. It lit on the third click. Tired of playing with the lighter he put it in the top desk drawer, thinking he needed some good cigars for his humidor. Reaching over to the biggest drawer in the desk, he put a key in the lock and turned it. With a smile the drawer was unlocked, Theodore pulled it open and gazed at the money. $347,989 dollars were in the desk drawer. Nothing larger than twenty-dollar bill was there.

Theodore started to take the money out of the drawer so he could indulge in his favorite past time of daydreaming, but he dropped the money in his hands back into the drawer and relocked it. Instead he drove into town to pick up a newspaper.

CHAPTER SEVEN

Major sat in his darkened living room, no lights on and no T.V. The only noise in the house was the sound of the refrigerator running.

Major had been sitting there since he arrived from the hospital. He wanted revenge, but he also was intelligent enough to realize that he had to consider all facets of his situation.

He had already called his superintendent from work and arranged to take a couple of weeks off as vacation time. His super was real understanding and was trying to help him out in every way that he could.

Then he had called up one of his black belt students Carl Hooper, to take over the teaching of his Karate classes for the same period of time.

Major had two full weeks to try and find "Alfred", if he could, and get his son back. If he needed more time he would take it, event if it cost him his job and business.

But for now Major had to think of organizing his plan of action.

He walked over to his dojo and turned on the lights. He stripped down to his playboy briefs and started to stretch out. A good work out would help him think. Finally the need for action prompted him to his feet and work out began.

Any workout or training he had worked through before was nothing compared to what he pushed himself through now. Each punch, each kick, each defend was delivered with lightning speed and thunderous power.

Nothing flesh and blood could've stood in the way of Major during this workout. The heavy bag jumped, jiggled and shuddered violently from each blow.

Three minutes passed then four, the five and finally after six full out, no holds barred minutes of unrestrained power released on the bag. Major suddenly stopped with a moan.

Hands throbbing, leg aching, lungs heaving desperately for more air, his head pounding loudly from the workout and the injury suffered from the blow of the club "Alfred" yielded, Major slumped to the floor unconscious.

Major awoke the next morning in more physical pain then he could ever remember.

Using his aching muscles, he slowly got to his feet. His head was hurting so badly that his vision seemed to be meshed in red. He pulled the bag gloves from his hands and tortuously made his way over to the house.

He climbed the long flight of stairs to the bathroom and kicked off his briefs as he climbed into the shower. He let the hot water burn him up to ease the cramping occurred as he stepped into the shower and gradually added cold water until the water was a normal temperature.

Finished, he toweled off and got dressed in jeans and a tee shirt, and went down stairs to make him something to eat.

After steak and eggs Major headed to the town library to get information on the previous kidnappings.

CHAPTER EIGHT

Theodore bought papers for Ohio and West Virginia and took them home with him. Taking them into his den he sat at his desk and opened up the first one. He carefully studied the paper all the way through and couldn't find a clue to what "Gravel Man" had alluded too.

He wanted a drink of scotch, but was afraid that he would miss something in the paper if he drank too much. He opened up another paper and studied through it. Nothing. He opened up another and studied it. Nothing. Irritated, Theodore reached for another and stopped. There it was on the front page. It had to be. A West Virginia socialite couple just back from Paris graced the front page of the paper. A small article accompanied the picture.

Fuerte's Return
Millionaire Peter Fuerte and wife Allison,
Just back from the streets of Paris, France
Will host a party in honor of Mrs. Fuerte's
Thirty birthday. Included in the invitations
Will be West Virginia Governor Ron Middletown

Shaken, Theodore sat back in his swivel chair with an audible thump!

The Fuerte's-Allegations of drug money!

Allegations of ties to the underworld, Allegations of murder. Allegations of everything illegal or sordid, as long as there was money involved.

Theodore went back into the den and poured himself a water glass full of scotch. Now he could get drunk. He was just tipping the glass back when the jingling of the telephone shattered the silence of the cottage.

Theodore let it ring four times before he answered it. If it was who he thought it was, four times was an "all" clean signal.

He picked up the receiver. "Yes?" He answered.

"Gotta another job for ya"

"What do you need?" Asked Theodore.

CHAPTER NINE

Major gathered up the papers he had researched at the library and took them to the desk.

"Thank you," he said as he walked back to the table where his notes were.

He had taken down the names of all the malls from where previous kidnappings had occurred. What he was going to do with the information was still evolving in his mind. Not being trained in police or detective work he had to try and figure things out for himself.

One predominant fact that he did notice was that all the children stolen were under the age of four. He mulled that fact over in his mind.

Children that age could be reprogrammed quicker then an older child, or could it be that someone could be placing orders for a particular kind of child.

He looked back through his notes. There were no outstanding similarities between the children. They weren't all blondes or red heads. There was no set pattern to the descriptions of the kids.

A light bulb went off in Major's head. "That's it!" He thought. "Someone is filling orders." "If you need a blonde hair blue eyed kid, no problem! Or a black haired green eyed child, well, just let me get back with you!"

Excited, Major gathered up his notes and headed for a gas station. He wanted to pick up a map of Ohio.

Major picked up his map at a BP station, it wasn't Sohio any more, and headed for the house.

He threw all the material he had gathered on the table and headed to the refrigerator. Opening the door he looked at the meager picking on each of the shelves. What he seen wasn't worth the effort to chew and ingest. Sighing he dropped some ham slices down from the freezer and ran hot water into the sink. When the water was steaming hot he plugged the drain and let the water build up enough to cover the ham slices.

He walked back to the refrigerator and got a sixteen ounce bottle of Pepsi, cracked it open, took a long pull and went back to the table while his ham slices thawed out.

Opening up the map he had obtained he started to find the locations from where each of the kidnappings had occurred. Using a blue magic marker, he marked each spot. The areas marked made a semi-circle around the eastern side of Ohio, as far south as Marietta, Ohio and as far north as Youngstown.

King's Mall, located in Greensville, was the mall that was furthest west of the other kidnappings.

Major went back over the time lapses of the kidnappings and noticed that the first one was the most southern one, and it went up the state line in sequence. Kings Mall was the only one to break away from that pattern.

"I wonder if he's working central Ohio now?" Major thought he went to the telephone and pulled the directory from the drawer beneath it.

He dialed Triple A's number and asked for assistance. A woman named Sherrie came on and started to fill in some blanks for him.

All Major wanted was the names of the major malls north and south of Greensville. When he got the information he needed, he hung up with Sherrie and pulled the wallet from his pants pocket. Searching through the wallet he found what he had been looking for. He held the card up to the light and reached for the phone as he read the card.

DETECTIVE RICHARD BREELER
F.B.I.

He dialed the number listed on the card and let the phone ring.

CHAPTER TEN

Theodore was cruising Central Mall; it was one of the biggest malls that Theodore had been to yet.

He was just getting the feel of things. The graveled voiced man wanted another child, (worth twenty five thousand dollars), by Sunday. Theodore liked to check out the location well ahead of the jobs. The Brown child was the only hurry up job that he had committed.

Central Mall was a huge mall and Theodore spent the rest of the afternoon checking all of the exits and entrances.

CHAPTER ELEVEN

Major was just about to hang the phone up when Detective Breeler answered.

"Hello, Breeler here."

"Breeler, this is Major Brown, do you remember me?"

There was a pause and a slight hesitation.

"Yes, . . . What can I do for you?"

"Well," Major hesitated and then began, "well, I've been checking up on the previous kidnappings and I think I've discovered a pattern."

"And what pattern is that?" Breeler asked with a bemused tone.

"The first kidnapping started south by Marietta and worked itself up. King's Mall was the first to change on that pattern. I think the next kidnapping will be the next major mall above the King's Mall and that is, ummm-let me see here, oh yes! Central Mall.

"How did you arrive at that conclusion Mr. Brown?"

Breeler sounded like he was trying not to patronize him.

"I went to the library and got information on the other kidnappings and found out how they went up on the map."

Major was starting to realize that Breeler wasn't taking him seriously.

"Well, Mr. Brown," Breeler's voice started to take some steel to it, "That's a very good theory, but I think you better leave the investigation up to the people who have experience in that area."

"I don't think you are doing very well with your investigations at this time, do you?," growled Major.

"We're doing our job, Sir. The best thing for you to do is let us."

Major heard a voice saying something in the background.

"But can't you get someone to check it out?"

"Mr. Brown, we're doing everything we possibly can. Please leave the police work to us!

He heard the voice in the background again, and although he couldn't hear the words the sound of the voice was strangely familiar.

"But Detective Breeler . . ."

Breeler cut Major off in mid sentence.

"But nothing, Sir!" Breeler barked. "The F.B.I. is handling your case. I know that your worried but you must let us do our work!"

"But . . ."

"We'll keep in contact with you Sir!" Breeler said.

Major was ready to hang the phone up in disgust when he heard the familiar voice speak again in the background.

"Tell the Bastard it was his fault it happened anyway."

Instead Breeler simply hung up the phone, but not before Major recognized the voice. It was Jill. His wife was at Breeler's house!

Major called back and the phone rang over and over and over again. On the fifth teen ring Breeler picked up.

"What's my wife doing there?" Major asked fury barely contained.

"She's filed for divorce, she is not yours anymore Brown!" Exclaimed Breeler with all friendliness gone from his voice.

Jill grabbed the phone from Breeler, "Major?" She asked.

"Jill! What's going on? Why are you there with him?"

"I told you once, Major! We're through! I'm my own person now that you destroyed our lives!"

There was a pause and then Jill said, "Oh Major, he's a lot better lover then you!" Then she hung up the phone.

Major ripped the phone off the wall and headed over to the dojo for another work out.

INTERLUDE

While Major was working himself into semi-conscious, Theodore was sitting at his desk playing with his money and drinking scotch.

CHAPTER TWELVE

It was now Saturday, a full week since Major's life was so callously destroyed. A lot of changes had come into his life recently, almost all bad, but if anything good had come from his trial and tribulations was his physical conditioning. He was in better shape then he was when he was tournament fighting. He felt great physically and was sharp as a tack mentally. He was ready for action. Time to start looking for "Alfred". Time to start paying back.

Major spent all day cruising Central Mall looking for his unknown nemesis, realizing that it was a distinct possibility that he could be misreading his information gleaned from the library's newspapers. He had to take the chance that he was right. He only had a week left of vacation time and he was scared that he would never find Alfred.

He finally parked his little S-10 and entered the mall. He started to walk around the huge complex, past diamond stores, clothing stores, toy stores, health food stores and even a store that specialized in exercise equipment. As Major walked about the mall, he thought about the circumstances that preceded Brok's abduction.

How did Alfred know where to attack him? How did he know to attack him when the restroom was empty?

Major sidestepped a couple of elderly "mall walkers" and then stopped in his tracks. "Of course," Major breathed to himself. "He watches the food court and sees who goes into the restrooms." Major remembered seeing Alfred sitting on the bench outside the restroom where he was assaulted.

A sense of excitement surrounded Major as he headed over to the food court and looked around for a seat that kept him partially concealed, yet allowed him a good view of anyone coming and going in and out of the rest room area.

Major scanned the crowd slowly and completely. He didn't see Alfred anywhere, but he knew he was where he needed to be.

He sniffed the air with appreciation and looked over the restaurants before he decided on fish and chips from an Arthur Treachers store.

He walked over and ordered his meal and leaned on the counter with his right elbow and slouched down keeping a close eye on the crowd.

"Six dollars and seventy five cents Sir," a voice interrupted his perusal of the busy area.

Major handed her a ten-dollar bill and received his three dollars and twenty-five cent in change back. He put it in his right front jeans pocket and walked away with his food as the waitress said "Thank you."

He sat in his original seat and started to eat his fish and chips. After eating a couple of chips, he went back for ketchup.

Before he reached the counter, he saw him.

There he was the man that haunted his dreams at night, the monster that had completely disrupted his secure home!

Alfred had come from the area where the movies were shown and the mall game rooms were at.

Major figured that he was checking out possible prey.

Major felt like he had been hit with an electric shock. His body was numb and didn't respond to his brain's commands. His vision had narrowed to the point that it looked like Alfred was in a tunnel. His stomach had tightened up and a splash of bile had entered the back of his mouth before he could keep it down. Major broke out in a sweat and his face felt like it was on fire.

Dimly, he realized that he was making a low growling sound, like a dog warning off another dog from his food bowl.

Major knew he had to get out of sight; he didn't want to take the chance that Alfred would recognize him, but he still couldn't move.

Suddenly someone behind him reached out and tapped him on the shoulder.

"Excuse me bud," said a man wearing a Cat hat and a U.M.W. jacket. "You using this table?" He asked.

Major turned part way and glowered at the man.

"Whoa, bud. You okay?" Queried the man.

"Yeah," Major said. "I'm not using the table, go ahead and take it."

"Thanks," said the man and he motioned his wife and two kids over.

Major eased his way back to the spot he had picked out in the beginning forgetting all about the ketchup. Moving the fish and chips to the side of the table, he put his face in his hands with his elbows on the table as he sat down to observe Alfred.

Major was upset with himself for freezing like he did. His martial arts training should have prevented an occurrence like that. He knew that he wasn't as strong emotionally as he should have been and he vowed to himself that it would never happen again.

He watched Alfred slowly walk around the food court observing the people there. He noticed that Alfred paid close attention to the people who had kids. Finally he sat down on a bench that was close to the restroom area and settled in.

Major hadn't planned ahead. He didn't know what to do. He couldn't call a cop and have him arrested because he didn't have any type of proof. He didn't want to approach him because he didn't want to scare him off.

As he observed Alfred he decided to watch him and follow him and try to get a license number if he could. He knew a friend who could get it traced for him.

Major and Alfred sat in the food court for over three hours. Finally Alfred got up. Looking splendid in his three piece suit he started to amble around the food court. Slowly he made his way out towards the main part of the mall.

Major got up then and left his unconsumed meal on the table.

Staying back, yet keeping the silver haired man in sight, Major followed him.

Although the mall was packed with people, Major had no trouble keeping Alfred in sight, because he meandered from store front to store front like a babbling brook in a meadow.

Finally Alfred went out the Central Mall's main entrance. He crossed the roadway into the parking lot.

Major stood inside the entranceway foyer and watched s he unlocked the driver side door of a gray LTD. While Alfred's head was down looking at what he was doing, Major left the foyer and walked towards the car directly behind the LTD.

By that time Alfred had entered his car and was buckling up his seat belt.

Moving quickly, but trying not to catch Alfred's attention, Major got behind the ford and looked at the license plate. NHQ982 was the number he read.

Alfred glanced around and pulled from his parking space and was soon out of sight.

"NHQ982-NHQ982," Major muttered to him self. Quickly he wrote the number down on the hood of a dirty car beside him. Not having a pencil or paper he was afraid he would forget the number.

"What are you doing? You jerk!" An angry voice exclaimed behind him.

Turning Major saw a muscle bound man in a sleeveless tee shirt striding angrily over to him.

"That's my car you messing with."

"Sorry buddy," Major said, "I needed to write the license plate number down and I didn't have a pen or paper with me."

"Well that's you problem." The man came up to Major and with the index finger of his right hand poked Major in the chest.

"No body messes with my stuff without paying for it."

The big man was trying to intimidate Major with his superior size and his big weight lifting muscles, and Major wasn't in the mood to be intimidated.

With his left hand he brushed the guy's hand away from his chest area.

"Back off, Mister!" Growled Major.

"You little pussy," the big man roared and drew his right hand back in a fist. "I'm going to knock your head off!"

As he started to throw a roundhouse punch to Major's head, Major threw his left hand up in a high single knife defend to protect his head. His right hand came upwards with the fingers straight and the thumb bent down in towards the palm. Using the muscle and bone behind the index finger and beside the thumb he viciously brought the reverse knife hand up in the thugs groin at the same instance he blocked the punch that was thrown.

"Ughh," grunted the man, his fist changing to a grasp as he tried to grab Major's arm.

Major brought his hand from between the man's leg and using the heel of his palm with his fingers straight in the air, he drove the palm heel to the man's solar plexus, the nerve center of the body. "Kiaaaa," he shouted!

The weight lifter stepped back a couple of steps and slowly slid down the side of his car unconscious.

Major looked down on him, and shaking his head he walked over to the hood of the car and once again looked at the number written there.

"NHQ982" he said and finally memorized it. He rubbed the number from the hood and walked away as a crowd started to gather, he completely put the fight from his thoughts.

CHAPTER THIRTEEN

Theodore left the mall and drove to a convenient store with a gas station. He pulled to the gas pumps and filled the tank with a ninety-four-octane gasoline. He went and paid the clerk, who pointed out the restroom. Theodore went in and washed his hands drying them on the paper towels that issued from the roller machine above the sink.

He walked out to his car and climbed in and headed back to Central Mall. He now gathered all the information he had needed for a successful abduction. His tank was full and he was ready to go to work.

CHAPTER FOURTEEN

Major left the mall in his S-10 and headed back to his father's house. As he drove he tried to figure out what he should do with the information he had.

He didn't want to go to the police with the license number because he knew they would direct him to the F.B.I. and after the conversation with Detective Breeler he didn't want anything to do with them or that asshole.

Pulling into his father's driveway, he waved a greeting to his dad's next-door neighbor, Timmy.

"Your parents aren't home," the neighbor said.

"Okay, thanks," said Major using the key on his key ring to let himself in the front door.

Once inside, he went directly to the phone and dialed his buddy's number.

On the second ring a small child answered, "Hello?" In the background Major heard his friend telling the little kid to give him the phone.

"Hey Pete, "Major here."

"Hi Major, what's happening?" Pete wanted to know.

"Can you do me a favor Pete?" Asked Major.

"As long as I don't have to leave the house, I'll be glad to help you, Major. I'm watching my kid."

"No problem Pete, I need a trace on a license plate number."

"What is it?'

"NHQ982."

"Ohio?"

"Yeah."

"Okay, Major I'll get back with you. Are you home?"

"No, call me at my mom and dad's."

"Okay, I'll get back with you."

Major cradled the phone as Pete broke the connection. He went to the kitchen and rummaged through the refrigerator until he came across some pressed chicken. He took it out grabbed a Pepsi and carried everything to the T.V. room and sat by the phone.

Using the remote control, he switched the set on and flipped through the channels, settled on a Cleveland Indians baseball game and ate his lunch.

Keeping the sound off, he watched the game, although if you asked him the score, he couldn't have told you what it was.

Suddenly the phone jangled, and Major picked it up.

"Yeah?"

It was Pete. "Got the trace for you."

"Give it to me buddy."

"Theodore Grant, age fifty, address county road 7, Guernsey County, Box 70.

"Thanks Pete, I owe you one." Major was grateful.

"No problem Major, you don't owe me anything for that!' Pete said and hung up.

Major downed the rest of his Pepsi, and cleaned up the remnants of his meal.

At last he had a name, but . . .

Should he get to the authorities?

No, screw them!!!

Major decided to check it out for himself first.

Leaving his parents home he went to his pickup a headed towards Guernsey County.

CHAPTER FIFTEEN

Theodore was feeling good.

He had stopped at a state liquor store, had bought a new bottle of scotch, and he grabbed a can of Mr. Peanut cashew nuts.

He had left his graveled voiced contact earlier with twenty five thousand dollars in cash and was heading home.

The job was so easy.

He didn't have to assault anyone this time. The mother had turned her back on the little black haired toddler that Theodore had wanted and the child had been separated from his mother by an arts and crafts booth. While she was checking prices on the crafts there, Theodore simply walked up and carried the child away!

When the boy started to cry he stuffed a sucker in his mouth and child had turned his attention to the sweet.

Easiest twenty-five grand he had ever made.

"Ha!" He laughed out loud. "They're probably still looking for him at the mall."

He slowed down as he neared his driveway and checked for traffic. Nothing was coming so he pulled in and parked his car.

Grabbing the sack with the scotch and cashews he got out of the LTD. Pulling open the back door he grabbed the sack containing the money and shut the door with his butt.

Theodore breathed in deeply and exhaled after savoring the long breath of air.

He headed for the cottage with a happy bounce in his walk. He didn't feel the weight of two hate filled eyes that followed his every move.

CHAPTER SIXTEEN

After three stops at two gas stations and a rural general store for information, Major finally ran across someone with the information he needed.

He was inside the general store and the clerk/owner was the type of person who knew everyone's business in the general area and probably the outlying areas too.

Major had spent some time checking out the store before he approached the old man, and he had carried a Pepsi and a bag of pork rinds up with him.

"Got a little of everything in here." Major commented.

"Yep, anything a man could use, and a lot that he wouldn't."

The old man laughed.

Major could see tobacco stains on the last four teeth in the old man's head.

"Needing anything in particular?" He asked with a hopeful tone in his voice.

"No, just this." Major said.

"That'll be one dollar and twenty cents."

Major reached in his pocket and pulled out a handful of change.

"Take what you need."

The old man rooted through the change and grabbed some coins.

"Thanks," he said, "Come back when you need something else."

Major started out the door and stopped. He came back partway to the counter.

"Hey, maybe you can help me."

"Well, I'll try to." The old man agreed.

"You wouldn't happen to know a Theodore Grant, would you?"

"Theodore Grant, Theodore Grant," the old man repeated it twice.

"Tall man, white hair, glasses?' he asked.

"Yeah that him!" Major said. "Drives a gray looking car."

"LTD." The old man said. "What about him?"

"I'm trying to find him, I've got his address but I can't find his place."

The old man studied Major up and down as if he was trying to memorize his every feature.

Major started to get uncomfortable and had decided to leave when the old man spoke again.

"Ain't none of my business," he said, "but he's a weird duck"

"Yeah I know." Major agreed.

"Three or four miles west of here, stay on route seven until you come to the first gravel road to your right, only it's not gravel but white limestone."

"Okay, thanks." Major said, excitement starting to tighten up his chest.

"Don't tell him I told you." The old man looked at Major with an expression that he couldn't read.

"I don't usually give out information to people I don't know, but I get a feeling that I don't want to know you."

With that the old man spit a stream of golden brown tobacco juice in an old Maxwell House Coffee can and turned away from Major.

Major went out the door to find Theodore's house.

CHAPTER SEVENTEEN

Theodore had showered and dressed. He had eaten a sandwich of goose liver and onions before he had shaved and he was going into his den to have a drink, a cigar and to play with his money.

Major had driven home, showered, shaved and was dressed in a black ninja outfit that Jill had bought him for Halloween four years earlier.

When he drove back to Guernsey County he had found Theodore's cottage right where the old man had said it was.

He was going to go directly to the cottage then but thought better of it. He wasn't prepared to face the man in his own home. Especially now, Major knew that he was a dangerous man.

He didn't know if Theodore had a gun, or if he had a dog in the house, and he wasn't going to take a chance on losing him from stupidity or over eagerness.

Fighting a muscle bound idiot in the parking lot was one thing, but taking on a man in his own home was another.

He went down to the gun case, reached up on top of the cabinet grabbing the key and unlocking the compartment meant for ammo. Pushing the .22 caliber shells and the shotgun shells aside, he pulled out his western style .22 pistol. Reaching in the back of the case he brought out a soft black vinyl case and carried it and the pistol to the kitchen.

Sitting down in the chair Major put the black case and the pistol on the table and contemplated on what he had to do.

Shoving the pistol to one side, he unzipped the black vinyl case and opened it up. Shining brightly under the glare of the overhead light, two martial arts weapons called sai's were contained within. Shiny chrome with black leather strapping on the handles, they looked like miniature pitchforks. The middle tine was longer than the other two tines by two inches and the other two tines had a slight outward curve at the ends of them.

Originally used for a defense against swords in the war torn days of the samurai, they were thick, sturdy and extremely deadly in the hands of an expert.

Although the sai's had been Jill's, Major knew how to work them.

Picking up one of the sai's, Major grasped the handle. It extended past the bottom of his hand by an inch. Swinging the sai handle first out of the bottom of the fists, Major could break bones with it. He put the sai down, picked up the .22 and carried it back to the gun case, put it away and locked it up.

Going back to the kitchen, he put the two sai's in his ninja belt around his waist.

He shut off all the lights in the house and headed out the door to his truck.

Time to go see Theodore.

CHAPTER EIGHTEEN

Theodore was kicked back in his swivel chair. He had eaten a handful of cashews and washed them down with a good snort of scotch.

Reaching in his desk drawer he withdrew his gun lighter and grabbing a cigar he soon had it lit to perfection. Smacking his lips around the cigar, Theodore reached for the drawer with all of his money, almost $373,000 dollars.

It was almost time to retire.

CHAPTER NINETEEN

Major took the S-10 between the old man's store and Theodore's driveway, pulled off at a wide space beside the road. Keeping the truck as tight as he could against the wood line. Shutting the engine off, he listened for a minute then pulled the hood lever. Turning on the four ways signal lights, he got out and raised the hood.

He reached through the open door grabbing his black ninja mask and the keys. Locking the truck up he headed into the woods.

Major hid his keys in the fork of a small maple tree and headed west through the woods along the road. Inside the wood line, far enough where no one could casually see him from the road, but close enough to the road where he couldn't miss Theodore's cottage he trotted the remaining mile and a half to Theodore's place.

Major slowly circled the cottage listening for the bark of a dog. Theodore's car wasn't there, so he wasn't too concerned about him. He didn't want to be surprised by a dog though.

He didn't hear anything unusual. Keeping an ear to the road he went to the side of the cottage and tapped on the window. Still no barking, he peeked inside and seen what appeared to be a study area. A big desk dominated the room with a T.V. on a stand opposite of it. The door was shut that went into the rest of the cottage, so Major went around back and rapped on the door there. Still no barking.

Major had to assume there wasn't a dog. If there was, he wasn't a very good one.

Major examined the back door and soon realized that it wasn't used very often. In fact it looked like it was painted shut.

"Well, that leaves the windows and the front door," Major murmured to himself.

He started to go around to the front of the house when he thought he heard something. Not wanting to take any chances he quickly slipped behind an elm tree at the edge of the wood line.

He was glad he took the precaution, because he could hear the tires of a car popping the limestone out from underneath them as a car moved down the lane.

Major heard the car pull to the front of the cottage and shut off. He quickly moved to another vantage spot where he could see who ever it was going to the cottage. Keeping out of sight, he could hear the car door opening as he quickly hid behind another tree. He could see the color of the car was gray but couldn't tell the make. He heard the car door shut. Suddenly Theodore came walking away from the car carrying two sacks. Major could see that Theodore was exceedingly proud of himself as he practically danced his way to the front door.

Major couldn't keep the hatred from boiling up from down deep in his soul, and his eyes glittered as the hate filled them up.

CHAPTER TWENTY

Dusk arrived with Theodore in his den. He was in a very contented mood. He had consumed half of the bottle of scotch, the whole can of cashews and was just lighting up his second 50 ringer of the evening.

His money lay on top of the desk divided by denominations. To Theodore it was one of the most beautiful sights he had ever seen. A whole lot better looking then the little tramp that had forced him into his life of crime.

Theodore leaned back in his swivel chair and puffed smoke rings and watched as they grew distorted when the drifted towards the ceiling.

Theodore closed his eyes and puffed the cigar and never seen the black mass hurtling towards the window in the den.

CHAPTER TWENTY-ONE

Major waited until dusk before he made his move. He had briefly considered that he should go to the front door and knock, taking Theodore out as he answered the door. But then again, if Theodore didn't answered the door it would screw everything up.

Major decided that he wasn't taking a chance on Theodore having time to get a gun or some type of weapon if he approached the cottage in a normal fashion. Only one other way to go, and that's through the window. Major stood back about twenty feet from the cottage and took off on a dead run. About four feet from the cottage, Major left his feet in a high jump turning his body into a ball as he turned sideways to protect his face.

Major's head was turtled down between his shoulders and knees into his chest when he exploded through the glass. Major hit the floor rolling, as he did and came up to his feet in an instance.

His hands flashed down to his sides and whipped the sai's out of his belt and held them ahead of him like a street fighter getting ready to knife fight.

Stepping forward Major held the sai in his left hand under the chin of the startled and still sitting, figure of Theodore. The other sai was held back ready to strike deep into the chest area.

"Don't move a muscle," don't even flinch!" Major said.

"Do you understand me?'

Beads of sweat burst forth on Theodore's forehead as he swallowed painfully against the sai.

"Yes!" a dry mouthed Theodore croaked.

Major stepped slowly away from Theodore and keeping a close eye on him he stepped back so he could see Theodore but also check out the room.

"Keep your hands on top of the desk," Major ordered.

Theodore didn't answer. Theodore didn't move.

"Where did you get all the money at?" Questioned Major.

"It's mine."

"That's not what I asked you."

"It's mine," was all Theodore would say.

Theodore couldn't believe it. He almost had enough money to do anything in the world he wanted to and now, a common thief, a robber, had surprised him.

Major stepped around the side of the desk, keeping at least a leg distance from Theodore.

Still brandishing the sai ahead of him, Major looked at where Theodore was sitting. He didn't see anything that he could use as a weapon against Major.

"Okay Theodore." Major said using Theodore's name for the first time.

Theodore's head jerked up at that. He had just realized that maybe this was no common thief.

"Who are you?" He asked.

"No questions unless I ask them." Major growled at him.

"Take your hands slowly from the desk top and raise them in the air."

Theodore complied.

"Now shove yourself away from the desk using your feet and stay in your chair."

Slowly Theodore did as he was told.

"Now get up and walk to the middle of the floor and lay down."

"Now wait a minute here," Theodore started to complain.

"Do it," shouted Major, leaping towards Theodore sai's swinging in an arc from the top of his head another violently downwards toward Theodore's belly.

"Okay, okay," screamed Theodore and fell from the chair to the floor.

"Crawl to the middle of the floor you ASSHOLE!" Screamed Major as he kicked him in the curve of his buttock to help him along.

"Now don't move." Major commanded.

"I'm going to ask you some questions an I want answers."

Theodore remained mute.

"Where did you get all of that money?"

No answer.

"What's your business?"

No answer.

Major glanced balefully at the prone Theodore.

"Whom do you sell the kids to?" Asked Major, fury barely contained.

That made Theodore react.

"What do you mean? What are you talking about?"

"Roll over on your back," Major told Theodore.

Slowly Theodore rolled over.

Major reached up and pulled the ninja mask from over his head.

"Remember me?'

Theodore's blood froze in his veins. He knew that face! It was Brok's dad!

"No, I've never seen you before in my life," lied Theodore.

Major controlled the muscles in his face and made him self look like he was in control. He turned as if to walk away from Theodore but suddenly turned into a spin kick that he used to drive his heel deep into Theodore's unprotected groin.

Theodore screamed and curled up into a fetal position, puke running from his mouth and tears from his eyes, the smell of the regurgitated scotch and peanuts causing him to puke and retch over and over.

"I remember you," Major breathed out.

"Where's my boy?'

Theodore couldn't answer because of the agony deep in his groin. He could barely breath, between the vomiting and getting kicked in the balls he felt half dead.

"Where's my boy?" Major asked again.

No answer.

Major walked over to Theodore, looking down on the monster that wrecked his life. Kneeling down beside him he grabbed Theodore by the shoulder turning him over on his back.

"Ummm." Moaned Theodore.

Major laid one of the sai's behind him. Raising the other sai high above his head he shook Theodore to get his absolute attention.

Theodore looked at Major with tear filled eyes. Shaking his head he squinted hard to allow him to see, "Wha-what are you doing." He asked Major.

Major didn't answer.

With Theodore watching every move Major brought the sai down with all of his strength and drove the sai through Theodore's right shoulder, pinning him to the floor. Blood poured out of the wound and started to soak Theodore's shirt.

"Shit!" Theodore passed out.

Major stared down at the unconscious Theodore and was surprised at the total lack of compassion he felt towards the man.

Shaking his head he left the den and walked to the kitchen area. He needed something to put the money on the desk in. Not finding anything in the kitchen, he then went to the bedroom. He pulled the pillowcase from the pillow and went back to the den to sack the money up. Holding the pillowcase to the side of the desk, Major whisked the stacks into the case, exposing the gleaming oak desk beneath.

Bringing the swivel chair back to where it belonged, Major started to open the desk drawers, looking for something to tie the pillowcase up with.

Major saw the bottle of scotch and was tempted to take a drink, not for nerves but to steel him for what was ahead.

Putting the bottle on top of the desk, he continued his search, running across the gun lighter. Flicking it a couple of times, he was pleased to see it light. Putting it beside the scotch he rummaged through the last drawer and finally found a shoelace. Tying the pillowcase he heard a moan from the other side of the desk.

Raising himself up from the swivel chair, and leaning with both hands on the huge oak desk, Major looked at the speared Theodore stuck so eloquently to the floor.

Starting to sit back down, Major caught a blemish on the surface of the desk. It looked like scribbling. It was scribbling, just like Brok did at home! Brok had been here! His boy had been in this very room. This was the final proof!

Shoving himself away from the desk. Major took a deep breath and slowly walked into the kitchen where he poured himself a pan of water. Coming back into the den he threw the whole thing into Theodore's face.

Sputtering, Theodore came back from oblivion and more pain then he had ever had in his life. His right side was numb, until he tried to move, then it felt as if a red-hot poker was thrust through him. Glancing over he saw the leather wrapped silver handle sticking from out of his shoulder and remembered everything. Looking up he saw Brok's dad standing above him. His face was an angry red and like a fly caught in a spider's web, Theodore watched his death coming for him. Theodore watched him reach down and pick up the other sai.

"My boy has been here." It was a statement not a question.

"I've seen the scratches on the desk!" The sai was being passed back and forth between his hands.

"If you want to live, you'll answer my questions."

Theodore didn't even consider lying.

"Where is my boy?"

Theodore had to pay close attention to even hear the whispered question.

"West . . . West . . ." Theodore couldn't get it out.

Major dropped to one knee on Theodore's left side.

Raising the sai high in the air he looked Theodore Square in the eyes.

"Tell me!" He commanded.

"West Virginia," Theodore screamed it out.

"Where?"

"Don't know, don't know," babbled Theodore.

"Look at me," softly intoned Major "and know that I won't ask you again."

Theodore looked at Major and knew he looked at death itself.

"Fuerte's have him!" Theodore said with his last erg of energy.

"Fuerte's have him!" He could barely get the words out now.

Theodore started to slip away into darkness again but a sharp pain to his head brought him around. Opening his eyes he realized Major had slapped him hard across his face.

"Don't pass out yet!" Major said, "I want you to see this!"

Looking past Major's head, Theodore realized that the man still had the other sai raised high.

"No!" Screamed Theodore.

"Yes!" Major said and drove the sai down through Theodore's other shoulder.

Blood splattered both Theodore and Major as the three-pronged sai hit deep.

Sighing heavily, Major stood up, looking down at the impaled Theodore, he felt drained.

Walking over to the desk, Major picked up the bottle of scotch and the lighter!

Walking over to Theodore he sprinkled the scotch literally around and over him.

Major had been in a bar one time and had seen a drunk spill some whiskey and then light it with a match. Major had always wanted to try it, and now was his chance. Grabbing some paper from the trashcan he piled it haphazardly around Theodore and poured scotch onto that also.

Saving the last little bit in the bottle he walked over to the pillowcase full of money and carried it over beside the window.

Walking back to the unconscious Theodore, Major put his right foot squarely in the middle of his chest and reached down and worked the sai back and forth until it came loose from the floor and the savaged meat of Theodore's right shoulder. It was like pulling an ax out of a stringy piece of hickory that just won't split. Wiping the sai on Theodore's pants to get rid of the blood, Major then stuck the sai back in the belt of his ninja outfit. He then repeated the process with the sai sticking out of his left shoulder. Theodore remained unconscious during the procedure.

"Too bad," thought Major. After all the heartaches he's caused to the parents of all the kids he's stolen, he deserves to feel pain.

Major shut out the lights in the den and sat down at the desk. He had to consider the consequences of what he had done. He knew that he would be unable to destroy all of the clues he might of left in the house. He wore gloves, so that was no problem, concerning fingerprints. He was going to torch the cottage and hopefully any physical clues that would link him to this would be destroyed in the flames.

Theodore had holes in his shoulders from the Sais and Major knew that if the F.B.I. forensics were any good at all, they would probably figure out that Sais were the probable weapons.

Major had no doubt the F.B.I. would be involved once the police had Theodore's description. They would match Major's "Alfred" to Theodore.

Then if Breeler was called in and they figured out that martial art weapons were involved, then Major would be a prime suspect. Major now wished he hadn't have called Breeler with his theory of the kidnappings. Well, that couldn't be helped right now. Major had a powerful motive for murder, and he knew Breeler would love to nail him.

Major shuddered. "Murder!' What a nasty, nasty word and now Major would be a murderer.

A groan from Theodore brought Major's attention back to the prone man. He wasn't dead yet. Major could let him live. He might be in serious trouble, but he could still stop now. Major considered this. Major was a Christian and a part of him was sickened by what he had done tonight. The Bible said that God would never let you be tempted past what you could resist and Major knew he could stop everything that he had started right now. But Major had read the Old Testament and knew what

God had done to His people's enemies. If it was good enough for God, it was good enough for him.

He stood up and went over to Theodore and hunkered down beside him.

"Monsters like this destroy everything good," thought Major, "this man would've sold his soul for thirty pieces of silver."

Major kneeled down on one knee facing Theodore. Inner turmoil boiled up in his soul.

"May God forgive me!" He cried raising his right hand high in the air in a knife hand, fingers slightly bent at the tips and thumb aimed down into his palm, Major savagely brought his hand down across Theodore's neck, hitting through it so hard that his hand actually hit the floor.

Theodore gagged once and his body arched up in a spasm. Theodore was dead meat.

Major stood up and turned away from the body, grabbed the almost depleted bottle of scotch he emptied the rest of it on the papers and Theodore and using the gun lighter he set the papers on fire.

Throwing the pillowcase with the money out the window, he climbed out. Reaching back inside, he grabbed the curtain and lit it also. He reached down and got the money and slowly walked away as the flames started to climb.

CHAPTER TWENTY-TWO

Allison Furete had her 30th birthday and everyone loved her newly adopted child. The party was considered a great success.

CHAPTER TWENTY-THREE

Jill and Detective Breeler were eating a late supper while Theodore descended to hell.

CHAPTER TWENTY-FOUR

Major made his way back to the truck without incident. Once there, he took off his gloves and threw them and the money sack into the bed of the pick up. He then opened the door and shut off the four-way lights and walked around the front of the truck and shut the hood. He went to the tree and retrieved his keys. Watching for traffic major stripped out of his bloody ninja outfit and threw it into the bed of the truck with the rest of the stuff.

Climbing behind the wheel in his bikini briefs, Major started the engine, put it in gear and headed for home.

CHAPTER TWENTY-FIVE

Major parked around the back of his house. He got out of the truck and pulled his underwear off and threw them in the back with the ninja outfit. He then went naked into the house and went up stairs and got a hot shower. Afterwards, he used a bathroom cleaner to scour the tub and poured a generous amount down the drain. He didn't know if the cops could find traces of blood in the drain, but he wasn't taking any chances.

He dressed, putting on sweat pants and a tee shirt. Grabbing a can of Amour-All, he went out with a roll of paper towels and swabbed the interior with a Amour-All treated towel, paying close attention to the driver's side seat and steering wheel.

With that done, Major went into the kitchen, grabbed a plastic sack that groceries come in and went upstairs again. He went into the washroom and picked up some soiled dark clothes and put them in the sack. He put on socks and shoes went down stairs and back outside to the truck.

Opening up the sack he added the bloodied ninja outfit to the rest of the contents.

He then took the sais from the back of the truck and carried them over to the side of the house where the garden hose was. He turned the spigot on and let the water flow over the sais from the open end of the hose. After getting the sais wet, he walked away from the still running water and going to the bank behind the house, he proceeded to drive the sais deep into the soil, over and over again. He was trying to get rid of any blood remnants. Stabbing the bank brought back dark thoughts of the evening.

It was still hard to believe that he had killed a man. No matter how you sliced it, he was a murderer.

One last hard stab to the bank and he pulled the sai from the dirt and carried them both back to the hose. Rinsing the sais off as good as possible, Major then wiped them off with armor-all, leather straps and all. He then went to the gun cabinet and put them back in their own case and put them in the bottom of the cabinet and locked them up.

Major grabbed his keys from the table and drove to town. He cruised past Centersville's two laundry-mats and chose the least busy one.

Carrying the plastic sack with the clothes in, he went to a remote washer and dumped the clothes from the sack into it.

Major had forgotten soap so he went over and put a dollar in the soap machine and got a small box of Cheer. He read the instructions on the box and did as they said. The box held enough for two washes, he would use them both.

After the second washing Major took the wet clothes and put them in the dryer and watched them spin around and up and down seeming to sometimes defy gravity. He had brought the extra clothes in case he ran into someone he knew. He could say he was washing sweat clothes. Fortunately, no one showed up that he was acquainted with and he would not have to explain his presence here.

Major finished up and took his clothes back to the house. He wanted to put everything away in case, Detective Breeler found a reason to snoop around.

Major didn't know if he had destroyed all evidence of Theodore's brutal murder that pointed to him, but he knew he had a good start.

Major spent the rest of the night washing down the truck. Then after another shower, he hit the sack.

Later the next evening Major put a skillet of stewed tomatoes on to cook and went over to the dojo to get a good workout in. Gone was any excess poundage. Major was in prime physical shape. Flexing his muscles in his upper body, Major looked at himself in the studio mirror. He impressed himself.

"Not bad," he said and nodded his head to the image in the mirror.

Major took his time and stretched out slowly. He didn't want any pulled muscles at this stage of the game. Major stretched out on the floor and then went to the ballet bar and used it to power stretch on.

Major then went to the heavy bag. He started out slowly not wanting to wear himself to a frazzle tonight. He wanted to start organizing his plan for Brok's rescue.

Major was working on a combination of kicks on the bag when he sensed he wasn't alone any more. Major wheeled around quickly and took an aggressive stance. Sure enough, leaning against the door jam and barely visible was Detective Breeler.

Moving inside the door he spoke.

"I didn't mean to interrupt your workout, Mr. Brown."

Major didn't say anything. He looked down at Breeler's feet, which were still encased, in his shoes. Major then looked Breeler straight in the eye.

"Shoes do not belong in my dojo."

Breeler looked down at his feet.

"Oh, sorry sir," he said with an insolent tone. "I didn't know," he said as he backed out of the room.

Major stood there eyeing the detective up and down. "Now you do."

"Look," Detective Breeler's voice took a business like tone, "We need to talk." He looked around the room. "Can we go some where?"

Major reached for the towel on the bench and mopped his face with it. Toweling off his back and under his arms before he answered

"What do you want to talk about?"

"I think we need to sit down and discuss what I have in mind."

"I asked you a question." Major said, his face set in stone, "Answer it or get out."

"We found your "Alfred," said an equally stone faced Breeler.

"Good!" Exclaimed Major, "Let's go into my office."

Major bowed out of the room.

"Why did you bow to an empty room?" Inquired Detective Breeler.

Major thought for a second, the answer ran through his mind. A dojo was considered a place of tradition and respect. It was almost like leaving the United States and entering a different dimension. Once you enter a dojo or training hall, you were supposed to forget all worldly cares and woes, and concentrate on obtaining total mental and physical harmony. How could Major explain this to an outsider. Why would he even want to try to explain this to Breeler? He didn't even care for the man. Major entered his office without answering Breeler and the detective followed him in. Major walked around the desk and sat down in his chair.

"Look Breeler, I'm the type of man that says what is on his mind and I'm going to be straight with you."

Major looked Breeler straight in the eyes as he continued to talk.

"I don't like you. I think you are a total asshole! You come walking into my dojo uninvited wanting to talk. Well, that's okay if it's about the case. Evidently you don't where my son is, or you would've told me as soon as you walked in the door."

Major leaned back in his chair, arms folded behind his head. "You want to talk about the scum sucking dog that kidnapped my boy." Major's eyes glittered as his anger started to build up inside of him. "You said you found my "Alfred" but you didn't say you arrested him so there must be some kind of problem there."

Major leaned forward hands on the desk trying to control his anger. "You've been shacking up with my wife and still have the nerve to come in here and ask me questions about an art that requires honor and respect?"

Now Major stood up with his body sideways towards the impassive Detective Breeler.

"Like I said, Breeler, I don't like you and I know that I can kick the shit out of you! So you have three choices here. One, tell me what is going on with the case, two, get off of my property or three, let's get it on!"

Red started up Breeler's neck and face as he flushed with a barely controlled anger.

"Theodore Grant," Breeler said through tight lips. That was the alleged kidnapper's name." Breeler's voice became more business like again as he started to regain control of his anger. He didn't want Major to see how upset he was. "We know all about him."

"Well if you know all about him, why don't you have him arrested?" Asked Major.

"Because he's dead!" Breeler watched Major closely to get his reaction.

"How did that happen?" Major kept his reactions under strict control as he eased himself into his chair. He didn't want to give himself away.

"We don't know all of the details yet, but we'll know more in the morning."

Breeler leaned against the door jam with his left shoulder and casually glanced around the office. "Do you have any martial arts weapons?" He queried.

"You know I do."

"What kind do you have?"

"Throwing stars, num chucks, a sword, a couple of bo staffs. Why?"

Breeler ignored the question. "No sais?"

Major stood up and with his hands on the desktop he leaned forward. Sparks in his eyes. "Jill has the sais."

"She doesn't have them with her now."

"Well, you should know."

"Where are they?"

"In the gun case where they belong."

"Can I see them?"

"No."

"Look Mr. Brown, I'm trying to take it easy on you. We can do this casually or we can do it with a search warrant. The choice is yours." Detective Breeler had steel in his voice.

"Get the search warrant," Major growled, "and don't come back until you do!"

Major walked around the desk and stood toe-to-toe, nose-to-nose to Breeler.

"Now get out or I'm going to throw you out."

"I have a search warrant here, Jill said you would be reasonable, I guess she was wrong." Breeler was trying to hit Major where it hurt, and he did.

Major put one hand on Breeler's chest and shoved him backwards out of the office.

Breeler took two steps back and stopped again. "Theodore Grant was murdered!" He said, "Murdered by someone using sais. I hope you were the one that did it. Because I want to nail your ass to the wall!"

Throwing the search warrant to Major, he opened the outer door and signaled to a couple of uniformed officers that were stationed out of sight.

"Now, let's go see those sai's."

Major took the detective and officers over to the house and took them to the gun case. Reaching up on top he grabbed the key there and handed it to Breeler.

Major stepped back and the two officers flanked him.

Breeler opened up the ammo compartment and looked in. Putting on a pair of surgical gloves he reached in and pulled the sai case out. Handing them to an officer, they went back into the living room.

"Have a seat Mr. Brown, while we take a look around."

Major sat down and hoped he had cleaned up any evidence he might have drug home with him. The money was well hidden in the hollow of an oak tree a hundred yards up the hill. So he won't be too concerned about them finding that. He had ditched the pillowcase at the gas station he had stopped at for gas. It wasn't his regular gas station, so he was hoping they wouldn't find it. The only thing he was really worried about was if he missed any blood evidence, on either the sais, in the truck or on the ninja outfit. He didn't have time to buy new ones and with Jill hanging around Breeler, she would know that they should have been there. But then, maybe he's worrying too much.

Major flicked on the T.V. set with his remote control and tried to watch the cartoon network channel, but his mind was racing over what he had done last night.

He had killed a man and had tried to hide the evidence, but did he do a good enough job? That was the question.

After searching the rest of the house Breeler and the two officers came back into the living room.

"Well asked Major?"

"Do you mind if we take these sais with us?" Breeler inquired.

"I don't think I have a choice."

"Not really, but I'm trying to be decent to you."

"Do what you have to do," Major said.

"Oh, we will definitely do that," Breeler said. "Don't leave town Mr. Brown." "We will want to talk to you later."

The detective and two officers left a very troubled Major sitting in his chair.

CHAPTER TWENTY-SIX

The next day Major drove into town and went to the public library. He got an atlas of West Virginia and started to study it. Three hours later he went to his father's house.

"C'mon in," his father yelled as he knocked on the door.

Major opened the unlocked door and entered the house. Major's dad was sitting in front of the T.V. set with a can of cashews beside him and a bottle of beer stuck in his crotch.

"How you doing boy? I haven't seen you since you were in the hospital."

"I'm doing okay dad, but we have to talk."

Mr. Brown looked sharply at his son and was troubled by what he saw. Major looked to be in excellent shape, even the bruises sustained at the attack when Brok was kidnapped was gone from faded to an unnoticeable shade of color. But there was a hardness he had never seen about his son before. A wariness that was never there before.

Mr. Brown had seen Major acting on instinct before, moving with a speed that wasn't possible if you had to think about it.

For the first time in his live, Mr. Brown could understand why some people feared his son. He was seeing a side of Major he had never seen before.

"Any news about Brok?" He asked.

"Where's Mom?" Major asked.

"Over at her father's house, we're all alone if that's what you want to know."

"I've got some serious talking to do with you."

"Well, no time like the present," Major's dad tipped the beer bottle up and drained the amber liquid with a gurgle. "Let me get another beer and you some pop." He got up and went to the kitchen. Coming back in a moment later, he handed Major an unopened can of Pepsi and opened up a beer for himself. He sat back down and took a drink of his beer. "Okay boy, lets hear what you have to say."

Major took a deep breath and leaned forward elbows on his knees and cracked open the Pepsi. He took a drink and looked at his father.

"You've always kept your word to me dad, what I have to tell you now can never be repeated." Major took another slug of pop.

"Give me your word that what I tell you will never be repeated to anyone. Any one at all!"

"You want me to lie for you?" Questioned Mr. Brown.

"No, just never say a word about what I have to say."

Major's dad leaned back in his chair and reflected a moment on what Major was asking him. It must be something mighty important for him to ask for complete secrecy.

"Okay boy, I give my word!"

Major grunted with relief. He needed someone to talk his plans out with. If his father hadn't agreed to keep his mouth shut he would've planned things out by himself and he wanted an objective mind working with his.

"I know where Brok is."

"Does the police know?"

"No!"

"Well boy, I suppose you have your reasons, but how are you going to get Brok back?"

"I'm going after him myself!"

"By yourself!" Exclaimed Major's dad.

"I didn't raise a fool did I?"

"No dad, but it's something I gotta do by myself."

"What does Jill say about this?" Questioned Mr. Brown with a frown upon his face.

Major leaned back into the chair and reflected on his answer. No one in his family knew that Jill had left him yet and that was the way he wanted to keep it.

"No dad, Jill doesn't know."

"You can't go against the law, son."

"Dad, there is a lot you don't know about and I can't tell you." Major took a swig of Pepsi. He was thinking about Theodore's death and his mouth was suddenly dry.

"I'm already on the wrong side of the law and I've got a feeling I'll never be back on the right side again."

Mr. Brown drained his beer and went to the kitchen for another one.

"Need another pop?" He called from the kitchen.

"No thanks, dad."

Mr. Brown came back into the room and sat down again. He cracked open the beer and studied his son again.

"Okay boy, he said, I'm not going to ask you any more questions. You tell me what you want me to know."

"I can't tell you much of anything dad." Major said with a frown.

"I need you to get a hold of brother Phil in South Carolina and have him come up here and right away."

"Why can't you call him?"

"I can't dad." Major was afraid that Breeler would tap his telephone line. "I'm sure you'll find out why soon enough," Major said as an explanation.

"Okay," was all Mr. Brown said.

"Tell him to bring a survival medical kit and a pocket water filter that goes down to 0.2 micron. Tell him to get enough beef jerky and dried fruit to last a week." Major thought for a minute, "That's all I need for him to bring up."

"Okay son, I'll tell him."

"Call him tonight dad, just make sure that I'm not here when you call him."

"Okay."

It was time for Major to leave. He had other loose ends he wanted to take care of before his brother came after him. He figured about ten hours for the trip and a couple of hours to get the items he had told his dad.

Major and his dad both stood up. Major knew that it was unlikely that he would ever be able to sit down and talk to his father again. Mr. Brown had inkling to this also.

"Dad, I . . . ." Major's voice broke with emotion.

"I understand boy." Major's dad had tears in his eyes. "Are you coming back?"

"I don't know." Major set the Pepsi on the stand beside the chair.

"Even if I get Brok back, things can never be the same again." Major didn't know how to explain himself.

"It's something that you would have done yourself if you would have been in the same position." Major cleared his throat, "It's something that a man has to do if he is a man."

Major hugged his dad and kissed his cheek. "No matter what happens dad, just remember I love you and mom with all of my heart. Will you tell mom that when things break loose?'

"Yeah, I'll make sure she understands."

"Okay dad, I got to go."

Major stepped back from his father. The grin came back to his face as he faced his father. "See you later dad!"

"I sure hope so boy, I sure hope so!"

Major left the room, walked out the door and climbed into his truck and headed for a pay phone.

Mr. Brown waited an hour and then called his son Phil.

Major pulled up to a phone that could be reached from his truck. He opened up the truck's ashtray and sifted through the change until he found a quarter. Putting it in the slot he waited for the tone to return and dialed his buddy Pete's number. After the third ring Pete answered it.

"Hello?"

"Pete, It's Major."

"Hey, did that address help you out, buddy?" Asked Pete.

"Sure did, but I have another favor to ask of you."

"Let me get a pencil and paper."

Major watched the traffic go by until Pete came back on the phone.

"Okay, I'm ready."

"Peter Fuerte, West Virginia. Wife's name is Allison. I need their address as soon as possible."

"Okay, are you at home?"

"No, I'm at a pay phone, I'll stay here until you call back. I'll give you the number."

"It might take some time."

"Be as quick as you can, Pete. Here's the number."

Major hung the phone up. While he was waiting for Pete to call back he whiled the time away watching some kids practice on some in-line skates. Ten minutes had not passed before the ringing of the phone jolted him straight in the truck seat.

Major picked up the receiver and said "Hello."

"Major?"

"Yeah."

"Holy cow man, you're picking on some heavy hitters here aren't you?"

"What do you mean?"

"The Fuertes' are big time, man!" Exclaimed Pete. "Heavy influence with the political scene!"

"What else, Pete?"

Peter Fuerte is reputed to be heavy in the cocaine market, but has enough power and money to keep the politicians and law enforcements off of his back."

"Got the address?"

"Yeah, but listen Major, This guy has body guards for his body guards. Do you understand what I'm saying?"

"Just give me the address."

Pete gave him the address and then hung up the phone. Major started his truck up and went home.

CHAPTER TWENTY-SEVEN

Major went to the house and called his superintendent. After a brief conservation about inanities, Major informed him that he was quitting. After a brief try of talking Major out of it, they hung up.

Major left the phone and started to gather up things he would need for the trip to West Virginia. He went to the closet and pulled out a backpack that someone had given him. It was an old thing, faded from a bright green to a pukey shade and it had some holes in it. Major carried it out to the kitchen table. It was ugly but it would do the job.

Major went up and dug his ninja suit back out of the closet and put it in the backpack. He went upstairs and got three pairs of socks from his sock drawer and some handkerchiefs from the top drawer of the dresser. He took them downstairs and put them on the table by the backpack He sat down at the table trying to think ahead for what he needed.

He wasn't worried about food or water, because his brother was supposed to bring up dried supplies and a water filter. Major was planning to get in and get out. He was not planning for an extended excursion. Hopefully he could get Brok out without any problems.

Frowning, he looked at the socks on the table. "What a dummy." He thought. "Can't wear socks with the ninja outfit. The tabi boots had split toes. Once again he thought about the handkerchiefs, and decided to take them. He could always use them for bandages if needed.

Major leaned back in his chair. He sighed deeply and wiped his eyes with his index finger and thumb of his left hand.

What kind of weapon would he take? Major didn't know what he should do; he didn't want to take a gun with him. He got up from the kitchen chair and went to stand in front of the gun case. He studied the shotguns there, from a single shot H and R Topper 12 gauge model to a double barrel Savage Stevens 12 gauge. Opening up the ammo compartment he pulled the Western style .22 out and slid it from the holster. He cocked the double action revolver to the first notch and spun the cylinder around to make sure it was unloaded. It was.

He reached down and pulled a box of long rifles shells from the ammo compartment and loaded it up. Carrying the loaded weapon outside, he aimed at a tree approximately fifty feet away from him and let off all nine shots one after another. The sharp reports made his ears ring. After he reloaded the pistol's cylinder he carried it back in by the gun case, picking up the discarded holster he slid the weapon into it. Opening up the door to where the shotguns were encased, he hung up the holster on one of the empty slots that was available for other guns. Shutting the doors and locking the case, a habit he had gotten into when Brok was born, he went back to the kitchen and sat down and thought.

He wasn't good enough with a pistol to feel secure enough to take it with him. The impromptu target practices proved that. He didn't really want to carry the pistol anyway, too bulky.

A rifle or shotgun was out of the question because of their size. Besides he wanted to move light and fast. Get in and get out. He was hoping to avoid the Rambo scene.

Even the heroes like Arnold and Sly always won in the movies with their exotic weapons and bombs, Major wanted to keep this extremely low key. He had already killed one man and he hoped to keep it that way.

Major got and paced around the kitchen for a few minutes and then sat back down.

The only thing he was deadly with was the Sais and num chucks and of course the bo-staff. Could he pull this off with only martial arts weapons? He didn't know.

Besides Breeler had his Sais and he couldn't order more or borrow any without raising the detectives' suspicions.

"Okay," he thought to himself.

"Bo staff and num chucks will have to do."

He got up from the table to go to the dojo to get his six foot oak bo-staff when a knock on the door interrupted his mission. Hesitating he slowly walked to the door to peek out. He hoped it wasn't Breeler with an arrest warrant. He cautiously moved the curtain on the door back so he could see who was at the door and looked out.

Jill was standing there with a brown paper sack in her hands.

Quickly he unlocked the door and threw it open.

"Jill," he said with joy in his voice. "I'm glad to see you!" And he truly was. He had not realized just how much he had missed her.

In spite of all that had happened to him and what he had done, he smiled and felt a great release.

He stepped forward to give her a hug, and stopped short. Taking a really good look at Jill he realized from the look on her face that she wasn't thrilled to see him.

His hands dropped to his sides and smile fled from his face.

"I see that this is not a reconciliation?" He asked, his heart breaking all over again.

"We need to talk."

"Okay Jill, Let's go in the house." He held the door for her and she entered.

Major glanced around to make sure she was alone. Survival instincts kicking in again. For a brief moment he forgot he was a killer and under suspicion.

They entered the living room and Jill went to a chair and sat down. Major sat in the same chair that he sat in the night before when Breeler had searched the house.

He looked at Jill, "Well?" He questioned.

She reached in the sack and pulled out the black case that held her sais.

"Detective Breeler asked me to bring these back to you."

"Why?'

Ignoring the question, Jill looked Major in the eyes.

"Major, what is going on?"

"Detective Breeler said to bring these to you an to tell you that you're lucky." She paused and continued. "He said to tell you that they could find nothing conclusive."

Major thought fast. He wondered if Breeler was trying to use Jill to get Major to entrap himself.

Major decided to see what information that Jill had.

"What else did he say?"

"He told me that he thinks you're playing a game that is going to land you in some serious trouble if you're not careful."

Jill's eyes grew red as she suppressed tears, "Major, please," she begged, "Does it have to do with Brok?" Her fingers played with each other in her lap.

Major looked at her closely. Although she was a beautiful woman, he could see what her sadness had done to her. She had lost some weight and lines were beginning to appear from around the corners of her eyes. Slight purpling from under the eyes attested to lack of sleep. No matter what had happened between the two of them, she was still his wife, but he had to find where her loyalty was directed to, him or Breeler.

"Jill," he started, avoiding her question. "Did Breeler tell you why he confiscated the Sais?"

"He said he thought they might have been used in a crime. She paused, "Oh Major, I told him that you were too honest and honorable to be involved with any aspects of law breaking!"

She patted the Sais case that was on her lap. "He told me to bring them back to you and warn you not to do anything foolish!" She sniffed.

Major stood up and reached for the box of tissues on the coffee table and walked over to Jill and handed them to her.

She took them gratefully and blew her nose.

Major knelt down on his knees in front of her, his hands on the chair arms. He looked deeply in Jill's eyes.

"Do you love him?" He asked unconsciously held his breath.

Jill couldn't meet his eyes and she looked away. Major didn't think she was gong to answer and was about to get up.

Jill met his eyes again.

"No Major."

"Then why are you with him?"

"I had to get away from you."

"Why? I needed you so badly!" Exclaimed Major.

A sob burst forth from deep within her breast. "You lost my boy, my heart!" Jill put her face in her hands and the tears broke with deep rasping sobs that threatened to tear her apart.

Major slowly reached forward and grasping her shoulders he drew her close to his chest and let her sorrow pour out, her tears soaking the front of his shirt. Slowly her tears began to subside as Major held her with one arm and stroked her hair with his free hand. After a few moments, Jill leaned away from Major and reached for the box of tissues.

"I didn't come here to break down." She said and blew her nose.

"Oh Major, I want to come home!'

Major's heart leaped in this chest and just as quickly dropped to his feet. He couldn't take her back at this time. Things were already in motion. Even if he could change his plans at this time, what about the death of Theodore?

There was nothing in this world that he wanted more then his wife right now, correction, nothing more than his wife and son.

He stood up and stepped back.

Jill looked at him tearfully. "Why are you moving away from me Major? Don't you want me anymore?"

Jill waited for his answer as Major stood stricken in front of her.

Major was in a quandary, he couldn't tell Jill what he had done or what he was about to do in fear of her saying the wrong thing to someone.

"Yes Jill," Major answered slowly. "I want you more than anything in the world."

Major backed up another step.

"Jill, there are a few things you don't know and I can't begin to tell you."

"Why not?"

"Are you going back to Breeler's house to get your gear?"

"I don't have anything there that I need." Jill looked pensive.

"Are you trying to get rid of me?" Jill stood up and stopped in front of Major.

"Do you want me to leave?"

"Major bridged the gap between them and took her in his strong arms. He pulled her savagely to his chest and held her tightly for a moment. Releasing her he stepped back still keeping his hand on her shoulders.

"I'm leaving tomorrow."

"Where are you going Major, Breeler said you were not allowed to leave town!"

"I can't tell you anymore! You're going to have to trust me!"

Jill's face started to redden, "That's what started all of this before Major." Her voice was barely a whisper. Trusting you is a real heart ache!"

Jill sat back down with her head in her hands and started to gently sob.

Major watched her for a moment and then went back to the kitchen and sat down at the table.

Well, at least now he knew what weapons he was going to take. Sais, num chucks, and his oak staff.

He went back into the living room where Jill was still softly weeping and took the sai case from her lap.

"Come out to the kitchen Jill, and I'll rustle up some chow for you."

He went to the pantry and pulled out a couple of cans of soup, both vegetable beef, and opened them with a hand operated can opener. Finding a pan in the sink that wasn't too dirty, he rinsed it out with hot water from the spigot. Dumping the soup in the pan and adding the appropriate amount of water he put the pan on the stove to heat. Turning around to get some dishes from the cupboard he almost knocked Jill down. She was standing directly behind him.

"I trust you, Major, was all she said as she moved into his arms. "I trust you."

Major carried her up to the master bedroom where they spent the next hour making love and getting re-acquainted.

Later Major left Jill sleeping in bed and went back down to the kitchen. The first thing he did there was adding water to the soup that was still cooking on the stove. It was about ruined, but Major saved it. It wouldn't be as good as it would've been if eaten earlier, but it was good enough for Major. After all, compared to not eating, it was down right delicious. Major finished up the soup and washed it down with a bottle of Pepsi.

Going back up stairs, he checked to make sure that Jill was sleeping. She was.

He went back down stairs and turned out all of the lights. Slipping on black sweatshirt and black sweat pants, he also put on a black Cat Hat and cautiously went out the back door. He slowly worked his way up into the woods to where he hid the money he had obtained from the deceased Theodore. Although the darkness covered him from a casual observer, he still tried to see if he could spot anything unusual. Using his eyes, ears and even smell he checked out the surrounding area. He couldn't see anything, the sounds of the woods seemed normal, crickets chirping and the rustling of small nocturnal animals, and he didn't smell any human scents. Being a squirrel hunter, Major knew how far the smell of tobacco or cologne could be smelled on the fresh winds of the woods.

Finally Major felt comfortable enough to retrieve the knapsack containing the money. He sat on the ground in front of the majestic oak tree and counted out twenty thousand dollars. Re-zipping the knap sack he put it back in it's former position in the fork of the tree.

Major tucked his sweatshirt into his pants and put the money inside the front of his shirt.

Instead of going directly back to the house, Major took a meandering route around. He wanted to make sure that the area around the house was indeed police free. After reaching the north side of his property Major angled back towards the south side. He crisscrossed this way several times and didn't see anyone.

Arriving at the back door, he took one last look around and then entered the house. Locking the door, he went to the light switch and turned it on. Going back to the table, he pulled the sweatshirt out of the waistband of his pants and dropped the money on the table. He counted it out and separated it into two piles. He loaded one of the piles into his backpack. Major put his clothes in on top of the ten thousand dollars. He took the Sais from their case and loaded them in too.

Going over to the dojo he retrieved his oak staff and a set of black 16-ounce ball bearing chains connected to num chucks. Taking them, he loaded the chucks into the backpack. He leaned the staff over in the corner by the refrigerator. Picking up the backpack, he threw it into the corner by the staff.

Straightening up the pile of money, he put it in the middle of the table.

He briefly considered going back up to the bedroom with Jill, but quickly squelched that idea.

It would be dawn in a couple of hours and his brother should be arriving at approximately 6:30 or 7:00. Major was itching to be gone.

Brother Phil pulled into the driveway at 6:45. Major was sitting on the front porch with his gear packed.

Phil was driving a small truck, Major took a better look and recognized it as an S-10 Chevy similar to his but a newer model, the deep blue paint job was streaked and dusty from the trip up from South Carolina.

Major stood up and stretched, then reached down and picked up his backpack and bo-staff. He walked from the porch and started down the steps to the truck, when Phil opened up the door and stepped from the truck.

"Hey brother," he said as a greeting. "I gotta take a leak, where do you want me to go?"

Major smiled, he was always glad to see his brother. He had a winning way about him.

"Go behind the tree there, Jill is in the house and I don't want her to wake up."

"Okay." Phil went behind the tree and let a pent up flow of urine fly.

Aaaah," he said in relief.

"You better drive Major, I'm whipped."

Major didn't say anything; he threw his backpack and staff into the bed of the truck and climbed in the opened door.

He buckled up and shut the door. His brother went to get in the passenger side but the door was locked.

"Unlock the door Major," he said.

Major reached across the seat and flipped the lock open. Phil climbed in and buckled up.

Neither man said anything for a moment. They sat there and eyed each other. Both men were solemn. Major reached out and grasped his brother's willing hand for a bone-crunching handshake.

"Thanks brother," he said his voice cracking.

"No problem, but fill me in."

Major started up the pickup and put it in gear. Before he released the clutch he looked up to the house. Major knew that this would be the last time he would ever be able to see it in this sense.

Jill was in there and she was going to be very pissed that he left without a more thorough explanation. Hopefully in a few days he would be back with their son. Or, maybe he wouldn't be back at all. Only God knew the answer.

He left ten thousand dollars on the table with a note explaining that he wouldn't be back for at least a week. Major also knew that Breeler would be angry that he left town without notifying him, but he could kiss his ass!

For the first time in the last couple of weeks, Major felt good. He wasn't sitting around anymore. He was moving into action. What would result from this action was yet to be seen, but that would come soon enough.

Major eased the clutch out and slowly pulled away from the house and life that he once had cherished.

"Let's stop somewhere and get a Pepsi and maybe some lunch meat for sandwiches and then I'll tell you everything I know.

"Good enough."

Major drove away from the old way of life and into a new one.

CHAPTER TWENTY-EIGHT

Later after a stop at a local Lawson Store, Major and Phil were traveling down Interstate 77, which would take them through West Virginia.

Major had told Phil about the kidnapping and about the F.B.I. Detective Breeler. He told him about how he figured out where Theodore would strike next, and how he was there to locate him.

Phil never said a word, even when Major told him about the brutal murder of Theodore. He sat there and occasionally took a sip of pop.

Finally, Major wound down the story and fell silent.

"Major, old brother," said Phil. "Sounds like you've had some serious troubles."

"Who has Brok?" Phil took a slug of pop.

Peter and Allison Fuerte!"

Phil choked on his pop.

Spitting some from his mouth and a quite a bit spraying from his nose, he did a fine job sliming up the truck's windshield.

Leaning forward, he grabbed a handkerchief from his back pocket, and then loudly blew his nose. Using the clean part of the hanky, he cleaned his face up as well as he could.

"Whew, I hate when that happens!" He barked out a laugh. Phil's face suddenly was old. Lines appeared from nowhere and creased his face. Major was amazed at the sudden transformation of his brother's face.

Trying to keep one eye on the road and one on his brother, Major slowed the vehicle down.

"You alright?" He asked with concern in his voice.

"Yeah." Reaching into the glove box, he found some wipes, the kind you get from a restaurant, and so you can clean the grease off of your hands after a meal. Tearing one of the packet open, Phil pulled the contents out and used it to wipe the snot and pop from his face. Discarding the used wipe on the floor of the truck, he opened up another one and used it to try and wipe the windshield off. Only partially succeeding he grabbed his handkerchief and smeared it around enough that he could see out again.

"You've got big troubles brother."

"Why is that?' Questioned Major.

"The Fueretes, that's why!"

Major glanced over at his brother.

"Why does everyone know about these people but me?"

"I thought everyone knew about them," Phil paused and thought for a minute. "I'm going with you!"

"No!" Major said flatly.

"You don't know what you're getting into!" Argued Phil.

"I know what I'm doing, and I don't need help!"

"Major . . ." Phil started to say something, but Major rudely interrupted.

"No!" He shouted. "My life is all screwed up now!" I don't want you going down the river with me!"

Phil didn't say anything. He sat facing the road. The silence was oppressive after Major's tirade.

"I just wanted to help you brother!" Phil's voice was barely audible, yet you could hear the emotion in it. He turned and faced Major.

"Once you find Brok, what are you going to do then?"

"I'm taking him back with me."

"Okay Major," agreed Phil. "How?"

"What do you mean how? I'm taking him with me!"

"What are you going to drive?" "How are you going to back home?"

Major didn't say anything.

"You didn't figure that part out yet, did you?"

Major was trapped, "No," he hated to say that single word.

"You're going to need help getting back." It was a statement of facts. Phil had his brother's attention now.

"Yeah, you're right." Major squirmed in his seat.

"Got any ideas?"

"Yeah, I do." said Phil, "Listen up!"

Major and Phil spent the rest of the trip laying out the plans for the trip back home.

CHAPTER TWENTY-NINE

Jill woke up reaching for Major and quickly realized that she was in bed alone. Sliding from the waterbed, she quickly dressed in the clothes she had discarded on the floor the previous night.

"Major?" she called and frowned when she didn't get an answer. The house had an empty feeling about it and as she went down the staircase, she was sure that she was alone.

Jill went to the kitchen to make herself some coffee when the stacks of money on the table caught her eye. She drew her breath in sharply as she saw the note beside the pile. Quickly, she picked the note up and read it.

Major had said the night before that he had something going on, but she didn't realize that things were going to happen so soon. Stunned, she sat at the table. Putting her head on her arms, she gently began to sob.

Major and Phil pulled into the gas station of a small town on a back road a few miles from I-77. They were a few minutes drive from the town that Fueretes' owned, and they wanted to check and make sure that Major had everything set before they went there.

Major pulled to the pumps and got out as an attendant slowly made his way from the slightly dilapidated station.

"Fill'er up and check under the hood," Major gave the grease emgrimed teen instructions.

Major and Phil went into the gas station and Phil dug some change out of his right front jeans pocket and treated Major and himself to a pop from a machine that still dispensed glass bottles. Using the opener on the machine, they opened the pop and went back out to the truck.

Phil went over to the attendant, "We on the right road to Macsville?"

"Yes," agreed the teenager.

"How far?"

"Eight miles the way you're pointing."

"Thanks."

The boy looked under the hood and then shut it.

"Ten bucks."

Phil paid him and climbed behind the wheel of the truck.

After Major was done checking things over, he followed suit.

"Excuse me, Mister."

Phil looked at the teen attendant. "Yes?"

"If your gonna take them pop bottles with you, then there's a deposit on them."

Phil and Major looked at each other with a grin. Phil grabbed a dollar from the ashtray of the truck and handed it to the kid.

"This enough?"

"Yeah, thanks." He turned abruptly on his heels and went back into the station.

Phil engaged the clutch, put it in gear and slowly pulled away.

"Are you satisfied with your equipment?"

Major thought for a second, "Yeah, I think I have everything."

"I got the pocket water filler, dried fruit and jerky for you, and I got a small first aid kit too." Phil paused, "Hope you don't need it."

"Me too, brother!" Major looked over at Phil. "Let's go find Fuerte's place!"

Phil shifted gears and picked up speed as he headed for Macsville.

Jill spent the morning picking up the house, running the vacuum, doing up the dishes and washing clothes. After she had everything tidied up, she drove into town and stocked up on groceries. Everything in the house was low and she was sure Major hadn't been eating very well. When he got back from wherever, she wanted to have everything nice for him. She didn't realize just how much she had loved him, until last night. She smiled remembering. A knock on the door interrupted her reverie. Se went to answer it and opened the door to Detective Breeler.

"Hi Jill. Can I come in?"

Wordlessly, Jill opened the door wide and let him in.

CHAPTER THIRTY

Major and Phil slowly cruised the main street of Macsville, looking over the occupants that were going about their business. It looked like a typical small town. Not much going on at all.

Major knew the address of the Fuertes, but he wanted to get a feel for the town also. He had watched too many movies not to at least peruse the place. In the movies the town people were always in cahoots with the villains, although it seemed there was nothing unusual about Macsville. Phil slowly headed out of town, going north on a county road that would lead to the Fuertes.

The area they were heading to was like most of the land around this part of West Virginia. Hills rising up into mountains areas, and what flat ground there was had been utilized to the maximum benefit of the town or of the town's farmers.

A mile out of Macsville, heavy woods and undergrowth appeared to be a rough and wild country. Even as wild and primal as it appeared, it also had a tremendous beauty about it. Major was awed by it, and even Phil was quiet as the country road narrowed down to a single lane gravel road.

Three miles out of town Phil and Major came across a mailbox with the Fuerte's name on it. Slowing down and looking back into the lane that the mailbox was marking, Major and Phil saw a magnificent view. The lane was lined with trees that had trunks as straight as arrows, following the lane as if they had been purposely raised for that reason only. The trees were all of the same approximate height. They measured about thirty feet above the ground. On either side of the trees the deep underbrush and woods took over again. The white crushed limestone gravel of the lane gleamed white compared to the greenness of the surrounding foliage.

About a quarter of a mile back in, the lane suddenly opened wide into an open area that looked to be manicured lawn. The house if you could call it a house, was situated in the middle of the green expanse of the yard. Then the house went out of view as Phil and Major drove past the point where they could see back into the lane.

"Wow!" Exclaimed Major. "Did you see that house?"

"No Major, I didn't see it." Phil said thoughtfully.

"How could you have missed it?" Major asked stunned. "That's the biggest place I've ever seen!"

"I was watching the guy in the fringes of the woods."

Major didn't say anything for a moment.

"If they got a sentry in front, there must be others posted else where."

"Yes." Phil agreed.

"It's going to be a lot tougher than I thought."

"Yes." Phil agreed again.

A mile passed before anything was said again.

"Better run me about five miles away, Phil. I want to take my time going in."

Phil didn't say anything, he kept driving. When five miles clicked on the odometer, Phil looked for a place to pull off the road.

Both men got out of the truck and walked around to the bed of the S-10. Major grabbed his knapsack and bo-staff as he walked by the side of the truck.

Major dug deep into the knapsack and dug out the ten thousand dollars he had there.

"Here's the money." Major handed it to Phil. "If I don't make it, there's more money in the big oak tree behind my house." Major paused, "Give it to Jill."

Phil took the money from Major and shoved it down the front of his shirt.

"I'll be cruising this road at dusk every night, after three days." Phil stopped and thought for a moment. "Today is Tuesday, that means Saturday, at dusk, I'll be watching for you."

"Okay, brother." Said Major, "Remember to get familiar with all of the ways out of here. We might need that knowledge later."

"You got it bro!"

It was about time for Major to start on his mission with Phil standing guard. Major slipped behind a huge boled tree and stripped out of his civilian clothes and slipped the ninja out fit on.

Cautiously he carried the discarded clothes out to Phil who threw them in the bed of the truck.

Phil and Major stood and looked at each other for a long moment. Both knew that this might be the last time that they would ever see each other on this earth. Wordlessly, they embraced, patting each other on the back.

Major fought the lump down and forced the tears back that threatened to well up in his eyes. Without a sound he reached down and picked up the knapsack that contained his supplies, grabbed his staff and melted into the woods.

Phil watched him disappear, waited a long moment, climbed into the S-10 and continued down the road.

CHAPTER THIRTY-ONE

Jill followed Breeler into the house. Breeler was looking around intently, looking for something or someone and not finding it or them.

Jill assumed that he would stop in the living room, but he continued on into the kitchen. Looking around he abruptly turned around and faced Jill.

"I waited for you last night."

"I've decided to go back to Major." Jill couldn't meet Breeler's piercing gaze.

"I thought we had something together!"

"Sorry Richard." Jill used his first name.

"Are you going to stay here then?" Questioned Breeler.

"Yes, Major and I need each other."

Breeler's eyes hardened as he looked around the room again.

"Where is Major?" He asked.

Jill didn't know what to say. She didn't want to lie, but she didn't want to tell him that Major was gone either. Not knowing what to say, Jill kept silent.

"He's not here, is he?" Breeler stepped forward to stand almost chest-to-chest with Jill. Reaching with his right hand, he gently lifted Jill's chin up so she was forced to look him directly in the eyes.

"Where is he?"

Jill didn't answer.

"Where is he?" Breeler used more force in his voice.

Jill set her jaw and decided that she would never tell Breeler anything.

Breeler could see the determination enter into Jill's eyes, as she made up her mind not to tell him about Major.

Breeler was a big man, who was used to getting his own way in most situations. To those who were not intimidated by his physical size, then a show of his badge was usually enough to make most people want to accommodate his requests.

Breeler was not averse to using his fists when needed and that included reticent women. With his index finger still under Jill's chin, he suddenly clamped his thumb over the top of her chin and squeezed hard.

Tears came into Jill's eyes, but she still didn't utter a sound.

"I'll ask one more time, sweety," Breeler said with malice in his voice. "One more time then I get rough!" He paused and then said, "Of course you might like it rough, huh doll?"

Jill was frightened. She had never seen this side of Breeler before. But then, how long had she known him? Less than two weeks? She answered her own question in her mind.

After living with the kind and gentle Major for over twelve years she was more or less sheltered from the abusive male. Although she had seen enough of it on T.V. and read about it in woman's magazines, she had never actually experienced it.

Major had trained Jill all of the way from a white belt to a first degree black belt, and he had taught her to always be confident of her martial arts skills. Still, Jill was frightened and she didn't want to make Breeler angry, so she didn't move.

Breeler seen that Jill wasn't going to answer, "Okay doll, have it your way!" Breeler grinned a savaged grin, his grin almost feral.

Slowly he raised his free hand up above his head and tightened his hand into a fist.

Jill knew then that Breeler was going to strike her and that knowledge spurred her into action.

"Kiaaa!" She shouted and brought a perfect upper cut up to the point of Breeler's chin. His head snapped back. "Uggh," he groaned as he released Jill and staggered back a step, his hands going to his jaw.

Jill's feet twisted into a perfect front stance, the body squared straight ahead, and hands up to protect her upper body and with her back foot she drove it hard and straight into Breeler's unprotected groin. "Kiaaa!" She shouted again.

This time not a sound came from the detective as his body spasmed downward and he bent over to grasp at his crushed balls.

Jill brought her right front leg back to a forward stance and again brought it from the rear into a beautiful short inside crescent kick to the right side of Breeler's exposed head. Breeler's head snapped sideways and blood flowed from a cut that appeared over his right cheekbone.

Not stopping there, Jill linked her fingers together and made a club with both hands locked together. Throwing her hands high over her head, she brought her hands down hard on the back of Breeler's head. Breeler dropped to the floor like a rock. Blood flew anew from when his nose made contact with the floor. Breeler was out cold.

Breathing hard, sick to her stomach, Jill stepped back away from the unconscious detective. One hand subconsciously went to her stomach and the other to her mouth as she fought off nausea.

A good thirty seconds passed before she snapped out of her stupor. The fear of the detective regaining consciousness before she could escape from him goaded her into action. Almost running, she headed for the back kitchen door to escape, when she suddenly stopped short. This was her house! Breeler was an intruder! That was easy enough to think, but what could she do? She didn't want to physically have to defend herself again. This time the detective would be ready. She didn't think she could over come the much bigger man a second time with out the element of surprise.

"Think Jill! Think!" Jill's mind raced. "What would Major do?" She asked herself Jill thought back to her martial arts training. "Use the environment if necessary, Jill." Major had said time and time again.

"There does not have to be honor in a fight for your life!"

"Major is right." Jill thought.

Quickly she went in to look at Breeler. He was starting to stir. Jill moved quickly to the gun case and fumbled for the key on top. Not finding it quickly enough, Jill stepped back and threw up a sidekick that shattered the glass in the case. "Kiaaa!" She shouted to release the power within her.

Blood welled up on a cut on the side of her leg soaking through her jeans. Reaching in, she grabbed the.22 pistol from the holster, hearing a noise behind her, she quickly spun around in time to see Breeler stagger through the door. Jill aimed the gun at Breeler and cocked the double action pistol.

"Stop right there!" She commanded.

Breeler stopped, swayed, and then using both hands, he pressed against the doorjambs to keep from falling.

"Put the gun down Jill." He said through clenched teeth, anger flashed from his eyes. "Put it down now, and maybe I won't arrest you."

A small smile was on Jill's lips.

"Arrest me Richard?" She questioned, sarcasm dripping from her voice. "For what?" The smile grew larger. "Are you going to tell friends that a woman kicked your ass?"

Breeler didn't say anything, but started to move towards her.

Jill didn't hesitate. She aimed the .22 away from Breeler's head by less then a foot and pulled the trigger. The sharp flat crack of the pistol echoed loudly in the small room. Instinctively Breeler stepped back.

The smell of gunpowder stung Jill's nose as she aimed the pistol dead center on the detective again and recocked.

"Leave and don't come back." Her voice was just a whisper.

"I'll leave now." Breeler's voice was hate filled. "But I'll be back to see your husband, and if I get a chance . . . you!"

"When I tell Major what you did . . ." Jill left the sentence incomplete. "Get out of here!" She commanded.

Quickly, Breeler turned and left the room. Major was right, he was an asshole!

Jill didn't move until she heard the front door open and close.

Slowly she went to the living room keeping her eyes open and the gun ready in case Breeler was trying to trick her. Hearing a car door open and close, she went to the window in time to see Breeler's car peel out in the graveled parking place down by the road. Jill ran and locked the doors of the house. That done, she went up stairs, taking the .22 with her and laid down on the bed. Too spent to discard her bloody jeans or to take care of the nasty cut on her leg.

CHAPTER THIRTY-TWO

Major went into the woods approximately twenty yards before he turned and started to walk parallel with the road. Like an idiot he had never thought to bring a compass with him and now he was paying the price.

"Wonder how many other things I'll need before this is over with?" He thought to himself. Grimly, he broke into a trot that would eat up some ground. It would be dark in a couple of hours and he wanted to be as close to Fuerte's land as possible.

It was a beautiful summer evening. The sun was sending spears of light in a slant through the branches and leaves of the trees. It made a mottled effect that Major felt would enhance his ability to maintain his secrecy.

With the bo-staff in his left hand, and the knapsack secured to his back Major quickly jumped the log falls and dodged the branches and other obstacles that were in his path.

The woods had looked extremely dense from the road, Major was pleasantly surprised to find it fairly open. Although the lay of the land had a down slope to it, going from Major's right to left it wasn't too difficult to traverse.

Major eyed the terrain to his right. After about one hundred yards the pitch of the hill went up drastically. Within a half of mile from the road that Major was traveling beside, the hill became a side of a mountain. How ever the distance from the road to the mountainous terrain became wider as Major moved back towards Fuertes.

Remembering, Major knew that the house had sat back in the lane at least a quarter to a half of a mile by a rough guess. It had looked to him that the house had some open area behind it, although it didn't appear to be that much, because he remembered the mountain rising up behind the house.

Major trotted what he figured was to be two miles and slowed to a walk. He had been jogging around 40 minutes, but he had to jump and avoid quite a few obstacles. Hopefully he was around three miles away from his destination. Time to pay close attention to the surrounding areas.

Major didn't know how far from the house the Fuerte's controlled. He had to assume that they owned quite a bit of land in the outlying areas. Assuming that they did, Major figured that there would be sentries or some type of warning devices. He ruled out motion detectors, since there was no fences that he could see, the wildlife in the woods would continuously set off the devices.

Considering the remoteness of the area and the smallness of Macsville, Major was hoping that the Fuerte's felt secure enough with a few guards. If not, well, Major would worry about that when he got to it.

While jogging, Major had hopped across several small runs of water, but the slow moving water in the beds of the small streams was turbid an even for the pocket filter, Major didn't want to chance drinking the water, but now Major came up on a ravine that was cut deep into the ground and wide across the top. Approximately forty feet separated the division. Major looked out the sides and decided he could make his way down to the water and could get back up without too much difficulty.

Major turned and followed the ravine to the road on which he and Phil had come down. There was a bridge there that Major didn't remember crossing over. The ravine went on down further and ended up into a small lake.

Major turned and went back into the woods. He worked his way down the side of the ravine, trying not to disturb the ground. The less sign that he left behind him the better. Once he got to the bottom, he took the knapsack from his back and retrieved the pocket filter from within. Sticking the input end in the babbling brook, he pumped it a couple of times to start the flow. The discharge he put directly in his mouth and let it go. The purifier would sanitize around one quart a minute so it didn't take Major long to sate his thirst with the cold water.

Opening the knapsack again he reached in and grabbed a couple of strips of jerky and a handful of dried fruit. Taking his time and savoring each bite he slowly consumed his meager dinner, that done, he set the picket filter back up and again sated his thirst.

Darkness was only about an hour away and Major needed to find a secure place to sleep. He climbed from the bottom of the ravine and still working his way toward Fuerte's, he payed close attention to his surroundings.

A few hundred feet from where he had drank Major came across a lightning struck tree. It was of good size, although in the waning light, Major couldn't tell what kind it was. Major laughed at himself. Even if it was broad daylight he probably couldn't tell what kind of tree it was. If it wasn't a maple tree or a hickory he had to guess at the species. Major always wished he knew how to tell different trees apart, but never took the time to learn. Even pine trees! Major called them all pines, even though he knew there was a vast difference in species.

The top of the tree hung down to the ground, still connected to the trunk by a twisted and split slab of wood. Major walked over to the tree and looked up. It looked like a pocket was formed by the lightening blast. Major grasped the treetop and started to climb up the tree. Once he got to the top, he was disappointed to see that shards of wood were sticking up like daggers where the main trunk had been blasted. He climbed back down to the foot of the tree. Looking the treetop over, Major decided to work his way inside. Taking his time, he managed to get to the center of the top without making it too obvious of a path. Once there, he pulled some of the leaves off and made a leafy bed in the fork of two branches that laid on the ground.

Darkness became complete as Major lay down in the fork using the knapsack as a pillow.

Major knew he needed some rest before tomorrow, but sleep wouldn't come to him. Images of Jill and Brok broke his sleep. Major wouldn't admit it to anyone, but he was afraid. Not so much for his life, though he didn't want to die, but for Jill and Brok. He knew how much Jill needed Brok, and intended to re-unite them.

Major knew that his life was essentially ruined. He had killed a man. The ghost of Theodore hovered in the back of Major's mind every second. He wished he had not of killed Theodore now. Prison was a very good likelihood after this adventure was over. Major thought that he would rather die then go to prison. He reflected on this thought for a while, finally he said the Lord's prayer and faded off to sleep.

While Major was fading off to sleep, Jill was just wakening up from her slumber. There were no lights on in the house, so she lay there in darkness for a few moments. Deciding to get up, a moan burst forth from here lips. Her body hurt! Jill had never thrown the type of power she had hit Breeler with. She was stiff, sore; hurt and she had the beginnings of a whopper of a headache. Slowly she crippled her way to the bathroom. Switching on a light, she went to the bathtub to start her water. Stripping out of her jeans and shirt, she climbed into the tub and let the flowing water cover her. Soaking for a while, Jill finally sat up in the tub. Grabbing a large plastic soft drink glass from the side of the tub, she soaked her hair and then washed it. After conditioning it, she grabbed a razor from the shelf above the tub. She finished her bath by shaving her legs and armpits. Letting the water out of the tub, she then rinsed off with the shower. Stepping out of the tub, Jill grabbed a towel and dried off.

Going to the closet, she slipped on a sweat pant and shirt outfit. Getting in Major's sock drawer, she grabbed a pair of his socks. Sitting on the cushioned seat of the commode, she put them on. Padding down the steps, Jill turned on lights as she proceeded through the house. Going to the kitchen, she brewed up a pot of coffee. In the few minutes it took for the coffee to be ready, Jill decided to go to the dog pound in the morning and get a watchdog. That decision made, Jill went to the living room with coffee cup in hand. Sitting in a chair with her legs under her she started worrying about Major and Brok.

CHAPTER THIRTY-THREE

(Wednesday) Major slept fitfully throughout the night. Awakening several times at the unfamiliar sounds of a strange woods. A beam of sunlight broke through the branches and leaves of the treetop that Major was sleeping in. The beam worked it's way up Major's body, fading in and out as it was blocked by a branch or leaf playing for a moment on Major's chin, it finally reached his eyes, causing Major to stir. Slowly, He came awake. His mouth felt dry and his body was achy and sore from spending the night outdoors.

Before he moved, Major used his ears and nose to try and detect if anyone was near his hideout. The wood sounds were all natural, birds singing and a chipmunk squeaked somewhere behind the lightning struck tree. Not smelling any cologne or tobacco in the cool clean mountain air, Major slowly arose.

Once he was standing up, he peered out through the branches and perused the landscape in a 360-degree circle.

Satisfied that he was alone, Major grabbed his knapsack and oak staff and worked his way from the previous night shelter. He went to a bush behind the tree trunk and with a sigh, watered it liberally with urine. That done, Major moved out into the sunlight and sat down. Reaching in the knapsack he grabbed some dried fruit. He wasn't particularly hungry, but he would need something in his system.

After eating he went back to the ravine, climbed down and drank his fill of water through the purifier. Muttering under his breath Major realized that he didn't bring anything for oral hygiene. His mouth tasted like a sewer. Climbing back out of the ravine, he went to a small bush. Reaching deep inside the foliage he broke off a small twig. He hoped no one would see where he snapped it off. First fraying the end of the twig and then using it to clean the surface of his teeth, he soon felt better.

Major went back to where he spent the night and slowly started to stretch out his leg muscles and upper body. He had a lot to do today and a pulled muscle could spell disaster. Feeling the blood rushing through his veins, Major felt ready. In fact, he felt more alive then he's ever felt before.

"Time to rock and roll," he thought. Picking up his knapsack and bo-staff, Major started casting to his left until he was about 60 feet off of the road, Major again began to move towards the Fuerte's.

Knowing that there were sentries posted, he wanted to spot them before they spotted him. His black ninja outfit was more adept for the night, and Major planned on using the night, but he wanted to spot the location of all the people that were guarding the Fuerte homestead.

Major was afraid he would overlook something at night. It was exceedingly more dangerous to be moving during the day, but Major felt he didn't have a choice.

Major was finally closing in on the Fuerte land when a noise froze him in his tracks. It was the sound of someone clearing his throat. Slowly Major sank to the ground. He knew about where he had heard the man, but he didn't see him yet. Keeping his body perfectly still, Major moved his eyes only. A small movement caught his attention. There! About forty feet ahead of him! He finally spotted the throat clearer.

Slowly, Major scanned the woods all around the sentry. He didn't see anyone else. He watched the man fidget move around, and in general, try not to be bored with his duty. At no time did the sentry turn and look behind him. Major stored that fact away.

Moving very easy, Major backed up until he had a little more greenery between him and the guard. Slowly Major started working his way around the area of the guard.

Marking a line out in his mind, he tried to figure out where the next sentry ought to be. One hundred yard further down he spotted him. Rather he smelled him. He was smoking a cigarette. Major thought it was kind of dumb to try and hide your self and yet smoke a fag. Marking the guard's position in his mind, Major continued on. Working his way towards the house he was approaching the open area of grass, so he went deeper into the woods.

He spotted one more guard before he had to detour around the manicured lawn. He went over a hundred yards past the last post that he had spotted yet he couldn't find another person in that area. Major continued to check the area out as he slowly crawled his way forward. He wanted a good look at the house and surrounding area. Stopping right where yard met wood line, Major cursed himself under his breath. "Binoculars," he thought, "how in the world could a man forget to bring binoculars?" It was another item that Major knew he would never forget if he had to go on another mission.

The house was big. It sat towards the end of the large grassy lawn it's back toward the mountain. There was a narrow section of grass behind the house. Major figured it to be less then one hundred yards of open area, then a broken field of rocks and scrub trees made up the terrain before the mountain side took over. Brambles filled the other spaces. All in all, Major thought it looked like a nasty place to be in. It didn't appear to be guarded, for which Major was grateful. He wanted to recon the far side of the woods from where he was at and he wanted to go through the area behind the house. Slowly he worked his way back deep into the woods. Once in, he kept low and crept forward to where fallen timber and small rocks started to appear quite frequently.

Before he started through the rock field he once again surveyed the area for any activity. Nothing!

Major took a deep breath and entered the rough area. Keeping an eye towards the house he slowly inched his way across the rough ground on his stomach. He had traveled about one third of the two hundred yards when suddenly Major froze.

While in the woods, Major had heard a dry rasping sound several times. He couldn't identify it, but was assured it was some type of beetle or locust or a bird that made the unfamiliar sound.

Major was already sweating from his stealthy activity, but now sweat broke out anew on his whole body, his mind screamed with horror. Two feet ahead of the sweat soaked and horror stricken Major was a coiled rattlesnake. Major didn't move a muscle. Time froze. Almost in slow motion Major watched the pit viper's tongue slide in and out of it's slit like mouth.

Major had two tremendous fears in his life. Well, two outstanding fears. One was a needle the other fear was snakes.

Major assumed that this was a timber rattler. He knew that they were located in Southern Ohio, but he had never given them a thought about being in West Virginia.

The only rattlesnakes he had ever seen were on television. This particular snake didn't look like a diamond back. It was too short and thick. Besides the markings weren't the same. One thing for sure though, it was definitely a rattler. Major winced inwardly. All those times he heard the buzzing in the woods. He never even thought of snakes! What if he had been bitten? What could he have done? Major tried to slow his frenzied mind down. He had been lucky in the woods, but he needed more then luck now if he wanted to get out of this predicament unscathed.

The rattler had quit buzzing it's tail but was still staring Major right in the eyes.

The snake was in the shade of a fairly large boulder and didn't look like it was going anywhere.

Major had his bo-staff in his left hand. The hand was out of the snake's eyesight, so Major, using just the wrist of his hand slowly worked the bo-staff forward. The buzzing started again at the movement from the tip of the staff that was sticking out towards the snake. Angling the staff away from his face, Major worked the tip of the staff towards the right of the pit viper. With tongue flicking in and out the snake gradually turned its wedge shaped head towards the end of the bo-staff. Sweat burning his eyes, wrist cramping from the effort, Major continued to inch the staff ahead. When Major had the staff a little more then an arm's length away from his face, he stopped moving it.

The snake was poised, ready to strike. Major was tense, his muscles tight with fear and exertion. Only his martial arts training had saved him so far. Major had controlled his body and mind, even though his fear of snakes was paramount. He forced his muscles to relax and maintained control of his breathing. What he would do in the next moment would determine if his mission would be a success or not. It could be life or death.

With a flick of his wrist, Major moved the bo-staff so that the end scooted back towards him. With a lightning strike, the timber rattler uncoiled and struck viciously at the end of the bo-staff. The Viper's fangs wrapped around the staffs bole and venom splattered on the wood. While the snake was stretched out Major instantly leaped ahead and grabbed behind the snakes head. Despite a deep loathing, Major gripped the reptile with all of the strength in his right hand the snake writhed up to Major's hand. Letting go of the bo-staff, he grabbed the snake near its rattles. Trying to control his breathing, light headed from an incredible adrenaline rush, Major slowly worked his way to his knee, all the while maintaining a death grip on the snake.

The boulder wasn't high enough to shield Major from anyone watching from the direction of the house, but he had to get rid of the snake. Rising up quickly, he threw the snake over the boulder and as far away from him as he could throw it. Just as quickly, he dropped back to his stomach.

Major put his head in his arms, like a schoolboy laying his head down on a desk for a nap. Now that the immediate danger had passed, the trembling started. Major knew how close to being snake bit he had come. He didn't know if he would have died from it's venom, but he assumed he would have. Major knew right then, that he was ill prepared for this rescue.

Suddenly Major rolled as his side. Pulling the ninja mask off, he puked. Gagging and trying not to make noise, he finished being sick Major had to get across this snake-infested area and get back into the wood. There were snakes there too, but at least he wouldn't be crawling around on his belly.

Thirst was beginning to be a factor now. Major had lost an enormous amount of water through sweat. Throwing up didn't help either.

Major had figured on crossing this section of ground in under a couple of hours. After all, it was only about two hundred yards. Now, knowing about the snakes, he would have to be extremely careful or run the risk of being bit.

Major put his mask back on, putting the bo-staff back in his left hand. Major scanned the area ahead of him. Slowly he starting working his way forward again.

INTERLUDE

While Major was facing the pit viper, Jill had went to the dog pound, where she had picked out a mongrel dog of about one year of age. She named him Sensei.

CHAPTER 34

It was the middle of the afternoon before Major made his way across the snake field as he called it in his mind. He had ran across three more snakes in his patch, but knowing what to look for now, he gave them a chance to escape. Timber Rattlers are shy reptiles and would rather leave then fight.

The total time spent crossing the field took around five hours. When Major entered the cool woods after being out in the direct sunlight for the extended period of time in a black outfit, it was a welcome relief. However he knew he had to find water and quickly.

Instead of starting to circle the parameter searching for guards, Major headed in a straight line hoping to find a small creek or even a pothole containing water. He didn't travel very far before he came to a small run with water meandering through it. Ever mindful of snakes, Major worked his way into the run. Slipping his backpack off, he quickly opened it and grabbed the pocket filter. A moment later, Major tasted the best water he had ever had the pleasure of drinking. Taking his time, Major stopped drinking and tried to catch his breath. He had needed water so bad that he quit breathing so he could drink faster.

After catching his breath, Major pulled the jerky out of his pack. Slowly he ate two strips. Drinking some more water, he then ate a handful of fruit. Before packing the filter he took one more long drink.

Cautiously he stood up and moved away from the run, back the way he came. Before he went very far, he stopped and urinated. Feeling a whole lot better now, Major was ready to recon this side of the woods.

Just as on the other side, there were three guards posted approximately one hundred yards apart on pretty much the same parameter.

"Okay." Major thought, "Time to rest up." He moved away from the position of the last guard and found a place that he could catch forty winks. Satisfied that he was safe for the time being, Major said his prayers and then drifted off to sleep.

INTERLUDE

Mr. Brown opened up his fifth beer of the evening and worried about his twin boys. He knew Phil had to be with Major. He had tried to call several times and there was no answer. The beer gurgled from the tilted bottle as he took along pull and waited.

CHAPTER 35

Bring-bring! The sound of the phone snapped Jill from the light slumber she had apparently drifted into. Jill let the phone ring several times before she decided to answer it. "It might be Major!" She thought to herself. With that thought in her mind, Jill rushed to answer the phone.

"Hello?" She made it a question.

"Good evening, Jill."

Jill recoiled from the phone. It was Breeler. Slowly she replaced the receiver back to her ear.

"What do you want?' Jill whispered.

"I'd like to speak to Major," commanded Breeler.

"He's in the tub." Jill lied.

"I'll wait, just tell him I'm on the phone."

Unsure of herself, Jill hesitated.

"He is there, isn't he?" asked Breeler.

"Uh . . . Sure!" Said Jill.

"I'm waiting." Said a suddenly patient Breeler.

Jill didn't say another word. She softly replaced the receiver back in the cradle of the phone and broke the connection. She stood by the phone a moment and then started to move away. The jangling of the phone stopped her. Slowly she picked up the receiver putting it to her ear without a sound.

"I'm going to nail him to the wall!" As Jill suspected, it was Breeler.

"He's going to get the chair!" Exclaimed Breeler.

"He's going to fry!" The detective was practically screaming now.

"He's going to die!!!"

Jill broke the connection still not saying a word. Bending over to the phone jack, she disconnected the connection. She went back to her chair and waited.

CHAPTER 36

Major awoke feeling refreshed in the cool of the dusk. The light was fading fast when he stood up. Night was here, and in the night he would reconnoiter the Furete house.

Major eased his way up to the guarded perimeter and checked for guards. He wanted to see if the posts were manned at night. They were. Evidently they have posted guards for twenty-four hours a day.

Moving quickly, almost invisible in the black ninja outfit, Major skirted the guarded areas and went back to the snake infested rock field. Working his way through it quickly, but carefully, he headed back to the east side of the house. A quick check revealed that the guard station was manned too. Major expected it, but didn't want to leave anything to chance.

Major went back to the rock field and pulled the knapsack from his back. Unzipping it he withdrew the sais from within. Pulling a black shoestring from a side pocket he quickly tied it around his waist like a belt. Picking the sais up he thrust them in the makeshift belt. They were almost as a gun fighter would have had his guns arranged. Zipping the bag back up, he hid it and the bo-staff behind the rock.

Major was going to investigate the house, and he didn't want his hands encumbered. Looking towards the back of the house, Major shook his head.

Every room seemed to be emblazoned with lights. He would have to be extremely careful to avoid detection. The perimeter guards were always watching the house, and Major didn't have a clue as to how many more there would be inside.

Slowly he worked his way across the open span of ground behind the house. Shadows cast by the house were used as lanes to get closer. Suddenly Major stopped, a figure had crossed in front of one of the second floor windows. It appeared to be that of a woman. The lacy curtains kept him from seeing greater detail, but she appeared to be talking to someone.

While Major was familiarized himself with the surrounding areas, he had kept a cursory eye upon the house. He hadn't seen anyone before this. Assuming that this was Allison Furete, Major marked the room's position down in his mind. He wondered briefly if it could be Brok's room.

Major had just started to slink forward again when the woman passed from his sight in the window.

Glancing around him, Major sensed that he was still undetected.

He was only about thirty feet from the house when the woman re-appeared in the window. This time she wasn't alone. In her arms was a small child. Major's throat felt closed and he had trouble breathing. Tears sprang unbidden to his eyes. It was Brok! It was his son in the woman's arms.

"Oh Brok!" Whispered Major.

"I'm coming for you!"

Major closed the gap to the house. He hid in the shadows of a small bush. Looking about, he tried to decide which way to go. Major was a little off center of the window that he had seen Brok in. Another window was directly below it. It was well lighted. Major eased up to it and cautiously took a peek inside. It was a gym.

A no neck well built man who was doing a sitting bench press using all of the weights in the stack on the machine was using a home gym. To the right of him was another no neck working out on a stair machine. Other muscled men were sitting around in shorts and sweat pants doing different work outs on different machines.

Major leaned back against the wall.

"Wow!" He thought. "I hope I don't have to fight with these guys!"

The men all appeared to be in good shape, muscled and big.

Peering back into the room, he counted eight men. Counting the six on duty, there were approximately fourteen goons, not counting Peter Fuerte himself, or any cooks, or other domestic help.

Shaking his head, Major looked closely at the window he stood beside. It had a wide casement on it. The whole frame protruded out about six inches. The window was head high to Major. Groping the top of the window and hoping that no one inside would see him, Major climbed to the top of the window. About six feet above him was the ledge of the window that he had seen Brok in.

Crouching slightly and bunching his muscles tightly Major leapt with all of his strength and caught the ledge with the fingers of both hands. Dangling there for a second, Major then used his arms to pull himself up to where he could look into the room.

Looking through a space between the lace curtains, Major could clearly see the room. It was a child's room. A dresser stood directly across from him, while a bed shaped like a racecar was in the right side of the room. An immense rack to the left held an enormous load of toys of every description. It was a well-lighted and airy room. The walls were a light yellow and the carpet matched the walls.

Major was disappointed. The room was empty.

The strength in his fingers were about to give out, Major was getting ready to drop down to the top of the window below, when the bedroom door opened.

A hauntingly beautiful blonde haired woman walked into the room followed closely by Brok and a dark skinned extremely handsome man.

The pain in his fingers was gone at the sight of his only son. Major inhaled sharply as Brok tottered into the room.

Allison Fuerte reached down and grasped the child's hand as she led him over to the bed.

Major could tell that she was talking because her lips were moving, but he couldn't hear what she was saying. The glass blocked the sound.

Peter Fuerte followed the pair over to the bed. He sat down on the nose of the racecar slope and watched his wife and newly adopted son.

Peter was a rich man. He had more money then he knew what to do with. He could have anything in the world, but he couldn't have a child of his own.

Allison had never said anything to Peter, but he knew that she was disappointed by not having a child with him. Unknown to Allison, Peter had contacted a crooked lawyer who specialized in illegal adoptions. After explaining his situation to him and telling the lawyer exactly what kind of child he wanted, Ernesto had arrived on his wife's birthday. Peter had never seen Allison so happy or alive. It was worth every dollar that he had spent to please his beautiful wife. He smiled as he remembered their night of passion; yes it had been worth it.

Major's fingers were about to give out, but he didn't want to leave just yet. A wild idea was forming in his mind. If the Fuerte's left within the next few minutes, he would try to get in through the window and get Brok out right now!

The casement of this window protruded too, so Major reached up and tried to position himself better. His entire upper body was starting to tremble at the effort of keeping himself up on the ledge.

Major hooked his left arm up on the ledge and then did the same with his right. Shifting his weight Major was able to half lie on the ledge. It was uncomfortable but it didn't have the strain his previous position had.

Raising his head, he was able to look back into the room where he saw Allison kissing his son good night.

Peter had risen from the front of the bed in preparation of leaving the bedroom when suddenly Ernesto spoke.

"Daddy!"

Peter whirled around and looked at him.

"Did you hear, Allison? He said Daddy."

Both Allison and Peter had big grins on their faces.

"Daddy!" Brok said again and reached out, not to Peter Fuerte but towards the window where Major laid.

Confused, Peter turned and looked in the direction that little Ernesto was reaching for. Glancing out the window Peter could catch a glimpse of something black, but he couldn't identify what it was. Using his right hand he reached inside of his shirt grasping the small two shot .25 caliber derringer concealed in an armpit holster.

Allison gasped in surprise at the sight of the gun. She grabbed Ernesto and quickly hid on the far side of the bed.

Peter quickly moved to the window and opened it. He couldn't see anything at all. Frowning, he searched the shadows. He still couldn't spot anything. Peter was about to attribute the whole scene to imagination, when he caught a glint of light off to the left of the window by a small bush. Without hesitation Peter fired both shots at the flash. He knew that a hit with either bullet was a long shot with the small gun, but he had hoped to flush out whatever or whomever was hiding in the bush. Beside the crack of the pistol should bring his guards running. Peter was astounded when the darkness of the bush erupted. A black shape had literally exploded from the bush and was headed towards the mountain. Judging by the way the shape moved Peter knew it was a man. He quickly lost sight of him as the shadows claimed him for their own.

The door behind him burst open as all eight of the guards in various stages of undress came through the portal, Pistols drawn and ready for action.

"We have had an uninvited guest tonight." Peter stated flatly.

"We will find him." Peter looked at his wife and son, "Then we will question him before we kill him! Secure the grounds!" He commanded

CHAPTER 37

Major had thought himself near invisible laying there upon the narrow casement of the window, so he was taken totally by surprise when Brok had reached out for him, calling him Daddy. Major had read his lips.

Major moved quickly, without thought he slipped from the narrow ledge and dropped straight down lightly on it, then instantly bounced himself up and off of the ledge, flinging himself backwards into a tight ball. Judging the distance to the ground perfectly, Major came out of the tuck and hit the ground with bent knees. He followed his momentum with a controlled back roll, and just like that he was on the ground unharmed.

Fluidly and without any hesitation, Major leapt into the shadow of the small bush. Looking up towards the window, Major was confident that the black ninja out fit that clothed him from head to tow would completely conceal him in the shadow of the bush.

When Peter Fuerte flung open the double-glassed windows Major froze. He knew that the human eye wouldn't be able to pick him out of the shadows as long as he didn't attract attention with motion.

Suddenly Fuerte swung towards him and let two shots off.

A searing pain in Major's left shoulder told him that he had been hit by the gunfire. Agony filled Major. He tried to control the pain and not give his location away, but the pain was too intense. He felt like falling to the ground and kicking around in circles like Curly used to do on the Three Stooges. Major had to move and move now! He burst from the shadows with a speed and intensity that only a man in physical agony could have achieved.

Major ran with all the speed of a world-class athlete towards where he cached his gear. He had to get to the knapsack and head for the woods. Fearing a bullet between the shoulder blades, Major tried to unsuccessfully eke out more speed from his injured body. Coming to the rock, which hid his staff and knapsack, Major went behind it and retrieved his equipment.

Looking back to the house, Major could see no sign of pursuit as of yet. Taking a moment, Major reached up under his top and felt the bullet wound. Sticky blood had already soaked the front of his outfit and had started to soak down into his pants. Unzipping the knapsack, Major reached in and grabbed a handkerchief and folded it into a square. He put the makeshift bandage on his wound and applied direct pressure in an effort to control the bleeding.

Major looked towards the house again, a noise had attracted his attention. The garage door at the back of the house was being raised by an automatic door opener. Major could see the light starting at the bottom getting wider as the door rolled up.

A group of men were found in the doorway with flashlights already probing the quasi-darkness that surround the house. A ray of light swept the rock field. Major ducked behind the boulder, grabbing the bo-staff and knapsack in his right hand. As soon as the light beam had passed him by, Major left the shelter of the rock and headed east. He was headed the way he had come in. He wanted to put some distance between him and the house. He didn't know if they would search for him tonight or not, but he had to get his wound tended to.

Major stayed even with the rock field so he wouldn't run into the sentry post a hundred yards to his right. He jogged quickly, yet silently and soon left the lights behind him. Slowing to a walk, Major knew that he was in trouble.

Blood was still seeping from his shoulder even though the worst of it had been staunched with the handkerchief and direct pressure.

After an eternity, Major came upon the ravine where he had drank the night before. Major laid his staff and knapsack down and gathered up some dry wood. He stopped when he had his right arm full. Walking back to where he had laid his equipment, Major reached down with his wounded arm and picked up the sack and staff even though the action sent waves of nauseating pain coursing through his body.

Major carefully worked his way down the side of the ravine. He was getting weaker with every passing moment, and he didn't want to risk a fall. As soon as he reached the bottom he climbed under a small overhang and laid his burdens down. He unzipped the knapsack and pulled the first aid kit out. He hoped that Phil had put everything in it that he needed. Opening it, Major managed a small smile when he seen the prescription codeine laced tablets that were there. However that smile soon changed to a frown when Major realized they were in a childproof bottle. Grabbing the container in his left hand he managed to get the top off, even though it cost him a jolt of pain.

Major shook four tablets out, hesitated then added 2 more. Capping the bottle, he replaced it in the medical kit.

Getting out the purifier, Major washed the pain killer down with a cool drink of water.

The pain was intense, but Major couldn't wait for the pills to begin to work. He arranged the wood in a wagon wheel fashion and lit the small twigs to get it going. Major helped the flame along by blowing on it. Once he had a nice flame started, he added more wood. The fire burnt hot, because the wood was so dry.

Major pulled the sai on his right side out of his shoe string belt and struck the long tine directly into the fire. Major was going to have to remove the bullet from his shoulder and he would have to cauterize the wound. Searching through the first aid kit, Major found a pair of scissors that were slender and about 5 inches long. He didn't have a probe in the kit, so he decided to use the scissors.

Swabbing them down with an alcohol pad that was sealed in individual packets, Major soon had them sterilized.

By now the codeine was working and Major felt detached from his body. In fact, truth is known he was high as a kite. His shoulder still hurt, but he didn't care. Major pulled the ninja mask off and pulled the ninja top off.

The wound was a small puckered opening located between the rotator cuff of his shoulder and his collarbone.

His stomach was caked with dried blood and he could smell the stink of body odor. Taking the scissors he opened them up so he only had to use one blade to probe with. Gently he entered the opening of the wound. The blade was inside of his shoulder by one half of its five-inch length, when Major felt the slug. Sweat broke out on his forehead and body when the contact was made.

Even with the drugs in his body, the pain was excruciating. Grimacing, but grimly determined, Major slowly worked the blade of the scissors beside and then partially underneath the bullet. Slowly Major started to force the slug from its burrow. Blood spurted anew from the wound as Major finally worked the bullet out of his shoulder. The slug fell to the ground before Major could grab it.

Major picked up the blood soaked handkerchief that he had used for direct pressure and once again applied it to the wound. Major was extremely light headed from the loss of blood and the painkiller coursing through his body. He knew what had to be done, but still he hesitated to do it.

Pulling the handkerchief from the entry of the wound, Major laid it aside. Reaching for the sai in the fire, he pulled it out and examined the end. It was cherry red. Major stared at the glow for a mesmerizing second and then slowly put the tip of the sai close to the still bleeding wound. With a quick motion, Major thrust the tip of the sai into the raw pulsating flesh. The hot sai hissed as the blood and flesh burnt and sealed it. Major left it inside for a long second and then pulled it from the now charred wound. A small wisp of smoke carried the nauseating smell of burnt flesh to his nostrils.

Major laid the sai down and tried to control the pain that soared through his shoulder. Bile came up into his mouth and he almost puked. Tears came into his eyes and he openly wept. Major had considered the possibility of injuries, but never in the world did he think that it would hurt so much.

Major folded his legs underneath him and resting his hands in his legs, Major rolled his head back to provide a clear passage for his airway. He started to breath in through the nose, out through the mouth. He let his mind wander away from his body. Slowly the pain ebbed and Major was able to relax a bit.

Between the meditation and the painkiller, Major was finally able to function again. He warmed the soiled ninja top by the now dying fire's heat before he put it on Between the blood and dried sweat on his body Major was a mess. He stunk.

Major kicked the fire from the rock it was built on into the small stream. Ashes and smoke flew up as the water extinguished the flames. Major let the flow of the water carry the burnt wood away. He knew that he had left quite a trail from the house to the ravine, but he couldn't do anything about that now.

Reaching into the backpack, Major pulled out his stash of jerky and fruit. The painkiller blunted his hunger, but Major forced himself to eat three strips of jerky and a handful of fruit. Washing it all down with a long drink of water.

Major put the ninja hood back on and gathered up his gear. He had to get away from here. He stood slowly and closed his eyes as he felt the world spinning around. He was weak and hurting, but he had to leave this area quickly. Major slowly made his way up the ravine. He made his way towards the mountain; once he hit the rocky area he turned left and headed west back towards the Fuerte's house. He covered about a mile before fatigue and shock finally overtook him. Looking around in the darkness, Major couldn't find a good place to hole up. Finally he walked over to a pair of boulders nestled together and curled up like a dog. Major set his mental alarm clock and hoped he would get up at daybreak. In seconds he was sound asleep.

CHAPTER 38

It wasn't daybreak that woke Major. Rather it was the chill of the morning. His weakened body didn't adapt to the chilly air without some type of shelter. Major awoke damp from the morning dew. His shoulder was screaming out in waves of pain, he had a headache, and his whole body felt like he had been a sparring partner of Mike Tyson. Tie all of the physical agony together with a terrible case of morning breath, body odor, soiled clothing and you had a perfect picture of Major. It wasn't right to be this pitiful.

Major got the pain pills from his knapsack and dry swallowed four of them. He sat in the false dawn and waited for relief to come to him.

The birds were tweeting and chirping when the raging pain became a dull roar. Standing, he directed a stream of urine against the side of the boulder he had slept beside. Feeling relieved he ventured to the nearest bush and broke himself off a toothbrush. After cleansing his teeth, Major discarded the frayed twig and picked up his gear. Slowly and painfully he made his way back towards the Fuerte house, hugging the boundary of the woods and where the rocky terrain began. He had fished a piece of jerky from his backpack and was working on it when he heard voices in the woods in front of him. Major moved up beside a bramble thicket and hid behind the thorny foliage. Peering through the thick brambles he could make out movement ahead and to the left of him. A group of men were walking in a straight line parallel from each other. They were all carrying a weapon of some type. "One, two, three, four, five, six, seven, eight!" Major counted under his breath. Major saw that there were eight of the searchers and that they were following the trail that he had left last night. Major had known he had left a track that a neophyte woodsman could have followed. They would find the ravine where he had built the fire, and maybe even where he had spent the night, but tracking him after that would be difficult. Major had taken pains to conceal his passing after he had left the shelter of the boulders.

The line of searchers passed within a hundred feet of his hiding place, unaware that the object of their search was watching them. They continued on slowly, carefully, watching for any sign of their quarry.

Once they had disappeared behind him, Major rose up from the bed of brambles and started to move towards the Fuerte's again. His body started to loosen up and the pain in his shoulder had diminished to the point where he could move his arm in small circles. He continued to work the arm around as he silently moved ahead.

Major was about a mile from the house when he decided to find a place of concealment. He knew that the guards would be sweeping back this way sooner or later, and he wanted to have a place that wouldn't be discovered when they did.

He found a slight depression by a massive oak tree and after gathering up a mixture of live plants and dead branches he covered him up and felt that he was suitably camouflaged. He briefly wished that he had taken the time to sate his thirst, but that passed as a great weariness over took him. He said his prayers and was soon sound asleep.

INTERLUDE

While Major spent the majority of Thursday sleeping and recovering from his wound, Jill spent the day with her new dog. Sensei was almost a grown dog, yet still had enough puppy in him to enjoy a good romp with Jill.

Although Brok and Major were still weighing heavy on her mind, Jill enjoyed herself for the first time in almost two weeks.

CHAPTER 39

In the meantime, Phil had bought an old extended cab Ford. It was the type with two seats behind the bench seat of the truck. After the purchase of the truck, he bought a local paper and perused the want ads. Finding a couple of ads proclaiming the sale of two used motorcycles, he tore them from the paper and went to investigate them. He bought the first one he checked out, paying the young man cash. The youth helped Phil load the bike into the bed of the ford and watched as Phil drove away.

Phil drove to the local gas station where he filled the truck's tank and a five-gallon can that he had in the back of the truck. After checking under the hood, he was satisfied that the truck was ready for action. Procuring a map that showed local roads, Phil took the truck with the motorcycle still in the bed out to cruise them.

After studying the map he found the road where he had left Major off. Following it out he finally found a grange road that intersected it approximately ten miles from the Fuerte estate. Phil drove the truck until he came across the narrow rutted and ill cared for road. It looked like it hadn't been tended to in quite awhile. Phil took his time going up the steep road, driving between the deep ruts that followed the contours of the road. Reaching the peak of the road, he quickly dropped down to the other side of the hill past the old grange hall that had fallen in disrepair. Phil had known that the road hadn't been used in quite a while. Arriving to the bottom of the steep and winding mountainous hill, he was pleased to see where the two roads intersected. There was a guardrail blocking off the grange road from this side. Phil backed the truck up until he came to a small turnaround off the road where he backed into it. Getting out, he went into the woods with a small hatchet he had purchased at a hardware store in Macsville. He cut some branches off various trees and used them to cover the pick-up. Satisfied that the Ford couldn't casually be seen, Phil unloaded the motorcycle and rode it back to town. He went to a used car lot and traded the motorcycle and roll of bills for a rough looking Camaro that still ran hot. Everything was in motion and Phil was ready. Now everything was up to Major.

CHAPTER 40

Peter Fuerte had spent the night considering the complexity of what had happened last night. The way Ernesto had reached for the masked intruder, plus the fact that he had called him "Daddy," convinced him that somehow, someway, Ernesto's father had found him.

Thursday morning, he waited impatiently for office hours to come around. At nine a.m. he picked up the phone and dialed a special number. It rang several times before a graveled voiced male answered

"Hello?'

"Dick, it's Peter Fuerte."

"What can I do for you?"

"We had an intruder last night, my friend," Peter said and grimly added, Ernesto called him daddy!"

"What did you say?" The graveled voice man was incredulous.

"You heard me." Said Peter.

"Could this be?" He asked.

"Yes I'm afraid so," a pause, then, "I lost track of him two days ago!"

"Fool!" Shouted Fuerte. "Incompetent!"

Peter snarled obscenities into the phone, not stopping until he ran out of breath.

"Do you need some help down there?" Asked the graveled voiced man.

Visibly constraining himself, Peter shuddered for control before he answered.

"No, counting myself, I have sixteen men here to deal with him."

Peter paused and then continued to talk, "We will find him, and he won't be around anymore to cause problems." A smile came to the handsome face. "Then all of our problems will be solved. No?"

"Just be careful Peter, this guy is serious!"

"He has never seen serious, until he has crossed Peter Fuerte!" Peter was strutting his stuff now. "I have the best people in the world on this estate right now!" He bragged. "What can one man do against so many?"

"Just be careful with this one, my friend."

A pause came to the conversation, and then, 'I have a bad feeling about this!'

"Don't worry Dick, my men and I will handle it!"

"Just don't let him get away from you!"

Peter laughed at the thought of one man escaping him and his men. "Okay, my friend, you don't have to worry!"

After they exchanged a few more words, they broke the connection.

CHAPTER 41

The silence of the woods woke Major up. The squeaking of chipmunks, the singing of birds and the rustling of leaves had not wakened Major, but the sudden silence told him that something or someone out of place in the woods was coming.

It was an hour or so before dark and the shadows were lengthening in the woods. Cautiously, Major eased the brush from around his face, so he could see what was going on around him. There! About one hundred feet behind him were two men working their way back to the Fuerte's house on a direct line with Major's hiding place. Leaving the knapsack and the bo-staff under the bush, Major eased himself out of the depression in which he had hid. They were within fifty feet now and he could hear them talking. "We should have walked the road back with the rest of the guys!" Complained the bigger of the two. "It's our job to be thorough!" The smaller man stopped and his gun came up. "What is it?" Asked the big guy.

"Thought I saw something up ahead!" Slowly, both guns at ready positions, the two men moved ahead, eyes searching for something out of place. They had come up on the depression where Major had spent the day.

"What is this?" Questioned the big man as he used the barrel of the uzi to point out the almost invisible shape of the knapsack.

Suddenly both men whirled towards the big oak tree guns up as a loud farting sound caught their attention. Suddenly from behind the tree a thick body of a timber rattler came flying through the air directly at them. The snake's body caught the big man around the neck where the pit viper instantly sank needle like fangs deep into the thug's exposed neck. Screaming loud and shrill like a terrified woman, the big man fell to both knees dropped the uzi and clawing at the snake's body, trying to pull it away from its deadly kiss. Venom was pumped directly into the jugular vein as the snake bit down again. The now whimpering thug was unsuccessful in pulling it away from him. The smaller man had stepped back in terrified relief. He was glad that his partner had stopped the snake, and that it wasn't him that sounded like a whining pup under the poisonous fangs of the pit viper. As the small man watched fascinated at the struggle between his partner and the snake, he was suddenly aware of a black mass hurtling at him from behind the massive oak. He didn't have time to bring his gun into play before the mass hit him.

Major had eased his way from his sleeping place and was behind the oak tree when the thugs had came up and spotted his knapsack.

He was lying on his belly and was wondering what to do if they took his knapsack, when suddenly Major sensed danger. Slowly turning his head slightly to his left, Major's blood froze in his veins. A timber rattler was coiled, ready to strike. Major gasped in surprise and the snake instantly struck. He threw himself violently on his left side causing his shoulder to sing out in excruciating pain. He felt the snake strike his chest and felt the venom searing his skin. His bowels loosen and he defecated in his pants. An explosively loud fart heralded the arrival of underwear full of feces. Major grabbed the snake around the head and tail to keep it from further damage to him. It took Major a long second to realize that the pit viper didn't bite him. It had struck the front of his ninja top. The violent roll that Major had executed had saved him from an agonizing bite. Knowing that the two men on the other side of the oak had to hear the noise that he had made while subduing the reptile, Major quickly got to his feet with the writhing rattler in his hands. Peering around the bole of the tree, Major could just see a little bit of the biggest man. Without hesitation Major threw the pit viper on him. Once he released the snake, Major spun to the other side of the trunk and counted to five under his breath.

Stepping from behind the tree, Major could see the snake bitten man still struggling with the timber rattler, his partner was staring fascinated by the spectacle, before him. He never even seen Major launch himself in the air with a sai in his right hand. Major was in mid air and ready to strike when the man looked up and seen him. It was too late for him. Major hit him like a bowling ball on a five pin and knocked him off of his feet, his gun flying away from him. While he lain stunned, Major drew his right foot back and threw a hard front snap kick to the unprotected groin, hitting with the ball of his foot.

"Ughhh!" Moaned the fallen thug as he rolled on his side, legs drawn up into a fetal position. With total lack of compassion, Major dropped to one knee beside the curled up hood. Taking the sai, tines side-facing outward, Major drew his arm back and suddenly thrust the tines up through the bottom of the fallen hood's throat. He rammed the sai in so hard, that the longest tine appeared like magic out of the top of the dead man's head. It was harder pulling it out of his head, then it was driving it in, but Major pulled it out with relative ease.

Turning towards his other foe, he saw that he had managed to get the snake off of him and had thrown it in the bushes to the left of them. He was holding his throat where he had been bitten when Major walked up in front of him and hunkered down. Blood and brain matter still hung grisly on the deadly sai, but neither Major or the dying man paid any attention to the gore.

Major never said a word. He pulled the ninja mask off and let the hood get a good look at his face.

"Are you going to kill me?" Gasped the hood.

"Yes!"

He stared at Major his eyes starting to glaze.

"Well do it then!" He said. "Do it!"

Major drew the sai back.

"Do you have anything you want to say?' He asked.

"Yeah!" The hood barked a short laugh.

"Man you sure do stink!" The hood laughed again.

The laugh changed to a gurgle as Major drove the sai deep into his chest. His eyes flew open and his hands flew to the shaft of the sai. Grasping the handle, he tried to remove it, but failed. Slowly he toppled over and died.

Major rolled him over on his back. Stepping on his stomach, he reached down and viciously jerked the sai from the dead man's chest. His wound had started to bleed again and the pain was starting to intensify.

Major pulled his knapsack and bo-staff from the depression. He got four pain-killers from the bottle and dry swallowed them. One thing for sure the dead man was right! He sure did stink.

Gathering up his gear and leaving the fallen guards where they laid, Major headed east. He was going to the lake he had spotted the first night he had been in the woods. It was time to clean up.

CHAPTER 42

Jill was sitting on couch with Sensei when the phone rang. She considered not answering it, already sorry she had plugged it back in but with Major gone and maybe needing help she felt obligated to answer.

"Hello?" She asked.

"Is he there yet?" A mocking Breeler asked.

Jill didn't answer. Sensei felt the tension and came over to get his head rubbed.

"Well? Is he?"

Jill still didn't answer.

"I know that he isn't Jill!" Breeler's voice became harsh.

"I know what he is doing!" A lilt came to Breeler's voice. "When I catch up with him, maybe I'll save the state some money!"

Jill hung up.

CHAPTER 43

Major had come to the lake and had stripped down. He dove into the cold clean water and swam underwater for a distance. Coming up slowly, he flipped over on his back and floated that way for a few minutes. Swimming back to the shore, he retrieved a handkerchief from the knapsack and proceeded to cleanse himself as well as he could. Washing himself he felt a lot better when he finally got the dried blood, snake venom, sweat and the crusted remains of the feces that he had fouled himself with.

Grabbing first the top, then the bottom and finishing up with the ninja mask, Major soon had his outfit clean. Reaching in the knapsack he got the handkerchief that he had used when he was first wounded and cleaned it up too. He wrung all the excess water from the outfit and hung it on some bushes to dry.

He took one more swim before coming out to relax on the bank. Getting the pocket filter out to set it up and took a long drink. He pulled the jerky and fruit packets out and started to eat. He was getting pretty tired of the simple food but it would sustain him for a couple of more days. He stood up in the bright moonlight and examined his wound. It was starting to heal nicely. He finished up his meal and polished it off with a good drink of water.

Major put his still damp outfit on and picked his gear up. He slowly started back up the way he had come in and headed for the woods on the north side of the road. Major took his time heading back to the Fuerte's residence; he wanted to reflect on the day's happenings. Even though he had no intentions on killing anyone, he had destroyed two human beings. Their bodies were still laying where the fell. Major had been sickened by his own lack of remorse and had left the area very abruptly. He knew that they would probably be discovered tomorrow, and that would heighten security. It would make things extremely difficult. However, Major knew that they would show no mercy to him if the caught him. Major had to make a decision before he proceeded further. Should he try to spare lives or not. There were probably only two innocent people in the house, Allison Fuerte and Brok, and Major wasn't sure about Allison.

After considering the problem for a few moments, Major knew he would do what had to be done. After being responsible for three human deaths Major was becoming immune to killing. Although his consciences bothered him after the fact, he was starting to consider the foes he faced as low as the reptiles that abounded in the wooded and rocky areas.

Major made his way back through the woods and closed within a mile of the Fuerte's place. He came upon the site where he had dispatched the two men, startling a couple of wild dogs, which were feeding on the carcasses. The two dogs faded back into the brush, but Major could hear the faint growls as he passed. He finally made his way to the open yard behind the Fuerte house and worked his way into the rock field. He wanted to go to the west side of the home.

He made it over with no problems and made his way quietly past the sentry posts. He walked westward and left the house behind. Major selected a huge bole oak tree and climbed his way up. He came to where two branches grew straight out and after checking it over decided it would do. Taking the knapsack off and using it as a pillow for his head and laying the bo-staff across his lap, he was soon fast asleep.

CHAPTER 44

Peter Fuerte was sitting in his den. The music coming from the stereo was classical. The cigar he was smoking was pure Havana. He was sipping a glass of imported beer when Pedro came in with his report for the days search. Pedro had been with Peter since they spent their childhood together. Peter trusted him implicitly. Pedro was a huge specimen of a man. At six foot two and two hundred ninety-pounds of solid muscle, he was used as a detriment for keeping the other men in line. No one wanted to have to explain to Pedro why something didn't go right. Consequently things ran fairly smoothly with Pedro in charge.

Peter didn't say a word when Pedro walked in. he simply raised an eyebrow. That was all the permission that was needed for his giant friend to speak. In a low voice that could be barely heard, Pedro gave his report.

"Hose and Franco are missing," he said flatly.

"Missing?" Questioned Peter.

"They did not come back with the rest of the search party!"

Peter puffed on his Havana and then knocked ashes into an ashtray shaped like a heart. He surveyed the lit end of the cigar, and then lifted his eyes to Pedro.

"Any one see anything?" He asked

"No." Pedro answered simply.

"Do you think they ran into our friend?"

Pedro considered the question carefully before he answered. "They were two of our most trusted men." Pedro thought for a moment, "Something had to have happened to them!"

Peter stood up and walked over to Pedro. His five foot nine frame small compared to the bulk of his friend. Handing Pedro a cigar, he lit it for him, after Pedro had bitten the end off. "That leaves us with fourteen men counting myself." He mused. He sat back down. "Double the perimeter guards." He ordered. "You and I will provide the safe keeping for the house." Peter smiled at his friend. "Do you think we will be enough, old friend?"

Pedro answered affirmative with a grunt. Without another word he turned and went to double the guards.

Peter gulped his beer down. It tasted so good that he poured himself another one.

CHAPTER 45

Major had awakened up several times during the long day. He had thought things through several times. He had to laugh at himself though. In the movies, the heroes never went to the bathroom, never shown fear and to his knowledge had never dropped a load in their pants. That was what tickled Major so much. After chuckling at himself he started to think about what he was going to do this very evening. He was going in after Brok, and no one had better get in his way.

Pedro had doubled the guards and gave them orders to alternate sleeping during the day so they would be fresh that night. Pedro knew that the masked man wouldn't come during the day. If he caught anyone sleeping that night, he would personally kill them himself! Satisfied that his orders would be done, Pedro strode back to the house to catch some shuteye himself.

Phil was lying in his hotel room trying to quiet his racing mind. Tonight he would make his first run up the Fuerte road. If everything went okay, they would be on their way back to Ohio tonight. Phil tried to relax, but the waiting was finally getting to him.

CHAPTER 46

Darkness came slowly and the light was fading fast, when Major made his way down the tree. He had eaten off and on during the day and the only thing he really needed was a cool drink of water and to hike a leg on a bush. After urinating he took stock of himself. He had four of the codeine tablets left and he dry swallowed them. There was only a little jerky and fruit left in the knapsack. Major cached the knapsack and bo-staff to the side of the tree, covering the sack with some brush.

He wanted to travel light. If he needed the first aid kit again, then he would be able to get to it . . . if he was able. Slowly he loosened himself up. Putting one foot against the tree and keeping his leg locked at the knee, he slowly put his head down towards the side of his leg. Bouncing slightly he stretched the hamstring and the muscles in his leg. He then changed legs and did it again. He used isometric exercises on his upper body, taking care to loosen up his left shoulder.

After all of the problems Major had with his wound, breaking it open over time and time again, he was lucky it wasn't infected. He swung his left arm around in large circles and was pleased to note that there was only minor discomfort. Of course the tablets he had taken was largely responsible for that. Major worked on stretching until he had a sweat worked up.

He had a few minutes until optimum conditions. The sky had clouds that obscured the moon, although an occasional break in the cloud would light the woods up like daybreak.

Feeling good, Major decided to start towards the guard posts. It was a little after nine. Phil would be coming through around midnight, and he wanted to have Brok with him by then. If everything worked out they would be headed out of here in less than three hours.

Allison Fuerte and little Ernesto, alias Brok, sat on his bed eating cookies and drinking a glass of milk, It had become a ritual for them since Ernesto had arrived over a week and a half ago. Ernesto really liked the soft and chewy chocolate chip cookies that she made special for him. She knew Peter had doubled the guards on the out post, and that he and Pedro were trying not to show that they were keeping an eye on the two of them. She figured it had to do with the intruder the night before. She had been shocked when she discovered that Peter was carrying a concealed weapon. When she had questioned him about it, he had implied that such things did not concern her. Allison had heard the rumors about Peter before they married, but he had treated her with so much love and respect that she didn't hesitate to marry him. She had wanted a child of their own very badly but once she realized that Peter was incapable of siring children she had put child bearing out of her mind. Yet Peter was so sensitive of her emotions, that he had adopted a son and surprised her on her birthday. It was a moment she would never forget. Now, it seems that Ernesto's real father had somehow found them. Well, Allison had faith in Peter. No one would take her son from her. Little did she know that Jill Brown had thought the very same thing two weeks ago.

CHAPTER 47

Although the ninja outfit was a little worse for the wear by now, the hole from the bullet and tears resulting from the bramble bushes had pretty much ruined it. The blood and feces stains were there, but you couldn't see them in the dark.

Major silently arrived at the guard post on the west side of the house and went to the one closest to the road. Without a sound he crept up on the two guards stationed there. A low murmur told Major that they were having conversation, although he couldn't make out what they were saying.

Major had a sai in each hand. He was about ready to step out and attack the pair, when one reached for a cigarette. Major held his position. He closed his eyes when the man lit the cigarette with a match. He didn't want his night vision to be compromised. He knew that he would have the edge after the flame of the match had taken away some of their night sight. The two guards were facing each other sharing the cigarette when Major stepped from behind the small tree. They were sideways to Major. He took two steps and was within arms length of them, which was plenty close enough with the sais in his hand. Before they were aware that Major was there he struck. Bringing both hands forward with the tines of the sais outward, he struck both men at the same instances. Aiming for the spot just in front of the ear, Major drove the sais deep into the brains of both men. Each dropped to the ground without a word. The only sound was the rattle of their machine guns and the thud of their bodies hitting the ground. He bent over the closest one and felt his neck for a pulse. Amazing enough his heart still beat, grabbing the handle that protruded from the man's skull, Major wiggled it up and down destroying the brain. He felt for a pulse again and couldn't find one. He pulled the sai from his head and checked out the vital signs of the other victim. There wasn't any, he was already dead. "Two down," he thought and moved to the next post.

One of the men was sitting down his back to the tree, and the other one was watching the area towards the house.

Major moved in and stood directly behind the tree where the man was sitting. He wasn't aware of Major, but Major waited before he struck. Stepping out beside the sitting man, he brought the sai down hard through the top of the man's head. He drove it in so far that even the two smaller tines imbedded themselves into the bone of the skull. The noise of the attack sounded like someone thumping a ripe pumpkin.

The alert guard instantly turned and seen his partner with a sai sticking out the top of his head. The guard brought his gun up searching for a target that already had moved away from the skewered man. Shaken the guard, gun ready to rock and roll, moved up to check his partner out.

A kick that he never seen coming broke his wrist and rendered his trigger finger useless, inhaling he tried to yell out to warn the other guards. A ridge hand across the Adams apple from the invisible assailant choked the warning cry off before he could get it out. Dropping the gun he grabbed for his throat, unable to breath, he panicked. He turned to run, when another kick that he didn't see coming destroyed his knee breaking him down to the ground.

Consciousness was fading in and out as he lain there in physical agony, he opened his eyes at a nudge from a tabi-shoed foot and looked up at death. All he could see on the black masked head was eyes and they shone without mercy. The guard closed his eyes, knowing he was going to die. Major obliged him.

Major dispatched the six guards at the next three posts in pretty much the same manner. None of them had seen him coming and by the time they were aware that he was there, it was too late.

Major had one more set of guards to dispatch and moved in quickly for the kill. As he closed in he noticed that both guards were alert and watchful. That would make things more difficult. The cloud cover that had concealed Major during his killing of the previous sentries was still there, but it was thinning rapidly.

Major eased up to the guard closest to him and positioned himself to strike. The guard was uneasy, as if he could sense Major was there.

Major was in the shadow of a tree that concealed him fairly well. He was about eight feet from the man and couldn't close in.

Fluidly he reached down and picked up a small stick. He waited until the guard's head turned away from his direction, and then he snapped the twig. The guard spun on his heels gun up ready to shoot.

"Hey!" He exclaimed to the other guard. "I heard something!"

"Check it out, I'll cover you!" The other guard stepped up to back his buddy up.

The guard warily stepped forward, eyes probing the darkness of the shadows, not seeing anything. He was within two feet of Major when he struck. The end of the handle was sticking out of the bottom of Major's fist by half of an inch. Major brought the sai sideways to his chest with the bottom of his fist outward. When the hood was close enough, Major swung the sai handle first, at the man's forehead. The man's skull splintered like a mirror that was dropped to the floor. His feet went higher then his head and he looked as if he slipped on a patch of ice.

After the strike Major dropped into a back roll and come back to his feet five feet away from where he was originally starting. It was a good thing that he had moved as quickly as he did, for when the stricken sentry went down, his partner never hesitated. He opened fire. Bullets chewed up the tree and surrounding foliage where Major had been, the noise was deafening. Major closed his eyes to the muzzle flash.

The remaining guard stopped firing and warily moved up to look at his partner. His wide staring, unblinking eyes told him that he was dead. His skull was shattered.

While he was kneeling over his deceased partner, the remaining guard heard a stick break behind him. Instantly he whirled, uzi blazing away. There was nothing there. He heard a noise to the left of him and again, he turned and fired. He pulled the trigger until the gun was empty. Panic caused the guard to throw his now worthless gun towards where he last heard the noise. Spinning in a circle he pulled a hunting knife from a sheath attached to his belt. He assumed a classical knife-fighting stance.

Feet spread apart, his left hand out ready to protect himself and the knife in his right hand ahead the blade facing up the handle at the bottom of his fist. He gulped in great drafts of air, trying to calm his racing heart. Slowly he started to get control of himself. Thinking he might have lucked out and hit the intruder with his gunfire, he thought he might have a chance of surviving this night.

A movement to his right side caught his eye and he turned to face a shadow that was moving towards him. The moon suddenly shone bright and lit up the woods as it came from bchind the cloudbank that had been keeping the woods in darkness. The hood could clearly see his opponent now. He was dressed in all black and he had a weapon in each hand. The moonlight glinted off of each one, although both seemed to have some type of a non-glare substance on them. A closer look convinced him that it was blood.

The ninja stopped a couple of paces from the guard prepared to attack.

"Wait!" Exclaimed the guard. "Let me go! I won't bother you!"

Major considered it. "Why should I?" He asked

"I don't want to die!"

Major considered it. Started to say something but stopped.

The frightened hood saw that he had a chance.

"Please, I don't want to die!" He said again.

"Put the knife down." Major commanded.

If he hesitated doing the simple command, he would die, but the man did it without hesitation.

"What's your name son?" Major asked.

"Anthony Thomas."

"Well Anthony, this is you lucky day!"

Major stepped forward. Give me your word you won't interfere with what I'm doing!"

"I give you my word!" Anthony drew himself up, head held high, chest out, and his right hand over his heart.

"It's funny," said Major, "I believe you!"

"Turn around!" He commanded.

Anthony turned and waited. He never felt the heavy blow that Major landed with his fist to the back of his head.

Major stood over the unconscious youth and considered killing him anyway. After careful consideration, he turned and walked away. He did believe Anthon's word and so felt honor bound to let him live. However if he showed up at the house, then his life would be forfeit.

It was time to go get Brok.

Peter and Pedro were in the house when gunfire caught their attention. They looked at each other and smiled

"Sounds like our friend was spotted."

Pedro nodded his head.

"Maybe you should go check it out." Said Peter.

Without another word, Pedro turned and went to the front door. Before he opened it, he shut the light off so he wouldn't be silhouetted in the doorway. He opened the door and went outside.

Peter went up to Ernesto's room where Allison and Ernesto were awakened by the gunfire.

"Are we safe, Peter?" Asked Allison.

"I think so, my dear, Pedro is going to check out the situation.

Peter went to the bed where his two loved ones were lying.

RODNEY L. BAUMBERGER

"It will soon be over, my love." Peter smiled, "Then we will be happy, yes?"

"Yes dear, we will be happy!" But Allison wondered how happy they could be with so much turmoil surrounding them.

CHAPTER 48

Major eased his way up to the house, the bright moonlight took away some of his invisibility.

All the guards in the out posts, with the exception of Anthony Thomas were dead. Major's gloves were blood soaked and his hands were sticky. His ninja bottoms had blood smears down the sides, where the Sais hung from his shoestring belt.

Major felt good! Physically his shoulder still wasn't as strong as it ought to be, but the rest of his body was in superb shape. Not an ounce of fat was on him and his muscles rippled as he moved. Mentally, he was sharp as a bowie knife. He had brutally murdered thirteen men in the last two days, but it hadn't affected him at all. It had been as easy as killing ants. It was very simple. They stood between him and Brok, bad news for them.

Major made a circuit around the house, staying on the border of the lights that were shining from the house. He saw no sign of any other sentries so it was without fear that he finally moved towards the house.

Only once had he seen someone around in the well-lighted windows and that was for a brief moment.

Major was hoping that most of the hired help were lying in the out post, stone cold dead, if not, well, he would face that problem one at a time.

Major had creeped up to the house and was making his way around the whole circumference of it. He had made his mind up. He was going through the front door. He would hit hard and quick, trying to surprise anyone waiting for him.

Major was easing around the west side of the house, and was just to the corner that led to the front, when he was suddenly laid low by a gun butt to the kidney. Major lay in the ground paralyzed by the pain. He looked up, and was shocked to see the barrel of an uzi aimed right between his eyes.

"Get up!" Commanded the huge man.

Major painfully got to his feet, his mind racing, trying to figure out how to disarm this huge opponent.

"My men, you've killed them all!" Growled Pedro.

"Take you weapons from your side."

Major slowly reached down and pulled the knot apart on the shoestring belt. The sais clanked to the ground.

"Step back."

Major did as he was told.

"Take your mask off!"

Major did.

"Now turn around slowly!"

Major turned around.

"You are without weapons?" Asked Pedro.

"Yes." Major's reply was simple.

"Good!" Pedro threw the uzi on the ground behind them.

"I will kill you with my bare hands!"

Pedro lumbered forward, Major came up on the balls of his feet ready to move in any direction. Slowly he gave ground as the big man came closer. With a grunt Major stopped and launched a front kick using the ball of his right foot to the groin of Pedro. Major's aim was true as he struck, driving Pedro's testicles upwards. Major followed through with a reverse punch that connected with the point of the big man's jaw. Pedro hardly blinked an eye as Major danced backwards.

Major knew that he was going to have to be very careful with him. He had used all of the power in his body, adding the perfect follow through on each technique. It gave him the hitting power of a heavyweight, yet didn't appear to faze the big man at all.

Pedro threw an awkward roundhouse punch with his rear hand. He stepped forward at the same time trying to close the gap to Major. Major let the massive fist pass over his head as he ducked in plenty of time. As soon as Pedro had flashed his fist past Major's head, he drove a right hand deep into the side of Pedro. He let loose with every ounce of power he had. It was like hitting a sack of redi-mix concrete. Major didn't stop with the one pummel; he threw a left hand in the same spot and followed the left with another right. For the first time, Pedro let out a grunt. Not of pain, but of annoyance. He brought his arm back and caught Major in the side of the face with a back fist.

The surprise blow took Major sideways off of his feet and dump him stunned to the ground.

Pedro grabbed Major by the ankle and swung him around in a circle like he was a rag doll. He released him towards the house trying to crush Major's skull against the siding. At the point of release, Major flipped in mid air, not thinking about it, but by instinct. He landed feet first against the house and catapulted himself off of the side, tucking himself into a ball he rolled up to Pedro. Pedro reached down towards Major to grab him again when Major suddenly uncurled and let a sidekick loose to the throat of the giant. Pedro staggered back, grabbing his throat unable to breath. Major came to his feet, he snapped a sidekick to the knee of Pedro, snapping the knee backwards, hyper extending the leg. Pedro didn't go down, but he bent over slightly. That lowered his head enough to give Major a shot at an axe kick. Shifting his weight to his left leg, Major brought his rear foot sweeping across the front of his body, extending the foot higher then his head, he lashed the leg downwards to the back of Pedro's neck, using the heel to crush the vertebrae. Pedro dropped to the ground, paralyzed from the neck down. Major rolled him over on his back, looking down at a face that was rapidly turning blue. Major had crushed Pedro's windpipe with the devastating sidekick that was used after the acrobatics off the side of the house.

Major stared impassively as he watched the big man die. He picked up the ninja mask and top, taking time to put them on. He picked up his Sais and finding the shoestring soon had them positioned around his waist. He looked up at the windows of the house, spotting the figure of a man in one of the lighted windows.

As soon as he looked up, the man moved away from the window, back into the room. Major was on the opposite side of the house from where he had located Brok's room. He had no idea what was on the second story, but he was going to find out. He moved around to the front of the house, walked boldly up to the front door and turned the knob.

Peter Fuerte was sick to his stomach. He had watched his best friend and confidante die beneath the hands of a madman. Peter was sure that all of his men were dead. Other wise the ninja clad assassin would have never made it to the house.

He had silently cheered when Pedro had taken the ninja by surprise with the gun stroke to the kidneys. He wasn't pleased when Pedro threw his gun away. He had the ninja dead to rights, and that's what he would have been if Peter had the opportunity, dead! Still, Peter hadn't been too concerned even when the ninja struck the first blow of their battle. Peter was sure the fight was over when Pedro threw the ninja against the house, He was stunned to see him flip in mid air and use his momentum to spring off of the house back into Pedro. He knew then that Pedro would lose this fight. Peter just didn't realize it would be so quick. What would he pay a man such as this to be his personal bodyguard? He would make him rich. Maybe he should offer the ninja the opportunity to make much money. Peter didn't think he would accept, but nothing ventured, nothing gained.

When the ninja looked up at the window where Peter had concealed himself, he flinched back. He pulled away from the window and went to join Allison and Ernesto in the boy's bedroom.

A time of reckoning was in the offing.

Major opened the unlocked door, and flung it open positioning himself to the side of the doorjamb in case anyone shot through the open door way.

There was no activity at all.

Major slowly peeped around the corner of the jamb, seeing nothing. He dove through the open door, onto a front roll and then diving beside a chair.

Still nothing. Major looked around using caution.

Nothing.

He stood up and surveyed the area.

No one!

He went to each room, watching for and expecting a trap.

Nothing.

It was a beautiful house. The downstairs reminded Major of the mansion that the Beverly Hillbillies had lived in on the old half hour sit com. Even the stairway leading up, looked like it came right from the hillbilly set.

Major went to the stairs, uncomfortable in the harsh lights that filled every corner of the house.

Major's face had been numb on the right side that Pedro had struck with his ham-like fist, and the feeling was coming back. Major was slowly losing sight in his right eye. It was swelling shut as it turned into a brilliant hue of purple and black. Major could feel wetness on the side of his face and felt there. His fingers came away bloody. He had sustained a nasty cut and hadn't been aware of it. Major took the mask off and wrung blood from it, and watched it splatter to the floor. He replaced the mask and silently glided up the stairs.

The upstairs had a small foyer with several rooms leading from it. All the doors were shut. Major didn't fool with the ones on the west side of the house. He wanted Brok's room and that was on the east side.

There were three doors on the east side. Major tried to position the room in his mind and so he chose the middle room.

Standing in front of the door, Major took a rear-fighting stance. He used the rear leg and threw a sidekick hard under the door handle. The door's wood splintered and then gave as it exploded into the room.

Major was going to go hard into the room, but surprised himself by walking normally into the room.

Sitting on the top of the bed, both hands around his son was Allison Fuerte. Peter Fuerte was sitting in a chair with an afghan over the top of his lap, hands out of sight.

"Uh oh!" Major thought to himself. "I bet he's got a gun under there!"

Brok reached for his father. "Daddy!" He exclaimed then laughed.

Allison Fuerte held him closer.

Peter Fuerte smiled, his handsome face lit up. "I thought I had the best men in the world stationed here." He said, "I was wrong!" Peter shifted in the chair. "You can work for me, I'll make you rich!"

Major looked Peter straight in the eyes, "I've come for my son!"

"You mean my son!" Peter smiled.

"One way or another, Brok is going back with me!"

Peter shrugged his shoulders. "You will have to kill me for him!"

"No problem!" Exclaimed Major moving forward.

Peter threw the afghan off revealing the .25 caliber pistol.

"Don't move any closer!"

Major stopped. He knew that it was a good possibility that he could be shot again, or even killed, but he was going to end it now.

He was bunching his muscles in preparation for a fatal leap, his or Peter's, it didn't matter anymore. Major was at the end of his rope. Shot, beaten, scared half to death; time and time again he was prepared to die.

"Wait!" A quiet voice broke the tension. Allison Fuerte looked at her husband, tears in her eyes. "Peter, you have to know how much this man loves his son." Tears spilled over her lower eyelashes. He has killed and is ready to die, all for the love of his son!"

The pistol never wavered as Peter listened to Allison.

"Please Peter, for all of our sakes, let it go!"

"No Allison." Peter said, "The boy is ours!" His eyes never left Major as he thought of all his men destroyed, lying in their own blood, night insects feasting in the aftermath of the massacre.

"You forget the death of Pedro . . ."

A gasp from Allison interrupted Peter.

"Pedro is dead?"

"Yes, at the hands of this man!" Peter pointed to Major using the gun as an indicator.

Allison looked at Major stunned. "You must be a very extraordinary man to defeat a man such as Pedro.

Major shrugged his shoulders.

"Allison, take Ernesto and leave the room."

"No Peter!" Allison was very pale her voice trembled. "We can adopt another child!" Her eyes pleaded, "Please Peter!"

Peter's face darkened as his anger grew. "No one takes from Peter Fuerte!" He yelled, "Here, I am king!" He looked at Allison rage replacing the love towards her.

Brok's face pinched up and he started to sob, as Pete's voice grew loud with anger.

"We were happy, until he came and tried to destroy our lives!"

Suddenly Peter looked back at Major and the crack of the pistol filled the room.

Major was ready to move, he was on the edge when Peter pulled the trigger. He threw himself to the left as he felt the small slug pass by his face. Just as quickly, he dove through the air, his left hand seeking and then finding Peter's gun hand. The chair that Peter was sitting in toppled backwards as Major's weight knocked it over with both men struggling all the way to the floor. The gun clattered behind the two men as they struck the floor violently. Both men came to their feet, still grappling with each other.

Peter had Major by the throat, using both hands he tried to throttle him.

Major thrust both his hands up between the clenching hands of Peter. Partially breaking the strangle hold. He brought his knee up violently into the groin of Peter. Peter released

Major and grasped himself as sickness over took him. He went down on one knee, spittle sprayed from his mouth, sick to his stomach. Peter knew that he had been foolish. Trying to fight hand to hand with a man who had so handedly beaten his best man.

Major stepped back from his defeated foe. "All I want is my son." He said. "There's been enough killing." Major looked at Allison who was comforting his son. "You see how much you love him in the few days you've had him!"

He looked at Peter, "I have loved him since he was born, and you have destroyed my life! I can never go back to a normal family life after this! Your disregard for other peoples lives has caused me to become what I've always despised, a killer!"

Peter's head was hung low as Major continued his tirade.

"I'm willing to give you your life for your wife's sake. Just let me have my son, and I'll leave you both unharmed. Major folded his arms across his chest and waited for Peter's answer.

Pete could see the pistol out of the corner of his eye. If he could only reach it!

Suddenly lurching into the room was the guard that Major had let live. He took two steps into the room and fell to the floor in a faint.

In the brief instance Major looked towards Thomas, Peter seized his opportunity to reach the pistol. Scrambling on his hands and knees, Peter reached the gun as Major reacted to the threat.

Major took one long step and catapulted himself in the air for a flying side kick, even as Peter was trying to bear the gun around in order to put a bullet in the masked man.

Peter was too late his vision was filled with the split toe tabi-boot as it caught him flesh on his head. His body was still turned sideways after the mad scramble for the gun, his head turned towards Major. The kick Major hit him with had all of his body weight, momentum and a perfect placement. His head snapped violently around and the last sound Peter heard was the bones in his neck breaking. Peter died instantly; the gun went off as involuntary spasms of the trigger finger caused it to fire.

The bullet hit harmlessly into the floor. Major spun around as Anthony Thomas struggled to his feet. His voice broke as he spoke with difficulty, "Couldn't let you hurt the Missus." He said. "Kill me if you have too, but let her live."

Major was moved. After all of the sordid events that have taken place in the past two weeks, such dedication gave him hope. Major set the rocking chair upright and went to Anthony helping him to his feet and then to the chair.

"I will not harm her."

"Thank you." The words faded as Anthony lost consciousness.

Major turned to Allison and his son. Allison let Brok go as he struggled to go to his father.

"Daddy!" He tottered over.

Major met him picking him up and holding Brok to his chest. Sobs racked Major's chest as he cried with both joy and sorrow. Overjoyed that he was holding his son again, ecstatic that he could, after thinking he would never see him again. Sorrowful, because he could never be the father to him that he wanted to be. He would be a fugitive from the justice for the rest of his life.

"Oh Brok, I love you!" Said Major. "Ma-Ma will sure be glad to see you!"

"Ma-Ma? Brok wants Ma-Ma!"

"Okay little buddy, we'll see her later."

Major looked at Allison Fuerte. She was sitting on the bed silently crying, her chest heaving up and down as she fought to gain control of herself.

Major looked at the clock that was hanging in the wall. Eleven O'clock. He had an hour to get to the rendezvous with Phil.

"I'm sorry about your husband," Major said, "I gave him every opportunity to live."

Allison Fuerte looked up.

"Please take your mask off."

"Why?" He asked.

"I want to know what our son will look like when he's grown."

Shifting Brok to his right side, Major pulled the mask over the top of his head.

Allison gasped when she seen the damage that Pedro had inflicted on his face. She took a closer look and seen that Major had suffered extreme physical abuse. "You're hurt!"

"I'm okay now!" Major held his son closer.

"Will I ever see him again?"

Major thought for a long moment. "I don't know!"

"If there is any way possible, please, I would like it."

Major started to leave, but then turned and faced Allison again. "After the authorities figure everything out you'll be a rich woman." Major paused. "I apologize for any unnecessary violence, but may I make a suggestion.

"Yes," whispered Allison.

"Find a good man and have your own children. You're a very beautiful and rich, it shouldn't be difficult."

Major put the mask back on. Took one more look around and started to leave.

"Wait!" Allison asked.

Major turned and looked at her.

"Please, here is my phone number!" Allison snatched up a piece of paper, found a crayon and wrote it down. "I want to know what happens to Ernesto."

"His name is Brok!" Major took the paper from her hand and left.

Allison looked at her dead husband, waited twenty minutes and then called the state police.

Phil had loaded up some supplies in the Camaro, and left the hotel where he had been sleeping for the past few days. He hoped that Major had gotten to Brok; He wanted to end the mission tonight. There were too many things that could go wrong if they extended the time factor. There was only a half an hour before he was to meet Major. He started the car up and took his time going to the meeting site.

CHAPTER 49

M ajor left the big house, son in his arms and headed into the woods going east. He wouldn't make as good time going through the woods, but it would keep any casual observer from easily spotting him.

Major spent most of his time here in the woods and didn't know how heavily traveled the road was, even though he had never heard any vehicles on it.

Brok laughed and talked in Major's ear all the way.

Major wasn't as wary as he normally would be, but then again, there wasn't anyone left that could stop him.

He quickly covered the three miles from the Fuerte's and having arrived at his destination set Brok on the ground. "Stay here a second pal." He told Brok. Pulling his mask off, he walked out in the middle of the narrow road and placed in the center. Major went back to his boy and sat down on a small tree fall. Brok walked over to him and held his arms out, so Major would know to pick him up. Major obliged him. Holding him, he felt better then he had in a long time.

From the distance he could hear the dull roar of a vehicles engine coming up the road. In the silence of the woods, the sound carried a long way. Major and Brok stood behind a tree and watched. Finally headlights swept around a bend in the road. The car was moving slowly, when the headlights passed over the ninja mask. They blinked bright, dim, bright, dim, bright then back to dim. Major knew then it was Phil. The Camaro stopped and shut out its lights. Even though Major knew that it was Phil, he still approached the Camaro with caution. The dome light kicked on and Phil was outlined within.

A grin came over Major's face. They were almost home free. He carried Brok to the passenger side and opened the door. He deposited his son in the back seat and climbed in. Without a word Phil engaged the transmission and started down the road.

"What's the situation?" He asked.

"I left the house about a half an hour ago, I imagine that if they called the police at that time, they will be here at any time."

Phil goosed the Camaro, a long plume of dust following them down the road. He drove the seven miles to the old grange road, quickly without a word. There would be time to talk later. They had to get out of this valley and fast.

Major kept an eye on the road behind them and also searched the sky for any aircraft. Phil spotted the guardrail that cut the two roads from each other and drove on past. He went another mile before he pulled over. They got out of the car went around to the trunk where Phil opened it and retrieved the two duffle bags.

"We have to hike back a mile."

"Okay." Major picked Brok up and followed Phil as he set a quick pace toward the hidden truck. It took them fifteen minutes to reach the grange road, where the Ford was hidden.

Major was flagging badly by now. The added weight of Brok and the injuries he suffered the last couple of days had finally taken their toll on his body. Yet, he endured it all, because he had accomplished his mission, he had his son.

Phil led them to the hidden truck, and threw the brush off the truck. Major opened the passenger door and put Brok in the back seat of the extended cab. Phil and he were about to get in the truck when they both stopped. Ears cocked towards the Fuerte place, they could hear the faint, faraway trill of a siren. Cutting it close, eh brother?" Asked Phil, as they climbed into the truck.

"She must have waited before she called!" Major shrugged his shoulders. "They should have been here before now!"

"I'm glad they're not!" Phil started the four-wheel drive and without lights, started up the steep and winding grange road. They made it up and over the top of the baby mountain, waiting until he was on his way down the other side, Phil finally flicked on his lights. He came to the end of the grange road and turned right, back towards town. It only took ten minutes to get to I-77 and an hour later, they were checked into a motel room.

Allison Fuerte tried to answer the questions that the state police were asking. She couldn't tell them a lot, because the man wore a mask. No, she didn't know why he kidnapped her newly adopted child, and yes Anthony Thomas saved her life from the hands of the killer. No, she didn't have any pictures of the child, and that was all she could help them with.

CHAPTER 50

Phil went to a fast food outlet and picked up some burgers and fries. He had been shocked when he had seen Major in the lighting of the room. He looked like he had lost a lot of weight. He had been even more shocked a few minutes later, when he seen Major's naked body, when he went to shower. The bruises on his face had been sobering, but the cuts, welts and abrasions on the rest of his body were vivid and angry looking. Not to mention the nasty bullet wound in his left shoulder. Phil shook his head as he paid for the food and headed back to the motel.

Detective Breeler was outraged. He had learned about the Fuerte massacre through a friend in the West Virginia State Police. He had all the details that the police had, sketchy as they may be, tied in with what he knew, he had a complete picture of what happened. Sooner or later Brown would be coming back to his home and Breeler would be waiting.

Major, Phil, and Brok spent the weekend in the motel, with Phil going out for their meals and drinks, Major kept a low profile. They watched the news with interest. The reporters were calling what happened outside of Macsville, "The Fuerte Massacre."

Allison Fuerte had made a brief statement, stating that neither she nor the lone surviving bodyguard could give any details about their assailant. State Police were at a standstill, and Federal investigators were called in. Some rumors were going around saying that they were investigating a possible drug deal gone badly.

One thing the newscasters were foreseeing on the fact that Allison Fuerte now an heiress of the Fuerte fortune, was a multi millionaire.

Phil finished packing the Ford with what little they had for the trip back to Major's house. Phil went to a store that had some clothes and outfitted Major with a sweat outfit. Major was still too stiff and sore to be clothed in jeans and such. He bought a change of clothes for Brok and himself. The supply of clothes that he had packed in the truck proved to be too big for Brok and too small for Major.

Phil went to square up with the motel management, as Major and Brok went to the truck and got in. Brok climbed into the rear of the extended cab and sat on the floor playing with a toy he had gotten from a fast food establishment.

Major had wrapped his sais in a motel towel and carried them out with him. He had spent time in cleaning the weapons once again trying to destroy any evidence that could be on them. He didn't have the leather strapping on them anymore. He was afraid of all the blood and gore that had soaked into them. He couldn't leave the sais; he wasn't about to be weaponless. He had a gut feeling that Breeler would be waiting on him, and he had a score to settle with him.

Phil came back, climbed in, and they spent the next eight hours heading home. Neither he nor Major noticed the unmarked car escorting them.

CHAPTER 51

Sensei alerted Jill to the activity that was going on around her house. She went up stairs shutting the lights off in each room as she went. She went to the bathroom window and gently pulled the curtain back enough to peer out. She saw men positioning themselves at different areas behind the house. She went to a different window at all four points of the house and discovered she was well surrounded. She was about to phone the police when a knock interrupted her dialing. She went to the front door and opened it to Detective Breeler. A mocking smile on his face, he tipped his hat to Jill.

"Good evening Jill," he smiled. "I think you'll be having company tonight!"

"What are you talking about?" Jill took a step back from the door.

"Aren't you going to invite me in?" Breeler lost his smile. "The place is surrounded Jill, your husband is on his way back tonight, and I've arranged a reception for him!"

"Those are your men hiding outside?" Jill asked.

"Sure are Jill, we're loaded for bear too!" The smile came back to his handsome face. "We're waiting on a mass murderer!"

"Oh come on Dick, you can't mean Major?" Anger crept into her voice.

"Have you heard about the Fuerte Massacre?" Asked Breeler.

"Who hasn't? It has been on the news since Saturday!"

"Your husband did it!" Breeler said, enjoying the shocked look that came over her face.

"No!" Exclaimed Jill.

"Yes!" Breeler was ecstatic. "Yes! They had your boy and now he's been taken by your husband!"

"You knew where my son was at?" Asked Jill with a quiet voice. "It hasn't been mentioned on the news."

Breeler smiled, walked through the open door forcing Jill back. Shutting the door, Breeler's smile turned vicious. "Yes Jill, I knew where he was at! I knew everything!" Without warning Breeler suddenly shoved Jill backwards using both hands, Jill tripped over a small throw rug and fell ungracefully to the floor on her butt. "It's a shame Jill, I really liked you, and we could have been very good together!" Breeler hunkered down in front of Jill. "But no, you went back to your husband!"

Jill slowly crawled backwards trying to keep a little distance between her and Breeler.

"Theodore and I had quite a lucrative business together. Your husband destroyed everything that I had worked for!" Breeler took his hat off and fingered the brim of it. "Now I'm going to take my revenge on both you and your husband!" He stood up and threw his hat on the couch. "Let me give you a scenario, Jill." Breeler paused reflecting on the moment. "Major Brown is going to come home with your son, but instead of finding you alone, he'll find you with your lover, which is me!" Breeler grinned. "He'll fly into a rage, kill you, and die in his attempt to kill me, but don't worry Jill, I already have a new home lined up for your son!"

Jill was enraged! She got her feet under her and started to rise.

Breeler reached inside of his coat pocket and pulled out a small .22 derringer, aiming it at Jill. "Not another move, unless I tell you! Commanded Breeler.

"I'll never work, Dick!" Jill added, "Major will find a way to beat you!"

"I don't think so, but it will be interesting." Breeler's eyes roved up and down Jill's voluptuous body. "Strip down!"

"What?"

"Take your clothes off!"

"No!" Jill shouted.

Breeler cocked the hammer of the derringer, aimed it at Jill's midsection.

"I suggest you do it very quickly, I'm fast losing my patience."

"Why? Just tell me why?"

"You're a smart girl, Jill. Figure it out!"

Jill didn't have to think very hard. Breeler wanted her naked so when Major came in the house he would think that they were still lovers, and that she was betraying him.

"Come on Jill, give me a show while you're doing it!"

Jill slowly started to disrobe. First her top then her bottoms, she stood in front of Breeler in a bra and panties.

"All of it Jill!"

Her face reddening her mind in turmoil, Jill finished disrobing. She stood in front of Breeler, naked but proud.

"Oh yes, very nice Jill." Breeler was appreciative of her nubile body. "Now sit down in the chair and let's wait."

CHAPTER 52

Phil and Major brought Brock across the state line and only had an hour and a half to travel before they reached their destination.

Major had been watching the car behind them for quite some time now. If he didn't know better he would say that it had been following them. Major thought about that for a while. Even if it wasn't following them, why take the chance.

"Phil gets off the next exit."

Without a comment, Phil turned off of the interstate at the exit that came up within the next mile.

They pulled into the gas station and stopped at the pumps.

"Might as well fill'er up while we're here."

Major never said anything; he got Brok from behind the front seat and took him to the rest room and then in the storefront.

Six teens stopped in and bought some orange slice candy. The slices looked good and he bought Brok some too.

Major and Brok went back to the truck and waited on Phil, who was taking his turn at the restroom. When he came back, they returned to the interstate.

Phil was going the speed limit, when they passed the car that Major thought had been tailing them. He was going slow, allowing traffic to pass him. Once the Ford went by him he picked his speed back up following them but trailing by one hundred yards. Major knew then that the gut feeling he had was right on.

He reached behind the truck seat and pulled out a duffle bag. Reaching inside he sorted through the contents until he found his tattered and torn ninja outfit. Stripping down while Phil drove, he then dressed in ninja black. Finding the shoestring in the bottom of the bag, he tied it around his waist. Unwrapping the sais from the towel, he thrust them through the belt.

Phil watched Major's preparations without comment.

Brok played unaware in the back seat of the extended cab.

Pulling the ninja mask out but he laid it on the seat between him and Phil. He was now ready for action. One thing he was grateful for, he was glad he took the time to wash his outfit at the motel. It had been quite rank before that.

"Do you know something that I don't?" Questioned Phil.

"Yeah! We have a tail. I figure it's the Breelers' men." Major opened up the bag of orange slices. He handed Brok a handful, offered some to Phil and then finished up the bag himself. "You'll go to dad's house with Brok!" Major thought for a second. "When we get to the turn in the road before dad's, you slow down, I'll jump out there."

"What are you going to do Major?"

"I'm going to my house. That's where Breeler will be." Major's thoughts focused on the task ahead. "I'm going to end this there!"

Phil looked at his brother, "You know they'll be waiting for you. Are you in good enough shape after that beating you took in West Virginia?"

"I'll do what ever it takes!" Major reached in the back seat and pulled Brok up to sit on his lap. His little face and hands were sugary and very sticky from eating the orange slice candy. Major played with Brok until they were close to their father's house. He put him in the back again and got ready to move. Taking a sai from his belt he reached up and smashed the dome light.

"Hey, we could have pulled the bulb out!" Phil laughed.

"Didn't think about it." Major replaced the sai and put the ninja mask on. As they approached the gentle turn, Major looked back and saw that the car that was tailing them was about two hundred yards back. "Perfect." He thought. "Well, see you later brother. I wouldn't suggest you leave dad's after you get there!"

Major touched his sais like a gunfighter resting his hands on his guns. "All hell is going to break loose." With these words, Major threw the door open and jumped, landing lightly on the balls of his feet he tucked into a roll and came immediately to his feet. He jumped quickly into a big ditch along the road, hugging the inside. The car that had been tailing them passed by without being aware that anyone had left the truck. After the car was past him, Major got up from the ditch and set a rapid pace towards his home and Jill.

The F.B.I agent who was driving the escort car went past the Ford that had pulled into Mr. Brown's house. The agent only saw two people out lined inside, the driver and a small child. He frowned as he went to a turnaround a tenth of a mile past the house. Keeping an eye on the rear view mirror, and quickly turning around, he watched as only two people got out of the truck. Thinking quickly, he picked up a cellular phone and dialed a number.

The ringing of the telephone shocked Jill. There had been no conversation since Breeler had made her strip. Breeler walked over Jill, pulling her roughly to her feet by her arm.

"Answer it." He commanded.

Jill walked over to the phone aware of Breeler's ogling eyes. "Yes?" Jill listened for a moment then handed the phone to the detective. She stood there trying to figure out what was being said by half of the conversation.

"He wasn't with him?" Breeler smiled. "Yeah, I figure that too! How long ago? I figure he'll be here at any time! No I have enough back up. Okay, thanks!" Breeler's half of the conversation didn't make a lot of sense to Jill, but Breeler seemed very pleased.

"Go lay on the couch, Jill."

"Why?"

Breeler took two angry steps to Jill grabbing her by the shoulders and shaking her hard, and then half flung her to the couch.

Jill stopped her momentum and turned back towards Breeler, her breasts heaving with anger. "Just remember what happened to you the other day Dick!" Sarcasm dripped from her voice.

Breeler's face clouded as he remembered the pain that Jill had caused him. "I remember Jill, now it's pay back time!" Breeler pulled his derringer and once again trained it on Jill. "Now lay down on the couch!"

"You coward!" Jill's voice was venomous.

Breeler cocked the derringer.

"Do it!"

Jill studied Breeler for a long second and then slowly lay down on the couch.

"Oh Major," her thoughts raced through her mind, "if you're coming, come quick!"

Major jogged on the road, getting off and hiding only when a vehicle came into sight. He was within a half a mile from his home when he cut up through the woods. Traveling quickly, for he knew these woods like the back of his hands, he came to the area around his house. Stopping he sniffed the air and listened. He could hear the rustling of the leaves on a bush to left and straight up the hill. Doing a slow stalk, he spotted the agent who was stationed there. Without a sound, Major came up behind him, he pulled a sai from the right side of his belt, aimed it high and brought it sharply down on the back of the unaware agents skull. It made a klonking sound as he slumped to the ground, out cold. Major checked his vitals and was relieved to see he was still alive. He didn't want to kill any of the F.B.I. agents unless it came down to self-preservation. Major left the unconscious agent and cast his way up the hill. He knew the place would be surrounded. Major didn't want to disable them all, so he would have a path he could use for the flight out. He found the next agent fifty feet up the hill and incapacitated him pretty much like the first. Major eyed the section that was now cleared of lawmen and decided he had enough room for an escape, when it became necessary. He cut straight down the middle of the hundred feet area he had made safe and headed for the house.

Breeler stripped down to his boxer shorts and folded his clothes neatly on the chair. Jill watched with interest. "What are you doing Dick?"

Breeler didn't answer, he walked over to the couch where Jill lay, keeping the derringer on her at all times. He sat down on the couch his butt against her waist. The pistol was in his right hand as he reached across Jill's body and put the derringer to the left side of Jill's throat. "You move, you make one sound, flinch or even blink funny, I'll kill you!" Breeler's face was serious. "We're going to look like lovers when your husband walks in . . ." Breeler was interrupted as Jill started to speak.

"But uggg!" She chocked as Breeler rammed the derringer into her throat.

"I said don't move!"

Sweat broke out on Jill's brow as she realized how crazy Breeler was acting.

Breeler kept the gun tight against her throat his left hand came up and started stroking Jill's breasts.

Jill trembled, but didn't dare move. Breeler stroked her breasts, softly, tenderly then clasped down hard. Jill gasped but didn't move. Breeler laughed nastily.

"I'm enjoying myself babe! Maybe we can do it for real when I finish with your asshole husband." Breeler stopped talking when a black shape materialized like magic on the landing of the stairs that led up to the second floor.

Major made his way to the side of the house undetected. He thought about walking through the back door, but decided it would be too risky. He walked over to the tower that held the antennae for his television. He didn't use it anymore since he received satellite broadcasts. There was a window about five feet from the tower. If he could get in through there he could enter the house unannounced. He climbed rapidly knowing the shadows would conceal him from any observers. Besides the two men he had deposed of would have watched this side of the house. He was opposite of the window and was glad to see that it still held a screen. He had been afraid that Jill would take the screen out and secure the window. She usually did it every summer because of bees entering the house at that point. Major had put the screen in when Jill was with Detective Breeler.

Major's blood boiled when he thought of Breeler. He had been a big part of Major and Jill's brief break up and if his reasoning was right a big part of Theodore Grant's kidnapping ring. How else would they have been followed all the way from West Virginia without prior knowledge from Breeler? Major was sure Allison Fuerte or Anthony Thomas didn't talk. Ergo, it had to be Breeler.

Major hooked his leg around the side of the triangle tower and leaned out with his upper body. Using a sai, he punched a hole in the screen and worked the sai back and forth to widen the hole. Putting the sai back in his belt, he used one hand to help hang on to the tower and the other hand to pull the screening from the frame. The window was now open. He pulled himself back to the tower taking a brief rest. Although he certainly felt a lot better then what he did coming from the woods in West Virginia, his strength and endurance were still not as good as what it should have been. Knowing that it wouldn't get any better, Major again reached for the window sill and reached it with his finger tips of his right hand. With a leap generated by the muscles of his toes and calves, he hopped over to the window guiding himself by his right hand but catching the sill with both hands. Dangling there for a second he climbed up and in the window. He slid to the floor headfirst taking care not to bang his knees on the windowsill as he did. He laid there for a second in the darkness of the washroom. Climbing up the tower and in through the window had taken more out of him then he had thought. He sat up and assumed a sitting position, legs crossed, hands on his knees. Head back, chest thrust forward to give him a straight airway to his lungs. Major began to breath and meditate. He didn't hear anything for the next five minutes as he re-established his strength and mental calmness. He didn't want to give Breeler an advantage by going down the steps angry. He didn't hear Jill choke when Breeler shoved the gun into her throat, but he was startled out of his meditation by a cold nose and a wet tongue on his face. "What the heck?" He couldn't see in the darkness very well, but he knew it had to be a dog. Thank God that it hadn't barked when he entered the house. Major petted behind its ears and was rewarded with another doggie kiss. Major smiled as he petted the friendly dog, but then his face grew grave as he stood up. He wasn't going to feel any better then what he felt now. Time to go to work. He moved forward out of the washroom, into the bathroom. The steps were straight ahead. The upstairs was dark, but the downstairs were lit.

Major tiptoed to the top of the stairs and listened, he could hear a voice, but couldn't make out what was said. The dog tried to follow him, almost tripping Major before he showed him back away from the stairs. The dog stayed there, confused by the shove.

Major eased down to the landing, looking over to the couch, his jaw clenched tight, his teeth felt brittle under the strain, his fists tightened into balls of stone, creaking as the tendons tightened. A red haze blinded Major's vision, and he almost screamed in rage.

There on the couch was his wife in an amorous position. He would kill them both! After all that he'd been through! Major was about to bound of the landing, he could reach the couple in one leap after that, when the situation suddenly became clear to him.

Jill was lying there with her arms straight, hands at her sides. She certainly didn't look to be in the throes of passion, and was her jaw clenched tight?

Breeler's left hand was definitely weapon free, although busy, but what about his right hand. It was buried on the other side of

Jill's neck. If Major had to guess, he would say that Breeler had a gun to Jill's head.

"Why?" Major asked himself. Thinking furiously it came to him in a rush of emotion. Breeler expected him to get past his men! He was going to summarily execute Major and if he guessed right, Jill would be next.

Major tried to think quickly; Jill's life was the first concern for Major. His life was in ruin, but Brok needed his mother. Besides, Major loved Jill with all of his heart, he always said he would die for her and Brok well now it was time to put up or shut up.

Breeler suddenly squeezed Jill's breast hard, and Major could see his obvious arousal, when Breeler turned and spotted Major on the landing.

Time stood still for several long seconds as each man took the measure of the other.

"Well, well, well, if it isn't the Butcher from Macsville!" Breeler again began to stroke Jill's breast." Come on down Mr. Brown, but come slowly!"

Major walked down the rest of the stairs and walked towards the couple.

"Stop right there!" Breeler commanded Major as he was in the middle of the room.

Major stopped, eyes blazing orbs, starring from behind the mask.

Breeler knew that Major was a man on the edge. "If you make a stupid move, I'll kill your wife!" Breeler raised his right hand just enough to show Major the glint of the small derringer that he had pressed against Jill's neck.

Major breathed in through the nose and through the mouth, breathing to keep himself calm and relaxed. When he had the opportunity to strike, then he would.

"Please Mr. Brown, don't be a stranger. Take you mask off and stay awhile!" Breeler chuckled!

Major slowly reached up with his left hand and removed the mask.

Jill's eyes opened wide, when she saw the damaged face of her husband. Breeler couldn't hide his glee.

"Did my good friend Pedro do that?" He questioned, "Too bad he didn't have the chance to kill you!"

Major spoke for the first time; "Then it is true! I figured you were in with Grant, and that you probably adopted my son to the Fuertes', but I didn't realize that you were connected with the Fuerte's organization.

Breeler was enjoying himself. He kept the gun tight to Jill's neck, and his left hand was still manipulating Jill's lovely breasts.

"Well, it's like this, Mr. Brown!" Breeler pointed his left hand at Major. "I was making a lot of money off of both Grant and Peter Fuerte until you came along!" "Illegal adoptions are quite a lucrative business, if you make the right connections." Breeler paused a second and then "Enough about business, tell me, I'm curious, how did you pull it off?"

Major cocked his head as if he didn't know what Breeler was talking about.

"Oh, come on!" Breeler's voice rose a bit. "How many men did you kill there? Fifteen, sixteen?"

Major looked at Jill, her eyes were boring into his, not wanting to hear his answer.

Breeler didn't wait for the response. "How did you like Pete's pets?"

"Pets?" Major's blood ran cold when he realized what Breeler was talking about. "You mean snakes?"

"Why yes! Peter didn't allow anyone to kill them in fact he raised the and turned them loose, cheap security, was what he called them."

Major knew that he was dealing with some real Looney tunes! Peter Fuerte was dead, and soon Breeler would follow. Major didn't really decide that Breeler had to die until that instance, but he had to suffer first.

A low whine behind him almost made him start, but he held himself in check.

Breeler's eyes left Major's as he peered past him and located the dog in the semi darkness of the stair well.

"After I kill you two, I'm killing the dog!" Breeler laughed! "She's first!" Looking at Jill.

Jill had been lying there waiting for a chance to move, but Breeler never released the pressure of the small gun barrel from his throat. When she heard Breeler say that they were all going to die, she knew then there was no sense in being passive.

Breeler's butt was still pressed against her waist, the pressure from the gun never diminished, but Jill had enough. Her eye squinted slightly, her heart started to beat faster, a blush came to her face. The adrenalin surged through her veins. She brought her left arm up threw it hard over top of her head forcing Breeler's gun hand up and away from her throat, she folded her right arm across her breast, then with a loud "kiaaa," she brought it back into a classic back fist, the knuckles of her index finger and middle finger making hard contact with the side of Breeler's head.

Breeler groaned and half fell from the couch, landing on both knees and used his left hand as a support.

Jill saw Major leaping in mid air and realized that Breeler was swinging the derringer around to meet him. If Breeler could get the shot off, then Major wouldn't stand a chance. Without thinking acting on instinct only, Jill flipped over on her right side swinging her lift fist hand at Breeler's shoulder. Before he could pull the trigger of the derringer, Jill struck.

Breeler lost all feeling in his right arm. It hung useless at his side. Eyes opened wide, he watched as Major Brown stopped his leap in mid air and twisted so he landed on his gun side. Major aimed a snap front kick at Breeler's right hand, knocking the derringer away from him, tearing the flesh and cracking bones in his fingers. With contempt Major casually slapped Breeler aside.

He helped Jill up from the couch, leading her over to where her clothes lay.

"Get dressed!" Major never wanted her more then that instance, but his work wasn't done. He turned back towards the fallen detective.

"Get up!"

Breeler tried to get to his feet, but failed. Major pulled the sais from his belt; holding them casually, yet threatening, "I said get up!"

Breeler made it to his feet on this attempt. He leered as he watched Jill dress.

"Enjoy yourself now, because you don't have long to live!" Major's voice was quite but deadly.

"How did you get the gash on your leg?" He asked Jill without taking his eyes off of Breeler.

"It doesn't matter Major!" Jill was distraught. "You're going to call the police, aren't you? I'll dial nine-one-one." Jill started walking to the phone.

"No!"

Jill turned perplexed. "Why not? Let the police handle this now! Please Major, I want to be a family again!"

Breeler was holding his right hand, but managed a short bark of laughter. "Tell her why she can't call the police Major!" Breeler sneered at him. "I'll tell you why Jill!" Breeler leaned forward. "Your honorable, darling husband is a killer."

"No!" Choked Jill.

"Yes!" Breeler was again in his glory. "He killed Theodore Grant and personally, individually brutally murdered at least fourteen men in West Virginia." Glee filled Breeler's voice. "You wonder why he doesn't want to call the police?" A pause the Breeler again spoke. "Ask him!"

Jill looked at Major, "Major is it true?"

Major's eyes were flint; his lips were pressed so tightly together they appeared as a slit. He turned to Jill without speaking letting the expression on his face tell her the truth.

Jill gasped and staggered back as if dealt a physical blow.

"No, Major, NO!"

Major's expression softened as his eyes caressed Jill. "I'm still the man you loved and married Jill!" He turned back facing Breeler, his face hardening again, "I did what needed to be done!"

A stunned silence filled the room.

"I understand Major," Jill's voice was a low sob.

"I'm glad, but now you better leave the room!"

"No Major! You can't kill him!" Jill's voice was firm.

"Why not? Give me one good reason to let him live."

"Because the killing must stop now!" Jill licked her lips, "Let the law handle him!"

Major was spent. He was so tired, both physically and mentally. He was ready to let it end here. Jill would have Brok; maybe a good lawyer could help him. After all he didn't think he could be connected with West Virginia. He knew that there wasn't any evidence pointing towards him from the Grant murder, otherwise Breeler would have arrested him before he took off to West Virginia. He reached up with his gloved right hand and wiped his eyes. He was so tired.

It was what Breeler was waiting for; he dove in the corner and grabbed the derringer bringing it around to bear on Major. He had to use his left hand because the damaged right couldn't hold it.

"You won't have to worry about the law now, Brown!" He aimed the gun at Major's belly, "Goodbye!" Breeler pulled the trigger of the derringer. The bullet struck Major on the left side of his body, the slug passing through the fleshy part of his side just above the waist. Blood, skin and shreds of the ninja suit splattered against the wall behind him.

He spun from the force of the slug passing through him continuing the spin he surprised the detective by leaping through the air, ramming into Breeler forcing him back into a sitting position on the couch.

Jill screamed and the dog yelped.

Major grasped the wrist of the hand with the gun exerting all of his strength forcing Breeler to drop the derringer, watching it drop behind the couch. He pushed off of Breeler and stood in the center of the room, weak and dizzy.

Breeler stood up, now that Major was in an obvious weakened state, he would attack.

One of the agents outside of the house heard a gunshot, a scream and a faint yelp. He took his cellular phone from its case attached to his belt and dialed the number that Detective Breeler had made him memorize.

ML

It rang three times before the woman answered. Asking for Detective Breeler, the woman had started screaming into the phone. Something about the detective had kicked her dog away from him, the dog bit and Detective Breeler shot it. One thing for sure, the woman was definitely mad. She told him that Breeler was in the kitchen tending to the dog bite and that she hoped he died of infection. She then hung up. Agent McDonald laughed to himself and wished he could have been there to watch!

Major knew that Breeler was ready to attack him. He stepped back into a classic back stance, ready to fight. Breeler almost jumped him, and then he stopped.

Hardly seems fair!" He stated flatly. "It's obvious that my right hand is broken, and my shoulder is still numb." He eyed where the slug had caught Major. "There you are with a lousy flesh wound, doesn't seem fair!" He repeated.

Major pulled the sai out of his belt. He had dropped the other one when Breeler had shot him, and he didn't know where it was. "Sit down!"

Breeler sat. Major handed Jill the sai and then using both hands he grabbed the bottom of his ninja top, pulling it up and over his head. He let it drop to the floor. He stood there in front of Breeler and Jill naked from the waist up. Jill gasped and tears sprang to her eyes. Large bruises dominated almost the whole trunk of Major's body. His back was a vivid bloody blue and shades of red, compliments of Pedro's gun attack to his kidney. The wound that Breeler inflicted on him was a raw pulsating hole that even now was still oozing blood. It looked like some type of wound high in the left shoulder and of course his face. His rib cage and his pectoral were shades of black from the brief but violent encounter with Peter Fuerte. He had lost weight since the night they had spent together, before he had went to West Virginia or where ever he had gone.

Jill had never seen a body that had been beaten as badly as Majors was. It was a wonder that he could even walk much less continue to defend himself and her. Yet even as her eyes surveyed the damaged body of her husband, her own body responded too. Her breath quickened and her legs grew weak as she realized that she wanted him, needed him, and desired him.

The spell was broken when Major spoke, his voice low, hard to hear. "I think we're pretty well even."

Breeler tensed his muscles and sprang towards Major. He landed in front of him and threw a hard roundhouse right towards Majors head, he hit nothing but empty air, and Major had disappeared! Confused Breeler glanced down and saw that Major was on the floor directly in front of him in a perfect split. "Amazing," he thought inwardly, "I've never seen anyone do that before!"

His thought were cut sharply off as white pain flashed through his groin. A high keening scream defined him. He realized that it was him screaming as he fell, backwards to the floor. His head hit with a loud "klonk" and mercifully lost consciousness.

When Breeler leaped at Major throwing his right hand, Major didn't hesitate. He dropped down into a split. His butt on the floor his legs straight out from his body, the bottoms of his feet facing away from the trunk of his body, his big toes resting on the floor. His right hand flashed up into the wide legs of the boxer shorts that Breeler wore. His seeking hand found Breeler's dangling testicles and grasped them; his thumb and index finger formed a tight circle high around the sac with the rest of his hand partially open yet with a firm grip on Breeler's bag. Major jerked down with all of his strength ripping Breeler's bag and nuts from his body.

With a face set in stone, he watched as Breeler fell over backwards. Major didn't know if Breeler would die from such an injury or not. Actually he didn't care. Breeler deserved everything that he had gotten. Major wished he could have done more to the man who was responsible for so much pain and agony in his life.

The sound of Jill's retching made Major take his eyes from the fallen detective. Jill was on her hands and knees throwing up. What she had seen had been too much for her. Major stood up and casually threw Breelers testicles to the dog, sitting with a cocked head on the steps. The dog promptly swallowed them whole bringing on another bout of retching from Jill.

While Jill finished being sick, Major put his shirt back on and gathered up the sai that he had lost. Walking over to Jill he used his gloved left hand to clean the remnants of puke from the corners of her mouth. Taking her in his arms he held her tightly to his breast. Neither spoke. Major gave her a final squeeze and stepped back.

"You know that I have to leave."

"Yes."

"Brok is at mom and dads."

Jill gasped. "Is he alright?"

"Yes, he's fine, he wants you!"

"Let's go get him!" Jill was eager to see her son.

A sad smile was on Major's face. "I can't."

Jill stopped and turned to Major. "Oh Major, what are we gong to do?"

"You're going to get our son and raise him up right!"

"What are you going to do?" Jill swallowed a lump in her throat." "What are we going to do?"

"Don't worry about a thing Jill. "He told her how to find the money he had hidden in the tree up in the woods. He would stop and get enough to get him away from Ohio, and then he didn't know what he would do. He stepped forward and took Jill in his arms again. "Call nine-one-one and get them here as soon as possible!" Major was worried that Breeler's men would try to exact revenge against Jill. "Make sure they know Breeler was part of the kidnapping ring.

"Okay Major."

Major squeezed her one more time and then stepped back. He kissed her deeply and passionately, ignoring the faint taste of vomit. He looked around and found his ninja mask. He petted the dog's head, prompting a tail wagging. He put the mask on, checked the position of his sais, took one more look at Jill and slowly went up stairs. He would leave the same way he came in. He heard Jill pick up the phone to call for help. He found his way through the dark upstairs to the washroom. He looked into the darkness that was illuminated by the moon and slowly climbed out the window. He didn't know what the night would bring but he knew that he would take it like a man.

Sick…Major hobbled along through the woods encountering the occasional bramble bushes adding thin bloody scratches to the wounds he already had suffered. Dizzy, He leaned his back against a small tree, species unknown to him, and pulled the tattered black ninja top away from the searing wound in his side. He had suffered worse wounds in the past two weeks, but this one pulsed with the beating of his heart. Major had second-degree burns that had not hurt this much. With a grimace, he looked at the angry entry hole caused by the bullet from the now castrated Detective Richard Breeler. (That image brought a ghost of a smile to his face!) Major thought it was only a flesh wound, but oh my, it hurt!

He pushed off the tree, ignoring the looseness of his bowels; the high-pitched buzzing in his head, and the queasiness of his stomach. (Please don't vomit.) He had to get out of the area and quickly. He had left his home only ten minutes ago, and he could hear the wail of sirens now.

Major had rescued his son from the hands of a dope dealer and had brutally extinguished the lives of fourteen? Fifteen? His mind wasn't functioning right now, but he remembered how Brok had felt in his arms and how happy Jill, his wife, was to know Brok was okay. He had been the star in the "Macsville Massacre", but it had not ended there. Detective Breeler had been waiting for him when he arrived home. Thank God he had the foresight (intuition) to drop Brok and his brother Phil off at his Father's house.

After a knock down fight, in which Major had received this annoying wound, he had ripped the big detectives balls right off of his body, throwing them to Jill's new dog, (Sensei)? The dog ate them! Unbidden laughter lurched from his throat, causing immediate hot pain throughout his body. Still the grin remained for a moment.

Sick . . . He staggered forward knowing he didn't have much time left he had to get away. He headed for the destination he had in mind. His mind buzzing now, weak . . . oh so weak, his stomach was threatening him with dry heaves again. He had them earlier when he stopped and picked up a packet of money from his stash in the old oak tree. When he had finished, he did not know if he could continue on, but he had forced himself.

Major arrived at the four-way stop when the first sheriff's car slowed, then barged on through. Lights were flashing and the siren screamed. It tore up the road towards his house only a mile away.

Major stepped out of the woods and went to the ditch beside the eight-foot tall stop sign. He crouched down and hoped he was hidden from a driver's casual view. He could hear more wailing coming from the town area. They were swarming like ground hornets, all making a beeline to the Brown's residence. Headlights came down the road towards him. It was a small pick-up, looked like a Ford Ranger. The driver eased up to the stop sign and stopped. He leaned out the window and heard then seen the lights of an ambulance. All of his attention was centered on the emergency vehicle and he never noticed the unsteady shape of Major Brown slithering over the side of his Ranger.

Major cringed as one of his Sais clinked against the bed of the truck, but the driver neither saw, heard nor felt anything. He rolled up tight against the cab of the truck and once again fought the urge to upchuck the contents of his violated stomach.

The driver thrummed his finger on the steering wheel, whistling softly as his way was again clear. He waited a few more seconds to see if there were any more lights or sirens to warn him of an oncoming patrol car or ambulance. There wasn't any so he dropped the truck in drive and slowly pulled away. While Major lay half conscious in the bed of his truck, the man listened to Herb Score broadcasting the Indians game. No one could call a game like Herb.

CHAPTER 53

Lights were flashing from the front side of the house and peering out through the side of the curtain, she could see the approach of two uniformed sheriffs and one suited man. The man in the suit directed the two sheriffs to either side of him and then continued to the front door with his back and sides covered.

Jill went to the door in answer to the loud, confident knock.

"Mrs. Brown?"

"Yes! Come in!" Jill said with relief in her voice. It was Major's old school chum, oh what was his name? Oh yes! "Jeff Conner! Am I right?"

"Yes Ma'am." Jeff glanced around eyes missing nothing, noting the shambles of the living room. His features hardened when his gaze passed to the prone Detective Breeler. Reaching in his pocket he brought out a small radio transmitter.

Flipping it open, Jill thought he had an eerie resemblance to Captain Kirk on Star Trek.

"Conner here, what's the situation?" He asked. The receiver crackled with static and then . . .

"House is surrounded by Breeler's men, Sir."

"Who are they?" Conner's voice was sharp.

"Anderson, Pettay, Smith, Gerber and Birks. We found White and Miller up on the hill wandering around. They've both have been assaulted, Sir, from behind."

"Are they able to come to the house? The paramedics are coming in now."

"We'll get them there, Sir."

"Any sign of Brown?"

"No sir."

Conner pursed his lips, considering, thinking and then, "Call for the dogs, get them here. I think he's already gone, but we can go through the motions."

"Yes, Sir!"

"Send in two men and search the house. Let's not leave any stone unturned."

"Yes Sir!"

The paramedics were bending down to Detective Breeler for the initial examination and both had cringed when they found the raw wound below his manhood. Another one, a woman, was hooking him to an I.V.

Detective Conner walked over to Breeler and hunkered down, his buttocks resting on the heels of his shoes.

Breeler reached out with his right hand and grasped Conner's hand.

"Get that Bastard for me, Jeff!"

Jeff Conner quietly disengaged Breeler's hand from his own. With a steely gaze he stared into the fallen detective's eyes.

"You are under arrest. You have the right to remain silent . . . !"

"What!!!" Screamed Breeler, in a remarkably loud voice and despite the type of injury suffered.

"If you give up the right to remain silent, then anything you say can be used . . ."

Breeler let loose a vile stream of expletives, his voice rising higher and higher drowning out Connor's voice.

Detective Conner finished with the Miranda rights and waited until Breeler's voice started to fall off. When he was done screaming, his voice cracked and if a voice could, bled. Conner spoke in a calm voice.

"We know it all Dick, If Mr. Brown hadn't of taken you down tonight, we would have picked you up tomorrow.' Contempt was clear in Conner's quiet voice.

"Conspiracy to commit murder, kidnapping, extortion, bribery, selling children. Tsk-Tsk, Dick, crossing state lines, its all Federal, you're going away for a long time."

"I want a lawyer!"

"You'll have one." Conner turned to a Sergeant. "Go with him and keep him under guard. I'll arrange for someone to be watching him all the time while he stays in the hospital. Do not let him out of your sight."

"Yes Sir!"

The paramedics were done with the field dressing and put Breeler on a gurney. They quickly hauled the disgraced detective out to the waiting ambulance. The Sergeant climbed in and the door shut and locked them both.

Detective Jeff Conner watched them go. Turning to the other Sheriff, he spoke. "The man who were with Breeler, take them to station. We'll need to debrief them. Smith and Pettay are dirty. Arrest them."

"Yes Sir!"

"Leave me a car, I need to confer with Mrs. Brown".

"Yes Sir," The uniformed Sheriff turned and left the house. Conner could hear him barking orders as he went.

"Good man," he said to Jill, "he'll do what needs to be done. You'll be safe here now." A frown appeared on his face. "Jill, do you know where Major was going? I think it would be in his best interest to turn himself in."

"No . . ." Jill didn't know what Major would want revealed or how much. She had betrayed him by being with Detective Breeler and she knew now that she could never hurt him again.

"No, he never said anything to me."

"Did he say anything at all?" Detective Conner prompted, "Any details that might help us find your boy?"

"My boy!" Exclaimed Jill, "Major said Brok was at his dads house! Can you take me there?"

Conner reached up and scratched his head. "Major brought your son Brok, from where?"

"I don't know." Jill lied, "But I know he's at his dads. Can you take me there?" She asked again, tears welling up in her eyes.

"I'll be glad too, but there's going to be a lot of questions that will need to be answered."

"You'll have to talk to Major." Jill said slowly.

"Okay." Conner broke off from detective mode, revealing a compassionate side of him rarely seen. "Let's go."

CHAPTER 54

Major laid in the bed of the truck fading in and out of awareness, he had no idea how long or how far he had been driven and no idea of where he was or where he was headed. It was enough to know that he was putting distance between him and the law. It didn't matter where he ended up. He could faintly hear the Indians ball game coming from the cab and the reassuring voice of their radio broadcaster, Herb Score, made him feel at ease.

He had just drifted off again when the Ranger pulled into a dark driveway and parked. The lack of motion and lack of the thrumming from the exhaust system (the Ranger needed Midasized) brought him to a groggy alertness. He tensed himself, preparing for action in case he was discovered, but the driver slammed the door shut and went to the house and entered.

Major rose up from the bed of the pick-up and warily looked around . . . nothing. He pulled himself up from the bed, using one hand on the side to give him support and haltingly climbed from the truck. His injuries had stiffened and he had to clamp his mouth tight to keep from crying out.

He started walking from the driveway, hesitated and then headed to the right. He still had no idea where he was, but he assumed sooner or later he would encounter a road sign to clue him in. Slowly but gradually increasing his pace as the stiffness left him; he made his way down the road. When headlights heralded the approaching of a vehicle he quickly left the side of the road and hid from it. In this manner, he soon left the Ranger behind.

Sick . . . He stumbled along, his flagging strength barely allowing him to place one foot in front of another. A shallow ditch was beside him now and he had to be careful he didn't sway into it. He had to find a place to hole up in, an old barn, an abandoned house . . . whatever. There wasn't more then a handful of houses he had passed so far. This road wasn't over populated. It was a two-lane job, but it seemed to be a State Route. No matter, he had to find shelter and soon. Major walked another mile in his dazed estimation before the inevitable happened, he stumbled into the ditch, face first. At first he tried to get up but his strength was depleted. He was all done in. Whipped. "Pussy!" He thought to himself before he passed out. A few cars drove by him, never noticing the black clad man lying face down in the ditch.

CHAPTER 55

He was so scared; he felt hot urine spurt inside the front of his underwear. He was on his knees, arms bound roughly behind him, in front of the meanest man he had ever encountered in his entire young life.

His right eye was closed and both of his front teeth had been broken off at the gum line. He had difficulty breathing and he was sure had several broken, not fractured, but broken ribs. Blood bubbled from shredded lips with each tortured breath he took. All the fingers on his left hand were broken and the thumb on right hand had been hacked off with a penknife for God's sake!

It had started out innocently enough. Dressed in a pair of tight blue jeans that had emphasized his bulging manhood and a tight sleeveless tee-shirt that show cased his powerful, rippling muscles, he had went to the strip tease bar located just outside of his hometown of Canton, Ohio. His snakeskin cowboy boots added two inches of height to his six-foot frame, making him look like a man to be reckoned with. He had felt powerful, the blood coursing through prominent veins that had been carefully cultivated by a couple years of weight lifting.

He had tired of watching the young girls shaking and displaying their nubile bodies, hoping to entice dollar bill tips from eager young studs and went over to the lone pool table hoping to hustle up a few bucks or at least a couple of beers. Instead he had come across a hustler that had soon nicked him for twenty dollars.

His opponent was of average height about five foot nine, five foot ten inches, but powerfully built. He had a loose fitting sweatshirt on, but even that didn't hide the fact that the man was solid, more then solid, and massive. He probably went 210-220 and not an ounce of fat on him.

When the man was ready to leave, he had asked for his money. That's where he had made his mistake. Surrounded by the crowd and thinking that the man would leave it alone, he had refused to pay, claiming that he thought they were playing for fun, even though they weren't. Oddly enough, he didn't argue or complain, just looked at him closely for a moment, nodded his head, then left.

Oh Lord, he wished now he would have paid, oh how he wished! He had drunk a few more beers and decided he had enough for the night. He walked out the door and walked over to his car, still feeling like he could whip the world when his world was shattered.

The snubbed pool player had come up behind him and kicked him in the right side. With a funny sounding wet snap, several of his ribs had let loose. When he grabbed his side, an opponent that he never saw coming had shattered his lips, teeth and any illusion of being tough. A gun to his head helped him into his opponent's car. The rest of the damage to his hands had come at the u-store-it shed that had sprung up at different locations around Canton.

With the gun to his head, he had been guided inside the 12-by12 area. The door shut behind them but amazingly, the man holding the gun had a kerosene lantern in there. After he had lit it the young man was surprised to see the shed was empty, except for the lantern and a single straight back chair. It looked like it came from a dinette set. He had been bound and then the man had went to work on his hands, ignoring the screams that was tore from his throat. Now he was on the floor looking at the floor, just now realizing that maybe he wasn't going to survive this.

"Well now, do you think we're still playing for fun?" The man sitting in the chair leaned forward. "DO YOU?"

"Please, let me go! I won't tell anyone!" He pleaded, "Please!"

"Not so bad now, huh boy! Sure I'll get you go." The man stood up and walked over to the bound man and untied the tightly wrapped rope, and then he stopped. "Hey boy, what are you going to tell the doctors at the hospital?"

"I'll tell them I . . . I . . . I was in a car wreck-yeah! That's what I'll tell them."

The massive man studied the broken young man for a long second. "Nah!" He said. He sat back down in the chair. The young man's heart almost burst when he saw what was pulled out of his seated antagonist's pocket. It was the gun he had used to force him into the car.

"Do you know why doctors hate to see some one shot with a .22 caliber pistol?" He asked quietly, a teacher now.

"Noo . . ." Pain wracked his body as he tried desperately to maintain his cool. He felt as though he might foul himself.

"Because the bullet is so light that it ricochets around when it hits something hard . . . Like a bone." He leaned forward. "A bigger caliber gun blows a hole right through everything. It'll either kill you or give you a chance to live. Ahhh, but a .22, like I say, you never know where it's going to end up at?" He cocked the double action pistol and aimed it at his untied victim's leg. "I wonder where this will end up at?"

"No! Don't," he screamed.

Krak! The report of the pistol was loud in the small shed. The slug hit him high in the thigh causing him to arch up and try to get to his feet.

Krak! Another slug found the upper thigh of his other leg. He fell to the floor, blood flowing from the two wounds. Agonized, mouth gasping for air, he puked up what was left of the beer and chips he had consumed that evening.

Krak! A slug in the shoulder.

Krak! A slug ricocheted off the hard shin bone pinged around for a long second before burying itself in the wood of the roof.

Krak! This time it entered behind the cracked shinbone and to his horror, he really could feel it bounce around inside his leg.

"No more! Stop please!" He screamed.

The silence was over whelming. Pain twisted his features, with great effort he managed to raise his head up. The bore of the pistol was aimed right between his eyes.

"Well, how 'bout it boy? Did you feel any ricochets?"

"Please!"

"Ahh shucks, I guess I got my twenty dollars worth by now." A grin glowed on his face. "But who's going to pay for my shells I used on you?" The grin disappeared. He reached down and grabbed the youth by the hair and jerked his head up starring him right in the eyes.

"You should've paid up, boy! But then you didn't know that I don't play for fun, did you, of course not. I never lose! I've won in everything I ever did all my life. I've never lost! Never!"

He cocked the pistol again still keeping it dead center between his eyes. "I've got things to do, boy, but pay attention! I want you to see this coming!"

The wounded boy's eye opened wide as the again smiling man pulled the trigger.

Krak! A hole appeared as if by magic between the boy's eyebrows. His body jumped and twitched as the nerves realized that their command center was breached.

The killer then stood up and let the head drop to the floor as the stench of voided bowels filled the small room. He stuffed the gun in the front of his pants and turned to leave. He shut the kerosene lamp off and carried it outside. Relocking the shed, he picked the lantern up and went to his car. He had used an alias to rent this place, so he could walk away without worry. The rent was paid for three more months, so the body shouldn't be discovered before that, unless the stench from decomposition hurried it along. Flies always seemed to find their way to a free meal. No matter, he had left bodies lying around like this before. He had read about their discoveries in the paper, but they still hadn't caught up with him yet.

As he started to drive away, a car pulled in, headlights flashed across his windshield, highlighting his features for an instance. Instantly his mind started clicking. Should he just leave? Or go back and eliminate a potential witness? He pulled out from the

U-Store-It area and started to drive away. Changing his mind, he braked and put the car in park. He quickly crossed the grassy area to where the lone man was unlocking his storage shed. Pulling the pistol from the front of his pants and without further ado, subdued him. He spent the next two hours repeating what he did to the welcher that had stiffed him for twenty dollars.

CHAPTER 56

Tears sprang to her eyes and sobs emitted softly from her throat as Brok tottered over to her saying; Ma-ma, ma-ma!" Jill held him close and swore never to let him out of her sight again. Phil and his father stood back and both were made uncomfortable by the intense emotion that was transpiring in front of them. Finally Phil tapped Jill on the shoulder.

"Jill? Where's Major?"

Jill tried not to cry as she told them the story about Major and Detective Breeler's fight, but she couldn't hold back her tears when she told them that Major had left her, wounded and once again alone.

Phil looked at his father. "Well Dad, I was going to go home, but I think I'll stick around for a couple of days to make sure Major doesn't need help."

"Okay boy, go get us a couple of beers." Mr. Brown looked at Jill and Brok and his voice softened. "I think you and Brok had better spend a few days here."

"I cant! What if Major tries to call me?"

"Don't worry about that. This will be the second place he calls."

"Yeah, I think you're right. I think it will be safer here."

Jill excused herself and Brok going upstairs to give themselves a much-needed shower and the some sack time. But sleep didn't come easy to Jill that night. She had seen the physical damage to her husband's body and even though she knew how tough her husband could be, what bothered her most was how much longer could he last. Even stone can be chipped then broken.

CHAPTER 57

Major lay in the ditch dreaming of a time before the emotional agony had filled his life. He knew he had to get up, had to hide. He had wounds to take care of too, but he couldn't manage to gather the energy needed to continue on. He was spent; at last his body had betrayed him. That saddened him. He kept himself in decent shape throughout the years, but before he had went to West Virginia to retrieve his stolen son, he had been in the best shape of his life. His martial arts training had contributed to that, but most important aspect of that training had been mental. He had never succumbed to the temptations of the dark side of the arts, namely chi power, but he wished now he had dabbled more in to that side of it. But then again Major was a Christian. His God demanded that he put no one before him and Major did his best to please God.

He had killed, yes; he had taken a lot of lives these past two weeks. But he hoped God would understand. After all it was in the old testament; "an eye for an eye." He hoped God would forgive him because he felt no remorse for what he had done. None! Those men were blight on the face of the earth. He had just pruned them from the tree of life.

A clopping sound roused him from his semi-delirium. What was it? It sounded like it was coming from behind him. Weakly, he raised his head and looked behind him. Fear sent his hear rate soaring. After thinking about his God, it looked like Satan himself was coming for him. Sparks flew from enormous hooves, and he could see pointed ears bobbing up and down in the faded moonlight.

A car approaching from in front of him made him duck his head. He could hear it roaring towards him, the engine blatting its power out through its cherry bomb mufflers. It came sweeping around the turn, slamming on its brakes, raising a cloud of dust that swept over the prone man.

Raising his head again, Major quickly looked behind him to see if the devil was still coming towards him. He almost laughed aloud. It was a horse pulling an Amish buggy. In his weakened mental state, he had imagined a demon from hell coming for him. Dizzy again, he laid his head in his arms and tried not to pass out.

Car doors slamming roused him again and he realized that the buggy had stopped too. Voices drifted to him like fog on a breeze.

"Well, well, well! What do we have here?" A voiced asked. "It looks like we don't have to go to town to have a good time." Said another voice.

"What do you think, Sam?" Asked the first voice.

A voice that Major had not heard yet answered.

"Ain't like we haven't had an Amish girl before." The voice proclaimed. "Besides, we know they love it, no matter how much they say they don't." Knowing laughter followed this statement.

"Three of them." Thought Major.

The three men walked past Major, never knowing he was there, too intent on the frightened young girl holding the reins.

"Please! I don't want trouble!" She said in stilted English. "I just wish to go home." The young girl was very frightened. She had heard of four girls in her community that had been gang raped by three men and she knew they stood in front of her now. She had wanted to be safely home hours ago, but she driven her buggy to a livestock sale forty miles from her home to sell homemade bread, pies and preserves for extra cash money. But she had not sold the last loaf of bread until almost dark and now she knew that she was in desperate straits. Her grandfather would have been with her but sickness prevented from making the trip. "Please let me go!" She clucked to the horse and shook the reins, but one of the men grabbed its halter, preventing it from going forward.

"What's your hurry, babe? We just want to get acquainted." Laughter followed these words. "Get out of the buggy!" It wasn't a request, but an order. When she didn't step down, one of the men stepped forward and grabbed her by the front of her blue homespun dress. Half dragging, half lifting, he pulled her to the ground. All three men gathered around her trapping the frightened girl between them.

The girl turned from one man to another, trying to avoid being touched by them. Their hands were everywhere! Pawing hand grabbed at her breasts and her buttocks and between her legs. The one who had pulled her from the buggy reached for the front of her dress ripping it with a loud tear to her waist.

"Hold her!" He shouted, and then put his hands on her. "Turn her around!" The two men had her by the arms and turned her around bending her over the buggy's wheel. The one who had tore her dress was behind her now lifting her dress up exposing her to him.

Sobs tore from her throat, along with unheard pleas. "No! No! Please I've . . . I've never been with a man! Stop! Please!"

Laughter, and then a sound she knew she would never ever forget, the grinding whisk of a zipper being pulled down. She redoubled her efforts to break loose, but they were too big, too strong.

"Hold her, boys!" The man said as he stepped up behind her. Major had heard and seen what was transpiring before his eyes. Blind rage consumed him. He was going to help her even if it killed him. Weakness forgotten he made his way to his feet and stepped up from the ditch. He only staggered once as he started towards them. Hands automatically going to the silver sais stuck in a make shift belt made from a shoestring.

"No!" He thought. "No more killing! I can take them!" He thought, but his strength was about gone. "Only if I have to!" He touched the sais and moved forward even with the man who was about to rape the young Amish girl. Gathering his strength, he brought his fist back, and then drove it as hard as he could manage into his kidney area. It was enough; he dropped without a sound, paralyzed by the blow. It had happened so quickly that neither of the other two understood what had happened. Major was still clad in black so the alcohol and marijuana impaired duo only saw what they thought was a shadow. The (shadow) brought a snap front kick into the knee of the thug closest to him causing the man to release the girl and fall squalling to the ground. Major never hesitated He finished him off with a sidekick to his head, rendering him unconscious. The last man released the stunned girl stepping back away from her.

"Who are you?" he asked, his voice trembling. "I have never seen anything like that before!"

"A friend of the Amish!" Major said, "I know what you've been doing and it ends here!"

The girl turned towards Major, stunned by the sudden turn of events. Major gently pulled her behind him. "I suggest you gather your friends up and leave, now!" He commanded.

The young man hesitated and then stepped forward throwing a hard haymaker at Major's head, hoping to tear it off at the shoulders. Without thought, the martial artist brought his left hand up in a classic knife hand block, hitting the pressure point located in the man's wrist with pinpoint accuracy. Numbed to the shoulder, the man dropped his arm down to his side and stared at Major.

"You son of a bit . . . erggg!!!" His words were cut off by the point of a sai that had been jabbed in the hollow of his throat.

"Now, now, now!" Said Major, "You forget we have a young lady here!" He pushed the point of the sai in a tad deeper. "I've had enough of you and your friends! I strongly recommend that you gather them up and leave."

Major slowly, very slowly pulled the sai back and replaced it in his belt. Ready to defend himself if necessary. He hoped the young men would do as he asked because the last little bit of action had taken its toll. Already bits of lights were floating in front of his eyes, threatening to impair his vision but to show weakness would be hazardous to his health.

"Why don't you take your little Halloween mask off dude? Let me see who you are. Or are you afraid of me?" Sneered the man.

Major laughed, startled that he was able to do so. Suddenly the sai was back in his hand, pointed at the man like a knife. "Sure I'll take my mask off." He said a smile still on his face. "But if you see my face, I'll kill you!"

"Yeah, right!" Said the man.

The smile disappeared from Major's face as he stepped forward. Before the man could move, the sai was once again embedded in the throat of his foe. He reached up with his other hand, preparing to pull the mask off. "What ever you want boy."

Something in the Ninja's voice or maybe his manner unsettled the young man.

No! Wait!" His adam's apple rode up and down under the unforgiving steel of the sais. "I'll get 'em out of here!"

"Smart move!" Major said and stepped back, but this time the sai stayed out. He was too weak to fool around now.

The man went over to the two men still on the ground helping the one that Major had given the kidney shot to his feet. He started to help him over to the car when the Amish girl spoke.

"Wait!" She said.

The two men stopped, one with his arm around the other, supporting him. They looked at Major, who nodded, "Hold it!

The girl came from behind Major, holding her torn dress up to cover her nakedness. With her head held high, she went over to the to men side stepping the now moaning man clutching his dislocated knee. She stepped in front of the pair, peering closely at each with a face devoid of emotion; she cleared her throat then spat in the face of the man who tried to rape her. She then turned and did the same to the other one that was supporting him. Still not saying anything, she turned away and went to the last of the trio.

Major expected her to shame him as she did the other two, but what came next was totally unexpected to him. The young girl drew back one black high-topped laced shoe and drove the tip into the injured man's groin. He let go of his injured knee and grabbed his groin, inhaling sharply, and then he started to cry.

Everyone stood stunned for a second Then Major spoke, "Get out of here!"

The two went to the car and the uninjured one helped his buddy into the vehicle. He came back and got the other one to his feet, then half dragging, half carrying the still crying man to the car.

Once they were all in the car, the motor roared to life. The driver gunned the engine to redline and peeled away from Major and the girl, throwing gravel and dust behind it as they left.

Major stumbled towards the horse and leaned on it, grateful for the support. He inhaled the sharp scent of the animal, feeling the wetness of it's now drying sweat. He had forgotten about the girl as he tried in vain to keep the world from spinning around him. Now that the men were gone, the pain from his open wounds was screaming throughout his body, threatening to overload his senses. He jumped when the young Amish girl spoke from behind him.

"Thank you!" She waited for a response and peered closely at the black clad man who seemed unable to respond. She touched him on the shoulder and repeated, "Thank you."

With great care, Major turned towards her, keeping his right hand on the horse's flank.

Concern now she carefully looked her savior over. "Are you alright?" She asked.

Unable to talk, Major simply nodded.

"Who are you? Where did you come from? How did you know I needed help?" Now that she was safe she couldn't keep from asking questions, not waiting for an answer. Not that it mattered, Major was beyond words. Realizing that she was now safe, she turned from him and went to the buggy and reached inside. Digging around for a moment, she found a black shawl and wrapped it around her upper body concealing her naked torso. After making herself presentable, she turned again to Major; surprised he was still using her horse for support. Something clicked in her mind and she knew that the man definitely was not okay. She went to him and caught him under the arms as he sagged to the ground. Raised around animals and having to home doctor herself and her grandfather for as long as she could remember, she did not go into hysterics as a city girl might have done when she discovered her hands were wet with the man's blood. Wiping the blood from her hands on her ruined dress, she tore off a strip of cloth from it and used it to make a compress and bandaged the newly opened wound Using farm hardened muscles, she managed to get the semi conscious man in the buggy. With the reins in her hands she clucked to her horse and shook the straps. A moment later they were trotting down the township road to her grandfather's house.

CHAPTER 58

Three days after he had butchered the two men at the U-Store-It shed Pete Sanford laid in bed half asleep, a cruel smile on his face. He had been reliving the murders of the two and it brought him great satisfaction. Naked, arms behind his head, lying on the sheet with covers rumpled around him, he was totally at ease. If someone could have observed him at this moment, they would have thought a very knowing woman had just pleasured him. But no fleeting orgasm could ever take the place of the exultation he felt when he was killing things. Anything! It didn't matter what it was, bird, animal or human, they all brought equal pleasure to his warped being. He remembered the first creature he had ever destroyed. He was ten years old and his father had trusted him with his old Zippo lighter and a pack of Black Kat firecrackers.

"Don't hold them in your hands when you light them, Petey."
He said. "Put them on the ground, light and get clear!" He took
one of the small cylinders from the pack and demonstrated
how to light one. A hot sizzle from the fuse and then a loud
crack had sent a surge of excitement through him. These things
could do some damage in the hands of someone who had an
inventive mine. His father had explained that he should ever
try to relight the ones that failed to go off the first time. "The
duds are the ones that'll get you, Petey!" He had cackled around
the long necked bottle of a Carling Black Label. He had sent his
young son to the woods where he would be out of the way of
some serious drinking.

Pete had wandered through the small woods setting off an
occasional cracker, but for some reason (fate?) he saved most of
them until he found something worthy of their small charge.

He happened upon a baby robin that had fallen from its
nest, looking up into the tree until he spotted from where it
came from. It was a branchy maple tree. He had picked the little
bird up from the ground preparing to return the fledgling back
to its nest when the bird chose that moment to deposit a load
in the small boy's hand.

"EEEWWW!" He had wrinkled his nose up, shifting the bird
to his other hand, flinging the waste to the ground, then wiping
the residue on his pants leg. While he was wiping his hand
off he brushed against the Black Kats in his pocket. Suddenly
the return of the small bird to its nest fled from his mind. He
reached inside his pocket and pulled one of the firecrackers
out. Turning the Baby robin upside down, he jammed it up the
bird's hole so only the fuse could be seen. The bird screeched
and struggled in his hand, but Pete was enraptured. He set the
bird on the ground and lit the fuse just like he had been shown.
Three seconds later it went off stilling the robin forever and
sending a streak of pleasure through that was so intense that he
had actually blacked out for a few seconds. He had climbed the
tree and found two more small birds and carried them down the
tree in his shirt pocket. The mother and father bird had flown
around him for a few minutes, then settled on a tree branch,
watching the fate of their young. Pete had repeated to the

two what he had done to first one he had found. The pleasure derived from the third bird was just as intense as what he had felt from the very first one.

He had searched the woods for other nests, blowing up the contents until he had run out of firecrackers. He had a blast. (So to speak.) He went back to his father and begged for more Black Kats. All he got was a backhand from his now drunk sire.

As the summer went on he became more and more inventive in ways of forced deaths. Rabbits, Possums even fish died terrible deaths by his now experienced hands.

One time a neighbor's cat had a litter of eight kittens that he had not wanted. Pete followed him as he carried the old burlap sack of squirming blind little creatures. He had thrown them in the creek that ran beside the woods where Pete had first learned to kill. When he left, Pete had rescued the mewing kittens. He spent the rest of the day torturing them to death. That night he had received a thrashing from his father for being gone all day, said he was worried. Hah! He didn't have anyone to fetch his beer for him.

As he grew, Pete graduated to bigger animals. Dogs were a favorite, especially when he was able to run across m-80s, a firecracker that packed the punch of a quarter of a stick of dynamite. One memorable day he had shot a lone Holstein cow to death to death with a .22 rifle (single shot.) He knew the farmer and his wife weren't going to be home till evening. He started shooting at her udder and went through three boxes of shells before the riddled cow had finally died.

Pete and his father had moved to Canton, Ohio during his teen years and then he was lost for awhile because animals were a lot harder to come by then. It seemed like everyone was watching everyone. You didn't have any privacy. Houses by houses stacked beside each other like eggs in a carton.

Once Pete earned his drivers license everything changed, Cleveland was just a short drive away and many a bum or wino were beaten bloody by his growing fists. It wasn't the same as killing, but it gave him pleasure to cause blood to flow from their broken noses and cut lips. He killed his first man in Cleveland. He didn't mean too. By then he had started to grow to his present size. A crashing blow from his huge right hand had broken the neck of a bulbous nosed, bleary-eyed drunk. He had spent several days at his home waiting for the police to come and arrest him. When no one showed up, he had realized just how easy it was to literally get away with murder. He made it a habit to go to different towns and find the dirtiest seediest dump of a bar he could find. There was always some drunk in there that no one would notice he was gone for several days. By that time he would be back home waiting until it was time to kill again.

He came across the idea of using storage sheds for prolonged torture by accident. He rented one to store some stolen stereo equipment. As soon as he seen the inside he had thought what a good place for killing. He went around in a hundred mile radius of Canton and rented sheds that were out of the way from normal traffic and used them for his sordid games. He always used a different name, but he wasn't naïve enough to assume that he would never be caught. He knew that the police had discovered all the bodies he had stored in the sheds throughout the past couple of years and they had to have a description of him by now. He knew sooner or later he would be caught, but he was in the process of laying plans for that right now.

His mind drifted to his father, dead this past year. Alcohol had eaten his liver up. His Mistress "Mabel . . . Black Label" had been the death of him. His mother had died when he was young, he couldn't remember her at all. He didn't even have a picture of her. No brothers, no sisters, no aunts or uncles, not even in-laws. He was alone, all alone but for his hatred. He didn't consider it strange to be friends with an emotion. Oh no! In face he preferred it that way. No hassle, no fuss, no muss. It was a constant companion, one he welcomed. Pete interacted with other people, but didn't really have them for friends. The men he ran with were like him to some degree, but none of them really had his total disregard for life, per se. Pete wasn't happy unless he was hearing a concerto of screams. Really want to get Pete off? Plead and beg for a mercy that would never be received.

Pete yawned, stretched his relaxed body and stood up. The sudden rush of blood going from his head made him dizzy for a second, but it would pass. He dressed slowly, dreamily in his mind still on his child hood. In his early twenties Pete had decided to enhance his fighting abilities. He checked out several martial art schools in the area before deciding on a school ran by an eight-degree grandmaster fresh off the boat from Korea. He had watched the grandmaster break eight boards with the first two knuckles of a small right hand, and even though the Korean stood no taller then five foot two and couldn't have weighed more then one hundred thirty pounds soaking wet, he splintered all eight boards with a loud "Kiaaa!" and little effort. There had been other demonstrations that had impressed Pete, but the mental image of that little dude stuck with him. If he could harness that much power in that little frame, then what could he have done with a body like his?

He started working out the very next day. He was one of the grandmaster's first students and by far the most dedicated. He earned his black belt within two years and was deciding whether or not he wanted to continue training or quit. He had never really set goals in the art, but by now he was bored with classes. There was no one in his dojo that would spar with him any more. The other students had enough of Pete's intense sparring sessions. A bloody nose or a black eye was usually a lucky night for anyone who was foolish enough to go against him. Broken bones, cuts and severe bruises were usually the order of the day. Even the grandmaster would not spar with him anymore. In a moment of pique, Pete had ignored blows that shattered wood and dealt the grandmaster such a blow that he lay senseless for several long minutes. That basically ended Pete's sparring in class. He couldn't even get a good fight going in the local bars. His immense size usually intimidated most of the regular rum-dums who frequented the bars, but when one did stand up to Pete, he made short work of them. Shoot, most of the time he did not even need to use his skills.

He had made up his mind to quit his school, but a poster hung on the bulletin board that proclaimed a tournament was what changed his mind. Pete realized that here was a chance to compete against opponents with presumably the same skill as he had. He checked the divisions and was pleased that they broke the black belts up in weight groups. Of course Pete was a heavyweight. He went to the grandmaster, who helped him sign up. He was so excited by the opportunity of facing opponents that could stretch his limits (hopefully) that he went out that evening. He celebrated by taking the whole night to slowly kill a one legged black man who had made the mistake of asking Pete for some spare change. Pete really enjoyed working on the stub of the maimed leg. He used a propane torch to slowly work his way up the man's body, slicing away the seared meat as he went. When the black man finally died, his bad leg was nothing but white bone, seared in places. The other leg was hamburger all the way to the hip. Pete really enjoyed himself that night although it took several days to get the smell of burnt bone and meat out of his nose and lungs.

He had destroyed the other competitor's at his first tournament. To make it even more enjoyable, it was full contact matches. Pete fought four times that day and four heavyweights were hauled away by the ambulance crew that normally did not see that many casualties in a dozen tournaments. Pete let the tourney director hang the gold medal around his neck and stood high on the 3-place stand. The other two places were empty, there was no one left to claim second or third. Pete laughed to himself. He was watching the crowd and what he saw pleased him. They were looking at him with fear and awe, all but one, a black belt; he looked like a middleweight.

Later Pete had found out that the black belt was indeed a middleweight fighter of some renown. Evidently he was an excellent fighter, undefeated in his division and well respected by his peers. That was the first Pete saw of Major Brown. It wasn't the last. Oh no! The second and third tournament that Pete participated in he kept a close eye on Brown. He had been impressed by the black belt's skill but he lost some respect for Brown because he would never finish his opponent, content to win by points rather then to risk injury to his competitor.

Pete, however, was a different story all together. He too was undefeated in match play. He had fought ten opponents in those three tournaments and ten opponents were carted to the hospital, all of his wins were by knockouts, usually within the first minute. The last tournament, two would stand against him, in the fourth and last one he ever attended, none would sign up.

The masters of the tournament had made a public appeal for some competitors to sign up for the heavyweight bracket, but not a one would throw his hat in the ring. Not a one!

The masters had conceded the heavyweight divisions to him and called him to the podium, where once again he stood alone. Major Brown had already won the middleweight division (both sparring and katas) but had stepped forward before the gold was placed around Pete's neck.

He went to his master and bowed, "Excuse me, Sir." The master had nodded his permission for Major to speak. The Hall where the tournament was being held quieted down. Instantly. Everyone there knew that Major Brown would have never interrupted his master with out a good reason.

"It is not right for an award to be granted to a man without his earning it." He said.

"What is it, do you wish?" Asked Major's Master.

"If it pleases you Master, I wish to fight Mr. Sanford to give him the opportunity to earn his glory or to give me the same opportunity to increase my honor!"

The hall had exploded in raucous noise. A middleweight fighting a heavyweight? Especially one as big and mean as Pete Sanford? Impossible!"

The Master paused as if in thought, secretly he was pleased his number one student had challenged the over bearing and murderous Sanford, then nodded his assent.

Win or lose, Major Brown's status and reputation had soared to unheard of heights. Renown was his without striking a single blow!

Pete was happy too, not for any honorable reason, but for the chance to dismantle another foe.

All eyes were upon the two as they bowed to the center referee and then to the panel of black belt judges. Breaths were held as the referee held his hand up high.

"Begin!" He shouted and stepped back.

Pete had leaped across at Major eager to close with him, but he was not there! A blow to his side caught him by surprise and knocked some of his wind from him.

Three two minute rounds later; Pete had yet to lay a hand on the speedy and elusive Major. Pete knew he needed a knockout to win by now and he concentrated on trapping Brown in a corner. Brown made his first mistake of the night; he stood toe to toe with Pete, giving him the chance to win this fight and to make the blood flow.

A left and a right cracked the smaller man's head to his right and then left. Pete was drawing back to unleash an upper cut when the time expired. The referee jumped in between them, and just like that the fight was over.

Pete had put everything he had in the only two punches he had landed, but Brown had taken them both and was still standing. The audience was going bananas screaming Browns name. They knew as well as Pete that the smaller man had whipped the bigger man. David versus Goliath and the giant had lost again.

Pete was angry, oh so very angry! He had never lost in anything in his life. Now he had suffered a defeat so devastating that he knew he would never again enter a dojo. He respected Major's victory but he hated the man, not because he was a bad person, but because he had taken something that belonged to Pete. His reputation and glory!

He left his fighting gear on the floor and walked out. He would never wear them again. From now on it was root hog or die. No more playing games.

Pete had challenged Major several times over the next couple of years, but he had been turned down firmly and politely. He could not even shame him into fighting him, although he had tried.

Brown had retired from fighting after beating Pete and opened up his own school. Each refusal fueled Pete's desire for revenge. He had to establish a way to get Brown to meet him for a fight. This time without referees, judges or so called masters watching. Oh, there would be an audience there and Pete had plans for that. Just like Pete had a plan in the works to make

Brown fight him. When this fight was happening it would be heard about through out the world.

Pete slammed his fist into the wall beside the bed, knocking a hole in the dry wall that matched several other holes through out his apartment. Pete didn't believe in holding feelings in, just ask his victims, if any could answer.

"Yes Sir!" Pete said aloud, "We've got a date you and me!" He imagined Brown in his mind. "When we meet again, one of us will die!" Believe it or not, Pete found great humor in this because he knew that this time more then one will die. It's going to be great!

CHAPTER 59

Phil waited two days at his father's house, waiting for a call from his brother. Knowing Major as he did, he knew if he wasn't contacted by now then he wasn't needed. He said his goodbyes to his mother and father. Jill and Brok walk him to his truck.

"When Major calls you get a hold of me." He told Jill. "I want to know what's going on."

"Okay," said Jill.

Phil reached down and caught the squirming Brok and pitched him high in the air. He caught him brought him to his face, kissed him and sat him down. "I'm glad you got him back, Jill. Real glad."

Tears filled her eyes. "Phil, I . . . I've got to know, was it bad there?"

"Yes Jill, It was a war zone!" Phil paused, "You have to understand one very important fact. What Major did there was for his family. Sort of like a soldier having to kill during wartime. Just think of it like that."

Jill leaned on Phil's shoulder and tried not to cry. "I just want my family back together."

"What are the charges now?"

"I guess they just want him in for questions about the murder of Theodore Grant."

"That's it?" Questioned Phil, "What about Macsville?"

"Detective Conner took a picture of Major down to Mrs. Fuerte and she said that he wasn't the one that killed her husband his men!" Jill wet her full lips with her tongue. "But I know better! Major admitted to me that he was the one who did all the killings there.

"She said that, huh?" Phil pursed his lips. "I thought they said on the news that they never seen his face. This could be a trap set for Major."

"No, I don't think so. Major told me once that when Jeff Conner gave his word it was a good as gold. He said that Major was wanted for questioning about the murder of Grant, he gave me his word that was all."

Phil thought about that bit of information for a moment. He too had gone to school with Jeff Conner and he also respected him. This put a different slant on things.

"Do you know what kind of evidence they have on Major?"

"No, but I think Breeler would have nailed Major's hide to the wall if they had anything at all. Oh Phil! Maybe Major can get out of this after all!"

"Well, we can't do anything until we hear from Major."

Jill's eyes dropped to the ground, she had to ask her brother-in-law a question, but no matter how she put it, the question would hurt. "Do you think Major's alive?" She held her breath.

"They haven't found him yet, nor a body. We have to assume he's holed up somewhere. If you would of saw what I seen of him in West Virginia, then you would know that there's a ninety-five percent chance he's alive. We just have to wait."

Phil kissed Jill on the cheek, rustled Brok's hair, climbed into his truck and left. Jill watched him go down the road and made a decision to go home. She had things to do. Hand in hand Brok and Jill went into the Brown's house, packed their bags, said goodbye and went home.

Jill unlocked the front door and entered. The living room was still a wreck from the fight that was waged there two nights ago. She went to the kitchen coming back with a broom along soap and water. She straightened up the furniture, swept the floor, then on her hands and knees, she swabbed up the bloodstains that came from both her husband and the rogue detective. Once started, she went from room to room making each one immaculate.

She called her neighbor who brought Sensei back to his home, started supper, (green beans, potatoes and ham baked together,) and played with Brok.

After her son was in bed, she called up the black belt that had been running Major's school since Brok had been kidnapped. After a brief conversation in which she both thanked and released him of his extra teaching obligation, she finally set down in her favorite chair with a cup of freshly brewed Lipton tea.

She stayed up that night, not going to bed until the wee hours of the morning. Two full days had passed since she had lost contact with her husband and the waiting was tense and unsettling for her. When Major had left her to go and rescue Brok had been a very bad time, but she could not of imagined Major being hurt then. Now she knew for a fact that he was injured and thinking he was alone and hurt was almost more then her broken heart could bear.

The next morning after breakfast with Brok, she could not take lying around anymore. She dressed in tight workout clothes and then hand in hand with Brok she went to the dojo. Brok was perfectly content to sit on the floor and play with a myriad of toys he had kept over on his occasional visits to the dojo.

Jill stretched out slowly, unease still troubling her mind. She couldn't articulate what she was feeling; she eerily duplicated the workout that Major had gone through before his sojourn to West "By God" Virginia. She didn't drive herself to the brink of exhaustion that her husband had forced upon himself, yet she was fatigued by the time she was done.

During her workout she had decided to take over karate classes. She supposed that was on her mind since she dismissed the assistant instructor the previous night. For some odd reason she felt she needed to get herself in true fighting shape. (For some battle yet to come?) She had handled herself well against the likes of Richard Breeler, but some portent warned her that she needed more than that.

Mind troubled, Brok and she went to the house and prepared to go to town for groceries. Thank goodness that major had the foresight to leave her money. The only income they had was from the school and that wasn't enough to live on. The one question she had not dared to ask herself? Where did the money come from?

Dismissing everything from her mind, Jill set down and prepared a list for the things she needed from the store. She added things that weren't necessary to her household, but things that would please Major when he came home. There was no doubt in her mind that he would not come home. Jail never entered her mind. After talking to Detective Connor, she thought that there was an excellent chance that Major would be set free. Then and only then, with her family safely reunited would she be free of these terrible feelings of foreboding she had endured for the past two days.

Even while Jill tried to dismiss these niggling thoughts from her mind, her subconscious felt something was about to transpire that would completely shatter any thoughts of normalcy any time soon. She reached down and petted (old faithful) Sensei, stroking between his ears. Instead of settling down as he usually did when Jill was petting him, he whined his unease. Troubled Jill sat there for a few minutes when a thought forced it's way to the forefront of her mind. It was so powerful, that Jill did not doubt for one moment that it wasn't true. Major was alive! Jill fell forward on the table, head in her arms and cried with unmitigated relief. Never questioning her premonition.

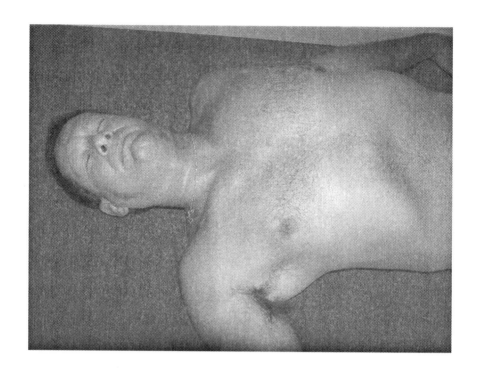

CHAPTER 60

Yes, Major was alive. For almost three nights and three days he had lain senseless, scaring the young Amish girl that had brought him to the humble log house, where she and her grandfather live. Neither of the two expected the feverish and out of his head stranger to live. The infections from the wound in his side had been difficult to treat, but with the man in a stupor part of the time, her grandfather had cut the infections away with the same knife that he used to make geldings from stallions. Home remedies and different concoctions pass down throughout generations had quickly controlled the poison that raged through the man's system. His fever had broken early this morning although he had not awakened his breathing and color was much better.

Onna Miller's grandfather, Seth, had not commented when she had pulled the buggy to the porch of their cabin, instead of going to the barn to unhitch and care for the horse. His keen eyes, he only needed glasses to read with, registered Onna's torn dress and the bloodstains that shone black in the light of the lantern he had held in his hand.

Still, with out question, he had helped her get the masked man from the buggy and helped her carry him into the cabin. Onna had assisted him in stripping the man to his waist, but it was up to him to do the final undressing. They placed him in Seth's bed and covered him to his waist. Onna had cleaned up the man's wounds and applied poultices to his many cuts. They had debated whether or not to take the mask from his head, but decided not too. Onna had felt under the mask and could not discern any fresh injuries other then some scabbing. So they had respected his privacy. It bothered Seth somewhat having an unknown man in his home, yet he had risked his life to protect his precious granddaughter. He knew four other fathers that would give anything to have their daughters whole again; a stranger in the house would be a very small price to pay.

Onna was at the wood stove, baking bread and pies. Supper had been finished two hours earlier and Onna had washed the dishes and put everything in its place. Seth was proud of her. He had raised her for eleven years now. Her father (his son) and mother had been hit by a huge semi-truck that a load of logs on it. They had been killed instantly. Fortunately, Onna had been with his now deceased wife when her parents were killed. The trucker's insurance paid for the burial and the logging company had donated the wood for the house in which was now Onna's and his home. All of their needs were supplied from the land. Wool from sheep for clothing, dairy products, eggs, grain everything, even the tobacco he used in his pipe came from his land. God had blessed them very well; it was too bad that Onna's parents couldn't be here to enjoy life with them. Seth knew they were with God and he looked forward to the day he would join them.

He had his Bible lying in his lap opened to Job. Now there was a man with problems. Whenever Seth thought his problems in life were too much for him to bear alone, he turned to the Bible and more often then not Job.

Seth carefully said a prayer eyes closed, hands together, lips moving silently, and then shut the Bible putting it on the little home made wooded sand by his favorite rocking chair.

He picked up his old corncob pipe tapping the old ashes out in an ashtray that had been chipped and fashioned out of a chunk of sand rock by Onna. He refilled the pipe with some of his home-grown tobacco tamping it in with the index finger of his right hand. He went to the kindling pile and selected a long sliver of wood, sticking it in the fire of the stove until it burst into flame. He used it to light his pipe, put the sliver where he could use it again, then sat down heavily in his rocker.

He was very concerned about how the stranger had been wounded. He knew what a gun-shot wound looked like and the man had two of them on his body. One was almost healed although a little leaky yet and the other was fresh, very fresh, and what about the money? When Seth had stripped the man of his clothes, his funny looking weapons (he assumed that's what they were after Onna told him what he had done with one) he had found a packet of money jammed in his underwear. If that is what you called them. Seth preferred long johns even in the summer. He had not counted it, but put it under the tick mattress where the man now slept.

He drew a long fragrant pull of tobacco in his lungs and slowly released it. Seth figured he owed the man a lot for saving his grand daughter's virtue, but if he were evil, then he would have to go. A curious man, Seth couldn't wait to hear the stranger's story. If he refused to confide in him or if Seth thought he was being lied to then he was to be removed from the hospitality of his home immediately, wounded or not.

He drew in another lungful of smoke and realized that the man's eyes were opened and aware. He released the smoke, blowing it upwards.

They stared deep in each other eyes for a long second and then the stranger spoke. "Wouldn't happen to have an extra one of those, would you?"

Seth stared at him, and then understood that he wanted a smoke. Seth rose and went to the dresser beside his bed, opened the top drawer and pulled out a brand new pipe he had fashioned from a cob less then a week ago. He filled it, lit it and handed it to the stranger. Onna now knew that he was conscious standing behind her grandfather secure in the knowledge that he would protect her.

Major took a deep drag on the pipe and took it into his lungs as if he smoked a pipe everyday. Major used to smoke but he quit when he went into training to go after his son. He took his time blowing the smoke from his lungs enjoying the light-headedness that came with the first smoke he's had in awhile.

He put the stem back in his mouth content for the moment. Major started to puff on the pipe again but stopped. Something was wrong. It took him a moment to know what it was. He still had his mask on.

"Any reason I need this on?" He asked pointing to his head.

"No, take it off if it is your desire." Seth said relieved that the man didn't feel a need to hide his identity.

Major pulled the mask and laid it on the covers. He saw the girl he had saved from rape . . . when? "How long have I been here?" He asked.

"This is your third night." Said Seth.

"Where am I?"

"You are familiar with this area?"

"Somewhat."

"You are in Amish Country beyond the town of Sugarcreek."

Major digested this bit of information. Evidently the truck he had stolen a ride in took him farther then he had expected. But that was okay. He imagined that the area in his neck of the woods had been pretty well searched. Major looked at Onna. "You are the one I helped, was I in time?"

A smile wrinkled Onna's face, highlighting her youthful prettiness. She would never be beautiful but a man could do a heck of a lot worse then this pretty young maiden in front of him. He judged her to be sixteen or seventeen years old, clean face with light blonde hair sticking out from underneath the little white kerchief she wore on her head.

"Yes thank you. It was wonderful what you did. Sometimes I wish I were a man!" Then I could do the things you did!"

Major answered her smile with one of his own. "You don't have to be a man to be able to do that." He said. "I could teach you how to take care of yourself."

"Ohh, could you?" She asked excited.

"Onna, our guest would like something to eat. It's been at least three days since his last meal.

"I'll get some him some broth and bread." Onna quickly went to prepare some nourishment for the man who saved her.

Seth turned to Major eyes showing deep thoughts. "My name is Seth Miller. My grand daughter's name is Onna." Seth took Major by the hand. "I too wish to thank you for helping her."

Major was embarrassed by the naked emotion showing on the old man's bearded face.

"I'm glad I was at the right place at the right time. She was lucky."

Seth went over and pulled a chair to the side of the bed.

"We are God fearing people. I am hoping we are not sheltering a viper under our roof." Seth paused, "What are we to call you?"

Major brooded over the question for along minute. "You can call me by my Christian name."

Seth's heart lightened at the words, "And that is?"

"My name is Major Brown. Major studied the old man's face carefully; he hoped that Seth had not heard of him.

Seth pursed his lips, brought the pipe back up and puffed hard to keep the coal in the tobacco lit. After several hard draws smoke again rose from the bowl in a straight line, going to the ceiling. He was about to speak when Onna came to the bed with a tray laden with broth, bread and foamy creamy milk Much to Seth's amusement she insisted on spoon-feeding Mr. Brown. Seth said a prayer, and then allowed Onna to feed him.

When the smell of the broth hit Major's nostrils it awakened a ravenous hunger in him. He was already in a semi reclining position but tried to sit up a little more. He could barely move his torso. Pain screeched from his side to a crescendo then faded off to a dull thump. He flopped back down under the careful watch of Onna then allowed himself to be fed like a baby. The first spoonful was sheer heaven, a simple broth, yes, but ambrosia of the gods to Major. He greedily ate all of the broth and bread washing it all down with that delicious glass of milk.

Not a word was said as Major was fed. When the last drop was ingested, Onna took the tray from his lap. "More for you?" She asked?"

"Later, I'm full right now. Thank You."

"Onna dimpled, then pivoted to again clean up dishes.

Again the two men studied each other. Seth rose taking the pipe Major used, filled the bowl and lit it.

"You are tired Mr. Brown?"

"It's Major. No. I guess we had better talk." Major shifted to get comfortable in the bed.

"I have heard of you . . ." A pause and then, "Major." Seth was not used to being overly familiar with a person he didn't know, but in this case, familiarity seemed the right thing to do.

Guarded, Major asked, "You have?"

"Yes, Onna and I watched you and your people put on a Karate demonstration a couple of years ago."

Major looked at him blankly.

"At the Tuscarawas County Fair."

"Oh yes I remember that." Major was relieved. Maybe these people did not know what has happened in the past month or so. They smoked for a moment.

Seth leaned forward pinning Major with his eyes. "Did they find your son yet?"

Major didn't answer. Without warning, Major was reliving the kidnapping of Brok, injuries he had suffered at the hands of the now deceased. Theodore Grant, the brief breakup of his marriage, the carnage in West Virginia, the fight with Breeler and finally his interruption of the attempted rape of Onna.

"I . . . I . . ." Major stopped talking thinking how to explain to the old man. "I brought him back. Yes he's with his mother by now."

"Is that how you became gunshot and beaten?"

"Yes." Major knew he had to trust these people; he desperately needed to get healthy and to have time to heal. Yet he didn't want to involve these gentle people with the dirtiness of his crimes. He started talking, slowly at first, then quicker as the words poured out of him in a torrent.

Seth never said a word. He refilled the pipes when the tobacco was smoked up but other wise did nothing to stop the flow of words from the tormented man.

When Major finally told the whole story, he felt at rest for the first time. He lay there, waiting for the old man to ask him to leave.

"So you are a wanted man?"

"Yes." Major agreed quietly.

Seth stood and stretched. "There is a night pan by your bed, if you need it. We will talk again in the morning."

"Seth?"

"Yes?"

"I need to contact my wife Jill. She knows I'm hurt. She will be worried.

Seth took Major's pipe and put it on the nightstand with his.

"In the morning. Good night." Seth went to the kitchen table and sat down. Onna was preparing for bed and he would soon follow, but first he needed to talk to the Lord. He clasped his hands together and bowed his head asking God for guidance. When he finished praying, he went to bed. He needed time to think. Onna kissed him good night, blew out the candles and went to her bed.

The house was quieting as Major tried to sleep. He pictured Jill in his mind. She was sitting at the table writing. Major started to drowse off, his mind reaching out to her. He saw the sitting Jill's head snap up as if she was aware of his thoughts. Oh how he wished that were so. He wanted her. There was no doubt of that. If they ever got this mess straightened out he would never leave her.

"Goodnight Jill!" He whispered and drifted off to the most restful sleep he had had for a while.

CHAPTER 61

Detective Jeff Conner sat behind his desk looking at a file laying there. It was the evidence that Detective Breeler had amassed against Major Brown in connection of Theodore Grant. There was nothing! Nothing at all, No witnesses, no physical evidence not a shred of facts that could incriminated Brown with the murder. All they had was the puncture wounds through each of Grant's shoulders and the holes in the floor where the weapon penetrated. They were most likely made by a martial arts weapon probably a sai. But Breeler had run tests on Brown's sais, which had, came up negative. Sure they fit the wounds, but how many sais were in circulation. No, they did not have a thing on Brown. Except for Breeler's absolute conviction that he was the one who did it.

As for the "Macsville Massacre," Conner had taken a photograph of Major to Mrs. Fuerte for identification. She had insisted that it was not Major Brown who had killed the bodyguards and her husband. She claimed to have seen the assailant's face during the fight in which her husband, Peter had been killed. Therefore any charges against Brown involving West Virginia were also moot. Sure, there was circumstantial evidence involving the martial artist, like how did he manage to get Brok back? Yet with out Allison Fuerte's cooperation then they had nothing. Unless they found something vital that they had missed, Conner would recommend that Major Brown be cleared of all charges. As far as he knew, Breeler was throwing them Brown to save his on neck.

A knock on the door interrupted Conner's thoughts. "Come in!"

The door opened and a sergeant walked in with some paperwork in hand.

"Excuse me, Detective, but three men claimed they were beaten and robbed by a man dressed in black wearing a mask."

"Where and when?"

"Three days ago near Sugarcreek."

"What took them so long to report it?"

"They reported it the next day, sir, I was reading the reports and thought maybe Major Brown was involved."

Conner leaned back in his swivel chair rocking it slightly.

"Any witnesses?"

"No sir, just their statements."

"Okay, leave them with me."

"Yes Sir." The Sergeant left the reports on Conner's desk and left.

The detective took his time reading them. After studying all three of them, he again sat back in his chair. He did not believe what was in the statements. No, not at all. Conner had no doubt that something did happen that night but he didn't believe these statements for one minute. However it was the first clue of the whereabouts of Brown.

After some heavy thoughts Conner decided to leave it be for right now. He had an idea where Brown was located, but without proof of any crimes why should he spend the man-hours looking him up? No it was best to leave things alone, besides he didn't want to spook Brown at this time.

Conner knew something bad had been going on in Amish Country just what he did not know, they didn't confide easily with others outside of their order. Especially since the courts ordered the two brothers who liked to hunt to wear orange which was against their religion. It was for their own safety yet the Old Order Amish went to jail before they would deny what they thought was their religious right.

Conner had a suspicion that these three men were involved with the problems that bothered them. He decided he would keep a close eye on these men and if his idea were correct at least he would have a starting point.

He got his telephone book from the desk and looked up the Brown's number. He dialed and on the fourth ring, Mrs. Brown answered.

"Hello?" Anticipation in her voice, that told Conner that Major had not contacted her yet. Conner had to admit, Brown had been very clever escaping Breeler's net that night, even more clever in losing the dogs. He would love to ask him how he did it if he ever has the chance.

"Mrs. Brown, this is Detective Conner."

"OHH!" Jill sounded disappointed.

"Have you heard from your husband yet?"

"No."

"Well, when you do, please let him know that there will be no charges filed against him for Macsville or the murder of Theodore Grant."

"Oh Detective Conner! That's great! I know that he'll call sooner or later. I'll tell him!" Jill was ecstatic. Her prayers have been answered. As soon as Major contacts her she would give him the news! They would be a family again. Tears rolled unchecked down her cheeks.

"Here's my number. Call me when he contacts you. I still need to talk to him." Conner gave Jill his number and hung up.

He felt better giving Jill such good news. There was no doubt in his mind that Brown was involved in all those deaths somehow, but without evidence and witness there could be no charges. He briefly wondered why Allison Fuerte would not testify if indeed Brown was the killer. Oh well, she wouldn't so he wasn't going to lose sleep over it. All the men that died that day were nothing but scum any way. Good riddance! He for one was going to let sleeping dogs lie. He picked up the three reports and started to reread them.

CHAPTER 62

Pete made his living by thieving. It was quite a ludicrous business. He had never had a lack of money and if he liked something he had stolen he kept it. It was not in his mind about getting caught with the goods (so to speak) because he knew he was not going to be nailed for something so mundane as thievery. No what he was going to go down for was murder. Plain and simple, he knew it as well as he was breathing. It didn't bother him a bit. Oh no! In fact he couldn't wait! Pete had invested a lot of time, money and effort laying plans in case he was picked up.

In fact it was time to go and check on the final pieces of his grand adventure. He was dressed in a tight fitting sweat suit as he stepped out into the street. He smiled at the occasional pretty girl that caught his eye. He didn't have to turn around to know that they were checking him out from behind. Let them check, Pete wasn't interested in wasting his time on a casual dalliance with some no-brainer that was more interested in his physique then his mind. Not that he was queer! If Pete thought that a person harbored that thought in their mind . . . well, shame on them. Pete had used to feel the thrill of a Saturday night hunt, the stalking, moving in for the kill, and the climatic, animal sex. Not lovemaking, sex. Although for the most part the young women Pete had centered his attention on usually wanted to "party" with him, his ending to the evening was almost rape. They protested, sure they did (most of them) but once Pete's blood was raging there was no holding back. Maybe some of them wouldn't have even minded the rough, animal, she mauling he dished out, but once he was finished, then he was finished. He didn't care if they orgasm or not. He just rolled off, dressed and walked out.

All of that ended when he was beat by Major Brown. It was hard to believe that something so trivial in the problems of everyday living would do so much damage to a man that was as strong as Pete, but Pete was strong physically, not mentally. No one could destroy the lives he has over the year and remain immune to it. He wasn't trying to psychoanalyze himself; he knew that there was something wrong in his mental make up. But do you know what? He really didn't care. He liked who he was and he liked what he was doing. He didn't believe in God or the devil, he believed in himself.

He jogged around for a half an hour before he headed to a warehouse he had access to. The equipment he had stored there didn't take up much room and the manager was more then willing to pocket a little cash under the table for the trouble.

Pete went straight to the office to pay his inside man and to make sure he could go in with out worry. Everything went without a hitch and he went straight to his equipment.

To the average person, Pete's stuff would be considered trash. There was an assortment of used martial art vests, called Hogos. They were used in classrooms and tournament situations where contact could be expected to the body. They were ribbed in sections of four inches with an open back that fastened like a shoestring. An inch and a half thick, they could diversify a blow protecting the wearer to some degree. Of course some martial artists could penetrate the padding with powerful pinpoint blows, Pete was one of these, Major another.

Pete threw the top couple of Hogos to the floor revealing a great number of new ones. He had five used ones, (he had stolen them from the different tournaments he had entered,) and one hundred new ones. He had taken the new ones to a seamstress and had zippers placed in the back doing away with the tie straps. He didn't do that with the other five because he didn't care if they worked properly when the time came or not.

Pete checked and made sure all of his stuff was still there and untouched. It was, good thing or the manager of the warehouse would have felt terrible retribution. Putting everything back in its proper place, he walked out of the warehouse. He had made arrangements for an associate to pick up the crates for the next day. The Hogos needed some extra attention before they were ready to be used.

Now he had to go and see an old Vietnam Veteran that Pete had use of. He needed some material that only he could get for Pete. Things were coming together now. Pete had to be ready for anything and he would be soon, very soon.

CAHAPTER 63

Major woke up the next morning with a full bladder. Seth and Onna were already up and about, the cabin empty. Alone yet embarrassed, Major reached under the bed to retrieve the night pan. With a pleasurable groan, he emptied himself. Done, he slid the pan back under the bed. He was naked under the covers, feeling barren without at least his underwear for comfort. He was ready to call out when the cabin door opened and Seth came in carrying a pail of foamy, frothy warm milk that had came straight from the cow. He always kept a jersey cow for their milk and dairy products. Seconds later Onna came with a basket containing eggs, still warm from the hen's bottom.

"Good morning, Major." Seth eyes twinkled, "We will soon have a nourishing breakfast, yes?"

Major returned Seth's smile with one of his own. "Yes Sir!"

Onna scurried to the stove, stoking it to high heat. She quickly sliced potatoes and onions into the biggest cast iron skillet, Major had ever seen. Soon bacon and eggs were frying right beside them sending wonderful aromas wafting through the cabin. Coffee brewing completed the collage of enticing smells.

Seth went to a room off of the one Major was in and came back bearing Amish clothing.

"Onna is repairing your outfit she brought you here in. But you can wear these if you like." Seth looked Major over closely. "If you let your whiskers grow into a beard and we cut your hair in our fashion, maybe you can pass for one of us." He handed the clothes to Major. "You may stay here as long as you wish, but it would be better for all of us if you were Amish."

"Does anyone know I'm here?" Questioned Major.

"I told only the elders of our church. Usually we shun outsider's company. Once I explained how you saved Onna, they were much more lenient."

"Do they know who I am?"

"Yes."

Major's heart sank. "I got to get away from here! I am a wanted man!" He did not blame Seth for telling his people who he was, but he didn't want to place them in danger. He started to rise, forgetting his nakedness in his anxiety. The covers fell from him as he stood up. Onna stared then blushed as she quickly turned away from him, busying herself with the morning repast.

Major was extremely weak. Weaker then he had imagined he would be. The room spun around in a crazy and surreal spin, tossing him to the floor where he landed awkwardly on his knees. He again tried to rise using the bed to help him up. It was too much for him. He fell heavily across the bed, letting the old man cover him with the blankets.

"As long as I'm here, I'm am putting you in danger." He said quietly.

Seth didn't answer. He put the clothes at the foot of the bed and went to Onna and said something to her in a low whisper.

Onna shook her head in disagreement for a second, then after more insistent whispering from her grand father she turned and left the cabin.

Seth came back to the bed, pulling up a chair and producing tobacco for the pipes. "I sent Onna out for a moment. What we have to say is for men." He packed the pipes and after lighting a sliver of wood used it to start them.

"You can trust my people."

"It's not your people that I do not trust." Major said. "You know as well as I do that sooner or later someone will be knocking on your doors looking for me."

"How do they know you are here? Even you had no idea where you were. How will they find you?"

Major had not thought of that. He had been so used to being hounded by Breeler and his men that he had not realized that maybe the circle had been broken when he had stripped the detective of his man hood.

"Good point." Major relaxed. "What will your neighbors say if someone does come knocking?"

Seth pointed to the clothes at the bottom of the bed. "They will say that there are three Amish people in Seth Miller's family." He smiled, "Besides didn't you promise to teach Onna how to protect herself? That would give comfort to an old man without a lot of years left."

"When I get my strength back, I'll be happy to show her." Major reflected for a moment, "Seth?"

"Yes."

"I have to get a message to my wife. She knows I was injured. She has to be worried to death."

"What do you suggest?"

"Can you get to a telephone?"

"Yes."

"Will you call her and give her a message?"

"Yes."

Onna came back in the door toting an armload of kindling. She dropped the wood in the box and immediately went to the stove turning the potatoes that were sticking and checking the frying bacon.

"Grandfather, are we ready to eat?"

"A few more minutes, Onna."

"Okay grandfather."

Onna turned to the stove, removing the skillet from the heat then going to the home made cupboards to get plates and eating utensils. After seeing how little strength Major had she made up her mind to tend to him until he could safely leave the bed. This breakfast would be a start. Not that she would let him gorge himself, oh no! She would feed him several times throughout the day. That is how Onna would help him recuperate.

Major explained to Seth what he wanted said to his wife. He didn't want Seth or Onna (who ever called) to stay on the line in case they were tracing all calls. He asked for and received paper and pen. A turkey feather and what looked to be home made ink did the job. He handed the paper to Seth who glanced at it before he pocketed it.

Major was embarrassed. "I'm afraid I have no money to pay for this."

Seth looked at him strangely, the reached under the mattress. He threw the stack of bills on Major's chest. "This was with you the night Onna brought you here. It isn't yours?"

Major looked at the bills lying on his chest, "Yeah, it's mine I guess I forgot I had stopped to get it." Major looked at Seth remembering, "That was a extremely hectic night." He looked around, "Are my sais here too?"

Seth reached down to where he had pulled the stack of money from and handed the two sais to Major. "Yes they are."

Major took the sais, feeling their familiar weight. These sais had drank deeply of human blood and caused numerous deaths. Scenes from West Virginia flashed through his mind. Major closed his eyes and tried to dispel them from his thoughts, but failing. The weapons felt too . . . good, too . . . right in his hands. He shuddered and opened his eyes under the scrutiny of a concerned Seth.

"Are you alright?" He inquired.

Major didn't know how to answer. Sure his physical body would heal, but what about his soul? When he was after Brok he didn't care if he lived or died, just as long as he could get his son out safely. Well his son was safe, his wife was happy and he was going to hell.

He flipped the sais over handles toward Seth. "I would appreciate it if you would get rid of these for me."

Seth reluctantly took the weapons and put them under the bed. "I will do that for you."

"Thank you!' Major said feeling somehow relieved.

Onna came over with a tray made up for Major.

"Grandfather please say the prayer. The food will get cold."

Seth, Major and Onna bowed their heads and listened to the old man thank God. After the "Amen" Onna placed the tray on Major's lap and once again began to feed him. This time Major refused help.

"Thank you, Onna, but I must start helping myself."

"But I don't mind . . ."

"I do." Interrupted Major. "I have to start building my body up. This is the start."

Onna made small talk about the farm as they ate, including Major in the conversation as much as she could. Major listened and nodded at the right times smiled when he should of but his mind was till far away. Where would he go after he recovered?"

Onna fed him throughout the day and by evening he was taking tentative steps throughout the cabin. He was dressed in her dead father's clothing and almost looked the part of an Amish man. Like her grandfather had said, "Let the whiskers grow."

The next morning Onna and Seth started out early towards town. Major wanted them to call Jill early so they would be sure to catch her at home. He said to stay on the phone only thirty seconds no matter what. Seth felt in his pocket for the umpteenth time making sure he had the message. They came to a telephone that was place low enough to make a call from a car and pulled up to it.

If anyone would have drove by that morning, they would have been treated to a sight they probably never seen before. An Amish girl in a black buggy pulled by a horse making a phone call on a pay telephone. Now that would have been one for the books.

Onna placed the coins in the slot like Major told her to do then dialed the numbers on the paper. She never had used a telephone before and was actually kind of excited. Ring . . . Ring . . . Ring . . . Ring . . . the phone was picked up.

CHAPTER 64

The jangling of the phone jolted Jill awake. She glanced at the clock; seven a.m. quickly she threw the covers off her and jumped to the phone. She fumbled for a second then raised the receiver to her ear.

"Hello?" She was hoping it was Major, but the voice was that of a woman.

"Jill Brown?"

"Yes." Jill thought it sounded like a telemarketer, if it was; well . . . she wasn't going to be very polite at seven o'clock in the morning.

"I have a message for you, please listen carefully.'

"Is it from Major?"

"Time is short, please do not interrupt." Onna cleared her throat and her voice dropped a couple of octaves. "Recovering from wound, miss you and Brok, will be in touch when healthy again, don't worry, I'm safe, I love you both." Without another word the Amish girl replaced the telephone in its cradle.

"Let's go home grandfather."

Seth shook the reins and clucked to his horse. Soon they were pulling into the lane that led to the farm house."

"Go check on Major," said Seth, "I will take care of the horse and buggy."

Onna entered the cabin and started on her daily chores after making sure the needs of Major were met.

Click, then a dial tone, the woman had hung up before she could say a word. Frustrated, Jill banged the phone down. She had been waiting for this call for four days now and when she got it she didn't get to talk. Major was still out there somewhere not knowing that he was free to come home. Not knowing that all of the charges that he thought were pending against him were so much fluff in the wind. She went to the bathroom, brushed her teeth and did her toiletry. She stared in the mirror for a long minute. Criminetly, was that a wrinkle in the corner of her eyes? Yes, there was. Oh man, a little gray on top? All this worry was getting to her. Well, thank you Major! As soon as she voiced that thought in her mind, she felt ashamed. Major had looked like he had aged twenty years that night he fought Breeler

"This damn business is killing us all. "She said aloud. She felt Sensei pawing at her leg and she looked down. "Sooner or late Major will come to me, Sensei. Then I'll never let him go!" (Little did she know how wrong that thought was.)

She left the bathroom and went downstairs to the phone there. Jill lowered herself in her chair, sitting on her legs. Sensei took his position at her feet. She dialed Phil's number in South Carolina and listened to it ring. After ten of them she was about to hang up when Phil answered

Jill gave him the meager information she had and both of them were truly blessed that they knew Major was safe and being tended to. She promised to call if she had any more information. After a couple more minutes of trivial conversation, they hung up. She called the Sheriffs department and asked for Jeff Conner. Jill was put on hold, (she hated that with a passion) for a minute or two before Jeff Conner answered.

"I received a message from Major this morning." Jill said.

"Great! Is he okay?"

"Well yes. I guess so. A woman called and told me that everything was okay."

"Well when he comes to you, remember I need to see him."

"Gee, Jeff, Major thinks that you people still want him on charges. He's not coming in at this time. He's going to contact me later."

"You don't know where he's at? No idea?"

"None."

"Okay, at least you know he's somewhere safe. If you hear anything let me know."

"Alright, thanks." Jill hung up.

Still frustrated she went up to Broks room and sat in the rocking chair. She rocked gently as she watched Brok breath in and out. Patience . . . Patience . . . Patience.

CHAPTER 65

D etective Jeff Conner sat at his desk and thought of his old friend Major Brown. Although they were never what he considered close pals when they were in High School, they had participated in sports together. Jeff liked major and knew him for what he was, a good man. Unfortunately, he became involved in Detective Richard Breeler's child napping scheme when his son had been taken. Breeler had been an arrogant man thinking he had nothing to worry about from the mild mannered Brown, but evidently he had turned into a superman. Sure, there wasn't any proof that Brown had been involved in the murders. Sure, a good defense lawyer would have shredded anything the State had as evidence on the killings and sure, Conner had no doubts that Brown did it. Conner liked to think that what happened in West Virginia would have been done by him if the situation were reversed. What he had told Jill the day before was true. He had told the grand jury and the prosecutor that they had nothing on Brown. Of course, the Prosecutor had insisted they file charges against Brown for assaulting an officer of the law. Conner had laughed in his face, almost losing control and braying into the suddenly red faced so-called guardian of the people. What an ass! If the public knew how many cases this man has blown and how many innocent people he had locked up they would have impeached him He was an egotistical, pompous, glory seeking little man who lived his whole life as a lie. No, the biggest concern Conner had at this point was he hoped that since Major didn't know he was cleared, he would not do something stupid and against the law.

He leaned forward, elbows on his desk, head in his hands. He studied a report on two more torture murders. They have been going on around the state for close to eight years now. Usually bums and winos were the victims, but his time the latest find had been two average citizens. They had died hard. Of course all of the victims throughout the years had not been given the luxury of a swift and merciful death. They had been slowly stripped of their humanity and many of their body parts to boot. They had questioned the owner-operators of the U-Store-It building and pretty much had the same description every time.

Big man, black hair, not so tall, no more then six feet, extremely well built. Always wore sunglasses. No distinguishing marks or tattoos.

Not a lot to go on, but better then nothing. Sooner or later they would catch him. Then maybe (Old Sparky) would light up after all these years of disuse. Trouble was, how many more would die before they caught up with this low life? Conner didn't know, but even he would have been surprised to know how many lives would be destroyed before they brought him down.

CHAPTER 66

Time passed slowly to Major while his body regained its vitality. Slowly his appetite increased and soon he was gorging himself at every meal. He had bought an occasional loaf of bread or a pie or two from stands that the Amish set up at different locations throughout his county, but he had never experienced the full depth of their cooking before. What was really great about the whole deal was everything was home made.

Major ate so much that it didn't take long to regain the weight he had lost in his adventures. He was helping out around the farm more and more as he rebuilt his strength back to where it belonged, so he wasn't overly concerned about getting fat or soft.

He started by walking slowly and stiffly to the hen house to gather eggs and taking them to the cabin. It took him so long that first morning that Onna came to look for him. She was sure that he had fallen and hurt himself. He had spent the rest of that day sitting in the rocking chair, smoking a pipe and resting. The next morning he again made the trek to the hen house, bringing back fifteen jumbo brown eggs in which twelve of them were double yoked.

Soon he was bringing in wood for the stove, happy to be making some type of contribution to Seth's household.

At night Seth read from the Bible and afterwards they discussed what had been said. It was interesting to all three of them on how their opposite life styles had cause the interpretations to be different from each other. Major enjoyed these nightly readings immensely. He had forgotten how much he liked to hear the stories from the Bible. These nightly meetings and discussions reminded him of his childhood. His mother always read from the Bible. Major read some off and on throughout his adulthood, but not as much as he should have.

Afterwards, he and Seth would smoke a pipe out on the porch of the cabin, content to sit and puff, not talking but feeling comfortable with each other in the silence of the evenings.

Soon Major was strong enough to do more arduous chores. He cut wood, split and stacked it. It took a lot of wood throughout the year to provide heat for the cabin and fuel for the oven. It was a chore that Major relished, It pumped blood throughout his body and he grew stronger. He helped scythe down hay and then stack it (all by hand) in great piles in the field. He remembered his Father talking about doing it that way back in the "Good old days." It was hot sweaty work but Major enjoyed it. It took his mind away from his troubles. Afterwards a swim in the pond took care of the "itches."

He helped Onna in the vegetable garden. Weeding, hoeing and caring for the plants that were so vital to the survival of the family. Onna "put up" all the extra vegetables she could. Those they didn't eat or can, they sold in a produce stand along the road. It brought in the extra money they used for medicine or other sundries they couldn't produce or make from their farm.

He helped Seth clean the barn out of the accumulated manure and helped haul it to the garden where it returned to the earth renewing the soil.

He learned to cut the seed out of pigs, horses and cattle. What he picked up from Seth would probably never be used by Major yet it was an experience that he never would have had under the circumstances. Then again, if Major didn't get his life straightened out, well . . . maybe he could use this knowledge to create a new life elsewhere.

He helped butcher chickens that were constantly being renewed by broody hens and an extremely proud (or maybe cocky) rooster, which thought the whole barnyard was his private domain. The big fowl had snuck up behind Major one morning after he had gathered the eggs and had been walking back to the cabin lost in thought. He had spurred him in the calf of his leg and flopped him with his strong wings. Major had dropped the basket of eggs, breaking over half of them. He wheeled around so quickly the rooster did not have a chance to run, peep or throw another spur. A lightning fast right hand had taken it around the neck causing the bird to emit a startled "squawk!! Major punted the bird a good fifteen feet before it could catch itself with it's wings, gliding to the ground. Major laughed so long and so loud that Seth and Onna had come out to see what had tickled him so. It took a while to get it out, but through wheezing, choking bits of laughter he had finally told them what had happened. Seth and Onna both laughed and if they had a chance would have loved to have seen it. After that Major had to watch his back when he went to gather the eggs. The rooster wouldn't risk a frontal attack, but thought nothing about taking him from behind. It was a game between the two A simplistic battle against two warriors. Seth said he would be glad to make a soup out of the tough old bird, but Major had refused, saying that it didn't bother him in the least bit. To tell the truth Major enjoyed the little game of warfare, and he thought the rooster did too.

It was over two weeks since Onna had brought Major to their home. Two weeks that returned life to Major's depleted body and soul. Mentally he had not felt this good since before Brok had been taken. Physically, he had a little ways to go. The wounds were basically healed over, yet still were tender. Each day they knitted together growing flesh and scar tissue to cover the entry and exit wounds. Bruises faded then disappeared.

It was on a Monday night after the chores were done the Bible read, discussions over and dinner plates and items put away that Major approached Seth about teaching Onna self defense.

"You wish to teach Onna martial arts?" Asked Seth.

"No. Self defense. To learn the art of karate would take years. Years that I don't have."

Seth puffed on his pipe for a time considering.

"When will you start?"

"If I have your permission, then it will be tomorrow evening."

Again a pause as Seth deliberated.

"Will I be able to watch?"

"You are more then welcome."

"Tomorrow evening then."

Amiably, they sat on the porch and smoked their pipes.

CHAPTER 67

It was a long two weeks for Jill. She never received another message from Major and she had stopped waiting around the phone. She was smart enough to know that sooner or later Major would contact her. She spent those two lonely weeks playing with Brok and working out. She had forgotten how gratifying it was to teach the martial arts. The classes had grown under her tutelage and after the last class a student had told her how much he had liked her teaching.

Brok had started to learn more and more and she would test him for his tenth yellow belt next week. He had Major's athleticism and it looked like he was going to have her family's size. A lethal combination when he grew older.

But ohhh how she missed her husband. She could not help but worry about him. If only she could get a message to him. She could have him home again if he knew that he was not a wanted man.

Breeler had been indicted on Federal charges for kidnapping and running an illegal child adoption ring. Jeff Conner said he was facing twenty years in a Federal penitentiary.

She went into the kitchen and made herself a sandwich out of homegrown tomatoes (can't beat them) and a peanut butter and jelly sandwich for Brok. They went out on the front porch with the sandwiches and a couple of Pepsis to watch the traffic go by. They ate slowly under the watchful eyes of Sensei, who hoped they would remember he was there. Of course Brok ate half of his peanut butter and jelly before he accidentally dropped it to the floor. Sensei had it scarfed up almost before it hit. That had brought a rare smile to her face and a frown to Broks. She went to the kitchen and pacified him with a Swiss Miss cake. They were a little too sweet for Jill, but just right for a little boy like Brok.

She hated to admit it but she was getting along just fine without her wayward husband. She missed him sure but she was managing very nicely without him, thank you.

A car went whizzing by blowing its horn at the pair. Jill and Brok waved automatically although it had went by so quickly they didn't recognize the occupants.

Soon it would be Brok's bedtime and then she would be sitting alone again. Maybe tonight she would watch a little television. Usually she would work out a little bit more, but Jill was in excellent shape. She noticed men checking her out when she was shopping. It made her feel good but she only wanted Major. She was toned and probably the best shape of her life. She had always been a "looker", but now thanks to her nightly workouts and the martial arts training she was a knock out. For some odd reason call it premonition or whatever, she had a terrible feeling she needed to be ready for . . . something.

Something in her mind was telling her she had to be ready for . . . for what? Jill didn't know, but she was ready. More then ready, willing.

Willing? Yes that was the word. Jill was willing and waiting for something to happen. Something that would not only shake her and Major's world, but would send tremors throughout the whole United States and maybe beyond.

CHAPTER 68

Pete had met with the former soldier who had spent a year in Vietnam before he was discharged for dealing in black market items. He had been lucky he wasn't sentenced to spend time in a military prison, but he had saved his squad three times in battle and his commanding officer had stood up for him. He had been dismissed from the army but maintained contact with the unsavory friends he had accumulated in his shady dealings.

It was through these friends he was able to obtain the materials that his massive buddy needed.

C-4 and the caps to set them off plus a transmitter that could be set to different frequencies. He had gotten enough to blow up a whole town if he wanted to, (and a little extra for himself. The vet wasn't entirely in his right mind.) It had cost quite a bit of jack, but Pete seemed to be very well heeled. Funny thing about C-4, without a cap or current to set if off, it was entirely benign. You could eat it, kick it, roll it in a ball, anything you wanted to do with it, simply silly putty. Put a charge to it though and watch out, watch the Rambo movies or the Norris movies and see what it could do.

It never occurred to the vet to ask what Pete wanted to do with the stuff. Sure, he and Pete were friends, well not friends, they needed each other for different reason but the vet was very, very frightened of the man. There was something wrong with him. He looked at people like they were snakes to be eradicated from the earth.

The former soldier had the C-4 crated in preparation to taking to where Pete wanted it. All he needed was a location and he would take it there. He would be glad to get rid of it.

A hard rap on the door directed his attention to it.

"Who is it?" He asked.

"Pete."

The vet walked away from his workbench and opened the door. He didn't have locks on the door; there was nothing in his desolate room to interest even the most desperate thief.

"C'mon in, Pete. I got what you wanted."

A rare grin lit up the massive man's face. It made his usually stoic face quite handsome.

"Good deal! Let's get it out of here." Pete stared hard at his rogue friend. "You want to make some beer money?"

"Yeah, sure, okay let's go."

Pete picked up the small crate, slinging it over his shoulder and grabbed the satchel containing the detonators.

The vet opened the door for him then shut it as they both left the room.

They put the C-4 and caps in the trunk of Pete's car and then made a circle of the town, weaving in and out of main streets and side streets. Making random stops at different stores and gas stations Pete was soon satisfied that no one was following them. Not that it mattered. Neither he nor the vet would have recognized an experienced tail anyway. But Pete felt better for it.

They arrived at one of Pete's rented U-Store-It cubicles an hour and a half later. Together they unloaded the material and after Pete unlocked the door they entered. He had the Hogos on a table inside and he put them on the floor so they could get the C-4 out of its container. He looked at it for a long minute. Then once again a big smile broke across his features.

"This is going to be a blast!" He said. "A big blast!"

He retrieved a Hogo from the floor and spread it out on the table inside of the protector up. He took a utility knife from a small toolbox from under the table and opened it.

"Pay attention!" He told the vet. "I'm only going to show you once what I want and you'd better do it right."

The vet paid real close attention. He definitely didn't want to upset old Pete Sandford, no sir, not him.

Pete slit one of the ribbed sections of the hogo the part that protected the diaphragm area. He unwrapped a brick of the explosive and pulled a fist-sized chunk off. (A normal fist, not Pete's ham sized fist.) He flattened it, rolling it in his hand until he had a long smooth snake like roll of it. He carefully fished it inside the slit he had made. He added a detonator cap and carefully sealed the slit with good old duct tape. He had checked the frequency of the detonator and in black magic marker wrote it on the front and back of the hogo.

"Each one of these detonators is on a different frequency. That way if I only want to blow up one at a time I can." Pete explained.

"I'll set each one so I can also detonate them in a continuous cycle, just by upgrading to maximum setting and hitting the button. That'll set off all the charges. Or just like tuning a radio, I can dial, hmmm, let's say one-oh-one point seven. I put that number on the indicator then hit the button, and then only that cap will detonate. Pretty cool, huh?"

"Pretty cool!" Agreed the vet.

After Pete set the hogo up with the C-4 and detonating cap he turned it over and showed the vet a small device located on the zipper.

"Now this here is a safety device."

"Safety device?"

"Yeah! A safety device for me." Pete sneered. He waited for a comment from the vet and when he realized that he wasn't going to ask any more questions he volunteered the information.

"Once the zipper clasp is pulled over top of it, the metal activates this switch. It's also set to the frequency of the caps. If someone tries to take the hogo off after it's been zipped up it will set the explosives off."

"Pretty cool." Said the vet. Nervous sweat poured down his face, he sure could us a drink. He didn't like the way Pete was sharing all of this information. The vet's mind stuttered over this. Could Pete be thinking about terminating their partnership? Why else would he be explaining something like this to a broken down alcoholic, dope smoking old man like him? Suddenly the vet wished he were anywhere but here. He picked up a hogo and tried to slit it the way Pete did the first one, but his hands were trembling too bad.

"Easy does it there old boy." Said Pete. "I'm going to need your help on this and I don't want any foul ups. Get me?"

The vet stared at Pete. "Is that all? You need me to help you? Is that why you're telling me all this?"

Pete laughed. "Yeah! Why were you afraid I was going to kill you or something? Ahhh, we're partners, you and me. I need your help. Not just on this, but on a couple of other things too."

The vet let out a relieved whoosh of air. "Anything you want, Pete! Anything you want!"

What I want is to get these hogos done. Let's get busy."

Pet and the vet spent the next twelve hours setting up the explosive protectors. At least that part was done, but now the vet was wondering what other kind of help the big man needed.

CHAPTER 69

"No Onna, that's not the way I showed you!" Explained a patient Major. "The thumb has to be in the middle of the hand in order to get enough leverage."

Onna moved her grip from his wrist and positioned it the way Major told her. With a quick flip she made him lose the grasp he had on her blouse top.

"Yeah, that's the way it's done, but you have to do it right every time."

Major grabbed her blouse, "Do it again?"

Onna reached across her body and grasped his hand in the correct hold, twisting it hard downward.

"Oww! Onna! Take it easy! You can really hurt me doing it that hard!"

"Sorry!" Onna tried to look contrite, but couldn't quite conceal the pleasure of doing the move correctly. She had wanted to learn how to do everything about the martial arts and she was an excellent pupil. The only problem was Major didn't have the time necessary to give her profiency at the art. He started out showing her simple self defense moves that although very basic and easily done by the young woman were also deadly.

He taught her how to get out of choke-holds, grabs from behind and the classic schoolyard hold, where they grab you by the head so they can punch you with the other hand. Simple stuff, sure, but Onna had never seen any of it and even the most basic move thrilled her. The techniques he showed her were lethal. Depending on the angle of the hand or the placement of the blow, it could be fatal to an antagonist. Major did not teach his martial arts student lethal blow until they were near black belt level, however in this case he was more then willing to show the young lady how to destroy an opponent.

He had been working with Onna for a week, teaching her different defenses for different types of attacks. He kept them simple and Onna picked them up very quickly.

He didn't show her all of Tae Kwon Do's fancy kicks she didn't need them. The only one he was trying to have her perfect was the snapping front kick. That way she could use either her foot or her shinbone on the aggressor's groin or knee area.

Although Major never mentioned it, he noticed Seth covertly watching the nightly sessions. Major knew the old man was uncomfortable about Onna learning such deadly techniques, but he knew that Seth would never stop the practices after what had nearly happened to Onna the night she brought Major under their roof. A fortuitous event for all involved. It had given him the opportunity to heal and the chance to pay them back in some way.

Major concentrated on what he was showing Onna, not seeing the small group of people that came to the cabin he knew that Seth had left his usual position, but noticed it only with a passing thought. He had so much work to do with Onna. He was sure she could defend herself against someone her size, maybe a bit bigger, but he wanted her capable of protecting herself against a much larger person. That required perfection in almost every nuance of a move.

"Do it again, Onna!" He knew that she was pleased that she could break free of him on most of the moves, but that wasn't good enough. He usually spent an hour with her pushing her memory for the holds and her instinct on when to use them. Finally Major called a halt to the class for the evening, he turned to go and take a swim in the pond, but Seth stopped him with a call.

"Mister Brown."

Major turned and looked inquiring at Seth, he had not been called "Mister Brown" since the night he awoke.

"Yes, Sir?" Major saw that Seth had company and realized the reason for the formality.

"Could you spare a minute for us, please?" Seth asked.

"Yes Sir." Major walked to the small group noticing the four young girls that peered out from behind the stern featured men.

Major self conscious of his sparse beard, rubbed his chin and waited.

The four men looked at each other before one of them stepped forward.

"My name is Olin Zimmer." He held out his hand.

"Pleased to meet 'cha." Major shook hands then stood back, silent.

Embarrassed the Amish man continued.

"Seth has told us of you. He told us you are teaching Onna to be able to protect herself.

"Yes, that's true."

"Our daughters . . ." He faltered, lost for words for a second, "our daughters were placed in a situation where they needed to be able to protect themselves, but couldn't."

Major knew that these young girls had to be the ones assaulted by the three men he had stopped from raping Onna. Tactfully, he didn't say anything that could be construed as uncaring or insulting.

"I am aware of the circumstances." He said quietly.

Again the eyes of the men flitted and met each other. Words passed unspoken between the four men. Zimmer turned to Major and met his eyes and never wavered.

"Could you help our daughters as you are helping Onna?" Head held high, stance and bearing never betraying the Amish man's discomfort of asking something so important from an "outsider." Only Major whose eyes were locked with his could see the pleading that was born from agony of his soul. Without disengaging the intense gaze Major spoke, "Onna, would you and the young ladies go to the cabin and get my pipe and tobacco please?"

Onna knew that Major wanted to speak to the men alone. She motioned to the girls and somberly went to the cabin. Once they were out of earshot. Major let his eyes pierce each of the men.

"I know who the men are that hurt your daughters. I don't know their names, but I will know them when I see them again.

"Yes, we know them by sight, if not by name."

"Do you wish me to exact revenge for you?" Major hoped not, but made the offer willingly.

"Revenge is a two bladed sword, no, Mister Brown. As much as we would like to see these young men twist in the wind, we do not wish harm to them."

"Then tell me what you want."

"Seth has been telling us that you are training Onna in self defense."

"Yes."

"We want the same opportunity for ours."

Major pursed his lips and thought. He had wanted to be leaving in a week or so. If he stayed to help these men's daughters it would be two weeks. He wanted to go to Jill and Brok, just to hold them one more time. Damn it! He wanted his life back! The Amish stood back and watched the different emotions cross Major's face somewhat taken aback at the storm clouds that appeared.

"Well," Major thought, "I can't have my life back, I'll help them with theirs."

"I'll help them."

"Thank you! Thank you very much!"

"I don't know if you'll thank me if they use it on one of your own." Major sighed. "Have them here tomorrow evening around seven o'clock.

"They will be here." The men turned and started away. Onna and the girls who have been watching from a distance came up to the group. She handed Major his smoking equipment and all three silently watched the group climb into their individual buggies and ride away.

"Are you going to help them?" Asked Onna.

Major took his time loading the pipe, lighting it with a stick match. "Yes."

"They will be happy."

"I'm glad."

Together Major, Seth and Onna walked to the cabin all lost in thought of things to come.

CHAPTER 70

Pete finished reading the local newspaper, throwing it on the floor. Every Saturday, wedding and engagement announcements were listed in it, along with pictures of blushing brides and horny grooms. Pete wasn't interested in that, he got the paper for the engagement pieces.

"Mr. and Mrs. So and So are proud to announce . . ." Big deal! Pete figured they had been doing the horizontal bop anyway, why would a guy give up his freedom for something he was getting for nothing?

He had his black bound notebook lying on the table beside him. He kept notes where all area weddings were to be located at. Not that he was interested in going to them, oh no, he wanted the dates of the rites. He knew where there were weddings; there would be wedding receptions. That is what he wanted to know.

He knew where all the reception halls were located at and how many people it would hold. Usually on Saturdays he would drive around and check out the ones he had considered an ideal place for his plans. There were several that suited his purpose and he made it a ritual to ride past them and see how the parking lots were being used. One in particular located just across the Stark County line in Tuscarawas County appealed to Pete.

It was a big rectangular building with front and back doors, no side doors and no windows. It looked like a shell building that had been converted to a meeting or reception hall. Bingo players and other various functions frequented it throughout the week. But every Saturday evening you could count on a wedding reception. It was the ideal place for the purpose that he had in mind. If Pete had the chance it would be the place he wanted to put his plans in motion.

He could chain the back door shut and not have to worry about being surprised by anyone trying to come in that way. It was big enough to hold a couple of hundred people and still give him plenty of room for action. The front had a fairly large grassy area that extended out towards the road seventy feet away from the door. Yes, when the time came, Pete would do his best to take this hall and use it for his nefarious plot.

He left the table going to the refrigerator for a beer. Everything that was needed for his plan was ready except for one detail. He carried the beer back to the table and picked up a pager he had purchased earlier. He would look up the vet today and give it to him He hated to rely n the old boozer, his drunken father had proven to him that alcoholics were very unreliable, but the vet was very important to his success. When all hell broke loose he had to have his help. Pete could probably handle everything but he needed some one to watch his back and to toady any small tasks that might arise.

The explosive ridden hogos were ready and stored in the trunk of an old beater car he had purchased. It was parked in a garage that was rented to him. He had enough brains to know that he probably wouldn't be able to use his own auto when the time came. He bought the car using an alias, giving him the chance to get to one of the halls when the time arose.

It had taken a lot of time and effort to get all of the equipment that was so essential to his plan. Now he had everything together and ready to go. He went over and over his ideas, making sure there was no weak links that would derail him before he had a chance to gain his revenge on Mister Major Brown.

Swigging the beer he glanced down at the paper that was lying on the floor. A caption caught his eye causing him to pick the front page up for closer perusal.

"Capture imminent for U-Store-It Serial Killer." It proclaimed. Pete read the article and laughed. It stated that various clues left at the scene of the double murder brought the police closer to the deranged killer. Pete started to laugh again, then stopped.

The article gave him an idea. Maybe he should leave some clues the next time he performed his medieval torture on his victim. That way he could perhaps have a time frame to work with. He definitely did not want to be captured before he had a chance to implement everything he strived for. In fact, Pete thought it was an excellent idea! He wasn't going to write his name in blood for the cops, but a game of cat and mouse appealed to his baser nature.

"Cool idea!" He said aloud. He would have to think it over on how he would proceed, but he thought that with in the next two Saturdays D-Day would be one of them.

He polished off the beer, clinked the bottle in the trash and went to look for the vet. As much as he hated to admit it, he needed the old drunk.

CHAPTER 71

Jeff Conner had read the same article that Pete Sandford had read. He sat at his desk, fingers forming a tee-pee and thought for a minute. Maybe the Stark County detectives found something he was unaware of. He looked at his telephone and decided to place a call to one of his friends on the force. He looked up the number and dialed. He talked to the detective for a few minutes before he replaced the receiver. Just as he suspected, they had no clues except for the general description of the man. The press had been hounding them for something to soothe a worried public and the department had thrown them a few general tidbits. Jeff figured the closest thing they had to a clue were the last two men they had discovered. They did not fit the usual victims that the killer generally prayed upon. That had to be their starting point. Why had he changed his methods? If he could find that out then they would have the lead they so desperately needed. People that the young man worked with said he had planned to go to a strip tease joint that evening and Jeff planned on paying a "unofficial" visit there that night. He was sure the Stark County squad had followed up on that, but being the methodical person he was, he wanted to make sure there was nothing left to chance.

He didn't particularly relish going to a strip tease bar, these places disillusioned him, but he couldn't expect the killer to come into his office and pull up a chair. Jeff laughed. It would sure make his job easier.

It seemed that every day something new was crossing his desk, threatening to divide his attention and therefore weakening his grasp of the serial killer's importance.

Breeler's case for example, he was being arraigned next week, Monday, he thought, and part of his force was still gathering up evidence that would damn him to what would be close to life in prison. If the populace knew that he was an ex-cop and they would of course, then his twenty years to life would be a death sentence. Oh well, that's Breeler's look out, not his.

His mind wandered to Major Brown. He was still missing. Jeff was pretty sure he was holed up in Amish Country somewhere, but he didn't have the manpower to spare for a search.

As much as he would like to see Major and his family reunited he was hand cuffed, so to speak.

Thinking of the Amish, Jeff knew there was a problem there too. The three men that he had being watched were up to no good somewhere in the close knit community. He still had no idea what was going on, but sooner or later he would find out. When he did he would sit down hard on them. The Amish were citizens of America and of his district and were due the protection that he was more then glad to provide, if they would only let him.

Add these problems with the murders of passion, thefts and other criminal activity then Jeff had more then a full slate to contend with. All crimes were important to the victims, but he and his department could only do so much. It would help if the prosecutor's office were more adept at their job. More often then not, alleged criminals were being released after the head buffoon botched their cases. No matter, Jeff's job was to apprehend the perpetrators not to prosecute them. Something would break soon. He just hoped his department would he up to the task when it did.

CHAPTER 72

Major was in Heaven. He was using an old cane pole with a cork bobber. His stringer was full of hand sized blue gills. He, Seth and Onna had decided to take the day off and fish. Major's help around the farm put the Amish ahead of their work, thereby giving them more leisure time then they normally would have had.

The cork dipped below the surface of the water and again Major set the hook on the slab fish. The limberness of the cane pole made the fight the bluegill put up seem so much more ferocious. Onna and Seth save all the fish they caught. The little ones were ground up and made into fish patties. The others were filleted or cooked whole. You had to be careful of the bones, but you got all of the flesh.

Major loved to eat bluegill. Some people swore that walleye or bass were the best eating, but Major disagreed. He would take the smaller fish over any other game fish any time he had a choice.

He brought the struggling bluegill into shore and added it to the heavy stringer. He replaced the bait with a broken piece of night crawler and flipped the line back into the water. They would have a good feed tonight.

He sat back and let the sun warm his face. He looked like an Amish man now. He dressed like them, right down to the straw hat, his reddish blonde beard although straggly, concealed his features well. If anyone chanced upon them they looked like a family on an outing.

Onna and the four girls had learned their lessons well. Even though Onna had a week on the others they had picked the self-defense up very quickly. Major thought their experiences made them hungry for the knowledge. He knew they were capable of defending themselves, but he didn't know if they could over come generations of meekness in order to damage another living person. But then again, he remembered what Onna did the night she was almost raped, so maybe he shouldn't worry about what they would or would not do.

Right now the only worry he had was the cork that was starting to bob again.

Today was Saturday. Tomorrow, they would attend church and have a day of rest. Seth said Monday they would be going to the Sugarcreek livestock sale. He could pick up some extra cash money by helping at the sale. Major had tried again to pay him out of the ten grand he had with him, but Seth had politely but firmly refused. Major wouldn't offer again. The old man had pride and he would do nothing to offend him. Major counted him as a true friend.

Onna, though, was an enigma. She was always doting on Major. If he didn't know better, he would say she had a crush on him. It didn't seem to matter to her that he was more then twice her age and married. Major made it a point to never be alone with her. He liked her a lot, but his heart belonged to Jill.

Thinking about his wife took a little joy from the day. Even though it was for the best, Major felt as if he was deserting her and Brok. He was planning on leaving Seth and Onna by next Saturday and one way or the other he was going to see his family before he left the area. He had not tried to get in touch with her since the initial phone call, but he knew she would understand. Major knew now that he could never spend time in jail. Never!!! He would die first. She would be better off without him anyway. He could never forget the look in her eyes when she learned he was the "Butcher of Macsville."

The cork went under again and Major's dark reflections were broken by the frantic efforts of the fish trying to get off the hook.

They fished an hour more before Seth was satisfied with the take. Seth and Major cleaned them while Onna prepared them for their supper. Fried potatoes and fish were the main fare, but both of the men felt like kings as they stuffed themselves.

Later in the evening Major drew Seth aside.

"I'll be leaving soon."

"Yes, I knew the time would come." Said Seth. "When are you planning to go?"

"I hope to be gone by next Saturday, if you don't mind my company for another week."

"You are more than welcome." Seth didn't even attempt to tell him that he considered Major as family by now. He could never replace his dead son, but he had enough love to accept Major as one.

"You will be missed greatly." Said a miserable Seth.

"Yes, I too will be sad." Major looked the old man in the eyes. "You will see me again."

"If you are not dead, or in jail." Said Seth.

"I might be dead, but I won't be in jail." A grim Major said with conviction. "I won't be tethered."

"Well, we have another week, Monday we will go to the sale. Did I ever tell you about the homemade vanilla ice cream sold there?"

Major laughed, dispelling the gloomy atmosphere. "No."

"It is heavenly, when you get some ask for strawberry topping."

"It is homemade too?"

"Oh yes, it must be tasted to be believed."

"Then I will make sure I eat some."

Onna came out on the porch wiping her hands on her apron.

"What is so serious that your faces are sad?"

"Just talking about ice cream, Onna. I can't wait to try some."

"Oh yes! The restaurant in the sale barn has excellent food. You will have to have a hamburger with the works."

"I believe I will try it, Onna. I like good food as you can tell!"

Major laughed and patted his stomach. He was pleasantly bloated from the huge amount of fish and potatoes he had consumed.

Seth and Major loaded their pipes and smoked contently. They watched the rooster strut around his hens as it viewed the barnyard as his domain. The rooster and Major still fought with each other, but the bird was slowing the warfare down a little. It was getting tired of Major's foot up its rear end.

The two men and Onna sat on the porch and watched the sunset. If Major had his family with him he would have been happy. But they weren't with him. Homesickness swept over him like a rain cloud blocking the sun on a hot day. He was leaving here next Saturday, that was true, but he was going home. He had to see Jill. He wanted to hold her again, make love to her and spend time telling her how much he loved her.

He would go to her and Brok to say goodbye. That was all that was left to do now. He figured on heading north. Probably Canada, if he could get across the border. He would have to start a new life; his old one was in tatters, a new name and endless possibilities. It all started next Saturday.

CHAPTER 73

Jeff Conner sat at a back table in the dark and seedy bar. Tired dancers flaunted their nakedness trying to inspire jaded old men and lusty college boys to depart from some of the dollar bills clenched in sweaty hands.

He shifted his attention to the pool table located at the rear of the bar. There was only a couple of players and judging by how they ignored the dancers, they were regulars.

Jeff picked up his long necked beer bottle and strolled back to the slate topped tables. He watched them play a couple of games, not saying a word. They were both excellent shots and Jeff enjoyed watching the competition between the two. The two men knew he was there, but didn't acknowledge him. After a while he moved a bit closer to them.

"You guys are pretty good."

The one racking the balls looked up. "Thanks. We play quite a bit."

"Yeah! It shows."

The other player was chalking his cue, making sure the tip was well covered with blue powder. He eyed Jeff up and down before he spoke.

"You're a cop." It was a statement, not a question.

"Off duty."

"Still a cop."

"Yeah."

"What are you doing here? I've been watching you. You're not the type for this kind of place."

"I heard this was where the guy who was murdered last week played at."

The two men looked at each other. The racker picked up the triangular holder and stepped back. Crack! The sound of a hard cue ball breaking the ordered balls into streaking colors of speed sounded loud to Jeff.

The man who broke moved from the table. No balls dropped into any of the pockets and he gave way for the racker's turn.

"Yeah, so what?" He asked.

"Thought maybe you could tell me if you were in here that night."

"Nope, I wasn't."

Jeff looked at the shooter. "How about you?"

"No."

Disappointed, Jeff pulled a twenty from the inside pocket of his suit jacket. He laid it on the railing of the table. "Thanks anyway." He turned to go; he was tired of this hole, when one of the men spoke.

"I said I wasn't here, not that I didn't know what happened."

Jeff turned back. "What happened?"

"The dude stiffed the big boy he was shooting with for a twenty."

"Know this big boy?"

"Just his first name. He's not a regular. Seen him now and then at different places."

"That's better than what we have. What's the name?"

"Pete . . . that's all I know. Pete."

Jeff reached back into his pocket preparing to throw another twenty down.

"Not necessary." Said the man. "The twenty you left will buy the beer and games tonight."

"Okay." Jeff turned again to leave.

"Hey copper!"

Jeff half turned back. "Yes?"

"The big boy is dangerous. Very dangerous, word is that he has something big planned."

"How big?"

"Dunno."

Jeff hesitated, and then pulled a business card from his wallet.

"If you hear anything, let me know. I'll take care of you."

"Okay."

Jeff left the bar, climbing into his car rather stiffly. He sniffed the air smelling smoke on his clothing and the fumes from the beer he had partially consumed. (No D.W.I. for him.) It was hard for him to believe that just like that he had a first name for the man that so many police departments were searching for. He would have to go undercover, but maybe, just maybe he could look up and find that murdering jackass before he could start doing "something big." He had his start. Now he had to work towards the finish.

CHAPTER 74

onday morning came and it was a beautiful August Day. The grass was shiny wet from the dew; the sun that rain bowed through spider webs and sky was a magnificent blue. Yes sir, a gorgeous day.

Major was happy. They were going to hitch the horse up to the buggy and drive into Sugarcreek to the livestock sale. The sale was held every Monday, although they had a sale on Fridays where they sold only horses, ponies and riding accessories. Major had been to the sale barn a number of years ago, but hadn't been back after they rebuilt it. There had been a fire and it pretty much destroyed everything.

Major was feeling good about getting out among his own people. Even though he would be dressed as an Amish man. Honestly, it felt great to be able to leave the farm even for a day. As long as he remembered he was Amish, he should be okay.

After a hearty breakfast of fried eggs and potatoes, they had prepared the buggy and were soon trotting down the road.

Major had never ridden in a buggy before, except when Onna found him. "That didn't count." Major thought, "I don't remember much."

It was an entirely different perspective from the open-faced buggy. Cars whizzing by, big semis rocking the buggy as they blew past, the clopping of the horse's shoes on the pavement added together provided an exciting if not a thrilling ride.

Major was astounded to see Amish men riding bicycles, driving cars, walking and of course using their buggies. He had thought they always used horses for transportation. Evidently he had never noticed them using any other mode of travel before.

Coming down the hill past the Garaway High School they turned right and went through the down town area. Once again Major marveled. The storefronts were styled after Swiss fashion. The buggy was slow enough to allow him an excellent look. Major had been through this way before but when he drove a car he sped through never taking the time to view the beautiful sights.

They traveled the last few blocks and drove into the parking lot of the sale barn. They turned left to go to the hitching post, where there were already ten to fifteen buggies and horses tied off.

Onna had put on her best dress for the day. A wine purple dress fit her stunning figure like a glove and the white cap tied to her hair offset the dress to compliment her features perfectly. Major helped her down by offering his hand. Onna took it but leaped nimbly to the ground. She didn't let go as they stood hand in hand and watched Seth slowly exit the buggy.

They made a handsome couple as they strolled hand in hand to the front door of the barn, Seth trailing behind. Major released her hand and stepped forward holding the door open for her and Seth. He followed them in and trailed them up the steps.

Once to the top they could look down into the selling arena. The kitchen was to their right, two doors were screened and being used by a steady stream of people. Seth left them here. He went around to the left and entered the stall area. He was one of the men used to guide the animals from the truck to their holding pens.

Major grinned at Onna, "Come on, I'll treat you to a hamburger."

Onna answered his grin with one of her own, "I would like that."

Major opened the screen door and followed Onna in. She chose a stool on the opposite side of the doors where they entered. Major liked it better that way. He could see everyone coming in. Even though he looked Amish, his training taught him to always be prepared for trouble.

They ordered, then sat back to watch. All kinds of different people came in the restaurant. Young men, old men and some kids. The kids were pretty young and all seemed to want ice cream.

Their orders came, both had hamburgers with the works and they bowed their heads and thanked God for the food. They ate slowly, lingering on their stools enjoying the fast pace that everyone but them were employing.

Sandwiches done, they pushed the plates to the waitress behind the bar and ordered the ice cream. Major's eyes lit up as he watched them put a healthy dollop of strawberry topping on it. They asked for and received plastic spoons for their ice cream, so they could go to the arena to watch the cattle being sold.

Onna and Major never talked. They shared an occasional smile and were relaxed in each other's company.

They finished up the ice cream, it had been delicious. Major took Onna's and his cups to the trash container and dropped them in. As the men's restroom was directly in front of him, Major decided he would go and use the facility before he and Onna wandered around more.

He walked through the door and immediately wished he had waited. The three men he had worked over more than two weeks earlier were lounging around inside. Major started to turn and leave when one of the men jumped in front of him halting his departure.

"Where are you going, Amish man?" He asked?" We're not going to hurt you!"

Major stood there staring at him. He decided to go around him, as he wanted to avoid him if he could. He didn't want to blow his cover at this time. He stepped to his left, intending to bypass the man but he again moved in front of Major.

"Where are you manners Amish man?" He sneered. "You have to say please!"

Major's body tightened up ready to strike. He drew in long breaths exhaling smoothly as he tried to control himself. Thirty seconds passed before he spoke. "Please?"

The three men laughed and the one-stepped to the side.

"See? That was all I wanted. You people have to know your place."

Major didn't answer or even look at him. He started for the door, grateful that trouble was averted. He was in mid-stride when one of the men punted him in the seat of his pants. He whirled without thought, leaping to the kicker, a hand like a steel claw biting into his unprotected throat, the other hand grasping for then finding the man's penis. He stood there for a long second, his steely eyes staring relentlessly deep into his foes eyes! The man's gaze flickered and then broke from Majors. Slowly like a man waking from a dream he released he hold from him. Mouths open, all three men stared at the Amish clad man, unable to believe what their eyes had shown them. Without a word, Major turned and with a long stride exited the restroom.

He walked over to Onna reaching for her hand. She stood up with his help and they walked from the arena. The auctioneer secure under the shoulder mount of a huge longhorn bull watched them leave. He knew who Onna was, but he had never seen her companion before. He didn't walk like any Amish he had ever seen before, but he auctioneer had to call the bids. He put Major out of his mind. Only later in the week would he realize whom he had seen.

Onna and Major strolled slowly along the various stalls. There were bulls in some of the pens that were so big they were put in on an angle so they weren't crowded. Major's head was even at the front shoulder of some of these massive brutes.

They went to the pigpens and watched six hundred pound sows fight each other. It wasn't long before the blood was flowing from razor sharp tusks. Major could have watched them fight a little longer, but Onna pulled him by the hand towards the horse section. This was her favorite section of the huge barn. She loved to look at the horses and try to imagine which one she would like to have for her very own. Major got a kick out of that. She was like a young woman in his world comparing cars to each other.

Major looked around and saw Seth leaning against a post during a lull in trucks. Walking over to him, he could see Seth was thoroughly enjoying himself. There were several Amish youths helping out, but Seth was the one they went to when they had a problem or was unsure of themselves. He and Seth looked over the big Holstein bull, admiring its great size. They moved down by the hogs watching them bite each other the high-pitched squealing out of place among the lowing of the cattle.

They conversed for a few more minutes then Major looked for Onna. When he saw her he knew she was in trouble. The three men who accosted Major in the rest room were surrounding Onna by the horse stables. From the look on her face she knew who they were.

Seth started to go and help her, but Major's hand across his chest stopped him.

"Hold on Seth!"

"Onna is in trouble! She needs my help!" Again Seth started over and again Major stopped him.

"Wait!"

Seth had enough respect for Major that he stopped but every fiber of his being wanted him to rush over to help his precious grand daughter.

The big one Major thought it was Sam was directly in front Onna, the other two flanked her.

Sam was trying to pat Onna's head but she kept ducking away from his hand. From the look on Sam's face he was having a good time teasing her.

Major and Seth stepped back where Sam and his cronies could not casually spot them Major was hoping that Onna would be able to take care of herself.

Sam looked around to see if they had attracted any attention yet. They hadn't. Thinking he was unobserved Sam grabbed Onna's breasts, one in each hand. He never expected the kind of reaction he got from her. Usually when he was playing with the Amish girls they tried to get away from him. After he felt them up Sam generally would let them go on about their business. Sure, they were upset and sometimes crying, sure they told their fathers, brothers or boy friends, but not once had anyone of them ever tried to stop them or even verbally chastised them. Sam figured that most of the Amish had enough sense to be frightened of them. "Doggone right!" He thought to himself. Onna suddenly threw up a palm heel strike under the nose. Blood and snot flew as she snapped her hips and pivoted perfectly into the strike. Sam staggered backwards tripping over his own feet, falling without grace to the hard wooden floor. The other two grabbed Onna by the arms to hold her, but she didn't stop there. Using them for a fulcrum, she again pivoted into the one holding her right arm. She brought her knee up sharply into the meaty thigh eliciting a grunt from the much larger man. Again, she used her knee as a weapon. This time he let her go.

Onna turned to attack the remaining assailant but he was ready for her. A hard right hand crashed into Onna's temple, dropping her as if she had pole axed.

Major was all over the man before either of them realized he had made a move. He spun the man around and delivered a short punch to the bridge of his nose, breaking it. The nose slewed off to one side and blood poured from it. Major didn't stop. A left, a right, and uppercut to the jaw, another left, another right. The hood's hands came up to try and protect what was left of his face. Major didn't care. He crashed a hard right hand to his gut, using his left to hold the punk up. He drew back and hooked it into the false ribs on his left side. Another hard blow to the ribs Major felt something give that time. It drove him to frenzy. He was throwing punches with abandon now. Hitting just to hit, hurting just to hurt. This punk had hit Onna! He had to pay! He beat the man to his knees, fists slimy with blood and still he wouldn't stop. Someone grabbed him from behind trying to stop the maddened Major. Catching a glimpse out of the corner of his eye, Major saw that it was Sam. Reaching back he hooked him behind the head and twisted hard. Sam came flying over top landing hard on his back, breathless, he was gasping for air.

Major leaped high in the air landing with a devastating double stomp to Sam's belly. He slipped off and spun a spin kick to his head. Sam moved, only received a glancing blow. He rolled over in a fetal position, unable to stop the kicks that were landing to his kidney area. One kick? Two kicks late he never knew what happened, he was out cold.

Major had lost control. He had turned into a snarling raging beast. He wanted to maim, to destroy. He moved to the head of the unconscious Sam preparing to fix his face the way he had done the one who had hurt Onna. He drew back his foot, preparing to put "boot city" to work, when he was seized from behind. The remaining hood had bided his time, he was too intelligent to try and confront the raging Amish man from the front. The man was an animal.

Wes was a strong man. He prided himself on the face that he could bench press four hundred pounds. He moved in behind the Amish man and grabbed him in a full nelson. Hold secured, he used his impressive strength to squeeze the man's head downward. Surely he could subdue this guy enough to get his friends out. It was the last thought that he formulated for quite awhile.

As soon as Major understood what hold the brute behind him was trying to employ, he countered. Throwing his hands and arms straight above his head he threw his feet out in front of him as if he were going to sit down. He slipped from the full nelson ending up directly below the head. He threw a kick upwards and caught Wes in the solar plexus. The big man grunted, already out on his feet Major brought his foot back down, cocking it. Faster then the thought that started the kick it was over. Wes was partially bent over from the stunning blow to his nerve center when the blade of Major's shoed foot took him hard under the nose. He went backwards feet higher then his head, landing on is shoulders and neck.

It was less then thirty seconds since Sam had placed his hands on Onna, thirty seconds these punks would never forget.

Major helped a groggy Onna to her feet. The silence in the big barn was complete. Everyone was staring at the bloodied

Major, most of them with their mouths wide open. Even the quarrelsome pigs were silent.

The Amish didn't know what to do, they had never encountered such a savage scene before and farmers didn't want to risk jumping in and taking a beating. Finally Seth moved forward, his movements jerky and slow as if he was in shock.

"You have better leave quickly." He said.

Major slowly looked around seeing the stunned faces of the spectators. "Yes maybe I better."

"Take the buggy. Take Onna with you. I will find a way home."

Too weary to argue, Major simply nodded. He guided Onna by the arm, and together they exited the barn. Once outside, Major could hear a siren growing closer quickly he and Onna untied the horse climbed in the buggy and went home.

CHAPTER 75

om Port the detective assigned to tailing the three hard cases did not know what to do. He had been keeping an eye on these yahoos for the past four days and had a pretty good idea of what their concept of fair play was. Three against one, simply put, they were the worst kind of hoods. They didn't bother anyone who they thought was a threat to them. They gave equal odds a wide berth. They were bigger in size then the average man, but they all had a yellow streak a yard wide down their backs. Young women were their favorite prey. They weren't averse to slapping around an inexperienced youth, but what they really liked was touching and feeling up young women.

Port noticed that they kept an eye on the gathering sites of the Amish but until a minute ago, he had never really seen anything that he could bury them for.

He didn't know how to feel now. He had watched the three men sneaking their way over to where the young Amish girl was standing alone. Before she had realized what was going on, she was already in trouble. Still he could not believe the cowardly trio would sexually accost her in the wide-open spaces of the barn. When the one named Sam put his hands on her he started to go to her aide, yet he had stopped. He had not the urge to blow his cover on this if it could be helped. He had been caught totally unaware as the girl had booted old Sam smack dab in the cojones, and even more surprised when she followed it up with another blow. He thought the Amish were supposed to be meek and mild. Whew! Shot that idea all to hell and back. He had almost cheered when it seemed she was going to break away from the two that was holding her, but once again a cowardly blow ended any resistance from her.

Port's feet were already moving to assist her when he was suddenly no longer needed. An Amish Man, medium build, reddish hair and beard, probably closing in on forty leaped to the rescue. What happened next sickened him. He had seen some great bar fights in his time if truth were known; he had also participated in them. There were almost always some serious facial and bodily injuries with copious amounts of blood flowing freely with the overturned beer. But the beating the three men took in the next thirty, forty seconds was by far the worst he had ever seen administered to anyone.

The man moved like greased lightning, catching them completely off guard. Blood flew off the man who had struck the young girl. It was coming off so hard and fast, that it reminded Port of a dog shaking muddy water off of its drenched coat. The gore actually was making a spray pattern on the wooden stalls and wall. He was glad when the other man jumped the Amish man. It would give him time to get down there to get things under control. Once again he had under estimated the prowess of the man. He had totally destroyed the piggyback rider even quicker then he had beaten the other dude up. Still he had managed to close the gap another thirty feet when the biggest of the three caught the Amish fellow in a full nelson. Now he would have time to get there.

Wrong again! In a dazzling move that Port could hardly believe even though he saw it with his own eyes, the big boys was flat on his back out cold. Port slowed down to a walk then stopped. The Amish man was helping the girl up, looking around checking the people out. For some unknown reason, (instinct?) Port did not want him to know he was a cop. He memorized the features of the man and let him go on his way. Port scurried to the restaurant to use the phone, but once again stopped as he heard sirens coming towards the sale barn. Someone else must have called them in. Port was relieved. No one would know he was a cop if he played his cards right.

He went down to where the three men were still out cold, lying bloodied in straw and manure. One of them groaned at least they were still alive. He decided to speak with the town cop and go with them to the hospital. Maybe he could figure out what was going on.

Port cocked his head to one side, tongue tip outside his lips. He thought long and hard. He was no dummy, but everything had happened so fast that he took a minute to slow down and try to figure out what he had seen.

He knew that the three men had been doing something nasty to the Amish and maybe he would never find out exactly what it was. But he had a feeling that the beating administered by the adept Amish man was a pay back. The total loss of temper and control meant that he wasn't trying to warn them off. Well, maybe he could find out what happened after they awoke. Although he doubted if he could believe a word they said.

The revolving lights from the bubble top of the town's old police cruiser broke him from his thoughts. He joined the small group of Amish and spectators waiting for the moment he could talk to the policeman. As it turned out it was after the trio were loaded and transported to the hospital.

CHAPTER 76

That night Pete was in a killing mood. He went out to cruise the bars. He had stopped at two already drinking a single beer at each one and moved on. Somehow they didn't seem right to him, so he kept on going until he found a seedy little bar that cried out to him. Parking his car he went inside.

Yep! This is where he wanted to be. A dark atmosphere and the smell of urine and cheap perfume hanging in the air told him that he would be able to find a victim here.

He ordered a beer and sauntered over to a small table in the corner. Here he could see everything that was happening in the bar, yet was partially hidden by the shadows.

He watched bleary-eyed old drunks drinking their life-blood down in gulps then sips as the fever left their brains. He watched blowsy old whores rubbing up against the drunks hoping to entice them into a few free drinks.

He picked out a grubby old man sitting by himself at the end of the bar. The only person he would talk to was the bartender. Anyone else was rudely rebuffed. The old boy sat with his eyes on his glass surrounding it with both hands. The hand that guided the liquor to his mouth had a slight tremor to it, but it did not stop him or cause him to lose a drop.

Pete smiled to himself. His selection would be perfect. It didn't appear that anyone cared for the old man or even noticed him after initialing seeing him upon entering the dump. He nursed his beer until it warmed and then he ordered another. He would wait as long as necessary. This guy was going to be the first one to die in order to speed up his great adventure. He couldn't wait to get started.

A young man and woman walked into the place fifteen minutes after Pete had targeted the bum. They went to the pool table inserted a quarter and bought a rack of balls. Pete watched them play two games before he put his quarter on the table. Both of them looked him over closely then looked at each other. They shrugged their shoulders and continued to play.

The girl won the game on a called three-rail bank, started to chalk the cue and said, "Rack 'em," to Pete.

Pete did so, stepping back to watch the break. She put her butt into it and broke nicely. She took low balls after the six dropped into the corner pocket.

Pete let her beat him pretty easy and put another quarter on the table. Again she beat him handily. The third game he offered to play for drinks. After a brief conference with her (boyfriend?) She agreed.

Pete lost the next two, paying up cheerfully. Now she wanted to play for five dollars a game. Pete agreed and promptly lost again. Pete played her like a violin. He started to win a couple, lose a couple, always making sure they were winning. Soon the pair had a few too many and upped the bet. Pete took them for everything they had won from him and more.

The man gave him his last five one and said, "That's it, man! You got it all!"

Pete waited to see if they were going to ask for their money back or try to sponge off of him the rest of the night. They did neither.

"Later man!" The man said and together they started to leave.

"Hey! Hold up!" Said Pete. "C'mon back here!"

The pair hesitated and came back. "Yeah?" Asked the girl.

Pete reached into his front pants pocket and pulled the money he had won from them out. He handed the wadded up ones and fives to her. "You guys are pretty straight. Here, take it, I don't need it."

They looked at each other and this time the guy spoke. "You won it fair and square, man! We don't welch!"

"No really, take it." Pete kept his hand out money lying in his palm.

"Nah, it's yours." The man hesitated, "But if you want to buy a six pack we'll drink it."

Pete turned and went to the bar. "Twelve pack of Millers to go."

The bartender filled the order, accepted payment and turned his attention back to the bar. One of the patrons were tapping a coin on the bar top to get his services.

Pete carried the beer to the couple and handed it to the guy.

"Here you go."

"Thanks man, we're grateful."

"No problem." This time Pete allowed them to leave without comment. They were luckier then they could ever guess. On the spur of the moment, he had considered them for tonight's fun and games, but since there were absolutely straight with him he would not bother them.

He ordered another beer from the bar again going back to his dark seat. He had enjoyed the games of pool and the honesty of the young couple. Pete did have a sense of honor, respecting those who lived up to their word, destroying those who did not.

He again eyed the original object of his attention. The old man was slowly becoming more and more inebriated still staring down into his glass of liquor. Pete drank three more beers before the drunk slid from his stool wobbling to the door.

"See ya tomorrow, Gil." Said the bartender.

Gil never reacted to the words, head down he mumbled his way out of the door. Pete grabbed his long neck, took one more swig and headed slowly for the door.

He followed the drunk out to the parking lot, letting the old man shamble to an unlighted side. Pete waited while the old man urinated on the door of a small car. Then as he hitched his britches back up, he made his move. He moved in beside him and grabbed his elbow in one of his big hands.

"I'll give you a ride, old timer."

The old man mumbled something then tried to jerk away. Pete kept a firm grip. "Come on, you'll be better off if you let me help you!"

Again Gil tried to jerk away but the iron grip on his elbow kept him glued to Pete. He could see he was wasting his time trying to talk to the old man instead he increased the pressure in his grip until the drunk had to move with him. Whimpering he stumbled along to Pete's car.

Pete opened the driver's side and forced him across the seat to the passenger side. Gil didn't try to get out he must have been resigned to ride with Pete. Pete started the car and pulled from the lot.

If he had paid closer attention to his surroundings he would have noticed the two he had played pool with earlier had been watching the whole scene.

Fred and Gwen did not entirely understand what they had just witnessed but even though Fred was very soused (and very, very aroused,) he took the time to write the license number down. That done he turned back to the willing Gwen and continued making out.

Later Pete was gratified to find out the old drunk could still talk, but scream better.

CHAPTER 77

It was later in the evening before Tom Port was able to talk to the three men who took such a beating earlier that day. He interviewed them one at a time getting three different versions of the beatings. One thing they all agreed upon was that they were not doing anything that warranted an attack on them. None of them knew that their interviewer was also an eyewitness to their discretions.

Port took notes and left statement sheets for the three to fill out. He quietly talked to the head nurse and asked if they could be kept apart for a long as possible. The nurse agreed to try and Port left the hospital heading back to the office.

He filled out a report of all he had seen and left it on Conner's desk. Port thought about the Amish girl and the Amish man who both were adept at protecting themselves. He wondered if Major Brown was responsible for their skills in self-defense. If he was well, he must be one heck of a teacher in order to show so much in so little time.

Port slammed on his brakes and swerved to the curb, throwing the car into park. Another idea had come to mind making so much sense that he couldn't believe that he did not see it from the very beginning. That Amish man who was so deadly with his hands and his feet, could that have been Brown? Yes! Yes, it could have been!

Port reviewed the fight in his mind, remembering how quick and adept the man had been with his martial arts skills. The way he had moved the way he had stood, his stance his attitude! That was no Amish! That had been Major Brown! Conner had been right. Brown was holed up in Amish Country. No! Not just holed up. He was Amish!

Port bet himself that if he found out the name of the girl then he would know where Brown was staying. He would clear it with Conner in the morning. Shoot! Conner might not want anything disturbed at this time. It's his call.

He put the car's transmission into drive and signaled his intention to pull back into traffic. Waiting for a gap, he smiled to himself. He finally figured out something on his own. He felt like a real detective now.

He pulled away from the curb, making his way home. It didn't take him long to make a "Dagwood" sandwich to eat and he opened up a soda to wash it down. A half hour later he was in bed. Eager to get started on Major Brown's trail in the morning.

CHAPTER 78

Major and Onna left Sugarcreek without saying a word to each other. Both were lost in thought. He was driving the buggy and his blood-speckled hand was always in his eyesight, grim reminders of lost temper.

He wasn't sorry he had beaten them so severely. Oh no! They had it coming and more. What had bothered him was the loss of control. Instead of just administering a severe beating he could of killed any one of the three. He looked upwards his mind racing talking silently to the Lord. "Thank you for stopping me Lord, Thank you!"

He eyed Onna sideways. She had a raised welt on the left side of her face, but it didn't look like it would bruise. She was leaning back eyes closed, tear tracks sending a silent message down her barn-dusted cheeks. Major was grateful she was unconscious when he had worked the three over. He had been proud when she stood up for herself never expecting her to be hurt. He should have went over as soon as he seen what had been about to transpire, but no, he wanted to see how much Onna had learned. She had picked up plenty and if she had a little back up she probably wouldn't have been hurt at all. Major blamed himself. It was him that stopped Seth from going to Onna before the incident had escalated. It most likely would of ended there. But no! Know it all Major had interfered. They were lucky to get away from the barn before the local police had pulled in. Major hoped that the mostly Amish witnesses would stay as closed mouthed as they normally were. Maybe he could get away with this. He was planning on leaving this weekend anyway, but that was till five days away. He needed to go back to town and get supplies, clothing shoes and toiletry. Major wasn't going to leave as an Amish man. He was going to shave, get a haircut and join the modern world. He still didn't know where he was going but he had almost a week to decide . . . if he wasn't forced to leave early.

Soon they were trotting up the long driveway to the cabin, still without sharing a word. Onna skipped down from the buggy without waiting for Major's help. She hustled to the cabin opened the door and disappeared.

Major took care of the horse and buggy before going down to the pond for a nice long swim. When he was done, he rinsed the blood from the clothing he had worn that morning. He left them to dry lying under a shady bush waiting and thinking.

He wondered if Seth would ask him to leave now. He would not blame him if he did. And what about the four girls he had been teaching? He figured that was done too. Their fathers had been working at the barn too, and he was sure they had seen it all. He had shown the Amish community what could be expected from the outside populace. Between him and the three rapists, they had really shown them the rectum side of their way of life.

Major stayed away from Onna the rest of the day. He didn't go to the cabin until Seth was brought home by one of the neighbors. He waited for a short period of time then slowly ambled his way to the front door. He opened it and entered.

Seth was in his rocker patting Onna on the shoulder as she knelt in front of him. Major turned to leave but Seth's quiet voice stopped him.

"Where do you go, Major?"

"Ahh, I don't know, I thought you and Onna needed some more time alone." Major's throat worked, "Maybe I should pack up and leave. I'm sure I've brought a pile of problems to your door steps."

"From who?" Questioned Seth.

"I believe most of your neighbors saw me today. I'm sure I'm not the type of person you people would want associating with your family."

"No I talked to them. They will be here in the morning. They wish to confer with you. Will you be here?"

"If you do not object."

"Onna and I would be honored!"

Major looked down at Onna, she was still being comforted by her grandfather's soothing hand. "Onna?"

Onna looked up, tears welling in her eyes. "Yes?"

"Is it alright if I stay? If you wish otherwise, well, I can be out of here quick."

"Why do you ask me such a thing?" She asked in a quiet voice.

"Because I can feel your anguish. I know you've seen a side of me that would scare anyone. If you feel threatened by me or my actions then it is best I go."

Onna sat with her head down for a long moment. "It is not your fault I feel this way, Major. I feel I let you down today. I thought you were ashamed of me."

"Ashamed of you? Why?"

"I could not defend myself properly! I was rendered unconscious! I did not do as you taught me!"

Major reached for her hand and helped he to her feet. "Your wrong! I was very proud of you. You took two of them out. It was the third one who nailed you. I know of only one other woman who could of done what you did today."

Onna looked into Major's eyes, "Who is that?"

"My wife, Jill." Major swallowed the lump in his throat. Just the mention of her name brought back a deep longing for her. He knew his plans called for him to leave Saturday night giving him the cover of the weekend crowds to camouflage his escape.

He planned on stopping at his home before he continued on. He wanted to take Jill in his arms to make love to her. To feel her body joined with his. He missed Brok and his little boy ways. He did not care what problems he had to endure to get to his family. He would risk them willingly.

"I was worried I failed you."

"You didn't fail me Onna! You made me proud."

"Yes Onna." Seth joined in the conversation. "You were, what is the expression you use Major? Oh yes! Bad to the bone!"

"Really grandfather?"

"Yes! Really!" Seth rubbed his stomach. "And now it is suppertime. Are we prepared to eat?"

"It will be ready soon, grandfather. Why don't you and Major smoke while I hurry it along?"

"Excellent idea, Onna. I could use a smoke." Agreed Major.

Onna went to the stove, a smile finally on her face while Major and Seth loaded up their pipes and went out on the porch. They sat down and lit up. They smoked quietly once again comfortable in each other's company.

With a quiet voice, Seth asked Major the question that had been preying on his mind all day. "Major?"

"Hmmm?"

"May I ask you a question?" Seth hesitated, "It may offend you."

"I don't think anything you ask could offend me Seth. We've been through too much together."

Majors answer pleased Seth giving him the courage to ask his question. "How did it feel?"

Perplexed, Major asked, "How did what feel?"

"Beating those men until they could not move. How did it feel?"

Major reviewed the morning once again. He had thought about nothing else. He had hidden part of the truth beneath the excuse of temper lost. But he wasn't so sure after he had reviewed the scene over and over that day. He wanted to be totally honest with Set. He was more then a friend. He was like family.

"It felt . . . good."

"Good?" A cloud of smoke was puffed upward.

"Yes. I guess I've been waiting for the chance to maybe discourage these people from bothering your women again." Major told Seth about incident in the restroom too. "They were ready for a lesson. It's just that the one they received was a little strong."

Seth smiled. "It was good that such an excellent lesson was taught. And even better I was there to see it."

"Dinner's ready! Onna called out.

"Okay, we're coming."

They knocked their pipes out, sending little streaks of burning tobacco streaming to the hard packed earth beside the porch.

"Yes, I was very glad I was there." The old man said again. "We pray that we can forgive the actions of our fellow men, but it's easier to forgive someone who has paid for their transgressions." Seth laughed and he and Major went to eat.

CHAPTER 79

Tuesday morning broke into a pleasant day as the temperature slowly increased into the mid eighties.

Tom Port woke up, stretched climbed from bed and went and showered. He was eager to get to the office today. He wanted to let Conner know what he had figured out.

After swinging through a McDonald drive thru and inhaling two Egg McMuffins he entered the detective parking facility. He parked, checked out his tire and went directly to Conner's office.

He hoped Jeff was in. He was. Tom knocked and was given permission to enter.

"I found Major Brown." He said without preamble.

Conner looked interested. "Where?"

Pleased, Port told the Head man about what he had witnesses the previous morning. To his great pleasure Conner agreed with what he had surmised.

"I figured he was hiding in Amish country, but I never expected him to be Amish." Conner mused. "Did you get any names?"

"No Sir!" Said Port, "I'm going to talk to the owner of the sale this morning to see who they were."

The phone rang before Conner could give his permission.

"Yes?" He answered. Conner listened for a moment before he hung up.

"Go ahead to the sale barn and find out who the girl was."

"Okay." Agreed Port.

"That's all! Don't try to follow up on it. I need you to help in another case. Do you understand me?"

"Yes Sir!" Port almost clicked his heels and snapped a salute.

"Our serial killer left another body last night. This time he didn't try to hide it."

"He didn't? What do you think that means?" Port asked.

"It means he doesn't care anymore." Conner rubbed his eyes.

"It means things are going to get pretty bloody around here."

"What about Major Brown?"

"What about him? He's not wanted for anything. As much as I would like to send him home to his family, I can't. We're going to need all of the man power we have to nail this sick bastard that's been slaughtering people for his own pleasure for years."

Port didn't want to leave anything uncovered. "Did you read my report on those three men at Sugarcreek yesterday?"

"Yes."

"What do you want done there?" Port knew what he would like to do but it wasn't his call.

Conner thought for a moment. "Charge them for disorderly conduct and sexual assault. That'll do for starters."

"Yes Sir!" Port turned to leave but stopped again. "Sir?"

"Yes?"

"After I find out who the girl was, what then?"

Conner wrote an address down on pad paper then handed it to Port.

"Take this. When you finish up there, go to this place. We'll be there."

"Yes Sir." Port left.

Conner leaned back in his chair. From what was said over the phone, it was a pretty gruesome murder. The body was found outside a U-Store-It Shed by a passer by. The police arrived quickly enough to find a fairly warm body, but no suspects.

Conner had a terrible feeling that a blood bath like none ever seen was about to start. This murder would be the escalation.

He sighed and got up from the desk. He put his suit jacket on and headed to the scene of the killing. It was in the tip of his county, just inside of his jurisdiction. It wasn't like he didn't have enough to do as it was. But with the three men in the hospital safely away from making trouble, he would try to spend more time and manpower on this homicidal idiot. He also couldn't fault the surrounding sheriff's department for the relief in their voices when they found the latest murder was not their baby.

All of the surrounding county and beyond were involved in the murders. The sick S.O.B. had left bodies everywhere in the state of Ohio. Jeff didn't doubt that there were probably more that they never would find too.

He gave his secretary the address where he could be found and left the building. He breathed deeply of the summer air, knowing that it wouldn't be long before fall reared its head up.

It didn't take long to get to the crime scene. Driving moderately, he was still there within a half an hour. He took his time getting out of the car and then strolled over where three other law enforcement agents were.

He perused the body silently as the other three watched him. The sight raised his gorge, but he didn't show any signs of distress. He would die before he showed any weakness in front of these men.

"Anything?" He asked.

"Take a look inside." Said the scruffiest of the three.

With a wary look, Jeff faced the partially open door and entered. The metallic smell of blood gagged him. Mixed with the fecal matter from the deceased, the stench was almost over powering. Knowing that eyes were watching him, he never let on that he was bothered at all.

On first glance, everything appeared to be pretty much the same type of scene usually encountered when they found one of his victims. Kerosene lamp and a chair, same as always. Jeff slowly turned around surveying the room as he did. When he came upon what the other three officers had been talking about, He was shocked. On the wall, drawn with the victim's blood, was an outline of a pretty good-sized man. The borders were wide and sloppy but you could tell that whoever drew it rubbed it close enough to his body to make an almost perfect silhouette. Above it was a name. Pete.

Well, Jeff guessed this was verification enough on the name he got from the two pool players. Judging by the size of the "self portrait" he was a big man.

Something on the wall caught his attention. The shadows in the room had concealed it at first. It looked like a lump of clay. Jeff peered closer but still couldn't tell what it was. He inched closer and instantly wished he hadn't of.

The lump was male genitalia, probably from the victim. They were nailed to the wall. On closer inspection of the outline, there were nipples where they were supposed to be. Looking up, Jeff saw that a pair of eyes was bulging at him. Under the eyes was a nose. Jeff still managed to keep a grip on his stomach, but what was under the ruined nose made him blow chunks in the corner of the storage shed. It was a tongue. Long slimy looking and looking like a bloody necktie, it shouted out to him, causing his senses to reel. He quickly left the shed wiping his mouth with the back of his hand.

"His?" He asked the detectives.

"Yeah. We didn't move the body but you can see the eyes and nose are missing if you squat down beside him."

"Looks like we're in for a rough one." Said Jeff.

"Yeah, he doesn't care anymore. I think he's going to try something big and pretty soon!" Agreed the scruffy one.

"Well, get pictures of everything and go over everything with a fine tooth comb. We don't want any mistakes." Jeff really didn't think they would ever get

Pete to trial; he knew that the killer would crash and burn before he would let himself be incarcerated. One thing for sure, something was going to happen and soon. This guy was gearing up for some climax that only he knew about. That was very scary to Jeff. Very scary.

CHAPTER 80

The mutilation and murder made the front page of the local paper the next day causing a stir among the citizens that lived in the area. The public had no real conception of exactly how many and the duration of murders that had been committed by this nefarious fiend. If they would have, then the outcry would have been so great that more then one elected official in more then one of the surrounding counties would have been booted out of office way before now.

It's a lot easier to commit an insolvable murder then what is generally considered. If a person is with out remorse or a conscience and cool and calculating in their approach, chances are they will get away with "the perfect murder." Usually what happens with you typical serial killer is complacency. They kill and kill and kill and get away with it. It becomes so easy that instead of staying sharp and concentrated on their activities they become careless, or so insane they just don't care anymore. Either way, sooner or later they are caught.

Some commit suicide, some are arrested without incident, some go out with a bang, taking anyone and everyone they can with them. They don't want to die alone.

Jill sat in her chair, Sensei at her side reading about the gruesome murder. She was around long enough to remember some of the worse killers that had shocked the nation with their heinous crimes. Bundy, Lacy, Speck, and Dahmer all ran through her mind, but the one who really jumped out in her mind? Charles Manson. She had watched a program about mass murderers once and he was interviewed in his prison cell.

Even through the television screen, Jill had been able to feel the evil sweeping off of him in waves. His cold dark eyes seemed to stare clean through her soul. That was through a screen measuring twenty-seven inches. Jill just couldn't imagine trying to interview such an evil man. He gave her the nervous shakes just thinking about him. Reading the story about the old drunk had caused the same type of reaction. She didn't know why, but something caused her to wrinkle up into good-sized goose bumps. She then threw the paper to the floor and petted Sensei.

"Hey Brok!" She yelled.

Brok came toddling into the room. He was walking so much better now. Jill could see he was gifted with a grace that could only herald great athleticism.

"Mama want Brok?"

Jill didn't answer, she held her arms out to him and he trotted over in such an endearing way that Jill's nervousness left her.

"I just wanted a kiss and a hug, Little buddy." Jill used the nickname Major always used. She squeezed him close and smothered his little face with kisses. Brok endured it for a minute and then wriggled to get down. He went back to the other room to continue what he had been doing. Leaving Jill alone once again.

Her thoughts went back to her missing husband. She wished he were home with her. She missed his presence, his strength, his love, loyalty and most of all she missed his quiet confidence.

He was the only man she knew that did not feel the need to prove himself over and over. Once he had mastered something, he moved on. It didn't matter if he was challenged to repeat past glories he simply refuse. He did not feel a pressing need to recapture any of past victories or to attempt to add to them No, he simply walked away from it.

It's been a long time since they had been able to sit together and hold an intelligent conversation. Jill missed that too. With Breeler, it had been sex, sex, and sex. When she did try to hold a conversation with him, it always concerned police work If she tried to steer thing around to a subject that she liked he rebuffed her and returned to what interested him.

But Jill had concerns. Big ones. She couldn't forget how Major's eyes deadened when Breeler denounced him as the "Butcher of Macsville." Could he have really of killed all of those people in cold blood? Yes . . . Yes, he could of, he as much as admitted it to her. And look how easily he had emasculated the detective. He did it without any regret at all. It was like pulling the wings off a fly.

Jill shivered at the memory. It still haunted her dreams. Could she live with a man she evidently didn't know as well as she thought she did? That was a question that had to be answered quickly. She had a strong feeling that she was going to see Major soon, very soon. She didn't know what would happen then.

She loved him but did she love him enough? It would be answered when she saw him again. She wished he were here. Jill knew that his presence would solve any and all questions. She couldn't wait.

CHAPTER 81

Pete spent Tuesday and Wednesday nights involved in a killing spree unparalleled in modern history. He went out to every bar and dive he could locate, picking and choosing victims at random. Men or women, it didn't matter anymore. His mind was eroding now. He killed just to kill, gaining animalistic pleasure from each groan, and each plea for mercy. He almost became orgasmistic at the spurting of blood from severed arteries.

In short, for these two evenings, Pete totally lost it. He indulged himself in any and every fantasy of torture and death that he could devise. He was inebriated with the power of it all. In that time frame he was completely vulnerable to capture. He had forgotten why he had started his unrestrained killings in his ecstasy.

He piled up bodies in one small shed at an U-Store-It Place near where he had left his "message," for the police to find. At first he made some more of the sketches with human parts like the one that had sickened Jeff Conner. By Wednesday night he had ran out of room on the walls of the small shed. That was okay though, the bodies were stacked around like a cord of wood making access to the walls difficult.

"Wait till they find this one!" He chortled to himself, over and over like a mantra.

Some of his victims put up tremendous struggles as he fought them to the door of the shed. Once inside though, their struggles turned to disbelieving shock. The sight and smell of all the bloating bodies over came the resistance of all but a couple of his unfortunate victims.

One middle-aged man totally spasmed out, Pete beat him to death with his bare hands enjoying every blow immensely. He lavished over the blood that splattered over him with each and every strike. By the time he was done with him, Pete looked like he had a bad case of the measles. Oh what a fun time he had those two blood drenched nights.

By Thursday morning sanity, if you could call Pete sane, finally crept back into his mind. He had almost forgotten that he started this slaughter to speed up his meeting with his old buddy Major Brown.

After he finished up with his last victim, Pete seemed to come out of a fog. Staring about the room he estimated that there were at least thirty bodies in various stages of mutilation and bloatation.

He drew in the stench of death and exhaled with satisfaction. He was totally at ease. In another hour it would be daybreak and he wanted this carnage to be found today. He reached down and grabbed one of the bodies by the hair, it was a barely recognizable woman and dragged her outside.

Looking furtively about without seeing anyone, he let the head drop to the pavement with a thump and simply walked away. It still filled him with amazement how easy it was to kill and get away with it.

He strode happily to a newspaper box, put his fifty cents in and pulled a paper out tucking it under his arm. He walked to his car whistling a tune from his childhood days. He unlocked the driver's side door and threw the paper on the seat. Sitting behind the wheel he smiled reliving some of the highlights from the past two nights. Putting the car in gear, he headed home.

Ten minutes later he pulled into his parking place on the street. He took the paper from the seat and slid from behind the wheel. Walking to the door Pete became aware of the fact that he was uneasy. No that wasn't the word for it, more like unsettled. Something was wrong. Without warning the hair on the back of his neck rose up like hackles on a cur dog getting ready to fight. Without moving his head, he rotated his eyes from side to side trying to pick up what his senses or maybe his instinct was warning him about.

Nothing. Even though he couldn't spot anything out of the ordinary, Pete trusted his intuition. He had studied the arts too long and was too dedicated to the dark side to be fooled into complacency. Something was up, no doubt about it.

He went to his door and acted like he was going to unlock it. He dropped his newspaper and in the act of picking it up he took a good look around. He didn't see anything out of the ordinary, but yet he knew something was wrong. Just as an animal senses danger.

He slowly picked up the paper and decided to play a gambit to see if he could draw anyone out. He simply turned from the door and sprinted down the street. Right before he turned the corner he took a quick peek back. The whole area was swarming with the police.

Not wanting to be captured before he exacted revenge on Brown, Pete turned and started to sprint again. Fortunately he had a back-up plan for just such an occurrence. Time to go to it.

CHAPTER 82

Jeff Conner spoke quietly into the radio; "He's opening the door. When he steps inside, we all move at once."

It had been a stroke of luck for his department. A young couple had come into his office with some "important information" as they put it. The front desk officer listened politely for a moment and was about to send them on their way when he realized they were talking about the drunk that was butchered a couple of nights ago. He got Jeff on the phone and received permission to send them to his office

He sat through their story disappointed they didn't have a name to go with the excellent description of the big man.

He asked them to go back out to the front desk to file a report of all they had witnessed and thanked them.

"Do you want his license plate number?" Asked Fred.

"Your telling me you have his plate numbers?"

"Yes Sir!" Said the girl. "We were in the parking lot when he left with poor old Gil." She sniffled a little.

Conner shoved a pad and pen over. "Write it down!"

Fred hesitated and pulled a scrap of paper from his pocket He shoved it to Conner. "Here it is, man."

Without looking at it, Conner grabbed the phone to call out to the front desk "Come in here, I have a number I want ran."

The officer came into the office taking the scrap of paper and checking out Gwen's legs before he left.

"This is the first solid lead we've had on this guy. We owe you a lot!" Said Jeff.

"He shouldn't of killed ole Gil!" Exclaimed Fred. "He never hurt anyone! He was just a little weird, that's all."

"Well, I'm sure sorry about your friend, but you'll help us catch his killer.

Hesitantly, Gwen spoke up. "We're not going to be in the paper are we?"

Jeff wanted to be completely honest with her. "If we take him alive, you'll have to testify against him. You two are the first to see him actually take a victim." Conner realized that there was something wrong between the pair as they exchanged sideways glances at each other. "Why?"

It was Fred who explained. "We're both married . . . but not to each other."

"Ohh!"

"We'd rather keep a low profile, if we could." Said Gwen.

"I can't promise you anything," Said Jeff, "but I'll try."

"Okay man!" Said Fred. He and Gwen stood up to leave. "We'll fill out statements, but remember, you hold our lives in your hands."

"I'll be as discreet as possible."

"Thanks." He and Gwen left.

Fifteen minutes later, Detective Jeff Conner had the information he had requested. The plates had spit out a name. Pete Sandford, five foot ten inches tall. Weight two twenty. A big man, how was he often described? Oh yes, massive. Bigger then what his measurements indicated.

He reached for the phone. He was going to need some help on this one. He called for all the sheriff departments that surrounded his county. He wasn't going to take any chances on Pete Sandford escaping them.

After making arrangements with them, Jeff had personally recorded the address that had been on the license.

Average neighborhood, average house; a little run down, but nice.

Jeff arranged for a search warrant. All told he had a task force of thirty men primed and ready to take Mr. Pete Sandford down.

Jeff positioned men inside of Pete's house and the areas outside. He had most of the block cordoned off. When Pete entered the house, they would act.

When Sandford had finally appeared, Jeff felt confident that he would be captured without a hassle. He had frowned when Sandford dropped his paper, but he was ready to key the mike on his transmitter, setting everything in motion.

He clicked it twice, the signal for "ready" when Sandford turned and tore down the street. Surprised, he clicked again and set the trap off. Only the target was rapidly disappearing from ground zero.

Police poured from the house and surrounding areas trying in vain to catch the remarkably fast man and restrain him. By the time they reached the end of the block Pete Sandford had disappeared from sight and of course from capture.

Frustrated, knowing that his failure would rest squarely on his shoulders, Jeff Conner uncharacteristically slammed the walkie-talkie down on the pavement smashing it to pieces.

CHAPTER 83

Major and Onna drove the buggy into town where Major drew curious stares from an overweight, nibby saleswoman that couldn't believe an Amish man was buying the type of clothing he was. Black bikini underwear, tight fitting white Tee shirts, white socks, clinging name brand jeans and a good pair of high top Nikes completed his wardrobe. As an after thought he added a pack of handkerchiefs. The big blue ones farmers liked to have hanging from their back pockets.

Going to the health section of the store, he picked out a three pack of disposable razors, deodorant, toothbrush, toothpaste and a bottle of Old Spice Cologne.

He paid cash for everything and carried his purchases out to the buggy where Onna was waiting.

"I have to get a couple more things." He said to Onna and turned up the street. He entered a small store and perused the pipe section. He picked out a good briar pipe and took it and a whole carton of filters to the counter.

"Thought you Amish made your own pipes." Said the clerk.

Major stared at him for a long moment. "I don't think that's any of your business."

"Sorry." Said the clerk, but Major knew he wasn't.

"Yeah, right!" Major picked up his purchases and left.

They drove the buggy back to the farm and unhitched the horse. Major brushed and rubbed it down before he put it out to pasture. He carried his packages to the house and put them under the bed. Onna assumed he had bought clothing and such, so he wasn't worried about Seth or her finding out about the pipe he bought him.

Later that evening Major held a conversation with Seth about Onna. At first Seth refused Major's request, but finally at his urging he accepted what he had to offer. Major had no idea what he could get Onna for a present. Seth insisted they needed nothing, but Major would not stop picking at Seth until he agreed to take money for a gift for her.

Come Monday, sale day, Onna would have her pick of any horse she wanted from the Sugarcreek Sale. Major hoped she would pick out a dandy. He wished he could help her but he knew he would be gone Saturday night.

He was finally prepared to say goodbye to his friends. He knew Onna and her girl friends were able to defend themselves now, although he doubted if the three that had terrorized the Amish would make a return appearance. He hated to leave the old man, but Seth knew that he must move on.

Major would miss the farm and it's active but laid back life style, but he had to get on with his life. He had to get out of the States and make a new life for himself. Maybe in a few years he could have Jill and Brok join him.

Jill . . . Brok . . .

A lump formed in his throat. He was going to see them Saturday night and he was going to take the time to love his wife. Man-O-Man did he miss her. One way or the other, he would be with her. No one could stop him! No one!

CHAPTER 84

Pete laughed as he had escaped the net the police had laid for him with ease. He was holed up in an old house that was destined to be torn down with-in a year. Pete had converted two rooms into a pretty snug little hide away. It had all the comforts of home; a small Honda generator supplied his electricity. He had more or less sound proofed the room it was in so you couldn't hear the little gasoline engine at all. A cot, refrigerator and portable television kept him comfortable.

He opened up the refrigerator and got a beer. Peering inside, he also with drew four eggs and a pack of krepples. Opening the beer, he swallowed down a charge and then cooked his super.

Tomorrow was Saturday. D-Day.

He had already contacted the vet and made arrangements for him to bring the car with the hogos in it over to pick him up. Tomorrow evening, all of his plans were going to come to fruition. He couldn't wait. Pete laughed.

CHAPTER 85

Saturday morning broke clear and warm. It was going to be a very hot day and very sunny.

Jill decided she needed some time for herself today. She called her babysitter and made arrangements for her to watch Brok that evening. She wasn't sure what she wanted to do, maybe a movie and a bite to eat afterwards. Even a fast food restaurant sounded good to her.

She spent the morning working out taking her time, luxuriating in the exercise. She finished up around noon and made lunch for her and Brok She picked out a sports bra and a pair of gym shorts to wear out. It was a sweltering day and she didn't think it was going to get any better by evening.

She laid down for a nap. She would bathe after she got up. Brok lay down with her and they both had a peaceful untroubled sleep.

CHAPTER 86

J eff Conner and his force were intensifying their search for Pete Sanford. Jeff wouldn't believe that he had gotten away from them.

A hysterical woman had called the station and reported Pete's latest atrocities. They were still hauling bodies out of the U-Store-It Shed. This time it was out of his district, so he concentrated on trying to find the maniac that had brutally slain so many.

He and his crew had managed to get some sleep Friday night, but they had all started searching again early Saturday morning and Jeff knew they wouldn't quit until totally exhausted or they found him.

He was totally jerked that he got away. Jeff still didn't know how Sanford had known they were there. By the time they got to the corner he was already gone. The big man definitely could move.

Jeff knew that any killings that Sandford committed now would always weigh heavy on his mind. He had him in sight and lost him! Jeff slammed his fist into his open hand startling his driver. He didn't offer an explanation; "Drive!" was all he growled. He couldn't wait to run into Sandford again. This time he wouldn't get away!

CHAPTER 87

Saturday morning broke and the dawning was beautiful. Major had made the effort to get up before daybreak. He wanted to watch the sun come up in the rustic Amish setting. The beauty of it was almost over whelming. He hoped to carry the memory of it forever.

He picked up his backpack and ambled slowly to the pond. He warily watched the rooster as he went through his territory. Major smiled, he would miss the tough old bird. He shed his clothes by the pond and waded out in the summer-warmed water.

Stretching and slowly limbering up he again admired the beauty surrounding him. It was a warm morning, foretelling a hot day and the birds were spreading their cheer throughout their world.

Smiling, Major dove into the deeper water, swimming effortlessly and easily around the pond several times. He rested for a moment floating on his back looking at the cloudless blue sky. Sighing, he turned and swam over to where he had undressed. He pulled a mirror from the pack and trimmed his hair with a small pair of scissors. The styling wasn't perfect or square when he was done, but it wasn't too bad considering he never cut hair before. He used the scissors to cut the long from his beard before a disposable razor debuted from the pack. He lathered up with a bar of soap and soon was clean-shaven.

Major laughed at his reflection. It had been a while since he had seen himself. It was almost the face of a stranger.

He reached inside the pack and pulled the bikini underwear out and donned them. Socks, jeans and a tee shirt felt good against his cleansed skin. He sat down in the grass and laced his Nikes up. The blue hankie and a Cleveland Indian's ball cap completed his war robe.

He peered into the reflecting surface of the pond, pleased with what he saw. The tee shirt hid the scars from his healed wounds but didn't hide the fact that he was one built son of a gun.

Muscles rippled as he flexed and stretched. His biceps bulged as he "made a muscle." The good food and hard farm work had left him in excellent shape. He had slowed down on the pipe and his wind was adequate, though not as good as it could have been. All in all, he was pleased with what he saw and felt.

He put his toilet items in the backpack and put it over one shoulder. Leaning down, he picked up the clothing and shoes Seth had let him borrow. He carried everything to the cabin getting an ill-tempered evil eye from the rooster that no longer recognized him.

He laid the shoes and clothes on the corner of the porch and put the backpack beside them. He didn't plan on leaving until dark and that wasn't until around nine o'clock

He had all day just to sit with Seth and Onna and relax. He knew it would be along time until he could ever relax again.

He opened the door and entered to the shocked stares of his Amish family.

"I did not know you could look so different from us!" Said Seth. "I did not know you at first glance."

Onna didn't say a word. She stared, blushed then turned away.

"What's the matter, Onna? It's still me." Said Major.

Onna concentrated on the stove readying breakfast. "You look so different, that's all."

Major smiled. He went to the table and sat down.

"All the chores are done, I did them early. Everything is already finished for the day." Major paused, "Well, except milking the cow this evening. I was hoping we could spend the day just being together."

Onna brought Major and Seth plates heaping with potatoes, eggs and bacon. "That sounds wonderful. Grandfather, we could have a party!"

Seth mused and then nodded his head. "Yes Onna, there are many people who will be sad to see Major go. This will be a day of good byes. Do you mind Major?"

Major did, but he would never say so. "No Seth, that's fine."

Onna tripped out the door to tell her girlfriends and families. All that day Amish folk came to Set's cabin to sit and talk laugh and joke with Major. All of them had heard what he had done to the three men who had been terrorizing them and they were grateful.

They didn't come empty handed either. Major never knew how many different ways there were to cook turkey, chicken, ham, pies and preservatives. He sampled a little of each and was astonished of how tasty everything was.

The day passed quickly and dusk was rapidly approaching before the majority of the people had cleared out.

Major had finally quit eating in the early afternoon because he wanted to get to his home before morning and that was going to take some physical exertion. He couldn't afford to be bloated. He felt good though. He was like a high-powered racecar racing its engine from zero to red line on the tack. Almost time to go.

Seth, Onna and he were sitting on the porch saddened by his soon to be departure when Seth looked up. An unfamiliar sound coming down his lane alerted him to the fact that a car was coming to the cabin.

The three exchanged quick glances and Major immediately got to his feet and entered the cabin. He kept the door cracked; he wanted to hear what was going on.

The car bounced and jolted it's way up the lane causing a cloud of dust to slowly move across and disperse over the pasture ground. It pulled up in front of the cabin and stopped, engine dying as the key was turned off.

The driver side and passenger side doors opened and two men got out. Seth could see a third person inside the car but couldn't make out whom it was. Neither he nor Onna greeted the pair standing on the porch with stone faces.

"Seth Miller? Onna Miller?" Asked the one who wasn't driving.

Seth answered, "yes."

"My name is Jeff Conner. I'm a detective for the Sheriffs department. I need to talk to Major Brown."

Onna breathed in sharply, "Who?"

"Please sir, ma'am, we have an emergency. I need to talk to Major now."

Again neither Onna nor Seth would answer.

"You don't understand. People are dying, we need Brown!"

"He's not here. He has already gone!" Said Seth in a faint voice.

"Then whose is that?" Asked Jeff pointing to the backpack that was still where Major left it early in the morning.

Seth reddened, caught in a lie he elected not to say another word.

Jeff turned to the car and motioned for the occupant to get out. The door wouldn't open from the inside. Tom Port stepped back and unlatched the door.

Jill Brown stepped out of the car still dressed in a pair of short shorts and a sports bra.

The fading sun gathered in her hair like a halo, enhancing her physical strength yet not taking away anything from her beauty.

Onna gasped when she realized who she was. Any idea of Major as a potential suitor fled her mind in that instance. She knew she could never compare to her. She was gorgeous.

"My name is Jill Brown. I'm looking for my husband."

Onna's temper flashed. "You would lead him to jail? A life locked up? He would die you know that! What kind of Judas are you?" She flared.

Jill was confused for a second. "Jail?" Then she understood. "No Miss Miller. All charges against Major had been dropped. He's free.

Onna's jaw dropped. "Free?"

"Yes Miss Miller. However there is another problem. One only Major can deal with. People are dying. We need him now."

The cabin door slowly opened and Major stepped out, sliding between Seth and Onna. They both stepped to the side and Major stood alone, his eyes on Jill, a hunger in them that caused her to blush and weaken.

Major shifted his gaze to Jeff Conner. "What's this about charges being dropped?"

"It's true, Major. No proof. I personally reviewed your accusations and couldn't find enough evidence to prove you were at any of the murder sites."

Major digested this then turned back to Jill. "Is it true?" He asked.

"Yes!" She breathed.

In two long strides, Major was off the porch and gathered Jill up in his arms. He swung her around twice before he put her feet back on the ground. He kissed her deeply, hungrily. She could feel his desire pressing against her stomach.

On the porch, Seth and Onna watched. Jeff and Tom Port stood fidgeting for a moment.

"Major?" Said Jeff. "We got a problem. We need your help."

Major stepped back from Jill, but not releasing her. She felt too good, too right for him to let her go.

"Something about people dying? What's that got to do with me?"

"You remember Pete Sandford?" Asked the detective.

At the name, memories flooded Majors mind. He shuddered.

"Yeah, I remember him. Why?"

He wants to see you."

Major stared hard at his old school buddy.

"We'd better go inside and talk. You can tell me what's going on in there." All six entered the cabin that no more then an hour ago held happy, but sad friends. Now it was a grim group that sat down for a serious conversation.

CHAPTER 88

Pete laid low until Saturday afternoon. He and the vet left his hide away and snuck over to where Pete had hidden the car with all of his gear in it. He drove out to the hall he had wanted to use in his plan and checked it out. Looking in his little book, he knew that there was going to be a wedding reception here late afternoon.

There weren't any cars in the parking lot and Pete decided to take a chance. He drove to the space marked "The Boss." After he parked, he casually strolled to the door resisting the urge to look furtively around him and tried it . . . locked.

Shoot! He went back to the car and left the parking lot. He figured he had a couple of hours to kill before anyone showed up to open up the hall.

He drove around until he found an oil well road that went off the road a ways and parked. He opened the trunk and rechecked everything. He put fresh batteries in the trunk earlier, but still didn't put them in the detonator yet. No sense in taking a chance on blowing himself up.

He reached under the pile of hogos and felt the hard shape of an uzi. He pulled it out and loaded it. He didn't really want to use it, but he knew it would be necessary. He loaded his pocket with extra clips and went back to the front of the car. He opened the glove box and pulled out a small baggie of marijuana and rolled himself up a log. He sat on the hood as he lit it and smoked it down to a roach before firing it into the weeds. He rolled up another one but this time he shared it with the vet.

"Not too much now! I need your head clear!" He cautioned.

They sat in the heat both sweating mildly; both stoned both thinking unspeakable thoughts.

Pete glanced at his watch, stood and shook like a big dog. "Time to go."

The vet simply nodded. They entered the car and headed for the hall. This time when they pulled up, the lot was pretty well filled.

"No screw ups!" Admonished Pete. "If you do, I'll kill you!"

The vet's eyes dripped to the floor. "I won't!" He said.

"See that you don't."

Pete's plan was simple. He would drive the car up to the door to eliminate having to carry his gear any distance. He would secure the hall and set his plan into action.

He eased the car into gear and looked sharply at the vet.

"Get the chain and lock ready to go."

Again the vet demurred. He put the heavy section of half-inch chain around his neck and shoulders, and then patted the pocket where he had put the lock. "I'm ready!"

Pete drove to the door bumping sharply over the raised sidewalk. He picked the Uzi up and quietly entered the door, the vet trailing behind.

The crowd was watching the newly married bride and groom toast each other. If Pete had been a romantic he would have appreciated the beauty of the scene. But he wasn't.

He brought the Uzi up to his waist ready to announce his presence with a burst of nine-millimeter slugs, but refrained from pulling the trigger when an old man noticed him and stepped over on an intercept course.

"What are you doing with that gun?" He asked.

Pete grinned at him, enjoying how wide the old man's eyes opened when he pointed the gun at his midsection.

"Why, telling everyone I'm here!" He said, triggering off a burst that sent the old man backwards spilling champagne and guts as he did a death dance before he fell.

Heads jerked around and bodies reacted to the loud gunfire in the hall.

"Don't anyone move!" Screamed Pete. He fired off another burst and shattered the head of a woman who was reaching for her child. "I said don't move!" he screamed again.

Children were screaming women crying but everyone froze for a hellish moment.

"What . . . what the hell do you think you're doing?"

The barrel of the Uzi swept to the groom as he started forward.

"You can't come in here like that!" The groom walked angrily forward, "I'll . . . I'll kill you!"

Bruppppp! The Uzi barked again, stitching a path from the groom's groin up to his chest stopping his advance and crumpling him in a heap to the floor, blood splattering.

The bride screamed and ran to her newly dead husband, dropping to her knees to cradle his head.

"Why?" She asked in a low voice. "Why did you do this?"

"Bruppppp! The Uzi barked again. The slugs knocked her backwards ripping the satin dress, changing the whiteness for red as the blood gushed from the wounds. Pete stepped forward and casually held the gun over the badly wounded woman.

"Because I felt like it!" Said Pete and pulled the trigger again. He brought the Uzi back up. "Everyone over there!" He ordered pointing to the wall on his left. "Now!" he screamed when they were slow in moving. One little boy tripped over a chair leg and fell awkwardly to the floor. Pete killed him with a small burst. Again screams and curses echoed throughout the hall.

"Shut up and move!" He fired a burst into the crowd wounding several and killing two more. "I'm not playing games!"

Quickly the people packed against the wall, unable to even help the injured because Pete was threatening them with the Uzi. He dropped the used clip and put a fresh one in. He turned to the vet. "Go lock the door!"

The vet hurried to the back door threading the chain through the dual handles making the chain short and taunt, locking it. Now the only way in or out was through the front door and no one was going that way with a maniacal king kong with an Uzi barring the way.

"Go get the stuff."

Again the vet ran out the door and started carrying the equipment in. Throwing it all in the center of the room, he hurriedly emptied the car of all the supplies. Once done, he backed the car away from the door and over into the parking lot. They wouldn't need it again.

The vet entered the door and stood uncertain of what was expected of him now. Pete was still covering the people not letting them move or speak. He sensed the vet was behind him and he turned to get things ready.

"I want all the women to move to the front." He quietly ordered.

Sobbing, crying aloud and in a dazed shock they moved to obey.

Again the Uzi sounded as the mother of the slain boy broke and ran to his bloody side. Mother joined son in a death embrace. Curses sounded loud and furious from some of the braver men, but not a one moved forward, they had finally understood that a madman was in control of their lives.

Once again an unnatural calm prevailed in the hall. The only sounds were the moans of the still living wounded and the harsh breathing from the frightened people.

Pete motioned the vet forward to the hogo pile.

"One at a time," he said to the women, "come forward and put one of these on." He pointed the Uzi at a trembling young girl on his left. "We'll start with you." She stepped forward with small steps, afraid to move, yet more afraid not to.

"Turn around and raise your arms." Said the vet. She did as she was told, standing still until he zipped it up.

"Okay." Said Pete, "You go to the other side." He pointed to the wall on his right. "Next!"

One at a time the children came forward. They ranged in age from six to thirteen years old. When the last child had been zipped into the killer hogos there were only twenty-three left. Pete looked over the remaining men, pointing at random at the youngest. "Gear up." He said as he pointed to the ones he wanted. When all of the hogos were gone he glanced at the men who were left without one.

He had all one hundred and five hogos in use and there were, how many? Fourteen men left without one.

"Turn around and face the wall. "Pete commanded them.

"Screw you! Yelled an older man, "You're going to kill us!"

Pete smiled, "You're right!" He said and leveled the Uzi on them. Brupppp!!! He cut them down dropping them like pins in a bowling alley. It was over in a matter of seconds.

Pete whirled and aimed his hot-barreled machine gun at the hogo-clad hostages.

"Anyone moves and you're dead!" He waited meeting their angry fearful stares until one by one they dropped their eyes. He had cowed them with his sheer will power. Of course the corpses lying around like broken rag dolls helped his case immensely.

"Watch 'em." He ordered the vet. He strolled over to each of the bodies one at a time dispatching any of the wounded as easily as stepping on an ant.

When he had finished, he moved back to the entrance of the hall and picked out ten of the biggest men.

I want all the tables and chairs to the back." He pointed to the bodies using the Uzi. "Move the trash too."

The men moved quickly to obey. Soon the hall was an open area half the size of a basketball court.

"Good job, fellows. Now see if you can find something to clean up all the blood. We don't want any slippery spots in here, now do we?"

The men used linen table clothes to clean up the gore. When they were done they rejoined the line.

The next half hour was spent setting up his portable television and antennae. He wanted to be able to monitor broadcast information from the networks. He wanted this escapade hitting all the news stations across America. He wanted everyone in the whole United States to know who Pete Sandford was. He would make his demands and they would listen. Oh Yes! They would listen or every one of these people would die, one at a time.

CHAPTER 89

Jeff Conner received the call while they were cruising the neighborhood where they had lost Pete Sanford.

The lady at 911 explained the situation to him in clear and concise details. Sandford had given her all the information necessary to cause his belly to burn with instant indigestion and his head throb with a headache like he had never had before. He dry swallowed six aspirin from the half empty bottle he kept in the glove box, hesitated and chomped up a couple of anti-acid tablets too. He didn't know if the calcium would block the aspirins properties or not. Frankly, he didn't care.

He transmitted the location to all his units and called dispatch. Jeff wanted help from the surrounding sheriffs offices, the more men the better. He had a hostage situation he had never in his life imagined.

His car pulled up to Breck's Hall and stopped from the outside everything looked normal, but he knew that inside was a form of hell for the people trapped within.

They stayed in the car until other units with flashing lights; some without came sliding rapidly into the parking lot. Soon, there were police everywhere. The building was surrounded as effectively as a castle by a moat. The killer wasn't going anywhere, but Jeff knew that was what Mister Pete Sandford wanted.

Jeff set up a communication center and tried to telephone the hall. No one would or could pick up. He had to try and establish communications with the killer. After several tries he used a megaphone telling the killer to pick up the phone. Still no response, Jeff was starting to prepare for along siege when the front door of the hall opened.

A young woman stepped out dressed in some type of padding. She had her hands high in the air and was moving slowly to the open area in front of the hall. Her stylish cut jet-black hair was sweat soaked and adhered to her head as if it was glued. Perspiration poured from her face in rivulets and she was actually shaking from fright. She walked fifty feet from the door and stopped, when she didn't move, Jeff knew that she wasn't going any further.

"Stay here. I'm going to her." He said.

"No!" Tom Port disagreed, "We need you here. Let me go!"

Jeff grinned nervously at his loyal friend. "Can't do it, Tom. I'm in charge. I'm going." He walked around the side of the car and with his hands held up so anyone inside could see he didn't have a gun in he hand, he moved to the girl.

"I'm Detective Jeff Conner." He said to her, "I'm here to help."

Without talking the young lady handed him a set of earphones that had been hanging from around her neck. Jeff turned them over in his hands and then put them on.

"Hello there!" A voice boomed form the earpieces. "Back away from the girl!"

Jeff slowly backed away, her pleading eyes staring accusingly into his own. When Jeff was fifteen feet away another order came through the earpieces. "Stop!" Jeff stopped.

"Listen very closely I want a television cameras here. Contact all major networks and I mean all of them! I have over one hundred hostages in here and I'll kill them all if you don't meet my demands. I want you to get Major Brown here!"

"Major Brown?" Thought Jeff. "Now what?"

"I want him here as soon as possible. Tell him we have some unfinished business to tend too. I will kill one hostage every half hour until the cameras and Brown are here. If you try to rush me or entertain any thought of rescue or I will destroy all the hostages at once. Do not try bother to try and contact me. When I want something, I will let you know. Oh, just in case

Brown doesn't want to come, tell him that Pete Sandford is waiting. Remember! One hostage every half hour!"

Blammm!!! The girl standing in front of Jeff was seemingly split in two as the upper part of her body actually separated from her torso and blew upwards in a gout of flame and blown up charred bits of flesh that struck Jeff on the front of his body as the force of the C-4 explosion knocked him backwards. The lower body actually stood for another second before falling sideways to the grassy lawn. He watched horrified as her head and shoulders flipped downwards striking the ground with the dull sound of an exploding melon. He chomped at his tongue trying to get the pieces of flesh and gore from his mouth. The spray from the dead girls demise had entered his mouth threatening to choke him. Her half lidded eyes stared off to his right reminding of a cheap baby dolls eyes. The smell of burnt hair and flesh caused him to fall to his hands and knees with uncontrollable retching.

All around him hardened police and sheriff's guns came up in reaction to the unexpected explosion. Some of them joined Conner in sickness although most would not admit it later.

Jeff stood, reaching for his handkerchief to wipe his mouth and to try to get some of the girl's flecks off of him.

The earphones crackled again, the cold hard voice came on.

"One every half an hour. Get those cameras and Major Brown here! I'll kill them all! Believe it!!!"

Jeff walked back to the car. "Get someone in to clean that mess up, if he allows it." He said to one of the deputies. "Tom, did you find where Brown was at?"

Tom Port's head bobbed up and down. Shock causing him to imitate one of those little bobbing dolls that you see in some cars, where their heads go up and down with every motion. "I don't know where he's staying, but I know who he's staying with."

They got in the car, lights flashing and quickly headed down the road. Jeff called dispatch. He wanted the Governor to be informed and he wanted to notify all the major networks. They would find out anyway, but if he could get them here quickly it might save some live. He also had Jill Brown called. He wanted to make sure she was home and ready to go when they got there. They had not time to lose.

The two-way radio barked out Jeff's name and he picked the transmitter up. "This is Conner, go ahead."

"Sir, we tried to retrieve the young ladies body, but he sent another one out telling us to leave the body alone."

Jeff rubbed his eyes, loosening a piece of flesh and hair that was stuck to the side of his face. He flung it to the floor with a shudder. "And then?" He asked dreading the answer.

"He blew her up too, Sir." The unseen voice cracked, "It was as bad as the first one."

"Okay. Everyone I can think of is notified. We'll be back as quick as we can. Keep me posted. Conner out."

Neither man talked as they sped to Brown's house. Siren howling, lights flashing enabled the pair to waste no time, as they arrived at the home in less then twenty minutes. Jill Brown was waiting at the bottom of the steps as they pulled up.

She was still dressed in her short shorts and sport bra. When the sheriff department had called she had put her shoes on and waited outside. She wasn't sure what was going on, but she wasn't going to make them wait on her.

"What's happening"" She asked Major's friend.

"We're taking you to your husband." Said Jeff.

"You know where he's at?" Jill was excited.

"Not exactly, but we have an idea." Jeff turned to her looking deep into her eyes. "We have a major crisis, Jill. What can you tell me about Pete Sandford?"

"Uh-oh." Said Jill.

CHAPTER 90

Pete was having a blast. He had almost lost it for a minute after he blew up the first girl. Never in his life had he ever been so excited before. He could still see the results in his mind. Wow! And that second one! Just as good as the first! He looked around at the hogo-clad crowd, one hundred and three more. He was actually hoped there would be a delay in the police meeting his demands. He wanted to watch more of his explosive handiwork. One thing for sure, the people had quieted down.

Pete glanced at the wall clock. It was almost eight-thirty, time to pick out another one.

"You!" He pointed at a young lady. "Come here!"

"No!" She screamed falling back into the surrounding people trying desperately to get out of his line of sight.

In three long strides, he was to her. He smashed a big fist into one of the men's faces as the fool-hardy youth tried to stop him. Blood stained the knuckles and fingernails on Pete's big hand, but if didn't stop him from grabbing the girl by the hair and dragging her to the middle of the floor. He slapped her hard across the face. Once, twice, three then four cracks were enough to finally pacify her enough for him to gain control.

"You either walk out there or everyone dies!" He said quietly.

"I . . . I . . . I don't want to die!" Tears streamed down her face, dripping off the end of her nose mixing with the snot running from her nostrils.

Pete put the Uzi under her chin. "Listen! He said, "You go out there and you have a chance that something will go wrong and you'll live." He pushed the barrel deeper causing her head to tilt backwards. "If you don't go then die now for sure! Your choice."

"Wait!" The young man Pete had punched stepped forward, blood still flowing from his shattered face. "I'll go!"

Pete never lessened the pressure from the Uzi on the girl's throat. He slowly turned his big head and stared menacing at the advancing youth. He let him approach within ten feet of him before he stopped him with the flick of his hand.

"Do you want to die?" He asked.

The young man spread his hands out in front of him. "No."

"Then why would you take her place?"

He shrugged his shoulders and didn't answer.

Pete looked to the girl. "Do you want him to take your place?" He asked.

"Yes!!! . . . No!!!" She said sure at first, but instantly changed her mind.

Pete shoved her roughly to the floor. "What's your name, boy?" He asked moving towards the young man.

"My name is Greg Henry." He stared defiantly.

"Go on out."

Greg turned to walk away, but stopped and turned back to Pete.

"You'll let her live?"

"She'll be the last to die. You have my word."

Without another word, Henry turned and walked out the door. Some of the men in the crowd started to mutter, but Pete shut them up by aiming the Uzi into their direction. He dialed Henry's number into the detonator but held back from depressing the button. He watched the young man's steady stride as he passed the bodies of the first two victims. Pete expected him to break and run but again he was surprised. The boy stopped just past the bodies the head of a triangle so to speak and turned back towards the hall. What he did next enraged Pete. He raised both hands and flipped Pete off! Not just flipped him but he was actually shaking his middle fingers at him!

With a snarl Pete pushed the button and grinned as he watched the defiant youth explode in a spray of blood, gore and disintegrated charred body parts. The mist of blood mixed with the flash from the flame of the explosion almost looked pretty as it drifted down to the grass, stirred by a restless breeze.

Later, Pete could see police personnel moving about, setting up giant generators and lighting systems. It was going to be dark soon but the area surrounding the hall would be lit up as bright as an August sun drenched day at noon.

He could see the television cameras setting up behind the police lines, trying to get the best angles for their viewing audiences. Pete turned from the door and glanced around the hall. He pointed at two men and had them use tables to rig up platform that could be used as a stage for a cameraman.

He gave the vet instructions and soon the old drunken dope addicted dummy had the television hooked up and turned to the news. The outside of the hall flickered and then strengthened into a quality picture on the screen. He turned up the volume and listened to the "On the scene" newscaster telling his listening audiences about the crazed serial killer that was trapped with over one hundred hostages with him. The camera panned the torn apart blood soaked bodies that lay broken and pitiful in full view of any and everyone who cared to look.

Pete turned to his hostages and picked out two women crying, they both stepped forward. He sent them out to converse with the police. Time to start pushing.

CHAPTER 91

Major held Jill's hand as he sat quietly and listened to Jeff Conner tell him everything he knew about Pete Sandford's evil and sordid past time. His fingers caressed hers and made her tingle from head to toe, causing her to blush under her tan and heighten the sensations that were trying to overload her senses.

Jill's eyes slowly took in the cabin she was sitting in, very rustic, yes but also very functional. Jill admired how the Amish were so skillful with their baking and craftwork, but she herself would never want to live as one. Judging by the excellent shape Major was in; he took to the Spartan life very well.

Silence broke her perusal as she realized that Conner was done with his briefing.

"Well Major, will you come?" He asked.

Major disengaged his hand from Jill's and stood up. He slowly walked around the interior of the cabin, head down, lost in thought.

"Pete's crazy. You know that, don't you?" He asked finally.

"Yes." Conner didn't have to elaborate any further.

"You know that I will have to kill him in order to stop him? There will be no surrender."

"Yes I know that too." Said Conner.

"Do you know what he will do if I lose?"

Jeff leaned back in the chair. "Yeah, everyone will die."

Major drew in a sharp breath, held it a second then released it. "What's my backup?"

Conner wasn't a man to lie. "There is no backup."

Major wheeled around, "What? No back up? What the hell is wrong with you?"

Jeff reddened. "Can't do it Major. We have no idea how many, their positions or one single piece of information we can use to take him or them out without destroying any chance of rescuing the hostages."

Major walked stiffly over to the table and placed both hands on it, leaning down into Conner's face.

"Then they're all dead Jeff! All of them!"

Conner was stunned. "Why? You beat him before! Jill told us all about it."

Major looked at Jill and for a moment his eyes softened, but turned to flint again as he once again held Jeff's eyes.

"That was a game of tag. There were rules to follow." He said quietly, "He hit me twice and if time hadn't ran out at that instance, I would been put down. There is no way I can beat him. No way at all." He held Conner's gaze for a second then pushed up off of the table. He walked over to the cabin door and opened it. He leaned against the jamb and looked out over the farm.

Conner heavily pushed his chair back from the table. He looked at Port and Jill and shook his head. "Well, I guess this is it then. Thanks Major, we'll try to figure something out." He and Port nodded their good byes to Seth and Onna and started to leave.

"Wait." Said Major. "I said I couldn't beat him, I didn't say I wouldn't go." He turned to the Millers. "Thanks." He hugged the old man and pulled Onna into a three-way embrace. Tears crept from his eyes. He knew that in all likelihood that he would never see them again. He released them and walked out the door. He picked up the knapsack from the corner of the porch and went to the car. He turned and looked at Jeff, Jill and Port, "Coming?"

The four left the porch and entered the car pulling away in a cloud of dust.

Seth turned to Onna, "Hitch up the horse."

"Where are we going, grandfather?"

"For the first time in my life," said Seth, "I'm going to watch television."

CHAPTER 92

The two ladies met one of the detectives Conner left in charge. They explained that Pete Sandford wanted a television camera set up inside and he wanted it in place before Major Brown arrived. They also explained that everyone was dressed in C-4 ladened hogos and if any attempt at a rescue were made then everyone would perish in one heck of a pyrotechnic display. Under prompting from the detective they explained where the hostages were standing and that there were two of them in command and both seemed crazy. Before the detective could ask any more questions, Pete decided they had enough time to deliver his directives and ended their lives as spectacularly as the previous deceased.

Inside, Pete started to pace. What could be keeping Brown? He knew that his hated foe had a high sense of honor and he had no doubt that he would show, but when? The longer this drug on, the possibility of something going wrong increased.

The hostages sat on the floor mumbling to themselves, yet afraid of catching his attention. They knew that whoever piqued Pete for any reason would probably be next.

Pete walked back and forth, back and forth, back and forth staring at the people. Suddenly he jumped forward and pointed at a young man.

"You!"

The young fellow tried to speak but his mouth had stopped being capable of speech. All the spit dried up instantly and a spurt of urine stained the front of his pants. He slowly stood on weak and trembling legs. He was scared to death, yet determined not to show it.

"Go tell them, I'm going to kill one every five minutes. I want Brown!" He screamed. "It's nine o'clock and he should have been here! Go tell them every five minutes!"

The youth staggered to the door trying to be courageous in front of the young women, but failing miserably. He opened the door then stopped. "Someone's coming." He said.

Instantly Pete leaped forward, smashing the Uzi to the side of the kid's head dropping him to the floor oblivious to anything. Pete looked out the glass and realized that a man was bringing the television camera like he ordered.

The man approached the door then stopped. Pete looked over and picked out another husky young man and motioned him over.

"Get the camera and come back in." While the young man hastened to do as he was ordered, Pete dragged the youth he had decked off to the side.

The husky young man re-entered the hall with the camera slung over his shoulder. "Where you want it?"

"Put it there." Pete used his head to point to the make shift platform they had made from the tables.

The man who brought the camera turned to leave but stopped when Pete shouted through the glass. "Wait!" He turned and walked back to the doors where again he stopped.

"When I'm ready to film, will it be on television?" He asked.

The man who brought the camera shrugged. "All you have to do is push start and aim. We'll take care of the rest."

Pete partially opened the door. "If that chicken hearted Major Brown ever shows up, tell him I'm ready!" Pete aimed the Uzi at him. "Now get out of here!"

The man ran.

Pete went back to the young man he had rendered unconscious. The boy was starting to get his bearings again. Pete held the Uzi in one hand and helped him up with the other.

"Okay boy, go give them my message."

"Wha . . . What?" He stammered.

"Get going!" The Uzi came up. The boy looked at the wicked opening at the end of the barrel, turned and walked out the door.

A detective came to meet him but this time he had a jacket or something slung over his shoulder.

The boy started to deliver his message when without warning the detective whipped what appeared to be a blanket around the youth's shoulder's and upper body.

Perplexed, suspicious then angry Pete pressed the button on the detonator. Nothing!" "What the heck?" Pete asked himself. Quickly he checked the frequency. It was the same as what was on the young man's hogo. Furious, Pete mashed the button again and again. As the detective scurried the boy away, Pete realized that the blanket had to be lead lined. It was preventing the radio waves from reaching the detonator switch. He watched in silent fury as the pair disappeared around one of the parked police riot vans. He was just about to pick out a new pair to take his place in death when an explosion rattled the glass in the doors of the hall.

Pete quickly looked over to where the two had disappeared and was gratified to see what appeared to be the boy's head and part of one shoulder flying a few feet above the van's roof before it turned and crashed to the ground.

A loud yell from the vet who was monitoring the television set sent Pete to the screen.

"What is it?" He asked.

"They were showing that boy on the air," he said, "They were unzipping the hogo when he blew up. Looks like he took a couple of cops with him." The vet laughed and looked at Pete. "Looks like your little booby trap worked!"

"Good! Snarled Pete. "Hope they learned a lesson from that!" Again Pete started over to pick out his next victim when once again the vet stopped him. "I think your buddy is here."

The big man turned and looked at the screen. It was bedlam. Reporters were thrusting microphones into Major Brown's face, trying in vain to get a comment from the granite faced martial artist. Police were finally forcing them back and Pete was able to get a good look at his hated enemy.

He looked to be in good shape and for that Pete was grateful. Too many so-called masters of the martial arts let themselves get fat and out of shape, relying on their reputations to commanded respect. Brown wasn't one of those.

Pete took a closer look when he saw the woman clinging to Brown's arm. Son of a gun it was his wife. She appeared to be in excellent shape too. Nice outfit. Pete didn't know why a looker like that was doing with Brown. She deserved someone like him. Well, he needed a cameraman maybe she would fit the bill. As a matter of fact Pete knew she would.

Pete watched the screen as a cop handed Brown a telephone. Seconds later the phone Pete left connected in the hall began to ring.

CHAPTER 93

Major's eyes swept over the carnage that was on display on the hall's front yard. Anger filled him, as he understood that they died in order for Sandford to force Major into a conflict he did not want.

He could feel Jill's hand on his bicep and found comfort in her nearness.

On the third ring, the phone was picked up.

"Took you long enough to get here." Said Pete in a low voice.

"Yeah, well I'm here. What do you want?"

Booming laughter came over the phone. Officers five feet away could easily hear it. "Why a rematch of course!"

"You're sick, Pete! All of this for a rematch? You're insane!"

"Hey, whatever Major old boy! All I know is that I have people in here that hope you can take me! Can you take me, Major?"

Major realized Pete wanted an answer. "I'll kill you, Pete!"

Strip down to your underwear and come on in! Let's get this show on the road!" Disgusted, Major shook his head slightly.

"What's the matter Mister Brown?" Questioned a young cop named Brandon.

Major grimaced. "It's hard to be tough when you're almost naked."

Major started to hand the phone to the nearest cop when Pete's voice came through. "Wait a minute! We need someone to run the camera! I suggest you bring your wife in. She'll want to see this first hand anyway!"

Major's knuckles turned white as he squeezed the receiver. "Leave my wife out of this!" He hissed.

"Either send her in or I'll be sending out more out to die! Your choice!" Snarled Pete!

"No!" Yelled Major into the phone. "No!"

"Major." Said Jill in a quiet voice, "I'm going."

Major pulled the phone from his ear. "What?" He sputtered.

"You heard me. I'm going!"

"But Jill . . ."

"No Major!" Interrupted Jill. "Too many have died now! I'm going."

Without another word, Major put the receiver back to his ear.

"All right Pete. She's coming!"

"Good!" Chuckled Pete. "Send her in."

Major looked deep into his wife's eyes and nodded his head. "I'll be with you in a minute, Jill."

Jill tried to smile but could only manage a weak grin.

"I love you, Major Brown. Be my prince." With the grin etched on her face, Jill turned and walked past the ruined bodies of Pete Sandford's victims and entered the hall.

Major watched her in a moment of reverie before the smooth voice of the killer interrupted his train of thought.

"Your woman has guts, Major. She'll be next to last to die!"

Another chuckle. "Come in when you're ready, but don't take too long!" Click! The connection was broken.

Major handed the phone to Conner and tried to pull himself together. To do this, he needed total concentration for the task at hand. Ignoring the shouted questions from the frenzied media, Major knelt down and prayed to his God. Eyes closed, hands clasped and head bowed Major did not pray for a victory, Oh no! He prayed for mercy and forgiveness. He knew he was most likely going to die in the next fifteen minutes and wanted to be prepared for it. A man who wasn't afraid of dying had a better chance of living.

Done praying he stood up slowly started to stretch out. He still didn't think he had much of a chance, but he was going to go all out. He didn't want any part of his body breaking down at a crucial moment because he didn't loosen up.

Inside Pete was bouncing up and down on the balls of his feet, arms working piston like on upper cuts. He watched his nemesis warm up via the television set. He could feel the power building in his body. He felt strong, powerful, and invincible! He was going to show the world how to destroy an opponent! Yes sir! Killing . . . class in session.

CHAPTER 94

All around the United States people were riveted in front of their television sets. Parents hushed the children and used them to retrieve snacks and drinks so they wouldn't miss a single second of the real life drama unfolding in front of their very eyes.

Phil Brown was in his favorite chair, quaffing an ice-cold beer and munching on barbeque potato chips. There were five more beers on ice beside the chair. He wasn't going to miss any of the epic battle. He wasn't worried. Phil knew of his brother's capabilities and he knew it would take an exceptional man in order to defeat him.

He watched as his brother finished warming his body up and silently move towards the door of the hall. "You da Man!"

Phil was taking a long swig from the brown bottle when he got his first look at his brother's opponent. Phil choked as surprise made him inhale sharply. This was no ordinary man his brother was about to face! He looked huge, massive. He reminded Phil of the body builder who used to play opposite of Bill Bixby on the old television show, The Incredible Hulk. What was his name? Oh yes! Lou Ferrigno!

He watched Major look around the hall the camera was filming from above the two men and on an angle from them. Phil couldn't see what caught his brother's attention in the back part of the hall, but whatever it was turned Major's eye to blazing orbs and his face to stone.

Major said something to-what name was the newscasters using?

Oh yeah! Pete Sandford! The words were hardly out of Major's mouth when Sandford rushed him.

Phil leaned forward in his chair. He didn't want to miss any of this.

Elsewhere, Onna and Seth were just sitting down at their friend's house when the battle was joined.

He and Onna held hands and silently prayed to their God for the safety of their friend.

Major's Mother and Father were also watching the two men lock horns.

Mister Brown loudly exhorted his son on leaning his body back and forth and shadow boxing along with the two fighters

Missus Brown fidgeted in her chair, crumpling, then smoothing a tissue. She had called Jill as soon as she found out that Major was the center of the attention on all of the major T.V. networks. She had been horrified when the babysitter told her that the police had picked Jill up and she was most likely already there.

Missus Brown watched her son on television and wondered how in the world thing could of ever progressed this far.

All across the nation people from all walks life watched the two men dancing across the screen. Some of the more faint hearted shut their sets off or turned to a different channel content to wait for tomorrows paper to find out the conclusion of the battle.

However people found out about the fight, it was a subject that would be told, retold and told again throughout the weeks to follow.

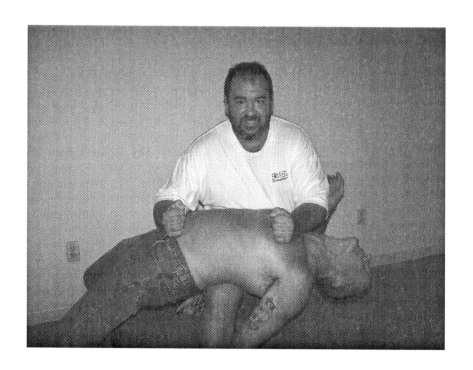

CHAPTER 95

Major finished stretching and nodded to Detective Conner.

"I'm ready."

Jeff nodded. "Good luck."

Major grinned weakly. Thanks." He stared for the door but stopped again as Jeff put his hand on his shoulder.

"Major, I just want you to know that if the worse happens. I'm organizing a volunteer squad to rush the building and try to save the hostages.

The martial artist thought for a moment and nodded. "I hope you don't have to." He turned away from his friend and walked away from the now silent crowd and entered the hall.

Pete was directly in front of him, forty feet inside the door. The hostages were to his right and all of them down on their knees. Jill was on a make shift platform to his left about eight feet off of the floor, she was manning the camcorder.

Major digested all of this as he moved further into the hall. He winked at Jill and studiously tried to avoid looking at the crowd. Their trusting faces pinned their lives on his strong shoulders never knowing how fragile their bubbles really were.

He watched a seedy looking man climb up on the platform with Jill. He carried what appeared to be a detonator in his soiled hands. That worried Major. Even if by some miracle he won then he would probably detonate the C-4 laden hogos. That would be a spectacular ending to a fun filled evening.

Major stopped fifteen feet away from the killer. He stood there, veins prominent, blood singing throughout his body. Major made his pecs jump, first together, then individually. He would let Pete move first.

As they stared at each other Major became aware of an olio of color behind Pete. A closer perusal revealed bodies stacked like cordwood. The different color clothing stained liberally with the spilled blood created a gruesome collage. His face set in stone he returned his gaze to a smiling Sandford. "You're one sick asshole!"

Major's words wiped the smile from the killer's face. With a loud scream Pete launched himself forward towards his hated enemy, wanting to crush Major to death with his huge arms.

Major held his ground until Pete was committed and then with perfect timing he turned out of the way, leaving his pivot foot planted. Pete grasped at empty air and tripped over the extended limb. He went down heavily, awkwardly, sliding on the industrial carpet burning a raw spot under his chin.

The hostages let out an involuntary cheer as he went down but were silenced as the big man bounced back to his feet. He wheeled around expecting the smaller man to press the attack.

Major wasn't stupid. He knew his only chance was to pick the man apart. He went up on his toes and danced. He waited for Pete to get in range, and then threw a stinging left jab to the right eye of the big man. A small split appeared, leaking blood.

Major easily moved away from Pete's counter attack dancing in a circle. He was working him from right to left, seeking an opening to press his attack. He threw a left jab to Pete's eyes then stepped forward with a powerful uppercut that snapped his head back. Major followed it with a knee to the groin.

Pete stepped back with a grunt, but otherwise acted as if he had never been touched. Again he moved in on Major. He swung a hard round house right to Brown's head, but the smaller man ducked. Pete grunted as one work hardened fist crashed into his false ribs. Pete shook his head in frustration desperate to slow the quicker man down. He could hear the hostages at each blow that was landed to his body, worse yet; Pete could hear the muted roar from the huge crowd that had gathered outside.

Major stepped forward landing a roundhouse kick to the back of Pete's left leg. He used the ball of the foot driving it in deep hoping to cripple him. It felt like he kicked a bag of concrete.

"Patience!" He admonished himself. "No mistakes!" He switched to a left-handed stance circling Pete the opposite way. He lifted a hard sidekick to the killer's stomach and was dismayed by how little it affected him. He followed the sidekick with a right handed back fist to the bridge of Pete's nose breaking the tear ducts, temporarily blinding the big man.

Major took full advantage of Pete's momentary blindness. He waded in with both fists flashing. He hit him hard and fast. His target started at Pete's midriff and elevated up. Major punished the stomach then the chest, a couple of haymakers to each side of the jaw then an uppercut brought from his waist exploded under the chin.

Still Sandford wouldn't go down. Major was perspiring heavily now, his breathing becoming labored. He was starting to wear down.

Pain lanced up through his arm as a knuckle on his right hand split on one of Pete's eye socket. The killer's face was blood covered and slick, blood flowing copiously from the damage inflicted by the smaller man.

Major took a deep breath stepping back away from Pete. His arms were heavy and he needed a moment to recoup his flagging strength before he would renew his attack.

Without warning Pete leaped forward and grabbed Major by his arm. He tried to pull him into his massive embrace but lost his grip on the sweat-slicked skin.

Major twisted away as Pete wiped the gore from his eyes.

There was no more time to rest now. The killer lumbered forward turning sideways to take a kick aimed for his groin on his thigh.

Major was stepping forward to send another kick on its way when disaster struck; he stepped in a blood soaked area of the carpet and slipped. He regained his balance almost instantly but it was already too late.

Pete brought a right-handed back fist from across his body catching Major across his right cheekbone laying it open to the bone. Sweat and blood flew as his head snapped around. He lost all sensation on that side not even feeling the blood flowing down his face, neck and chest.

Half blinded Major sensed rather then saw Pete closing in on him. With both eyes closed he snapped a palm heel outward that caught his foe under the nose. Again he started to unleash his punches but this time he wasn't near fast enough.

Pete blocked the first two punches, ignored the third one then smashed a huge right hand square between Brown's eyes. He staggered backwards but caught his balance. Before he could protect himself, Pete struck again.

Major felt some ribs break as a blow came from nowhere. He couldn't breath; tunnel vision instead of normal and he couldn't hear the crowd anymore. A quick glance over to them proved they were still screaming him on but he couldn't hear them now.

Ka thump!

"Wait a minute!" Thought Major as his numbed body took another blow he couldn't feel. "What's that?" He thought perhaps Conner was mounting an attack while Sandford was involved with the fight.

In between blows, Major realized he was hearing his heart.

Ka-thump!

Pete grabbed his left arm and snapped it across his knee. Major thought he might of screamed, but he wasn't sure.

Ka-thump!

Major was done. He stood swaying in front of Pete Sandford totally unable to lift a finger to save himself.

Ka-thump!

He clenched his right hand into a fist and weakly struck out a Pete. He refused to give up.

Ka-thump!

In one fluid motion, Pete avoided the weak blow and moved in. With his right hand buried in the Y of Major's groin and his left gripping him by the throat he effortlessly hoisted his broken opponent high above his head.

Ka-thump!

He paraded the bloody man in front of the hostages, taunting them!

Ka-thump!

He faced the camera that a stunned Jill was manning and broke Major across his upraised knee. He threw Major across the floor towards Jill and the camera.

Ka-thump! Major landed hard ending up on his back. It took everything he had, but he slowly turned his head so he could see his wife.

Ka-thump!

Jill left the camera running stepping away from it so she would have no barrier between her and her stricken husband. Her eyes met and held Majors.

Ka-thump!

"Jill, Jill. Jill!" Thought Major, "Lovely, lovely Jill!

Ka-thump!

Major tried to pour all of his love out through his eyes. He drooped his lid into a half wink.

Ka-thump!

"I love you! He thought "I . . . I love . . . youuu!

Ka- . . .

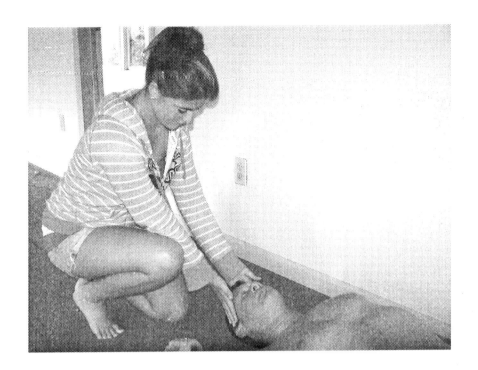

CHAPTER 96

A nation shared Jill's anguish as they watched the life leave the valiant martial artist's eyes.

Silent rage built up inside of her as quickly as lightening strikes. While people continued to stay mesmerized in front of their sets, Jill exploded.

Pete was standing over her husband's body his back towards her, head threw back roaring with triumph. She chose that unguarded moment to act.

Turning to the vet she unleashed a reverse knife hand that landed square across his neck. He dropped the detonator, reaching for his throat with both hands. Jill dropped him with a right cross that would of delighted Muhammad Ali.

The vet fell along eight feet to the floor, where with a dry snap of a broken neck ended all of his worldly concerns.

Without hesitation, Jill made the short run off of the table and threw herself through the air. Her left leg folded underneath her right leg cocked she flew towards the devil who had killed her man.

Pete sensed danger behind him and turned to meet it even though Jill was hurtling towards him. He might still have been able to thwart her attack if he had not tripped over the body of his dead foe.

He staggered back, arms flailing trying to regain his balance before Brown's wife could reach him. He was too late.

Everything was happening in slow motion. Jill could see the killer's nostrils flare, his eyebrows bunched up. She watched, fascinated as a drop of blood coursed down his battered cheek. Then she was on him.

With perfect timing, Jill unleashed the flying sidekick. The heel of her foot crushing Pete square between the eyes. He went down hard, the bone in the back of his skull breaking like an egg on the edge of a cast iron skillet. He lay motionless as Jill's momentum carried her beyond him. She landed lightly on her feet, turning to continue the attack if it was necessary. She turned to her left as a movement caught her attention. It was the young girl who had her life spared by the courage of Greg Henry. She ran to the inert Sandford and dropped to her knees behind him and grasped his hair in both hands.

Sandford was still alive and weakly tried to reach up with his hand to make the girl release him.

With a curse, the girl started pounding Pete's head up and down on the carpet, covered concrete. On the second strike, Pete quit resisting, on the third his body arched and he voided himself. Four more strikes, later Pete Sandford was dead, half of his head mush.

With a loud bang, the door of the hall was shattered as Jeff Conner and his volunteer suicide squad came bursting in.

"Get these people out of here!" He held his hand up to stop the talking and screaming. "Don't take the hogos off! Go with my men. They'll take care of you."

The hostages did not move. Slowly they moved up in a semi circle surrounding the body of Major.

Jill was down beside her husband trying to find a spark of life. There was none. She shook him, trying to shock him back. No good. She started CPR and was grateful when Conner dropped down beside her.

"I'll do the compressions, you breath." He said. "Get the paramedics in here as fast as you can!" He commanded over his shoulder.

Jeff could feel the broken ribs under his hands as he began to perform the life saving action. He hoped he wasn't driving a bone into the organs, but he knew he had to take the chance. Brown had given his all for people he didn't know; Conner would give his all to attempt to save his friend.

The crowd split open to allow the paramedics through. They took Jeff and Jill's place and continued to try and save Major.

Jill staggered backwards, brushing up against the make shift platform, shaking it. The television camera crashed to the floor, breaking it and causing a watching world to groan almost simultaneously as losing a direct contact with the bizarre scene. It would be hours before the world found out the fate of one of its valiant heroes.

CHAPTER 97

Phil drained the last of his beer and decided to nap before heading north. No one would release any information over the phone to him and he couldn't get a hold of his parents or Jill.

He leaned back in his chair and slept dreaming of a time when he and Major had no cares in the world.

Seth and Onna went home. They were sure that Jill or one of the detectives would be by to let them know about Major. They would wait a long, long time.

After word

Thank you goes to my wife Joni. I write everything in long hand and she had to decipher every word as she typed. She also took the pictures that are in the book.

Thank you to my son, Brock for having his pictures taken for this book.

Thank you to Kristian Hoffman for allowing me to use her picture.

Thank you to Ralph Baumberger I for posing with me. He made the perfect father.

Thank you to Brandon Burkhart for the difficult poses he had to endure.

Thank Joni. Without you, I would have never challenged myself to write a novel. You are the best thing that has ever happened to me.

Thanks to my brother Roger. He was the inspiration behind Phil.

Some of the places depicted in this book are actual places. The people are a figment of my imagination.